HOMES AND HEARTHS IN LITTLE WOODFORD

Catherine Jones

HEAD
of ZEUS

An Aria Book

This edition first published in the United Kingdom in 2020 by Aria,
an imprint of Head of Zeus Ltd

A CIP catalogue record for this book is available from the
British Library.

ISBN 9781838938093

Typeset by Siliconchips Services Ltd UK

Cover design © Cherie Chapman

Aria
c/o Head of Zeus
First Floor East
5–8 Hardwick Street
London EC1R 4RG

www.ariafiction.com

HOMES AND HEARTHS IN
LITTLE WOODFORD

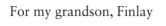
For my grandson, Finlay

I

One Saturday morning in April, Maxine and Gordon, happily married for over forty years and now both equally happily retired, were making the best use of having an empty nest by enjoying a post-coitus lie-in. It was a large 'empty nest' now it was just the two of them but, shortly after they had fallen in love with each other and married, they had fallen in love with Little Woodford and the big Edwardian villa they had found there and where they had lived ever since. It was a place they had bought to house the large family they'd planned but, despite their best efforts, they'd only managed to produce the one child – their daughter Abi. Sometimes Max did think that it was a tad ridiculous for the pair of them to be rattling around in the five-bedroomed house. They turned off the heating in the unused bedrooms and shut their doors but they both knew that one day they might have to think about downsizing. Maxine was thinking vaguely about that future prospect as she lay snuggled under the duvet but she also knew that the counter-argument was that if Abi and her partner ever got around to producing grandchildren, it would be nice to have the space to allow everyone to come and stay for big celebrations – like Christmas or significant birthdays.

But it promised to be too nice a day to worry about the long-term future so Maxine pushed such thoughts to the back of her mind, stretched luxuriously, yawned and sat up in bed.

'Tea?' she offered.

'Mmm,' murmured Gordon. 'That'd be nice.'

Maxine slipped out from under the duvet and pottered, stark naked, down the stairs to the kitchen. As she waited for the kettle to boil, she had a surreptitious swig out of the milk container. Through the big bi-fold doors at the far end of the room, she could see her garden, bathed in spring sunshine and the tops of the trees in the town's nature reserve beyond. Closer to hand was the bird-feeder on the patio where the starlings squabbled over the suet pellets. The garden was looking rather nice as lots of the spring bedding plants were still at their best although the grass could do with a cut. At the bottom of the big lawn, which sloped gently towards the boundary with the reserve she could just see the roof of the summer house that she used as her studio, dappled by the shadow of their ancient copper beech – the pride of their garden – which was just starting to come into leaf. Her 'studio' was a recent addition and she absolutely loved having a space where she could leave out her current painting and her materials and not feel the least bit guilty about the mess. Really, she thought, life couldn't get much better than it was right now; lovely husband, gorgeous house, great life-style, no money worries, daughter settled... all-in-all everything was pretty bloody perfect. It was hard not to feel a little smug, she thought, but she couldn't help it. She really did have it all.

She moved her thoughts to contemplating the day ahead; a quick swish with a hoover and duster round the house to bring it up to snuff while Gordon had a go at the lawn. Later, they'd walk to the pub to read the paper or chat with mates from the town, maybe have a bit of lunch and then drift home to snooze on the sofa for an hour before watching sport or tosh, then supper and bed. Sundays were much the same but weekdays started with the alarm as, invariably, one or other of them had something planned. Despite being retired, weekdays were go-go-go.

Maxine's eyes refocused from the garden beyond the window to her reflection in the glass. God, she was putting on weight. She really ought to do something about her tum. She sucked it in. That was better but she couldn't hold it. She let it sag again. Maybe she ought to do more exercise...

She was miles away and so jumped out of her skin, nearly dropping the milk container, when a horrified voice behind her said,

'Mum!'

Cold milk trickled down her chest. She grabbed the dishcloth to mop it up before she turned to face her daughter, cloth in one hand, carton in the other, her heart hammering with the shock of the unexpected interruption.

'For God's sake, Mum, what *do* you think you're doing? And supposing I had Marcus with me?' Her daughter's short blonde curls bobbed with indignation and her blue eyes were narrowed. She was a pretty girl, or she was when she smiled, with a classic peaches-and-cream complexion, a slightly retroussé nose and beautifully shaped eyebrows which were currently almost meeting in the middle in a frown.

'Well, if you'd rung the bell...' Maxine still felt a bit wobbly from being so startled but it was mixed with irritation that her daughter still thought it was acceptable to barge into her parents' house unannounced. For the umpteenth time, Maxine wondered how Abi would take it if she did it to her?

Abi gave her mother a withering look and stamped out of the kitchen. She returned a few moments later with Maxine's mackintosh which had been hung on the newel post at the bottom of the stairs. She thrust it at her mother.

'Do you and Dad often walk about with no clothes on? I mean, I'd have expected you to have been up and dressed ages ago.' She looked pointedly at the clock which read nine forty-five.

Maxine shrugged it on, grabbed another mug from the cupboard and returned to making the tea while she tried to regain her composure. 'No, dear,' she fibbed. As she and Gordon both slept in the nude, they quite often made their early morning tea in the all-together when the weather was nice or if the heating had been running long enough to have made the house warm. Why shouldn't they?

'Good, I'm glad to hear it. I mean... at your age too.'

Well, she might *be* sixty-five but she didn't feel like it. In her head she was still only twenty-six, which meant it always came as a shock when she caught sight of an unexpected reflection of herself. Besides, wasn't sixty the new forty? She decided to move away from the subject of her age. 'Anyway, why have you come over? You must have set out really early to be here now. What's so urgent?'

'I've got something to tell you. Go and get showered and dressed and I'll talk to you when you're decent.'

Maxine took the two mugs and returned to the bedroom thinking, as she tramped up the stairs, that she couldn't make up her mind whether Abi's tone sounded ominous or good. Twenty minutes later she and her husband sat in the sitting room waiting for Abi's news. In the privacy of their bedroom they'd speculated on what it might be: pregnancy; promotion; Marcus leaving her...

'And that's not outside the realms of possibility,' Maxine had said, gloomily. 'Let's face it, Abi can be quite tricky. And it's not as if they're married.'

'She just gets easily stressed. And she's a perfectionist. She's always set herself high standards,' said Gordon defending his daughter as he ran his fingers through his sparse hair, but his normally smiley mouth was in a thin line as he took on board Maxine's supposition.

'Standards which she expects from all and sundry,' said Maxine as she'd brushed her pepper-and-salt, shoulder-length hair before she gathered up the front section and clipped it neatly at the back of her head, a hairstyle she hadn't changed for forty years. Expecting perfection was a commendable trait, unless you couldn't meet Abi's requirements in which case, she could become quite tough. Still, thought Maxine, her bosses must reap the benefit of Abi keeping her subordinates in check. She wasn't quite sure what Abi did – apart from the fact it had something to do with HR. Marcus, a qualified accountant, worked for the same company but in the finance department.

Now, in the sitting room they sat opposite Abi, who was munching her way through a couple of croissants that Max had bought for her and Gordon's breakfast.

'You don't mind, do you? Only I found them in the fridge and they're on their sell-by date.' She was also drinking the last of the fresh orange juice.

Maxine *did* mind, rather a lot, but she supposed she and Gordon could make do with tea and toast. And it was too early in the day for an altercation so she let it go. 'It's fine,' she said as brightly as she could. 'So, what's the big news?'

'Marcus is being moved.'

Abi sounded up-beat about the prospect so Gordon ventured to say, 'And is that a good thing?'

Abi nodded. 'He applied for a job at the head office at Cattebury and got it.' She smiled at her parents. 'So, we're going to be moving nearer to you. Much nearer.'

'That's great, darling,' enthused Gordon.

'And...' Abi left a dramatic pause as if she was about to produce a rabbit from a hat. There was almost a drum roll. She smiled at both her parents. 'And, they've promised to relocate me too, although, given what Marcus will be earning, it's the ideal opportunity for us to think about starting a family. Just think, it'll be perfect and you'll be able to see much more of us than you would if we were in London.'

'Oh, darling, you're right, it is perfect. Isn't it, Max?'

Maxine took on board the news and its implications. Gordon was obviously chuffed to bits but Maxine was finding it hard to share his enthusiasm.

'Isn't it, Maxine?' he repeated, firmly.

'Lovely,' she said, weakly. 'That'll be... nice. Wonderful, even,' she added hastily.

'I knew you'd be pleased.' Abi beamed at her parents. Max was relieved she hadn't picked up on her misgivings. 'So, I'm here to go to all the estate agents in the area and see what's on offer.'

'Wouldn't it be as easy to look on Rightmove?' asked Gordon.

'We're doing that too, but I want to persuade the local guys to alert me to things as early as possible – you know, as soon as they go on the market, not when they make it onto the website. It's cut-throat out there and, if you want to get something that perfectly matches your requirements, you need to be proactive not reactive. If you're not ahead of the pack you'll miss out on the best properties.'

And 'missing out' wasn't something Abi liked doing.

'And your flat is already up for sale, is it?' asked Maxine.

'Yup.' Abi nodded vigorously and then brushed the crumbs off the front of her sweater oblivious that they fell directly onto the carpet. 'The estate agents think it'll get snapped up and, with the stupid prices of houses round us, we should be able to get something much bigger and nicer here. We think we'll have about four hundred thou to play with. Of course, it may take a while to find exactly the right house...'

'Well, obviously,' said Gordon. Abi wasn't good at compromising.

'So, when does Marcus move?' asked Max.

'In a few months.'

'OK,' said Maxine. 'And if you haven't found somewhere...?' She had an idea of what the answer might be, but judging by the happy smile on Gordon's face he wasn't looking at anything other than a big fat silver lining on the cloud that was lowering over Maxine's vision of the future which, she feared, might involve being an unpaid, full-time childminder. Abi popped the last remaining piece of croissant in her mouth and said, 'That's not going to happen. We're bound to find something suitable.'

Maxine didn't doubt it – what Abi wanted, Abi got. But she hadn't mentioned anything about moving in with her parents while they house-hunted so maybe that wasn't on the cards. Maxine began to relax. She wouldn't mind Abi and Marcus living with them for a bit, a week or so, but anything longer might be disastrous. Her relationship with Abi had been a bit edgy since Abi had seamlessly segued from terrible twos to teenaged raging hormones without drawing a single breath. Someone had once said to Maxine that kids were like fine wines – they got better as they got older. But how much older? While Abi didn't throw monumental strops any more if she got thwarted, she had a knack of making life difficult if she didn't get her way. Not that Gordon saw this side of her, because he adored his only child unequivocally and indulged her shamelessly. Since Abi had moved up to London Maxine's relationship with her had, mostly, improved massively but all that rapprochement might evaporate in a moment if she moved back. Which would be regrettable, thought Maxine.

'Yes,' continued Abi, 'all we want is a normal family home and with our budget I really can't see it being a problem.' She glanced at her watch. 'Best I get moving if I'm going to get round all of the estate agents.' She leaned forward and dumped her plate on the table, next to the half-drunk glass of orange. 'Thanks for the breakfast,' she said as she stood up scattering a few more pastry crumbs off her trousers. She eyed the carpet. 'And I hope you're going to clean the house today, Mum. I mean, do you ever get the hoover out?'

Maxine regarded her carpet; it might need more than a *swish* around with the hoover. Thanks Abi.

'Good luck with the house hunting. Let us know how you get on. Will you be dropping by before you go back to London?' asked her father.

'I might. What's for lunch?'

'We were thinking of grabbing a bite at the pub.'

'Ooh, that'd be nice, I might join you.'

'That'll be lovely,' said Gordon.

'Yes,' interrupted Maxine swiftly. 'We're probably going to walk there at about one, one thirty.'

Gordon looked at her questioningly as they usually went to the Talbot at around twelve on a Saturday. Maxine shook her head at him to shut him up.

'Oh,' said Abi. 'I don't want to hang around all morning. Seeing estate agents is only going to take a couple of hours... maybe another time.'

'When you move here there'll be lots of other opportunities,' said Gordon.

Abi left and Maxine leaned against the door after she shut it and shook her head, despondently.

'I know I *should* be pleased...' she said.

'It'll be fine. Truly. And if she does have kids, won't it be wonderful to be able to watch them grow up?'

Which Maxine had already taken on board. 'I know.

That'll be lovely. But you know she'll expect us to be unpaid childminders, don't you?'

'Don't be silly, darling. She'll respect that we have our own busy lives.'

Maxine raised her eyebrows. 'Good luck with that,' she muttered knowing full well that Gordon wouldn't take issue with Abi if she didn't.

Across the town, Olivia Laithwaite left her home and shut the front door behind her. She had over an hour before her shift started at the local hotel, Woodford Priors, and she had a few errands to complete in the town of Little Woodford before she went on duty behind the reception desk. For a start she wanted to go to the Oxfam shop to buy another black skirt. The ones she wore to work had seen better days and, since she'd been told by the hotel manager the previous day that she was being promoted, she thought the time had come to invest in some newer and smarter ones. If the Oxfam shop couldn't oblige, she'd buy skirts off the internet but, after several years of having to be careful with money, she would rather not spend more than was absolutely necessary. She could, of course, go into the next town of Cattebury, which was much bigger, and had several fashion outlets, but that would necessitate an entire morning being set aside and Olivia, frankly, had more than enough to do each day without spending forty minutes on a bus each way in order to buy such basic items of clothing.

She unlocked her bike from where it was hidden behind the hedge, mounted it and rode decorously down the road, over the railway line and onto the high street. As she rode into the main market square a small car swooshed past her, a bit too close for comfort, causing her to wobble slightly.

'And that's never thirty miles an hour,' she muttered under her breath as she watched the car brake heavily before it pulled into the car park in the square. If the driver was still around once she'd parked her bike, she had a good mind to have a word. Olivia wasn't one to let people get away with anything that she considered anti-social. To some people she was a paragon of good citizenship, to others she was an interfering old biddy who should mind her own business. Either way, Olivia didn't care – she did what she considered her duty and that was that.

She locked up her bike and headed towards the little car but the driver was already striding off, locking the doors with an imperious flick of her key fob. Olivia watched the woman go, aware that she recognised her – the slightly disgruntled look that spoilt an otherwise attractive face was definitely familiar. She rummaged around in the recesses of her mind... she was a friend of one of her older children. Mike? No, he hadn't had much time for girls before he'd gone off to university. Tamsin? That was more likely. She remembered Tamsin coming home from school with gaggles of giggling girlfriends whom she would whisk upstairs to her room whence shrieks and yells and too-loud pop music would echo around the huge space of the barn conversion that had been her old house.

Her old house... which she'd assumed would be their forever home in the days when she had been a Somebody in the town: when she and Nigel, her husband, had lived in the biggest house in town; when they had been golf club members; had had invitations to the Lord Lieutenant's parties; when she'd been president of the local WI and an esteemed town councillor. Before Nigel had got hooked on internet gambling and had nearly ruined them. But that was in the past, and their present life and their tiny three-bedroomed house on a brand-new estate was somewhat different. Olivia sighed.

Abigail Larkham. The name of the car driver popped into her head out of the blue. Of course, Maxine Larkham's only child. Quite a tricky little minx, thought Olivia. She seemed to remember Tamsin complaining that if Abi didn't get her way, she could throw a strop like no one else. Olivia often wondered where this trait came from because it would be hard to find anyone more equable or easy-going than Maxine and Gordon. Which reminded Olivia – she hadn't seen Maxine for an age.

That was the trouble with her job; she'd been working shifts since she'd had to take up employment to help with the family finances and that meant it was nigh-on impossible to get to things like the WI, the book club or the other groups she'd belonged to, on a regular basis, so she'd let her memberships fizzle out. But, now she was being promoted, she'd be working office hours. It was time to pick up the threads of her old social life.

And she'd start by dropping in on Maxine for a brief chat on her way to the hotel. Fired up with hope and enthusiasm, Olivia strode into the Oxfam shop to see if they had anything that would fill her needs. Ten minutes later she exited with a perfect A-line, knee-length skirt which she put carefully in her bike basket before she remounted her trusty old cycle and rode up the Cattebury Road, past her old house, to the turning to Maxine's house. Two minutes later she rang the doorbell.

2

Abigail Larkham had hoped to be in Little Woodford earlier but the M25 had been a nightmare to negotiate with stop-start traffic for most of the journey. She'd also rather hoped to bum a free lunch off her parents, but she wasn't going to hang around for hours just to score a sandwich at the pub. She had too much to do back in her flat in Bow to waste time in Little Woodford. She slammed the car door shut and then headed across the market square to the first of the estate agents on her list. The bell pinged as Abi opened the door and a young blonde looked up from the monitor she was studying.

'Good morning. Can I help you?' the girl said breezily.

'I sincerely hope so.'

'Buying or selling?'

'Buying. Well, buying around here, I'm selling a flat in London.'

'Cool. Take a seat and would you like tea… coffee…?'

Abi pulled out the chair on the far side of the desk and sat. 'Tea would be lovely. Milk, no sugar.'

The girl went to a machine in the corner, pressed a couple of buttons and returned a couple of minutes later with a steaming plastic cup. 'Right, Miss… Mrs…'

'Abi. Abi Larkham. Miss Abi Larkham.'

'And I'm Marie. So what sort of property are you looking for? And what sort of budget?'

'My partner and I are selling a one-bed flat in Bow – we're hoping to get in the region of three hundred thou for it.'

'Well, I think you'll be able to get more than a single bedroom round here for that sort of money. So, what'll be your budget?'

'We haven't spoken to our mortgage broker yet but we're hoping that with my partner's promotion and the equity we've got in the flat that we'll be able to go for something in the region of four hundred thou.'

'Very nice and we've got some lovely properties around that price.' Marie stood up and went over to a filing cabinet where she pulled out several sheaves of papers. She handed them to Abi who put them on the desk without even a glance.

'So… rather than waste time looking at things we really won't be interested in, let me tell you the things that my partner and I agree are absolutely essential.' Which wasn't quite true as Abi's list of essentials had been drawn up without any reference to Marcus at all.

Marie pulled a pad of paper towards her and picked up a pen, making notes as Abi reeled off her list.

'… and off-street parking and a south facing garden,' she finished.

'You certainly know what you want,' said Marie looking at the long list of Abi's requirements. 'Are they *all* completely essential?'

Abi stared at her. Duh? 'I wouldn't have included them if they weren't.'

'It's just, in my experience, it's rare for any buyer to get the absolutely perfect house. And you can always make alterations once you've moved in.'

'Yes, well, I appreciate that, but my partner and I are both *very* busy people and would rather find somewhere that we don't have to spend money and time on.'

'Fine.'

The two women stared at each other until Marie dropped her gaze.

'Let me take some contact details,' said Marie, all semblance of friendliness now gone from her voice. She clicked a retractable biro several times to vent her feelings.

Three minutes later she had everything she needed and Abi stood up.

'I expect to hear from you with a suitable list of available properties in the very near future,' she said.

'And I would remind you that you'll have a better chance if you are prepared to be more flexible.'

Abi narrowed her eyes slightly. The woman hadn't filled her with confidence and this last comment didn't seem to demonstrate the kind of enthusiasm and drive she expected. But never mind; there were other estate agents in Little Woodford and if this one missed out on the commission the sale of a four-hundred-thousand-pound house would bring them, then it was their tough luck.

Abi picked up her coat and handbag and with a faked cheery 'goodbye,' swept out of the office leaving Marie looking somewhat irritated.

The other three estate agents in Little Woodford received similar treatment which elicited similar uncertainty that she would achieve every goal on her wish-list. And Abi didn't like compromise. Surely there had to be a property that was modern but not a new-build, with open-plan living, three bedrooms, two bathrooms, one en-suite, gas heating, south-facing garden, in the catchment area for a good school, shops and services within walking distance... But apparently not, if those wretched people she'd spoken to were to be believed. Where were Phil and Kirsty when you needed them? she wondered.

On hearing the ring of her front doorbell, Maxine grimaced and put down the duster and polish. What now? She suspected it was going to be Abi back again with a list of jobs for her mother to do on the house-hunting front while she disappeared back up to London.

'You don't mind, do you, Mummy?' was a favourite phrase of Abi's. And if Maxine dared to protest that it might not be terribly convenient, she was invariably told sharply by her daughter that she ought to be grateful to have something to do to fill her days. She'd tried telling Abi that she and Gordon didn't just loaf around, watching daytime TV and reading the papers, but Abi didn't seem to understand that, even though they no longer had full-time jobs, it didn't mean they didn't have other responsibilities, plans and commitments. Part of Maxine could see Abi's point of view; Abi and Marcus had relatively high-powered jobs and a hideous commute meaning they had zero spare time during the week, which couldn't be said of her and Gordon. But it was hard not to feel a twinge of resentment when Abi's demands upset her own plans.

Her feeling of faint dread was replaced by delight

when she opened the door and saw Olivia on the doorstep, her bicycle propped against a nearby shrub. As always, Olivia looked neat and tidy in her classic skirt-blouse-and-blazer combo, her shoes shined to a mirror gloss, not a hair out of place and her subtle make-up perfect. How, wondered Maxine, did she achieve that look and ride a bike?

'How lovely! And what a surprise. I haven't seen you for months and months. Quite possibly years. How are you? And come in.' She threw the door wide. 'You've got time for a cuppa, haven't you?'

'I've got time for a quick one. Got to be at work in,' Olivia glanced at her watch, 'about forty minutes.'

'Perfect.' Max led the way into the kitchen. She filled the kettle and said, 'To what do I owe this honour?'

'I saw your daughter in town and I suddenly remembered that, as you have so rightly said, we haven't seen each other for an absolute age. My fault entirely but I decided to put things right.'

Max smiled. 'It isn't your fault. It's the fault of circumstance. It can't be easy juggling everything and shift work.'

Olivia shook her head. 'I've got better at it. And Nigel has finally learned how to switch on the dishwasher.'

'And empty it?' asked Maxine with a smile.

'Come off it. One step at a time.' She leaned against the counter and looked out of the kitchen window. 'Your garden is looking so lovely. You and Gordon must work like Trojans on it.' She turned around. 'That is the one advantage of the new house; I can practically cut the lawn with nail scissors the garden is so tiny. But I miss the old one, even though keeping it nice was such hard work.'

'Gardens are a lot of work,' agreed Max. 'But worth it.' The kettle boiled and clicked off. Maxine poured the fizzing and spitting water into two mugs, added milk, proffered the sugar bowl to which Olivia shook her head and then handed her the mug.

'Anyway,' said Olivia, 'quite apart from wanting to see you again, I also came to tell you that I'm being promoted to the management team at the hotel.'

'Oh, Olivia, I am pleased. And about time too! You are wasted as a receptionist – all that talent and ability.'

'Thank you.' Olivia was genuinely touched by her friend's words. 'But I'm not fishing for compliments but to let you know there'll be no more shift work. Nine to five each day and most weekends off. Of course, I'll have to be on call now and again and work one complete weekend a month but it means that I can get to things like the book club and the WI on a more regular basis.'

'That's great. I've missed you at the book club. I can't remember the last time you managed to make it.'

'I know and I've missed being there but there was no point. Half the time, if I read the book, I couldn't get to the following meeting when it was discussed or, if I could make the meeting, I hadn't had time to read the blessed book first. It seemed pointless to carry on.'

'But not anymore. Brilliant! So, apart from being promoted, how is everything?'

'Just fine. And you? You look well.'

'You know, mustn't grumble.'

'And Abi?'

'Yes, she's fine.' Maxine gave Olivia a run-down on the reason that Abi was in town. 'Having her close will be so much easier than having to flog right the way round the M25 to visit her,' she concluded. 'And your lot?'

'We've just got Zac at home now and he won't be with us for much longer. 'A' levels next year and then uni. An empty nest – which, given the size of the house, will be very welcome.'

'I know. It's welcome even with a bigger house. I shouldn't really say as much but I love it now Abi has gone. It is so nice to have our house to ourselves, especially now Gordon has retired. I mean, I know Abi was never really underfoot what with the size of the place and everything but it's just grand not having to think of anyone but ourselves. Does that make me sound dreadfully selfish?'

'Not at all. I think it sounds perfectly wonderful. As does retirement. I'm looking forward to when Nigel can give up work too, but after…' She paused. It wasn't as if the entire community wasn't aware of her husband's past gambling problem which had resulted in the family almost being declared bankrupt, but she still found it incredibly painful to talk about it.

Maxine put her hand on Olivia's arm. 'I understand.'

'Thanks.' There was another silence for a second or two as Olivia composed herself. 'Anyway, with yesterday's news it's just possible that his retirement might be achievable sooner rather than later. What with that, and the extra free time I'm going to have, morale is somewhat better than it has been for a while.'

'That's great. Actually, I might have something to offer you to help you fill all those empty hours.'

Olivia laughed. 'All those empty hours. I wish. But it'll be nice to have my weekends and evenings back.'

Maxine reached behind her and pulled a home-made poster about an art club she planned to start, off a pile of papers on the work surface. She showed it to Olivia.

'Art club? Oh yes, I remember now, you were an art teacher, weren't you?'

'I was and I'd like to try to inspire grown-ups to have a go. And it'll be so much easier to teach people who want to learn rather than kids who have to.'

'Goodness, yes.' Olivia looked at the poster again and then said, 'I used to muck around with watercolours when I was much younger.'

'Well, then...' Max looked at Olivia expectantly.

'I'll think about it.'

Maxine raised her eyebrows.

'No, I mean it, truly. It sounds fun and undemanding. Calming,' she added. 'I like things that are calming. I've had quite enough of stress, thank you, to last me a lifetime.'

'The plan is to meet at the community centre in the evenings on a weekly basis but to have some awaydays at weekends to try our hands at landscapes and stuff like that. And, I hope it's going to be as much about being sociable as it is about painting.'

'Sounds perfect.' Olivia glanced at her watch and then sipped her tea. 'Must keep an eye on the time,' she muttered.

'Yes, you don't want to be late – not a good example for the management to set the workers.'

'Heaven forefend.'

'But we must have a proper catch up – over a drink or coffee.'

Olivia nodded. 'Before I go, when's the next book club meeting?'

'Next week. We're reading *Jude the Obscure*. We'd love to welcome you back.'

'Jude? Oh, yes – a laugh on every page... not. I read it at school and I might be able to remember enough of the story to make an intelligent contribution to the group. I'm not quite sure I've got time to re-read it properly.'

'We won't care about that. It'll be lovely to see you there.'

Olivia drained her mug and put it by the sink. 'I ought to get going.'

They bade each other farewell and Olivia made her way to the hotel feeling quite uplifted by the encounter. She'd forgotten how much she liked Maxine and furthermore she'd forgotten how much she'd got out of the various clubs and societies that she'd belonged to before Nigel's catastrophic actions had so upended her world. Things were never going to be the same but they'd managed to dodge total ruination and their future was looking reasonably secure. Exotic holidays, expensive meals out and luxury cars were never going to be a part of her life like they had been in the past, but she and Nigel had a roof, they could pay the bills and they could afford to eat well and healthily. And, thought Olivia as she parked her bike at the back of the hotel, that was more than many people could say.

Maxine put her poster back on the counter and made

a mental note to take it into town on Monday to get it put up on the town hall notice board. She'd already conducted a straw poll of some of her acquaintances to see what level of enthusiasm there was and she'd been encouraged. But she knew that there was a monumental gap between people expressing an interest and then actually *committing* themselves to paying for membership and coming along to the meetings. But, she thought, nothing ventured, nothing gained.

She returned to her dusting still feeling cheered by Olivia's visit. There was a woman who had shown immense dignity and fortitude in the face of adversity, she thought.

When the reason for the sudden sale of Olivia's old house had become apparent to the locals, a mixture of schadenfreude and sympathy had washed through the town. On the one hand were those who gloated gleefully about the fall of one of the town's most recognisable and influential residents and, on the other hand, were those who felt that it was the kind of calamity which could happen to almost anyone. But through it all, Olivia had held her head high and had refused to complain or rail against her change of circumstances and had, instead, got on with getting a job and downsizing. Maxine wasn't entirely sure she would show quite such strength of character if the tables were turned. And who knew when tragedy or disaster might strike? The news had certainly shaken up her and Gordon and made them count their blessings. And they had plenty to count. It couldn't, thought Maxine for the second time that morning, get much better.

She finished dusting and cleaning the downstairs – she'd do the upstairs on Sunday – and padded across the tiled hall into the big kitchen, pushing the hoover ahead of her to put it away. Much of the house hadn't changed much since it had been built and it boasted a wealth of period features. It was the cornicing, the tiles, the fireplaces and the like which had made both Maxine and her husband, Gordon, fall in love with it completely and which had convinced them they should buy it even though they knew that they would have to live extremely frugally for years in order to afford the mortgage. But it had been worth it and Maxine felt no less love for the house than she had back then. The sole alteration they had made to the fabric had been to extend the kitchen out into the big garden and install some huge bi-fold doors so that in the summer the garden and the house became one. And, last Christmas, Gordon had built Maxine the summer house at the bottom of the garden which she used as a studio. Other than that, Maxine always felt that the original occupants from a hundred years previously would have recognised it and still felt right at home.

As she put away the vacuum in the utility room, she could see Gordon working on the garden, digging over a bed for some spring planting. Above him the cherry tree was in full bloom and the daffs and tulips beneath it were swaying gently in the light April breeze. Maxine smiled, her heart lifted by the gloriousness of the flowers, before she tapped on the window to get her husband's attention and made a 'T' with her two hands. Gordon nodded in response.

Five minutes later, carefully carrying two steaming mugs, Max went into the garden.

She handed one to Gordon.

'Cheers,' he said as he took a sip.

'Olivia just popped by,' she told him.

'You should have said; I'd have come in and said hello.'

'She didn't really stop; she was on her way to work. She said she'd spotted Abi in town and it reminded her that she and I haven't seen each other for an age – not properly, since she had to get a job.'

'How is she?'

Maxine related the gist of her conversation. 'Not that we had time to have a proper catch-up but we promised each other that we will, and soon. And I tried to persuade her to join my art club.'

'Still not enough members?'

'I think I'll be all right, but I won't know for sure till it gets going. The community centre could take up to thirty with ease and I only need about ten to make the project wash its face, but the more the merrier. And the more we have the more we'll have in funds to pay for awaydays.'

'I suppose.' Gordon put his empty mug on the bird table and picked up his spade. 'I'll finish this bed and then we'll go to the pub, yes?'

Maxine didn't need asking twice. Just then her phone pinged with an incoming text.

Need to see you before I head to London. Over in five mins. Lunch would be nice

'The pub's off,' said Max as she showed Gordon her phone.

'Bugger.'

'So, how did you get on?' asked Maxine when Abi had shrugged off her coat. Gordon was still in the garden digging over another bed now the chance of a lunchtime drink had gone.

'Honestly, Mum, I don't know why I bothered. How difficult is it to understand that when a client has a list of *essential* features, it's not a list of things they'd quite like? I mean...' and with that Abi launched into a tirade of how useless the estate agents in Little Woodford had been. As Abi ranted Maxine went into the kitchen, followed by her daughter, and began to make some sandwiches.

'Have you thought of widening your net?' asked Maxine when her daughter drew breath. 'Trying somewhere like Cattebury?'

'Cattebury?' screeched Abi. 'Mum, that's a place people move away from, not to!'

'Or some of the other villages round about?' Maxine began to slice off the crusts.

'Maybe, but I *like* the idea of coming back to my roots; all those happy memories; maybe seeing old school friends. Lots of the kids in my class still have parents who live round and about and they come back to visit them. It'll be nice to hook up with them again, talk about old times...'

As Maxine recalled, Abi hadn't been able to get away from the town fast enough when she went off to uni. She seemed to recall the words *stultifying, boring, crap* and *dead on its feet* featuring quite a lot. And she hadn't thought much better of half the kids in her class either. *Lacking in ambition and drive and brain-dead morons* had been her assessment of some of her peers. She forbore to remind her daughter of her previously held opinions and just said, 'Well, I expect your friends' parents are a bit like us – they like the quiet life because it *is* very quiet here. Would that suit you after living up in London?'

'We'll get the train up to town if we want a bit of excitement,' said Abi.

'Which is fine till you start a family.'

'I don't see what that's got to do with it?'

Maxine did. Although it had been some years since she'd been to a theatre or a concert, she didn't remember babies and small children being welcome in the audience. Or being welcome in night clubs for that matter. 'Well,' she said, 'once kids come along, going out won't be as easy.' She got out a plate and began to move the sandwiches on to it.

'I don't see why not. It isn't as if you and Dad ever do anything – I'd have thought you'd jump at the chance to bond with your grandchildren.' There was a loud sniff. 'Maybe I was wrong.'

'Of course, Dad and I will help out where we can... we'd love to.' She meant it; she was looking forward to being a granny. 'But that's all for the future.' Maxine paused. 'It is, isn't it? I mean, you're not...' She glanced at Abi's stomach.

'No, Mum.' Abi rolled her eyes. 'I want to get settled. We're not going to try until everything is sorted. Anyway, I came back to ask you to keep an eye on the estate agents' windows and the local press. I don't trust them to keep me properly in the loop – I mean, they might have promised to but after their almost universal display of incompetence...'

And with that Abi gave her mother a list of instructions as to how she could best help with the house-hunting. Maxine tried, and failed, not to feel put-upon.

3

The following week, Olivia strolled towards the sole pub in the town, a battered and dog-eared copy of *Jude the Obscure*, which she'd managed to unearth in one of their bookcases, clutched in her hand. The state of the book was a result of it being a set text for her exams, back when she was eighteen. When she'd flicked through it the previous weekend to reacquaint herself with the story, her pencilled notes in the margins reminded her of what a dreary book it had been. She wondered why the group had chosen it. She suspected Miranda, the rather highbrow woman who had moved into her old home, The Grange, might have had something to do with it. Miranda, thought Olivia, had mellowed a little since she'd moved to Little Woodford and had given up trying to change the ways of residents to her way of thinking – encouraging them to embrace veganism and minimalism – but it was more than likely that she still felt it her duty to try to raise the townsfolk's cultural awareness. And good luck with that, thought Olivia as she reached her destination, pushed open the pub's front door and greeted the landlady who, as always, had a genuine and welcoming smile on her face.

'Hi, Belinda.'

'Hello, stranger! I haven't seen you for a while.'

'I know. That's the trouble with shift work – it totally buggers up one's social life.'

'But, all better now, back to a nine to five job... or so Maxine told me.' Belinda tucked one side of her page-boy bob behind an ear.

Olivia grinned. She didn't mind that the town's rumour mill had already swung into action. At least this time she could be thankful that it was good news that people were sharing. It made a pleasant change from the last time she'd been the hot topic of conversation. 'Yes, it's nice to be able to establish a proper routine and to plan ahead.'

'And... and I hope you don't mind me saying this... but the pay rise must be nice too.'

Olivia shrugged. 'I won't say it isn't handy but we've kind of got used to a more basic lifestyle so I don't think we'll be splurging the extra very much. I'll tell you something, though – I *am* considering having Amy back to work for me, if she's got any free time. I hate housework and say what you like about Amy,' which a lot of people in the town did, because she was an inveterate gossip and sometimes got her facts hideously wrong, 'she's a bloody good cleaner. Anyway, enough chitchat, I need to get a drink and get to the book club or Miranda will tick me off for being late!'

'Red?'

'Please. And best I buy a bottle to make up for my shocking attendance record.'

Belinda reached below the bar and picked up a bottle of the house red. She cracked open the screw top and handed it over. 'Nineteen fifty, please. And how many glasses?'

'Give me three. We can always get a couple more if needed,' she replied as she handed over the money and waited for her change. 'Anyone else here yet?'

'Quite a few. Heather, Bex, Miranda, Max – the usual suspects.'

'Cool. Well, I'll see you later. Always assuming we haven't been reduced to topping ourselves by picking over the awfulness of Jude Fawley's life.' She waved her book at Belinda and then tucked it under an arm so she could gather up the bottle of wine and the glasses.

Belinda laughed as Olivia made her way through the bar and up the stairs to the pub's function room. She could hear the animated conversation from the bottom of the stairwell.

'Hello,' she called to the group of around ten women standing around the low table that was placed in the middle of the room, a circle of chairs surrounding it.

Her friends turned and greeted her.

'Olivia!' said Jacqui, the doctor's wife. 'How lovely!'

The others in the room echoed the sentiment.

'Thank you,' said Olivia, suddenly feeling slightly bashful at the effusive welcome. 'I can't tell you how nice it is to stop working shifts.' She gazed around at the women in the room. 'I have *so* missed my social life. Anyway,' she said putting her bottle down on the table, 'what were you all talking about? It sounded very lively.'

'Husbands,' said Heather, the vicar's wife.

Olivia snorted. 'Well, where do I start?' The others laughed. 'Although, as I said to Max only the other day, he *is* getting better.'

'Well, I won't have a word said against Miles,' said Bex, a young widow who had recently remarried to the pub's chef.

'Yes, but you're still in the honeymoon phase,' said Heather.

'*And* he can cook better than most women,' added Maxine.

'*And* he enjoys it,' added Jacqui.

'Don't blame me for being a good picker,' said Bex with a laugh. She looked around the room. 'Anyway, your husbands are all lovely.'

'Oh, they are. Mine is a paragon, except when it comes to housework, cooking, cleaning, ironing, putting out the bins, picking up his dirty clothes off the bathroom floor... the list is endless,' said Jacqui.

'Has he been taking lessons from Brian?' said Heather.

'Aren't they born like it?' replied Maxine.

The sound of more voices and footsteps drifted up the stairwell and a few seconds later another half dozen women piled into the room and the noise level rocketed. Olivia drew Maxine over towards the window.

'I know you said so the other day but retirement *really* is good, isn't it? It *did* seem so when I saw you but... you know... Let's face it, as one who knows all about putting on a brave face, about dissembling to friends...'

'No, honestly I'm not putting on a brave face. I absolutely love it. And so does Gordon.'

'I'm glad. Some marriages aren't strong enough to cope with all this sudden *togetherness*. Not that I've never thought that you and Gordon are anything less than a wonderful example of why marriage is a good thing.'

Max felt herself blushing slightly at this praise. 'To be honest, we're hardly under each other's feet at all. What with his golf and my studio there are some days when our paths hardly cross.'

'Studio?'

'Of course, you didn't have time to see it when you popped over last week. It was my Christmas present from Gordon. It's really a glorified summer house at the bottom of the garden but I love it. The thought has crossed my mind that he bought it for me to get *me* out from under *his* feet...' They both laughed. 'You must have a guided tour next time you pop over. I can paint there undisturbed by the phone, the internet or real life. Honestly what with one thing and another we're busier than ever. And that's before I take into account the WI, the book club, my art club, the occasional lunch with friends plus working in the Oxfam shop.'

'And how is the art club going?'

'We start next week – Thursday evening, at the Community Centre. Fancy coming along?'

'Possibly.'

'I'm going to charge a hundred pounds a term which will cover the room hire, paints, brushes, sketchbooks, acrylics, really basic easels... all the kit to get everyone started.'

'Goodness, that's some investment you've made.'

Maxine nodded. 'It's seed corn money really. If people get keen, they'll probably want to buy their own stuff and, if they do, I can review the fees.'

Olivia was about to reply but was interrupted by Miranda pinging a wine glass with a pen and the imperious ding-ding-ding cut through the conversation.

'Shall we make a start?' she asked.

'I'll make a real effort for Thursday,' said Olivia as they took their seats.

'Please do, it would be lovely to have you join us.'

As the book club, in the upstairs room of the pub, was discussing the ghastly events that had dominated the life of Jude Fawley and wondering if Thomas Hardy was a complete kill-joy, Amy, the cleaning lady to several of the town's residents, strolled into the pub downstairs. As always Amy seemed to have one too many buttons undone on her blouse and her skirt was a good few inches shorter than was entirely decent. Belinda wondered why she wasn't catching her death.

'Hiya,' said Belinda. 'Meeting Ryan?' Ryan was Amy's new boyfriend and a vast improvement on her previous one, Billy Rogers, who was still inside doing time for burglary. Most of his victims had been local townsfolk and no one had felt the least bit of sympathy when the local magistrate had sent him down for three years. Belinda had never understood what Amy had seen in him – nasty weaselly man with a quick temper.

'I certainly am. Well, I am, assuming he hasn't had a shout.' Ryan was a fireman so his and Amy's plans were sometimes ruined if duty called. 'And a G and T please.' Amy extracted a tenner from her bag in readiness. 'And a pint of Guinness, too, please.'

'What if he can't make it?' said Belinda as she pushed a glass under the gin optic.

'Let's cross that bridge when we come to it.'

Belinda picked up a pair of tongs and deftly dropped in ice and a slice before she squirted in the tonic from the dispenser. 'And I might have some good news for you.' She handed the drink through the beer pump handles.

'Really?' Amy took a gulp.

'Olivia was in here just now – she's at the book club upstairs.'

'Mrs L? I haven't seen her for a while. How is the old bat?'

Belinda sucked in her cheeks to stop a smile. 'She's fine. She also mentioned that she's thinking of asking you to clean for her again.'

'You're kidding me.' Amy was genuinely surprised. 'What, after that business with Billy and her mum's engagement ring?'

'Yes, but *you* didn't nick it. Billy was a low-life and you were as honest as the day was long.'

Amy blushed because that wasn't the exact truth – both Heather and Olivia had caught her helping herself to little treats from their biscuit tins or their gin bottles. But she'd learnt her lesson and she hadn't done it since. Well, not much. Or more accurately, she was more careful about not getting caught.

'Have you got any free time?'

'Wednesday afternoons. Mind, I quite like that bit of time as I can get me smalls washed and sort me own gaff out.'

'True, but it'd be another few quid each week.'

'And her new place is only titchy,' said Amy, thoughtfully. 'I could get it all done and dusted in a couple of hours.'

'Exactly. Extra money and still home in time to get a wash on.'

'I'll pop round and see her, shall I?'

Belinda pursed her lips. 'Maybe it'd be better for her to come to you. She didn't say she'd made her mind up for definite.'

'I suppose.'

'And, let's face it, if she's going to get a cleaner the only person she's going to ask is you, isn't it? Hobson's Choice is what she's got.'

'What?'

'There was a film… never mind. It means she's got no choice at all. Who else cleans round here?'

'Yeah, good point. Or if they do, I bet they don't clean as good as me.'

Belinda looked over Amy's shoulder. 'And here comes your young man.' She went to pour the Guinness as Amy turned and greeted Ryan with a big kiss on his cheek. She had to stand on tiptoe as he was six foot and she was only a shade over five. And given that he was rugged and hunky with swarthy good looks and she was blonde, blue-eyed and curvy, they couldn't have been more like chalk and cheese, but somehow they managed to look good together. Belinda smiled fondly at the couple and hoped that this boyfriend was going to prove to be a keeper for Amy. She might have her faults but she deserved a happy relationship.

'Good day?' Amy asked her bloke.

'So-so. I'll be better when I've had a drink.'

'Did you get a shout?'

He grimaced as he nodded. 'An RTA. A nasty one.'

'Ooh, yuck.' Amy pulled a face. 'Don't tell me the details, I don't want to know.'

'No, you don't, trust me.'

'Here you go,' said Belinda, as she handed over the drink. Ryan went for his wallet. 'No, Ames paid for it.'

'Cheers, Ames,' said Ryan with a broad smile. 'I might just hang on to you.'

'Cheeky bugger,' she responded. The pair went to sit at a corner table. 'I might have just had some good news.'

Ryan's brow wrinkled. 'I'm not with you. Either you've had good news or you haven't.'

'That's just it. Belinda told me that one of the ladies I used to clean for is thinking of taking me back on again. So, if she is, it is good news but I don't know for definite yet.'

'OK, I'm with you now but have you got the time? What with the Post Office and your other cleaning jobs it seems to me you hardly have time to draw breath. Between your jobs and my shifts, we see little enough of each other as it is.'

Amy sipped her drink. 'I know but the cash would be nice.'

Ryan sighed and stared at his Guinness. 'Good point.' He paused, then said, 'I suppose...'

'Yeah?'

'This is going to sound a bit cheeky...'

'And?'

'What about if I moved into your place?'

'But you've always said you like your flat, you like your own space.'

'I like you more, Ames. And I'd pay half the bills and the rent and everything, and we'd see more of each other, and I'd do my bit round the house. I'm quite handy with a duster and an iron, and they always say that two can live as cheaply as one—'

'Three. I'd have to ask my Ashley.'

'Of course. Absolutely.'

'He'll probably say he's cool with the idea. He likes you. He never liked Billy.'

'No... well...' No one had liked Billy – except Amy and

that was only because he'd flashed the cash he'd made from drug-dealing and pinching stuff. 'And with me working shifts means there'll be lots of time when it'll just be you and Ash.'

'But what about when you're on nights and need to sleep during the day? Especially at weekends. I don't mind creeping around and being quiet, but it's not fair on Ash.'

'That's why they invented ear plugs.'

'You sure?'

Ryan nodded. 'And your Ash isn't exactly a hell-raiser, is he? I mean if he had a drum kit and needed to practise, I might think twice, but I expect I can sleep through a bit of music or him chatting on his mobile.'

Amy started to smile. 'If you're sure.'

'Never been more sure in my life.'

'How soon do you want to move in?'

'Just as soon as Ash says it's OK.'

4

The following Sunday, as Ryan, helped by Amy and Ashley, was packing the last of his personal possessions into his elderly Corsa, Gordon and Maxine were getting ready to walk across the nature reserve for a lunchtime drink at the pub. They'd done everything on their list of jobs for the morning: outside the grass was cut, the edges strimmed, the washing was blowing on the line; inside the house was dusted, the floors swept and mopped and they both felt they deserved a reward.

Maxine gathered up the paper and shoved it in her handbag so they'd have the crossword to do while they enjoyed their drink and Gordon went round the house, closing the windows and checking all the doors were locked. Two minutes later they were shutting the front door behind them when an unknown car swept into the drive.

'You expecting anyone?' Max asked Gordon as she stared at the Mini.

He shook his head.

Maxine thought for a moment. 'Didn't Judith say something about buying a Mini?'

'Yes, but it's not like your sister to drop in is it? She's never been a fan of this town – no bright lights, no cocktail bars, no Michelin-starred restaurants... Besides, she'd have rung first.'

Gordon was right about Judith liking a bit of hedonism. Actually, she liked *a lot* of hedonism so their contact was pretty much reduced to regular phone calls, which made the relationship much easier on every level and always had done. Gordon disliked Judith's husband Mike, whom Gordon thought was a knob, and it didn't help matters that he also thought his sister-in-law was a spoilt, over-dressed narcissist. Of course, he was polite and tolerant when they met but such encounters were never completely relaxed or easy and over the years they had reduced somewhat. Maxine had tried to convince Gordon that Judith wasn't as bad as he thought, not really, but that her attitude was the result of being the much-longed-for second child who had arrived after Maxine had gone to secondary school and who had been indulged from day one by her doting parents. That she'd always been a bit spoilt hadn't been helped by marrying someone who apparently worshipped the ground she walked on.

The car door opened and out stepped Judith in a faux-fur leopard-print coat (at least Maxine *hoped* it was faux-fur since Mike always seemed to think nothing was too expensive or over-the-top for his wife) and with immaculate hair and huge Jackie O sunglasses. Maxine smiled to herself – how like Judith to wear sunglasses even though the day was overcast.

'Judith? How lovely. We weren't expecting you,' she said, genuinely pleased by the surprise as she hugged her sister. 'You should have rung.'

Judith disentangled herself from Maxine's grasp, raised her glasses revealing a tear-stained face. She was obviously upset about something but whatever had befallen her hadn't stopped her from giving her long blonde hair an elaborate up-do and making up her eyes with liner, mascara and brown eyeshadow which, Judith had always insisted, made her eyes look even bluer. Of course, there was the possibility that the news had come after she'd got up but given that she wasn't an habitual early-riser and it had only just gone midday, Maxine wondered, a bit cynically, if the need to look beautiful outweighed the tragedy. Judith began to sob – loudly and theatrically.

'Judith! What on earth's the matter?' She saw that Gordon had the front door open again and she dragged Judith towards the threshold. 'Is it Mike? What's happened?' she asked as they both got into the hall. Max shrugged off her coat and helped Judith off with hers. 'Gordon, pour Judith a drink. She looks like she needs one.'

'Gin?' offered Gordon. He took Judith's wail as an acceptance and went to pour it.

'Come and sit down,' directed Maxine. She led the way into the sitting room and Judith collapsed onto the sofa. 'So, what's going on?'

Judith rummaged up her sleeve and pulled out a tissue and blew her nose.

'It's Mike.'

Maxine had guessed as much. 'Is he…? He's not…?'

Judith looked up sharply, her sobs ceasing instantaneously. 'Dead? He will be if I have anything to do with it. The bastard's leaving me.'

'No!' Maxine was totally shocked. She'd never have thought Mike would have had the balls to walk out on Judith. 'But why...?'

Judith blew her nose again. 'Oh, go on... guess.'

'Another woman?'

Judith nodded. 'A thirty-year-old. Young enough to be his daughter.' Not that Mike and Judith had any children. She'd flatly refused to even countenance having a baby as it would have ruined her figure.

'Shit,' breathed Maxine.

'Yup, that was pretty much my sentiment.'

Gordon came in with a large gin and tonic and handed it over. He gave Maxine a quizzical look. She mouthed 'Mike' at him, then 'he's left her.'

Gordon pulled a face.

'It's all right,' said Judith. 'You can say it out loud. I won't disintegrate.' She gave them a wan smile. 'Or no more than I have already.' She sniffed then swigged her drink. 'Thanks, Gordon – just what I needed.'

'You'll stay the night, won't you?' said Maxine. She was going to roast a chicken for supper and there'd be more than enough for an unexpected visitor. The spare room bed was made up – it would be no trouble.

'You sure? I did throw a few things in a case... I can't bear the thought of being alone.'

'I wouldn't have offered if I didn't mean it. Although, I'm not quite sure what we're going to have for lunch,' she admitted. She and Gordon usually had scrambled eggs for lunch on a Sunday and she knew she didn't have enough for three.

'Let me take you out,' said Judith. 'While we still have a

joint bank account, I have every intention of spending as much of Mike's money as I possibly can. Bastard.'

'That'd be very kind. Let's go to the pub – then we don't have to worry about driving back.'

Judith necked her drink in three large gulps. 'That's a plan then.'

Ten minutes later they pushed open the pub door, hoping that it wouldn't be too busy which it often was on a Sunday. Luckily there was a vacant table which Gordon and Maxine bagged while Judith went to the bar to collect the menus and a bottle of wine.

It was almost three when they got back to the house by which time Judith was quite maudlin and either crying again or bitterly insulting her ex-husband. One bottle of wine hadn't been enough as far as Judith was concerned so she'd ordered a second, despite Max and Gordon's protestations that they had had plenty and then she'd finished off the meal with a large brandy.

'I think I might have a lie down,' she announced as she staggered into the hall.

'Good idea,' muttered Gordon. More loudly he said, 'Give me your keys and I'll get your case in.'

Judith sat on the bottom step of the stairs as she rummaged deep into her handbag. 'Here they are,' she announced as she hauled the car keys out with a flourish. She hiccupped loudly. 'Oops, manners.'

Gordon fetched in an ominously large case which he took up to the spare room and then Max shepherded Judith upstairs, hovering behind her just in case her sister's sense of balance failed her – which, given how much booze she'd shipped, wasn't entirely unlikely.

Having got Judith safely to her room the couple returned to their sitting room and collapsed.

'Hell's bells,' said Maxine. 'Who'd have thought Mike would have dumped her like that.' She gazed at Gordon. 'And I don't want you getting any ideas.'

Gordon rolled his eyes. 'Come off it, Max. Just because Mike's having a mid-life crisis doesn't mean I'm going to follow suit.'

No, he was right and Max instantly felt bad for having made the suggestion. She moved her train of thought away from men and mid-life crises. 'It's a big suitcase – it certainly isn't *a few things*. How long do you think she's going to stay?'

'Why are you asking me? She's your sister.'

'She looks like she brought enough with her for weeks.'

'She can't stay that long. You know what they say about visitors and fish.'

As Gordon liked to tell her whenever *anyone* came to stay, that both stank after three days, she certainly did. 'I can hardly tell her to sling her hook when her three days are up, can I? She's in a terrible state and supposing she's got nowhere else to go?'

'Then, she'll need to find somewhere. Besides, as Mike's floozy is thirty, she surely has her own place so, he can, presumably, move in with her.'

'Maybe. Unless he's moved *her* in with him. In which case...' They both considered the ramifications of Judith being homeless. 'At least,' said Maxine gloomily, 'if she stays for any length of time, as she's a grown-up I can leave her to her own devices while I get on with my own life. She might be miserable and upset but she can't expect me to put everything on hold.'

'Huh,' snorted Gordon. 'Your sister...? Not want constant attention? Good luck with that.'

Maxine sighed... She loved Judith dearly but she wasn't good with only herself for company. Gordon might have a point.

Judith awoke with a banging headache, a vile taste in her mouth and a total loss of orientation. Where the hell was she? Her heart raced for a second before she recognised the chintz curtains and remembered that she was at her sister's house in her oh-so-twee spare room. Judith gazed at the decor and wondered why on earth her sister had such an affinity for antiques, mahogany and cretonne when the rest of the world had moved onto birch, light oak and clean modern lines. Still, chacun à son goût, although she thought Maxie's *goût* was very iffy. Maybe it was Gordon's taste. She wouldn't put it past him – old stick-in-the-mud. She knew Gordon didn't particularly like her – she wasn't stupid, even though she was equally aware he thought she was.

She shifted her head on the pillows and pain lanced behind her eyes. Ah, yes... there had been gin, and lunch at the pub with wine, and then a brandy. As she stared at the ceiling she wondered if the brandy had been entirely wise. From somewhere in the house she could hear the sound of a television and someone, presumably Maxine, was clattering about in the kitchen. Outside the window she could see it was definitely dusk. It was, wasn't it? It wasn't dawn, surely.

She levered herself onto one elbow and flicked on the radio next to the bed.

'Listen to me, Adam...' she heard Brian Aldridge say. Ah, The Archers, not the Today programme so definitely Sunday evening not Monday morning. She flicked off the radio again, swung her legs off the bed and sat up. Her head clanged as if there was a lead weight rolling around in it. She sat perfectly still for a second or two as the pain subsided and then tottered into the bathroom to grab a glass of water. As she filled the tumbler, she opened the cabinet over the sink in the hope there might be some ibuprofen or paracetamol. No such luck, so she gulped the water and went to find her sister.

The kitchen, when she reached it, was full of steam and the smell of roasting meat. She gagged. Oh, gawd, she didn't think she could face a massive dinner, not feeling like she did. Maxine, standing at the sink with her hands in soapy water, hadn't heard her come in, but she must have seen movement reflected in the window as Judith saw her visibly jump.

'Jesus, Judith, did you have to creep up on me like that?' her sister yelped.

'And do you have to shout?' retaliated Judith. 'I've got a dreadful head. You haven't got any painkillers, have you?'

Maxine raised an eyebrow in that way that had always annoyed her, before she reached into a kitchen drawer and chucked a packet of pills across. Judith snatched them out of the air.

'Thanks.' She popped a couple out of the blister pack. 'Water?' she asked.

Again, that raised eyebrow before Maxine picked up a

glass from the dish drainer and filled it. As she handed it to her sister a pan on the hob began to boil over and Maxine let out an audible 'tut'.

'Look, sorry, I am being such a monumental inconvenience,' said Judith as she took it, her headache making her tetchy. 'I didn't plan to have my life ruined by my crappy husband. I didn't plan to be left high and dry and I'm sorry I'm such a bother.'

'No, no, you're not,' said Maxine, turning down the gas and taking another saucepan off the heat. 'I didn't mean it like that, but you've been here enough times to know where I keep things.' She was juggling the pan and a colander as she drained the veg, then she tipped the broccoli into a dish which she shoved in the oven to keep warm. 'Look, if you'd like to make yourself useful, you could make the gravy.'

Cooking? Shit no. 'To be honest, Maxie, I'd only spoil it.' She put the glass and the rest of the pills on the counter. 'Maybe it'd be better if I got out from under your feet.'

She missed Maxine rolling her eyes as she drifted out of the kitchen and into the sitting room where Gordon was glued to some football match or other. She perched on the sofa. Surely there had to be something better on than footie? The trouble was, Gordon seemed to be quite enjoying it. Well, she wasn't and she was the guest here. Besides, whether it was the pills or the water she didn't know, but she was starting to feel better. And a nice gin would complete her recovery – a hair of the dog and all that – which might be on offer if she could tear him away from the sport.

'Good match?' she asked.

'It's OK,' was the reply.

'Who's winning?'

'Fulham.'

'I didn't know you supported Fulham.'

'I don't.'

'Then why? I mean, why watch if you don't care who wins?'

'Because... because...'

'There, you see. You're just watching for something – anything – to watch.'

Gordon sighed and switched off the TV.

'There, that's better, isn't it? We can have a nice chat now. How long till supper?' asked Judith.

Gordon shrugged and glanced at the clock on the mantelpiece. 'Dunno, twenty minutes, maybe.'

'Good,' said Judith. 'Just time for a pre-dinner drink then. I'm sure Max could do with one too.'

She smiled at Gordon as he stomped into the kitchen to fix the drinks. She leaned across the table and picked up the remote. A second later the theme tune to a banal game show blared across the room. Judith settled herself down to enjoy the entertainment. Football might be rubbish but this programme most definitely wasn't.

Just as Gordon, Maxine and Judith finished their breakfast the next morning, the phone went. Gordon answered it and mouthed 'Mum,' to Maxine as he left the kitchen to chat to his aged parent. Some people described Anthea as 'fiercely independent' but Maxine preferred the phrase, 'cussed old biddy'. She hoped all was well because, if Anthea gave Gordon cause for concern he would, like as not, jump in the car and drive the two hours to her place to make sure with his own eyes, that she was still capable of living on her own in the rambling house where she had resided for the best part of sixty years. Her house was, as Max frequently observed, hopelessly inappropriate for someone of Anthea's age and with limited mobility and vision, but she flatly refused to move out. It had trip hazards between almost every room because of the different levels throughout the building and as for the number of threadbare rugs scattered about it... Her sole concession to her age was to have a cleaner, Dot, who came in twice a week and who, as well as giving the house a once-over and doing the laundry and ironing, shopped on-line for her.

'We'll just have to hope Dot doesn't find her dead at the bottom of the stairs,' Max had said, when the arrangement had been put in place.

'Actually,' said Gordon, 'apart from the shock to poor Dot, it wouldn't be a bad solution; no persuading Mum to go into a care home, no slow decline into dementia, no battling for lasting power of attorney...' The latter was an on-going fight they were having with Anthea.

'I'm not losing my marbles and I resent the implication that I am,' she snapped whenever it was mentioned.

'But, Mum, supposing you did or you had a catastrophic illness? People do, you know, and if that happened there would be nothing I could do for ages to sort out your affairs.'

'If,' said Anthea with a gimlet stare in her son's direction, 'that happens and *if* you dare allow the medics to resuscitate me, when I finally *do* manage to shuffle off, I'll come back and haunt you.'

And Max and Gordon didn't doubt it. Anthea had very

firm views on nature being allowed to take its course. But until that happened, Anthea and Gordon phoned each other about once a week and once every couple of months Gordon felt duty bound to race across country because he had a gut feeling all was not well. Usually his fears were unfounded, but it was, as he often observed, just a matter of time before his mum's grumbling about 'feeling under the weather' actually turned out to be pneumonia or bronchitis. However, the snippet of conversation that Maxine had overheard before Gordon had moved into the sitting room and out of earshot, seemed to indicate that Anthea was still very much in the land of the living and was positively hale and hearty.

She got to her feet and started to stack the dishwasher. She pushed her concerns about Anthea to the back of her mind and turned her attention to her sister instead. Judith's life might be in total crisis but she'd still appeared at breakfast, coiffed, made-up, wearing a smart, silk shirtwaister and some very fetching sandals, looking like something out of a fashion magazine. Maxine, in her habitual jeans and plain cotton shirt felt frumpy in comparison.

'So,' she said, 'you've told me that Mike's a shit and a shyster and that he's got a younger woman but...' she paused. She knew she was being prurient but she felt there was something in Judith's story that didn't quite stack up. 'There's got to be more to him buggering off than having a wandering eye. I mean, a married man having a fling is one thing, dumping his wife is something else.' Across the kitchen table sat Judith, her eyes downcast as she toyed with a cup of coffee, a half-eaten piece of toast on the plate in front of her. 'I mean, presumably he's been carrying on with her for some time so why does he suddenly want to up-end the apple cart and leave you?'

Judith shrugged. 'I can't really see the details are any of your business.' She looked up and glared.

Maxine met her sister's gaze steadily, pulled out a chair and sat down opposite. 'You're my sister, of *course* it's my business. You've been hurt, horribly. Mike's jacked in twenty-five years of marriage... there has to be a reason.'

Judith looked away and pushed her plate across the table. 'Your guess is as good as mine.'

Maxine knew she was hiding something; Judith might have always been an inveterate fibber when it suited her but she'd also been a crap one. However, if her sister wasn't going to level with her there wasn't much she could do. She stood up again. 'Finished?' she asked as she picked up Judith's plate.

Judith raised her eyes. 'Are you talking about breakfast, or my life?'

Maxine sniffed. 'Don't be so melodramatic. You'll be all right. Despite what you've been saying, you know as well as I do that, deep down, Mike's a decent bloke, he's always been generous and he'll make sure you're OK financially.'

Judith's eyes flooded with tears. 'Easy for you to say,' she snapped. 'It's my life that's ruined. He's had my best years and now he's just chucked everything away. I don't want to live on my own. I'm not like you; I'm not good with my own company.' She sniffed and wiped away her tears with her fingertips – careful not to spoil her make-up. 'What'll I do? What will become of me?'

Maxine looked at her sister. If anyone was ever destined to come out of any situation smelling fragrant, it was her sister. She'd no doubt wind up with a huge settlement and be able to live out her years in the lap of luxury – and that was assuming she didn't meet another man, which, considering she was remarkably well-preserved and still a beauty, wasn't outside the bounds of possibility. Not that this was the moment to point it out. Instead she said, 'Your house is worth a mint, you'll be entitled to half of it. You don't need such a big place—'

'When I'm a lonely old lady?' peeved Judith. 'I'll just need a bed-sit and a cat, you mean?'

'Noooo, that's not what I meant. Seriously, supposing you downsized, got a nice flat somewhere so you didn't have to worry about the garden or maintaining such a big place. You'd have squillions left over; more than enough to see you right for the rest of your life.'

'You don't get it, do you? I don't want to be *seen right.* I want Mike. I want company, I want *MY* husband.' Judith got up and stormed out of the kitchen leaving Maxine none the wiser as to Mike's decision but certain there was more to it than just tiring of his wife.

5

Judith stayed for three nights at the end of which both Maxine and Gordon were beginning to realise the old saw about fish and visitors *was* completely true. They both sagged with relief when she announced after supper on the Tuesday that Mike had texted her to say he'd cleared all his things from the house. Now it was empty of his presence she was going to return to it. She'd leave in the morning. Quite apart from the gin bill, they heard more than enough about Mike's shortcomings to last them a lifetime.

'If he really was that bad, why did she put up with him for so long? She's no martyr, is she?' said Gordon to Maxine in the privacy of their bedroom as they got ready for bed. 'And I don't remember Mike being the bastard she's portraying him as. A knob, yes, but not a bastard.'

'I think it's a case of *hell hath no fury…* et cetera, et cetera,' responded Max. 'I also think she wants to try and convince herself that she's better off without him. It's a coping mechanism. I'm still wondering why he upped and left, though. I can't get a thing out of Judith. She says she doesn't know why – beyond the fact he's got a younger woman on the go. Which I suppose might be enough but it seems so out of character for Mike. He's always indulged her so much. Spoilt her, even. Why would he do this now?'

'Why don't you ask him?'

Max stopped brushing her hair and stared at her husband. 'You don't think that's...? No, I couldn't.'

'What, being too nosy? Let's face it, you've only heard your sister's side and you've often told me she can fib for Britain.'

'It's just... I'd be betraying her. Wouldn't I? Siding with the enemy?'

'I don't see why being in possession of the facts is a betrayal.'

'Judith wouldn't see it like that.'

'Just make sure she doesn't find out. If you don't tell her and Mike doesn't either – and why should he? – who will?'

'I dunno. I'll think about it.' Maxine resumed brushing her hair for a bit. Suddenly she put her brush down on the dressing table and turned to face her husband. 'You haven't got some bit of crumpet squirrelled away anywhere, have you?'

'Oh, come off it, Max. Me?! Besides, where was I going to find some willing and able totty on my field trips.' Gordon had been a geologist for a major petro-chemical company and had spent a lot of his working life in the back of beyond looking for oil fields accompanied, mostly, by burly blokes who would do the heavy engineering if he felt further exploration might yield pay dirt.

'You went to conferences too,' she pointed out. 'I bet there were women at those.'

Gordon nodded. 'Probably. But, as the immortal Paul

Newman once said, "why go out for burgers when you've got steak at home."'

'Well, much as that's very sweet of you to compare me to Joanne Woodward you've got to remember that, firstly, he was married to *Joanne Woodward* and I am nowhere near her league in looks or talent... or earning capacity, come to that and, secondly, he isn't immortal, he's dead.'

Gordon grinned at her. 'Details, details. Anyway, never mind Judith or Mike, let's just be grateful she's going home.'

'Although I worry about what she's going to find. I mean, she said that after he'd broken the news, she threw some stuff in a case and lit out to us. Mike could have used the time since to completely empty the place... and the bank accounts.'

Gordon shook his head. 'As I have just said, he's a knob, not nasty.'

'Let's just hope and pray you're right because, if you're not, I've got an awful feeling she'll boomerang right back here.'

Abigail put her phone on the coffee table in their tiny sitting room and rubbed her face with her hands. It had all seemed so easy when she'd told her mum and dad about her and Marcus's planned relocation – sell the flat, find a new house, move in – what could possibly go wrong? But now, almost a month on, she knew the answer to that question; it was *lots*. Plenty of people had viewed the flat but most had gone no further. And now, she'd had a call from their estate agent telling her that the couple who had expressed a real interest in their flat had decided against a second viewing. No, it was all a horrible mess but the move had to go ahead. There was no backing out now because Marcus wasn't going to be able to commute to head office on a daily basis and, even with his promotion, they couldn't afford to rent a place in the country and pay the mortgage on the London flat.

Marcus pushed his glasses off his face and into his thinning hair. For someone who was in his early thirties he had hair more suited to a seventy-year-old. What with that and his thick glasses he looked exactly like the accountant he was. 'We'll find a buyer.'

'Huh. I mean what's wrong with people these days? Fifteen minutes from the station isn't *so* far to walk to get the train. We manage it.' She glared at Marcus as if the distance was his fault.

'But it's not just that though, is it? No garden, no off-street parking—'

'This is London, what the hell do they expect?' She didn't stop to think that the lack of amenity space or car parking were two of the things that she didn't like about the flat either.

Marcus held his hand up to stop her rant. 'Maybe those things, plus the fact the flat is quite small.'

'They'll be lucky to get anything bigger for the money we're asking. And no, I don't think we should drop the price. We'll need every penny if we're going to get what we want near your new job and Mum and Dad.' Marcus didn't reply. 'Aren't you worried that we may not have sold when you have to move?'

Marcus nodded. 'We might have to get a bridging loan. It wouldn't be too bad with interest rates as low as they are.'

'I suppose. But that's if we find somewhere to move *to*.'

Abi looked at the pile of estate agent details on the coffee table, all printed out on the office printer because she found it so much easier to compare what was on offer on paper rather than on the internet, and the company was better placed to absorb the cost of printer ink than she was. 'It isn't as if we're after something outrageously unusual… Three beds, two bathrooms, gas heating… I mean, all quite normal stuff. If we wanted a home cinema or a heated swimming pool, I'd understand that there mightn't be much to choose from—'

'There certainly wouldn't be for the money we've got.'

'Don't be facetious, you know what I mean.' She pushed at the pile of paperwork. 'Which is more than the bloody estate agents do. Two thirds of these houses are hopeless.'

'But we could compromise. I don't mind if it isn't perfect—'

'—well, I do.'

Marcus ploughed on, bravely. 'Just because a house isn't *completely* perfect, it doesn't mean we couldn't make it so.'

'But the expense, the mess.'

'Short-term pain, long-term gain,' reasoned Marcus. 'And we might add thousands to the value, especially if we bought somewhere that was a doer-upper.'

Abi considered his argument for all of a few seconds before she dismissed it. 'No. Besides, I couldn't live in a place that was over-run with builders.'

Marcus leaned over and picked up the pile. He shuffled through them, reading each one carefully. After a few minutes he rifled back to one he'd noticed and pulled out the pages from amongst the others. 'This one is a case in point.'

Abi barely glanced at the sheet of A4 he held out to her. 'But look at the state of it.'

He studied the pictures. 'It's all cosmetic.'

'But it's gross.'

'I agree, the kitchen and bathroom are vile but replace those, get rid of the wallpaper, put down new carpets and it'll be lovely. And it's reflected in the price; it's way below our budget.'

Abi took the details and had a second look. 'It's only got one bathroom.'

'The main bedroom is huge, vast. Plenty of space to put in an en-suite. You could probably fit in a dressing room as well.'

'I suppose…'

'None of the jobs are tricky. A few stud walls here and there, new units… a built-in wardrobe or two. You want modern – well, it would be when we've finished with it, and a half-decent builder and a painter and decorator could have the whole job done in a couple of weeks. I reckon, once we've done the work the house would be worth another hundred thou.'

'You think?'

Marcus nodded. 'It'd be a fantastic investment.'

'And only two weeks.' She didn't stop to wonder what Marcus, a non-practical, DIY-averse, money-man knew about house building and retro-fitting? Instead she pondered the prospect and the price and the huge mark-up they might achieve when the work was finished. There was certainly a lot of bang for your buck – it was a much bigger house than anything else they'd been offered. Abi didn't like compromise but, on this occasion…

'And with a garden that size,' added Marcus, 'there'd be room to extend if we wanted to. That would add even more value. And it's handy for the school and the village shop and,' he looked at the map, 'not that far from your parents.'

Abi nodded. He had a point. 'Maybe we should go and see it. I'll fix a viewing in the morning for Saturday and then ring Mum. We could stay the night with them – make a weekend of it. Mum and Dad would like that.'

The next morning, Judith parked her car on her driveway and stared at her house. In some ways she was glad to be home because staying with her sister had been tricky. When she'd fled there, three days previously, it had seemed like a good idea; a bolt-hole in which to hide while she licked her wounds after Mike's appalling bombshell. But she'd barely arrived before she remembered how much Maxine and Gordon could irritate her with their air of faint superiority, of being better, just by being older. The last straw, as always, was her sister's barely concealed implication that her life would have been so much more fulfilling if only she'd had children. Really? Like, having stretch marks, saggy tits and a vastly depleted bank balance would have been the great panacea. Besides, despite what she'd told Maxine about Mike's faults, they weren't as bad as she'd made out and she *had* been happy, *very* happy, right up until the moment he'd buggered off.

She pulled her keys out of the ignition and stared at the bunch for a second or two. She was dreading going in, she was dreading living on her own, she was dreading the future… she was dreading everything. Wearily, she undid her seat belt and got out of the car. She went round to the boot, popped it and hauled her case out. Time was she'd have got her husband to do that... no more. She grunted as she dragged it to the front door and over the doorstep. She let herself in and gazed at her empty house – nothing obvious had changed, except everything had. The atmosphere was different and it wasn't just because it had been left empty for a few days. Heavens, she and Mike had left the house empty every time they went off on a cruise but it never felt 'abandoned' when they returned – which is how it felt now. And cold.

She took off her coat, hung it on the newel post, banged up the thermostat and then went into the kitchen to put on the kettle. What she really wanted was gin but even under the circumstances she couldn't bring herself to crack open the bottle for elevenses. Besides, drinking alone was the way to ruin and one thing she had decided on was that she was going to get even with Mike and, for that, she needed to be focused. He had had her best years and she was going to make him pay.

While the kettle came to the boil, she went upstairs to check that Mike had indeed gone and removed all evidence of his presence. She opened his wardrobe and found a few old suits and a couple of pairs of down-at-heel shoes but the rest of the hanging space was empty. This actual proof of his departure hit her unexpectedly and she collapsed, sobbing, onto the bed. She was all alone. No one loved her. What was to become of her?

After about ten minutes of self-indulgent sobbing, Judith's tears dried up. With no one to feel sorry for her or to say 'there-there' crying seemed rather a waste of time. She blew her nose and sat up. She returned downstairs and switched the kettle on again. While she waited for it to re-boil, she sat at the table in her vast kitchen and took stock. Maybe, she thought, her sister was right. This house was huge, it was worth a mint and, much as she liked it, it was going to seem awfully big and lonely when she was rattling around in it on her own. If she was honest, it wasn't as if she and Mike had had a load of friends in their town. Maxine had always said she'd missed out on school gate friendships because she was childless and, at the time, she'd poo-poo'd the whole concept but, in retrospect, Maxine did seem to know a lot of people in Little Woodford and it wasn't just because of the number of years she'd lived there. She and Mike had lived almost as long in West Myring and they hardly knew a soul. OK, since Mike had taken early retirement they'd spent half the year on cruises or other holidays so they hadn't been around much, but even when he'd been working, Judith had preferred to spend her days up in London, drifting around the high-end shops of Bond Street or being pampered in a luxury spa rather than spending her money in her own neighbourhood. West Myring was a nice-enough town but its main attraction for Judith had been the fast train to Waterloo which meant central London was only thirty minutes away.

The kettle crescendoed and clicked off so she made her tea and returned to the table with her mug. She wrapped her fingers around the warm china and continued with her line of thought. The hard fact was there was no particular reason for her to stay in this house. She mulled over, in turn, the idea of a swanky London apartment, or maybe a little mews house in Belgravia or perhaps a smaller place here in the village... But she'd still be lonely. She'd still be living on her own. If she had a crisis, a problem or was ill, who could she turn to?

The answer came to her like an epiphany. Her sister. Maxine might be irritating and Gordon mightn't be her greatest fan but she didn't have to see that much of them and to live reasonably close might be very useful – for a start, Maxine would know all about the local amenities and tradespeople so Judith wouldn't have to grope around in the dark, finding things out for herself. The town might be as dull as ditch water, but the spa at the local hotel would pass muster at a pinch and it had great train links to London. Maybe the city wasn't thirty minutes away but it was still less than an hour. Yes, as a plan it worked.

As Judith was considering her options and her future, her sister was staring at her mobile. Should she? Shouldn't she? Maybe it would be easier to text? Less intrusive. Besides, as her sister had very forcefully pointed out only a week ago, the reason for Mike's departure was no one's business but Judith's. Which was undoubtedly true but didn't do a single thing to allay Maxine's curiosity. With a sudden burst of determination Maxine picked up her phone and hit the button to call her ex-brother-in-law.

'Max?' Mike sounded incredibly wary.

'Hi, Mike. I'm just ringing to say how very sorry I am about you and Judith.'

'Yes... well...'

'And I want you to know that Gordon and I don't have an axe to grind with you.'

'Really?' He sounded sceptical.

'Look... I know Judith can be quite demanding. I am her sister when all's said and done and I know jolly well she's always been quite high maintenance.'

'She likes nice things.'

'Indeed.'

'And if you're worried about me doing the dirty on her... well, you needn't. I'll make sure she gets everything she ought to.'

'That's very noble of you. But what about...? I mean, you'll have enough left for...'

'Enough left for my new family, you mean?'

Family? That made it sound like there were kids involved. Maybe his new bird had a child or two from a previous relationship. 'I'm sorry, I don't know anything about your...' Shit, what did she call this woman? Mistress? Bit on the side? Girlfriend?

'My fiancée,' said Mike firmly, 'is called Trina.'

'Sorry,' said Maxine again. 'Judith didn't tell me her name.'

'That sounds like Judith. She was a great one for ignoring things she didn't like in the hope they'd go away. Only this time it didn't work.'

'No.' Obviously not.

'Anyway, I've moved into Trina's flat and we're going to marry just as soon as the divorce comes through.'

'Gosh.' Not hanging around then.

'I'm hoping Judith isn't going to cause problems. I'm letting her divorce me, I'm the guilty party in all this. I won't make any difficulties about the finances involved. I want this all over as quickly as possible. Call me old-fashioned but I want my baby born into wedlock.'

'Baby?!' Maxine couldn't help herself.

There was a pause. 'Judith didn't tell you about that, either.'

'Er, no.'

She heard a dry laugh. 'No, well... I suppose I never thought I wanted children. Jude convinced me they were a dreadful expense, they'd ruin our life-style, we were happy with just each other, we didn't need anyone else in our marriage; the excuses went on and on. And then I met Trina and she is everything that Jude isn't.'

'Jude has her good points.' Maxine felt duty bound to defend her own flesh and blood.

'She has. Loads. But Trina is just so different. She's so passionate about the planet and wildlife and she puts her money where her mouth is. She's utterly committed to recycling, to reducing the use of plastics, to living sustainably—'

Which no one could ever accuse Judith of doing. 'And she's pregnant,' said Maxine.

'Well... yes. And that's the key issue; that's the ultimate reason why I'm leaving Jude. It absolutely wasn't planned – Trina's pregnancy is a complete accident but it's a miraculous accident. When Trina told me she... *we*... are having a baby it was like I was hit by lightning. Suddenly I knew that this was the one thing in my life that would make me happy. That right up to that moment all the things, all the consumerism, all the travel and trips and hedonism were all just stuff I was using to fill my life with, because the one thing that would have made me complete – a child – was the one thing I didn't have. And which I wanted more than anything.'

The cynic in Maxine wondered if Trina's pregnancy had been quite as accidental as Mike believed. Really? In this day and age with modern contraception? 'Well, I'm glad you sound so happy,' she said. I hope it lasts, she added mentally. She had her doubts. He'd certainly made his bed and now he was going to lie in it. He obviously thought it was one of roses. Nasty things roses, though, despite the pretty flowers and delicious scent they had all those thorns and a tendency to greenfly and other parasites. 'Just one thing, Mike, don't tell Judith I phoned.'

'God no. Consorting with the enemy? No, don't worry about that.'

Maxine disconnected. Part of her wished she'd never made the phone call because it was going to be bloody difficult pretending she didn't know about the baby when she spoke to Judith.

6

Having finished talking to Mike, Maxine decided to make the most of Judith's departure and the decent weather by sitting in the sun with her book. Ah, the bliss of not having visitors. Her enjoyment was cut short by her phone ringing. Abi.

'Hi, darling, how are things? How's the house buying and selling going.' She half-wished she hadn't asked the question as she listened to her daughter's rant about the buyers who had pulled out and then felt her heart sink as Abi told her about their planned visit to see the doer-upper. So much for your long list of non-negotiables, thought Maxine.

'And we thought we could stay over on Saturday night and go back to London Sunday afternoon. That's OK, isn't it?'

'That's lovely, dear,' said Maxine.

'Good. We've got a viewing at two; we'll come to yours afterwards. Oh... and what have you got planned for meals?'

'I don't know, I hadn't really thought,' she lied.

'Only Marcus and I have gone vegetarian.'

'Vegetarian?'

'And it wouldn't do you and Dad any harm to cut back

on your meat consumption. Do you know how much grain goes into producing a kilo of meat? And as for industrial abattoirs.'

'Well, dear I'm sure not all of them are—'

'Don't be ridiculous, they're all the same. So, food… something yummy and veggie would be nice, only not quiche or pasta – we eat a lot of that.'

Maxine felt her blood pressure rising. 'Of course, dear, Anything else?'

'No, thank you.' It was apparent from Abi's airy tone that she hadn't picked up on her mother's irritation.

'Good. What time can we expect you on Saturday?'

'About three. See you then.'

Maxine put the phone down and wondered what the hell she could feed them. Gordon was very much of the meat-and-two-veg school of dietary requirements. She didn't think he was going to be thrilled about a meat free weekend. The back door clicked open and Gordon came in, toeing off his wellingtons as he did so. He logged the expression on his wife's face.

'Bad news?'

'Abi and Marcus are coming to stay at the weekend.'

'That's nice.' He saw Maxine wasn't in complete agreement. 'And?'

'And they've gone veggie.'

'Bugger me. What are you going to give them?'

'I haven't the first idea. I suppose I'd better get busy with the internet.'

'It'll be nice to see Abi, though.' He paused then added, 'I wish I had more in common with Marcus. I always find him such hard work to talk to.'

'I know, dear.'

'I mean, what do I know about accounting?'

'He's not that bad.'

Gordon's face perfectly reflected his disagreement. And Max could see his point of view. He and Marcus were never going to be soul mates. All his life Gordon had worked surrounded by out-doorsy types who were weather-beaten, swore, drank and took whatever life threw at them on the chin, while Marcus's complexion indicated that he loathed fresh air and his attitude to life was quite timid. Maxine often wondered what Abi saw in him given how strong her personality was – but maybe she liked having someone to boss around. She sometimes wondered how long it would be before Marcus got fed up with being ordered about, or Abi got tired of always having to make the decisions.

'God, this place is even worse than it looks in the pictures,' said Abi, as she and Marcus drew up outside Wisteria Cottage. The gravel drive was covered in weeds and the grass either side was waist high.

'But you can't say it was mis-named,' said Marcus as he stared at the pale mauve climber that covered the front wall of the Georgian style house. It was, according to the particulars, older than it looked with a facade added in the eighteenth century. It had two sash windows either side of the front door and three above. In the roof there were a couple of dormers and at each gable end there was a tall chimney stack. It looked like a classic doll's house. To the right-hand side was a large single-storey extension which had been fairly sympathetically done and blended in with the original building pretty well.

The noise of another car approaching spurred them to get out of theirs.

'Hi,' said a smooth man in a suit. 'Miss Larkham, Mr Stockwell? I'm Tim.' He pulled some keys out of his pocket with one hand as he proffered his other one for them to shake.

'Abi and Marcus,' said Abi. 'Let's get on with it, shall we?'

'So,' said Tim, 'as you can see this is a period cottage, set in a large plot—'

'Yeah, yeah,' said Abi, 'let's cut to the chase shall we and see what it's really like?'

Tim gave her a hard stare but headed for the front door. It creaked loudly as he opened it. 'Nothing a bit of WD-40 won't fix,' he said.

Abi stepped into the house onto a flagged floor and sniffed. 'Well, it doesn't smell of damp.' She sniffed again. 'Or vermin.' They looked at the big hall which ran the depth of the house, with stairs to one side leading up to the first floor and which had two windows overlooking the back garden. The walls were wainscotted up to a dado rail about waist height in dark oak. 'This is a lot of wasted space,' she said then she pointed at the panelling. 'And that'll have to go. Far too dark and old-fashioned.'

'The previous occupant used it as a dining room.'

'Still a waste of space if you ask me. Dark, wasted space.' She swept through it to the door on the right-hand side. She opened it and peered into the kitchen. 'God, this is a disaster – and more panelling.' She went in and Marcus and Tim followed her. She stared at the cracked lino on the floor. 'This'll have to go too. Quite apart from being hideous, it's a health hazard.'

'New units, a range cooker... It's very big,' said Tim. 'You won't get anything this size in a new-build,' he added. 'And here,' he added, throwing open a door, 'is the pantry, and here,' he took a couple of paces to his left and opened another, 'is the boot room.'

'Or we could knock those rooms into this and have a massive open-living space,' said Abi, thoughtfully.

'Let me show you the drawing room.'

After thirty minutes the pair had seen every square inch of the house, including the attics and, despite Abi's dislike of the decor, she could see it had huge potential.

'And, as you have no doubt deduced, it's vacant possession,' said Tim. 'No onward chain.'

'Yes, thank you. We'll let you know.' They left Tim to lock up and went to sit in their car.

'What do you think?' said Marcus.

'Superficially, it's got a lot going for it but all that work to strip it out...' Abi sighed. 'Are you sure it'll only take a couple of weeks?'

'The stripping out will be quite quick and I can't think it'll take more than a couple of weeks to fit a new bathroom and a kitchen. The alteration upstairs might take a bit longer... maybe three weeks, four tops.'

While Abi and Marcus enjoyed a lie-in on the Sunday morning, Maxine was pottering around her kitchen, emptying the dishwasher. As she worked, she thought about her daughter's enthusiasm for the house they'd viewed. Maxine decided she needed a second look at the details, in the cold light of day and without the benefit of a glass – or two – of wine. She put down a handful of clean cutlery and went into the sitting room to retrieve the estate agent's particulars. She read through them again as she returned to the kitchen and sat down so she could concentrate properly.

On the face of it, Abi and Marcus were right – it had huge potential. The rooms were all much bigger than you'd get in a modern build and there were quite a few nice period features: the stable door from the kitchen to the garden; the big fireplace in the sitting room; the antique balustrades with the polished chestnut banister; some pretty cornicing... But it was old and had been empty for a while. However, the estate agent had assured them that the house was sound – well, he would, wouldn't he? – and Marcus was sure there would be a massive profit to be had from doing it up. And Abi was full of ideas for how to get the most out of the spacious rooms. Turning the massive kitchen into a huge open-living space was a no brainer and making the little sitting room into a study also seemed sensible but some of Abi's other rather grandiose plans...

'The attic is huge, it runs the whole length of the house so it would be perfect to make it into some sort of giant rumpus room – maybe a home cinema,' she'd said.

At least, thought Maxine, with giant screen TVs being widely available and modern speaker-technology making surround-sound fairly run-of-the-mill, this idea wasn't as completely outrageous as it first sounded.

As Max looked at the pictures and the estate-agent-speak words, she recalled that neither her nor Gordon's parents had been encouraging about them buying this house. *You're over-stretching your finances and think of the work,* had been a couple of comments, and *why on earth do you want a big house like that?* had been another. She and Gordon had ignored them and had pig-headedly gone ahead and, in retrospect, it had been absolutely the right decision. Most of the work on their house had been done by themselves and the house had been totally sound structurally so, although it had cost a great deal in time and effort, it hadn't been financially draining. To counsel her daughter against buying a house that needed love, attention and hard work – exactly like her own house had done – would be hypocritical in the extreme, except that Maxine was sure it was going to need a lot of cash as well. Marcus and Abi couldn't possibly do very much of the work themselves and professional tradesmen didn't come cheap. Still, Marcus was the accountant and if he thought the sums stacked up, they probably did. What Maxine didn't stop to consider was that Marcus's knowledge of anything practical was absolutely zero – as was Abi's.

7

'I was talking to the estate agent today,' said Abi on Monday evening as she and Marcus walked back from the Tube station to their flat, their arms linked.

'What about?'

'Selling our flat.'

'And?' Marcus sounded cautious.

'He suggested it would have a better chance if we were to move out; put our stuff in store, give the flat a good going over, maybe a lick of paint, make it into a blank canvas so anyone viewing it can see what a lovely place it is.'

Marcus stopped in his tracks, jerking Abi to a halt too. He frowned at his partner. 'Storage? That's going to cost. *And* we'd have to rent somewhere here for a month and it's hardly likely anyone will give us such a short-term deal, not without a massive bill attached. I mean we're looking at Airbnb here, or a hotel,' he said. 'I thought you wanted to save as much as possible of the relocation money.'

'I do. But the clock is ticking – we've *got* to move up to Cattebury by July, so going a bit early isn't going to make a massive amount of difference. Look, I asked my boss about the chances of us getting a spot of gardening leave, and he didn't say no. Plus if we take some of our annual leave we could have as much as four weeks.' She looked at Marcus for approval. 'If we move up in June, we've got the whole month to get everything sorted, the new house fixed, the old one done up *and sold* – which I'm sure we will, once it's empty. The estate agent was really positive, says empty ones get snapped up in no time.'

'He's said, right from the get-go, the flat would get snapped up.'

'Yes, well... But he was really positive about our chances if we do as he says now. Seriously, it's a great plan.'

The pair set off along the pavement again.

'But there's no guarantee we *will* sell. We might end up paying two mortgages *and* the storage costs.'

'Ah, I've thought about that.'

Marcus's frown returned. 'And?'

'And...' She paused for dramatic effect. 'You know that ridiculous studio Mum's got in the garden.'

'Of course, and it's not really rid—'

Abi cut him off mid-sentence. 'We could shove all our stuff in there. I mean why does she need all that space just to paint some third-rate watercolours? It isn't as if she makes any money out of them. David Hockney, she ain't.'

'I think you're being a bit harsh, Abi. And your mum is pretty serious about painting – she's started that art club in town which, from what she was telling us, sounds pretty popular.'

'Says her.'

'And I rather like some of your mum's pictures.'

'Really?' Abi gave a snort of incredulity. 'Anyway,

it's almost summer – she can paint outside, and that shed is heaps big enough to put our stuff into. Let's face it, it's only our bed, a couple of sofas and some pots and pans.'

'I think it's a bit more than that.'

'Hardly.' Abi looked sharply up at Marcus. 'And even if it is, we could put anything that won't fit in, in their house. Just look at all that space they never use.'

Marcus didn't respond.

'Are you suggesting it's not a good idea?' said Abi.

'No... well... I mean it's a bit of an imposition on your folks, don't you think?'

'Come off it, Marcus, it'll only be for a few weeks. We're hardly moving in for good.' Abi exhaled an exasperated sigh. 'The clock is ticking, we *have* to relocate, we've found a house we both love – well, we will once it's properly sorted out – and we *need* to sell the flat.'

'I suppose.'

Abi ignored the scepticism in Marcus's voice. 'Good, that's sorted. I'll ring Mum as soon as we get home.'

Maxine put down the phone and sank slowly onto the saggy old armchair in the kitchen. On the face of it everything Abi said made sense, except... except fundamentally she felt she was being bounced into something she didn't want, hadn't asked for but could hardly refuse.

Gordon bumbled into the kitchen. 'Have you seen my...?' He stopped. 'What's up, love? You look like you've seen a ghost.'

Maxine looked up at him, her lips pursed. 'Not a ghost. I've just had Abi on the phone.'

'Oh, yes. And?' Gordon spotted the glasses he'd been looking for and picked them up. 'Why do I get the feeling what you're about to tell me isn't unalloyed good news.'

'They still haven't had much interest in their flat. Abi wants to move out so it's on the market as vacant possession.'

Gordon considered this. 'She might have a point. People are wary of getting stuck in a chain. Worse in London, I'd imagine.'

'Quite possibly. But she wants to use my studio as a storage depot.' She gazed bleakly at Gordon. 'Apparently, as,' she raised both hands and drew quotation marks in the air, 'it's nearly summer, I can paint outside, and anyway I don't make any money from my paintings so it isn't as if it's important.'

'Abi said that?'

'Pretty much.'

'What did you say?'

'To be honest, I was so taken aback I didn't really say anything.'

'I suppose,' mused Gordon, 'it's big enough for all their kit.'

He didn't get it, thought Maxine, still feeling raw at her daughter's less than veiled insult about her art. 'But it's *my* studio.'

'I know, but it won't be for long. And you managed without it before you got it.'

Which was true.

'When's all this going to happen,' he added.

'In a few weeks, maybe less. Abi says they're going to ask the company if they can take a bit of gardening leave between jobs, move up here and then they'll be on hand to keep an eye on the work being done on the new house.'

'So they'll be living here too.'

Maxine nodded. 'She *says* it'll only be for a couple of weeks.'

'That's all right then. We'll manage.'

Maxine shrugged. She was fairly certain she'd be the one who'd be doing the managing – not Gordon.

'Have they done anything about getting quotes for the building work yet?' asked Gordon.

'I didn't ask. I imagine they have. You know how organised Abi is. She'll probably have a spreadsheet with it all worked out.'

'More than likely.'

'She was telling me her plan; they're going to hire a van, pick it up after work on a Friday, pack it that evening, bring it here first thing on the Saturday, unload, and then race back to London to clean, paint, tidy, sort... And would we like to follow them in the car to help?'

'It'll be a quicker job if we do.'

'They say we'll just need to lend a hand with some cosmetic stuff. Many hands make light work and all that. Abi says it'll be done and dusted in a few hours and we'll all be back here the same day.'

'In my experience,' said Gordon, 'once you start doing a bit of decorating you have to paint everything, otherwise anything you haven't done looks terribly shabby in comparison.'

Maxine tried to look on the bright side. 'It's only a tiny flat.'

'Just wait till you start renewing all the white gloss – it'll seem blooming massive then.'

8

A few days later, Maxine stood at the front of the Community Centre and looked at the semi-circle of chairs that were grouped around her. Fifteen expectant faces smiled at her.

'Good evening, everyone. And welcome to another session of the art club. I thought today we'd try our hands at some abstract painting.' She moved to the table at her side and switched on the projector which was connected to a small laptop. On the screen behind her appeared a series of dots in various shades of black, white and grey.

'This is called *Hesitate* and it was painted by Bridget Riley. Now, whether it makes you feel giddy or confused, whether you love it, loathe it or are indifferent, I don't think any of us could dispute that it's a very clever bit of graphic design.' There was a murmur of assent. Maxine clicked the touch pad and the picture changed to a rectangle of multi-coloured splatters. 'And this is a Pollock.'

'It's a load of...' said a wise-cracker.

There's always one, thought Maxine.

The image changed to big rectangular blocks of colour separated by stark black lines. 'Mondrian,' said Maxine. She tapped the touch pad at intervals of several seconds.

'Klimt, Klee, Matisse…' She showed her class about twenty paintings in all. 'So, as you can see there are as many styles of abstract painting as there are modern artists. Well, almost. There is no right or wrong and whether you like something or not is all a matter of taste. If you need inspiration, I've some books of modern art here and you are welcome to flick through them but let's all have a go and see what we come up with.'

Behind the ring of chairs Maxine had put out half a dozen large tables so some of the group moved over to sit at these and immediately opened their big A3 sketch pads and got busy with pencils while others began to gather round the books. A hum of conversation filled the room.

Olivia stayed put and stared into space.

'Looking for inspiration?' asked Maxine.

'Kind of. I think I'd like to have a go at something a bit like some of Bridget Riley's stuff but I suspect that it'll be harder than it looks.'

'Give it a go – it's the only way to find out. Sometimes the *prospect* is worse than the reality.'

'So very true.'

'There's a whole raft of Bridget Riley's pictures in one of those books. They don't all involve circles – some are swirls, some are zig-zags. Some look deceptively simple.' Maxine moved towards the table at the front and picked up one of the glossy publications. She flicked through the pages. 'Ah, here we go.' She showed Olivia the pages. 'And while I've got your undivided attention can I ask for some advice.'

'Ask away,' said Olivia as she studied the pictures. 'I'm not sure how much use I'll be.'

'When Jade moved back to yours, before she moved out

to the vicarage, how did you cope? I mean, did you set down ground rules from the get-go or did you work out how to rub along as time passed.'

Olivia snorted. 'Huh.' She rested the book on the table. 'It was ghastly. We nearly came to blows and we had the mother and father of all rows. Honestly, she might have been twenty-three when she moved in, used to independent living and earning a wage but the instant she stepped over the threshold she reverted to being a small child. She couldn't even put her own stuff in the dishwasher and as for helping around the house...'

'Oh lordy. That bad?'

Olivia nodded. 'And when she moved down to Heather and Brian's she wasn't much better. I felt ashamed of what I'd dumped on them. In the end, even their Christianity was tried to the limit. They had to read her the riot act to make her realise that leaving a trail of chaos and mess behind her was unacceptable.' Olivia stared bleakly at Maxine. 'It really made me question my parenting skills. Again.' She didn't have to explain to Maxine that she'd first had to question them when it transpired that her youngest, Zac, had got himself heavily caught up in the local drug scene. She exhaled a deep, heartfelt sigh. 'Anyway, why do you ask?'

Maxine told Olivia about Abi and Marcus's plan. 'Of course, they've promised it'll only be a couple of weeks.'

'For a complete refurb of a house?'

'So they say.'

'I hope they're right.' Olivia sounded incredibly doubtful which exacerbated Maxine's concerns. 'Have you seen what needs doing?'

Maxine nodded. 'Gordon and I went over a few days back. It's horribly dated but a new kitchen and bathroom and a lot of fresh paint will make it really nice. Maybe they're right about it only taking a few weeks.'

'Hmm,' said Olivia, 'good luck. But regardless of the length of time I'd get some ground rules in place before they move in; like when they're going to cook, when they can use the washing machine, who unloads the dishwasher. I know it sounds prescriptive but it'll be easier in the long run, believe me.'

Maxine felt her heart sink. Everything that Olivia said mirrored her fears about having a grown-up child return to the house. And worse, she knew that Olivia was right about laying down some rules but she could imagine Abi's reaction. And if things got as bad as Olivia had intimated things had with Jade, she couldn't see Gordon taking things sitting down – even his patience would be tested. It wasn't going to be for long, she reassured herself. Abi and Marcus's circumstances were very different from Jade's, who had returned because she'd broken up with her boyfriend and was homeless and jobless. And Abi wasn't like Jade in that she was a bit of a control freak who couldn't bear mess and muddle so at least Maxine's house was unlikely to be reduced to chaos like Olivia's had.

'Look,' said Olivia, as she put the book down, 'I'm off this weekend and I still haven't had the guided tour of your studio. How about I pop over for coffee on Saturday and give you some of my considered thoughts on how to handle boomerang children.'

'Olivia! Would you? I won't lie to you – I am dreading

having Abi back and, I know Gordon is much more forgiving, but even so...'

'He probably won't handle it any worse than Nigel did and we survived.' Olivia smiled. 'I still have flashbacks to the day Jade called Nigel and I *emotionally retarded fuck-wits.*'

Maxine boggled. 'What?'

Olivia nodded. 'Nigel, as you can imagine, didn't take it well.'

Even Gordon, thought Maxine, who indulged his daughter in almost every way, would find that unforgivable. Olivia was right – that sort of scenario was to be avoided at all costs and if ground rules were the answer, so be it. But, she had a horrible feeling that no matter how diplomatic and sensitive she was in suggesting them, Abi might find grounds to take offence. She resolved to discuss the matter with Gordon in the morning and shoved the problem to the back of her mind. The trouble was, the problem refused to be *shoved* and she woke up several times in the night worrying about the issue.

Judith sat on her white leather sofa with her feet up and pressed the button on her phone to ring her ex-husband. She was shocked when a woman's voice answered it. That bloody little trollop, she thought. She almost disconnected there and then but she needed to talk to Mike and the sooner the better.

'Can I speak to my husband?'

'He's on the toilet.'

'Well, when he's off the *lavatory*—' God, toilet. How common. '—please tell him I rang.'

'Certainly. Can I tell him what it's about?'

'Nothing that concerns you.' She ended the call.

A couple of minutes later Mike phoned back. 'And there was no need to be rude to Trina, like that,' he said after they'd exchanged perfunctory greetings.

'I wasn't.'

'Have it your way. What is it you want to talk to me about?'

'I've sold the house.'

'Already?'

'It barely made it onto the market. And I got the full asking price so as soon as it goes through, I'll send you your half, less the fees.'

'I'm paying the fees, am I?'

'As I did all the work selling the blasted place, I think that's only fair.'

There was a sigh. 'If you think so.'

'I do.'

'Have you found somewhere to live?'

Judith thought he didn't sound terribly interested but then why should he be? He was all right, shacked up with his bimbo. 'Not yet, but with the best part of a million to play with I think I'll be able to find a very nice flat.'

'Are you staying in West Myring?'

'No. I'm moving closer to Max, not that it's any of your business.'

'Have you told her?'

'Of course I have,' lied Judith. 'She and Gordon are delighted.'

'Oh, I'm sure they are.'

Bastard. She was certain he was laughing at her. 'I'll let you know when the money's on its way. After that we probably won't *ever* have to have *anything* to do with each other.'

'Suits me.'

'And me. Goodbye.' But Judith was lying again, this time to herself and she felt a tear trickle down her cheek. She blew her nose and sniffed. Twenty-five years of marriage down the Swanee. What a waste. All that love and attention she'd lavished on Mike, and what had she got to show for it? She didn't stop to think that she had a wardrobe full of designer outfits, a *lot* of good jewellery and half the proceeds of a house that had sold for almost two million quid.

She picked up her phone again and called her sister.

'Ah, Maxie. Is this a good time, I mean you're not dashing out are you because I need to have a chat – I've got a favour to ask.'

'No, it's fine. What's the favour?'

'No need to sound so wary, it's nothing terribly onerous.'

'Good.'

'I want to come and stay for a few nights. I've taken your advice, sold this place and I'm going to move nearer to you. Won't that be lovely?'

'What?' Maxine's outcry was so loud Judith flinched.

'It was your idea. You suggested it.'

'Yes… yes… I never expected you to take my advice. You don't usually.'

'Because, usually, it isn't worth taking.'

There was a silence of several seconds before Maxine said, 'You want a favour. You may not be going the right way about getting it. There's a very nice hotel down the road.'

'No, you're right, I'm sorry. That was uncalled for.'

'And wrong.'

God, she was going to have to eat humble pie. 'Yes, yes, it was an off-the-cuff remark and I was out of order making it. Forgiven?'

'I suppose. So, when are you planning on coming to stay? Only I've got Abi and Marcus wanting to do the same thing and it looks like this house is about to become very crowded.'

'How lovely, that'll be nice,' said Judith.

'Given they may be staying with us for some weeks, I think the *loveliness* might wear off rather quickly.'

'Goodness, Max, you're grumpy today. You really sound as if you got out of bed the wrong side this morning.'

'To be honest I had such a rubbish night's sleep I'm quite surprised I managed to get out of bed this morning at all; right side or wrong side.'

'Oh, I'm sorry. But never mind that; back to me coming to stay... *I* won't be staying with you for long. I want to have a look round the area, see what's on offer – you can help me. You know where's desirable and where isn't, if a property is close to local amenities, that sort of thing. It'll be fun.' The silence from Maxine stretched a bit too long for Judith's liking. 'Won't it?' she prompted.

'Wonderful.'

'Good. So, given you've got Abi and Marcus planning on moving in, maybe it'd be better if I come sooner rather than later. I'll come over, tomorrow – does that suit? – and we can go house-hunting together.'

'Tomorrow? But that's Saturday... yes, I suppose so but make it after lunch – I've got things planned for the morning.' Maxine's lack of enthusiasm was almost palpable but Judith wasn't going to be put off by it.

'Splendid. See you about two. We'll still have plenty of time to hit the estate agents. Byeee,' she trilled as she killed the call. Really! She was only asking for a bed for a couple of nights, not a kidney donation.

9

'This is glorious,' said Olivia, cradling a mug of coffee as she stood on the veranda of the big summer house that was Maxine's studio. 'I love May. I think it's my favourite month.'

Beside her Maxine leant on the rail that fenced the front of the summer house like an old-fashioned American stoop, and in the corner were two rattan arm chairs with cream cushions and a small glass-topped rattan table. They looked over the low hedge and across the wild flower meadow at the centre of the town's nature reserve, to the big stand of trees on the other side. They were all coming into leaf and the vibrant shades of the new foliage were stunning. 'I bet you've painted this view in all the seasons.'

Maxine nodded and pointed to a big stack of canvasses in a corner by the door. 'And I've got a whole heap of watercolour studies as well. I really ought to think about doing something with them but I never seem to find the time or the energy.'

'Like hold an exhibition?'

'Not really my style. It's a bit *look at me... look at how good I am.*'

'I don't think so.' Olivia put her mug down and moved

over to the painting. She chose one and pulled it out of the pile. It was a view of Maxine's garden in full bloom with the trees in the reserve making a backdrop. 'Gosh, this is glorious. I love the flowers but I love the background. All those greens.'

'And all those greens have some splendid names – chartreuse, citron, emerald, mint, aquamarine, turquoise... well, maybe not those last two; too much blue for leaves. No, I never tire of the view. Of course, I am so very lucky to have this place – but not for much longer.'

'I don't understand.'

'Its loss will be temporary but irritating all the same: Abi and Marcus want to store all their furniture in here. Abi told me that, as it's summer, I can paint outside.'

'Cheeky minx.' Olivia put the picture back. 'Now then,' she said as she sat in one of the chairs. 'While we're talking about Abi... let's talk ground rules.'

'Hang on a tick.' Maxine dived through the door and came back a couple of seconds later with a notebook and pencil. 'Shoot,' she said as she sat down next to Olivia.

'Just because you're retired and they are working doesn't mean you are here to look after them. The jobs must be shared. They managed to do their own cooking and housework in London; they can manage it just as well here.'

Maxine scribbled as Olivia spoke.

'Your bills are going to go up. They can pay half of the utility ones – it's only fair especially as they'll be saving money; no council tax, no water rates, probably a cheaper commute as they'll be driving to Cattebury not taking a train into London. Laundry – have set days when they can use the washing machine – or, if they need a few things done urgently, ask them to liaise with you about sharing loads. There is nothing more irksome than having an overflowing laundry basket and a nice drying day to discover that your machine is being used to wash a couple of pairs of smalls and a T-shirt.'

Ten minutes later, Maxine's hand was starting to ache as Olivia said, 'And finally, have an agreement with everyone that if anyone does things that start to annoy them it needs to be dealt with sooner rather than later. That's things like where cars are parked on the drive, leaving lights on, taking stuff out of the fridge without checking if it's needed for a recipe...' She paused. 'I think that's about everything.'

'Wow,' said Max. 'That's quite a list.' She flicked back several pages and wondered if she had the courage to share the tips with Abi. In her heart she knew that every word Olivia had said was totally right but she had a feeling that Abi might take a different view. Not that Abi was moving in for a bit so she had time to think about it. 'Another coffee?' she offered as she put the notebook on the table.

'No, you've got your sister coming and I've got my old cleaner coming round to pick up a set of keys as my promotion means I can afford to employ her again.'

'That's a real bonus for you. I bet you're happy about that. And I'll let you know about how my happiness quotient fares although I suspect, despite your cracking advice,' she patted the notebook, 'it may not be quite as positive as we'd both like.'

Abi finished taping up a box of possessions, got out a large marker pen and scribbled 'kitchen utensils, various' on the side and heaved it onto a pile of similar boxes stacked in the corner. She then pulled a piece of paper from her pocket and consulted her list.

'Right,' she muttered, 'winter clothes next.'

She pulled another flattened cardboard box towards her and swiftly and efficiently assembled it into a cube. She went into the bedroom where Marcus was taking down the pictures on their photo wall and putting them on the bed. The wall was covered in an abstract pattern of white rectangles, studded with picture hooks, against the grubby paintwork.

Abi looked at the mess. 'It seemed like a good idea at the time,' she observed. 'Maybe in the new house we ought to cut back on banging nails into the wall.'

'I don't think it'll take that much to make good. A few dabs of *Polyfilla* and a lick of paint...'

'But it's another job on top of all the others.'

'We don't have to get it done over the weekend we move out. We've got gardening leave – we can always come back to finish off. We'll have to come back anyway to hand over the keys to the estate agent.'

'I suppose. It just seems such a waste of time to be thundering up and down the road to London and back when we'd be better off there, keeping an eye on the builders and doing what we can ourselves.'

'We can't do *that* much.'

'We can start on the garden, get carpet fitters in to measure up and give us quotes, choose kitchen and bathroom fittings... there's masses we can do.'

'If you say so.'

'I do. Really Marcus, we need to be on top of this every

step of the way otherwise the project will balloon in terms of time and money.' Marcus didn't respond. 'You're not having cold feet, are you? You were the one who was so keen on the house in the first place.'

'No, no, of course not. Except…'

'Except what?' Abi snapped.

'You read the surveyor's report. He couldn't examine the roof timbers because of the false ceiling in the attic, nor could he look at the floors because of the fitted carpets, nor the state of the walls because of the wainscotting.'

'It's a bit late to have doubts now. You said the surveyor's overall conclusion was the house is structurally sound.'

'Yes. Good solid stone walls and no missing slates on the roof.'

'Well?' Abi still sounded irritated by his cautiousness.

'I don't know. The builders' quotes were all rather more than I hoped and not one of them would commit to a fixed fee. They all wanted wiggle room in case of unforeseen circumstances.'

'I know that but if the house is solid…? And, let's face it, we've been offered a mortgage so the building society can't think it's dodgy.'

'Yes, you're right. I'm just being overcautious. But we need to make our mind up which builder we're going to go with. Everything being well, we'll be completing soon.'

'It's all going to be fine, you'll see.'

'Right,' said Maxine at midday. 'If I'm going to have the patience to traipse round estate agents with my sister this afternoon, I need a swift trip to the pub beforehand.'

'Is that wise?' asked Gordon, dubiously.

'Too bloody right it is.' Maxine picked up her handbag and her coat. 'I know she's my sister and I know blood is thicker than water but she can be *totally* demanding *and* difficult and I just know I'm going to be squirming with embarrassment by the time we've finished this afternoon.'

'If you say so.'

'I do.'

The pair reached the pub shortly after opening time and pushed open the door to find they were the first customers of the day.

'Hi, Belinda,' they chorused as they approached the bar. They noticed a very pretty forty-something brunette standing next to her. Or, at least, she looked forty-something till they got up to the bar. Maxine, with her artist's sharp, observational eye, noticed a slight crêpiness of the skin on her neck and crow's feet around her eyes. But the paint job, she had to admit, was good – right up there with Judith's standard. Maxine was reminded of Catherine Zeta- Jones – all tumbling dark curls, a Hollywood smile, smouldering eyes and cheekbones to die for. Her eyes flicked down to the woman's hands which were resting on the counter. No wedding ring. Which begged two questions: why wasn't such a lovely looking woman married; and why was she working part-time in a bar? Maxine's thoughts were interrupted by Belinda.

'Hello, you two. This is my new assistant – a replacement for Bex.' Bex had been the previous part-time barmaid who had married Belinda's chef and then produced a baby – a sister for her other three children.

'But Bex has been gone an age,' said Max. 'Must be a year since she left to have little Emily.'

'I know. Sheer laziness on my part that I didn't get around to advertising before. Anyway, Ella is here now so, Ella meet Maxine and Gordon, Maxine and Gordon meet Ella.' The three shook hands through the beer pumps.

'The usual?' asked Belinda.

'Please,' answered Maxine. Gordon seemed to have lost the power of speech.

They watched as Ella was coaxed through the process of pouring the drinks and then entering the order into the till. 'Nine pounds fifty,' she announced finally.

As Maxine and Gordon took their drinks over to a window table Max muttered to her husband. 'Put your tongue away, darling. It's hanging out so far you're going to trip over it.'

'Don't be silly,' he said. But he was blushing.

Busted, thought Max. She didn't blame him. Ella was a stunner and anyway it was only window-shopping. Besides, despite the fact Max loved her husband to bits she reckoned he could window-shop all he liked because there wasn't a snowball's chance in hell of a reciprocal interest – not with Ella looking the way she did and Gordon looking... well, much more ordinary.

'What time is Judith arriving?' He took a slurp of his beer.

As a topic for changing the subject it was pretty lame. 'Two, as you well know.'

'And will you be going to all the estate agents?' Little Woodford boasted four.

'More than likely.' Maxine sighed heavily. 'Why she needs her hand holding beats me.'

'It's because she values her big sister's opinion.'

'Huh.'

Judith stood in the middle of the market square and looked at the pretty Georgian town hall, at the lamp-posts decorated by hanging baskets trailing petunias in every shade and fronds of ivy, at the planters which were neatly spaced along the pavements and filled with colourful bedding plants and at the higgledy-piggledy roofline of the shops along the main street. It was quite charming, she thought. A bit chocolate-boxy but there was a buzz and a bustle and an air of cheerful prosperity. All the shops were occupied, the town had all the amenities she might want – a bank, a pub, a little supermarket and, of course, the railway link to London. It even had a hairdresser, although Judith would want proof of their skills when it came to colouring hair; her stylist in East Myring did a wonderful job and would be a hard act to follow. She had to admit that she could see why her sister liked the place.

'So,' she said to Maxine. 'Where to first?'

Maxine pointed to the estate agent across the road. 'Let's see what they have to offer.'

She led the way in. 'Hi,' she said to the young lady sitting behind the desk. 'My sister is hoping to move here. She wants somewhere central and not too big. Can you help?'

'Hi,' said the girl, 'I'm sure I can. I'm Marie, by the way.'

'And I'm Maxine Larkham and this is Judith Crowther.'

'Larkham?' Marie's eyes widened and her smile became forced.

'Yes.'

'I think your daughter was a client.' She sounded wary.

'Abi? Yes.'

'And do you have a list of requirements?'

'Darling,' said Judith, and she winked at Marie. 'I'm very easy-going, trust me. A couple of bedrooms, one en-suite, and a bit of garden so I can sunbathe in the good weather, somewhere in the town – it's all I want. After that...?' She shrugged to indicate how easy-going she was. 'I've got a wad of cash to spend and I'm not in a chain – show me what you've got, eh?'

Marie visibly relaxed.

10

'Today's the day,' said Maxine, a week after her sister's visit. Her face was as gloomy as her voice as she toyed with a piece of toast and butter. 'The big move.'

'It won't be so bad. And it isn't forever.' Gordon barely looked up from the morning paper as he spoke. 'Let's face it, you survived your sister and it'll be nice having Abi nearer.'

'I suppose. But at least Judith knows she's a visitor. Abi still thinks this is still her home – even though she's got one of her own.'

'She's not that bad. You've just got to be firm from the outset. You've got all that advice from Olivia, which you *know* makes sense – and so will Abi. Set out the boundaries then everyone knows where they stand.'

'Hmm.' She stared at Gordon across the big table in the kitchen – would he enforce the boundaries with the apple of his eye? 'I just worry it's going to end in tears.'

'Now you're being a drama queen.' He put the paper down and gave his wife his attention. 'Aren't you?'

'Huh. It wouldn't be so bad if they were going to be at work all day but they've got gardening leave till July.'

'I expect they'll be over at the cottage most of the time,

supervising the builders and trying to tame the garden.' He returned to the leader column.

'Giving the builders hell, more likely,' muttered Maxine.

The phone rang and stopped further speculation from Maxine about the future. She got up from her chair and picked the handset off the counter.

'Hello,' she answered.

'Hi, Max, it's Dot.'

Max's heart sank. Why would her mother-in-law's cleaner phone at the weekend? It had to be bad news. 'Morning, Dot.' Gordon looked up from the paper. 'What can I do for you?' she asked as she hoped it was something trivial.

'Anthea's had a fall. The ambulance is on its way.'

'Ambulance?'

Gordon got to his feet. 'Ambulance?' His worry was almost palpable.

'Look, it might be easier if you talk to Gordon,' said Max as she handed over the phone.

She listened to his end of the conversation with an increasing sense of doom. It didn't sound good. Finally she heard Gordon say, 'Yes, yes, you must go and let the medics in... Yes, I'll come immediately and meet you at the hospital. And thank you. Thank you for letting me know and for looking after Mum.'

He put the phone down. 'Sorry, Max.' He sounded contrite but Max forgave him. It wasn't his fault his mother had had a fall.

'How bad is she?' she asked.

'It's not looking great. She must've fallen last night, carrying her supper tray into the sitting room and she's been on the floor all night. It was just luck that Dot had agreed to go over this morning to help Anthea put away a supermarket delivery that was due first thing. If it hadn't been for that...' Gordon shook his head as the prospect of 'what might have been' hit home. 'She could have been there till Monday. Dot doesn't know exactly what's wrong with Mum but she's unconscious – Max, this is really serious.' He stopped and gulped. 'I know we both joked about it being better if...' Gordon swallowed again and shook his head. 'It's not so funny now. Anyway, Dot called 999 before she called us and the paramedics were at the door as I rang off. They'll know what to do.' He looked close to tears.

Max put her hand on Gordon's arm. 'Your poor mum. Go and pack. Don't worry if you can't get back tonight or tomorrow or next week for that matter. We'll cope without you.'

'But—'

'No *buts*. Your mum needs you. Stay up there as long as you have to. I'll ring Abi and tell them what's happened. She and Marcus may have to cope with redecorating the flat with just me to help – not that I'm much good at *that* sort of painting.'

Gordon went to grab an overnight bag and enough clothes for a few days.

'Give me a ring when you get there,' said Maxine when he'd returned downstairs. 'Let me know how your mum is and send my love. Now, go.' She handed Gordon his car keys and almost pushed him out of the door.

After Gordon had gone Max sat on the bottom step of the stairs and thought about the implications of the news. Anthea, tough though she was, was still well-over eighty and spending a night unconscious on the floor would have been very serious even for a person half her age, let alone someone so old. But this fall really underlined the fact that her house was totally unsuitable for her to live in on her own. Something would have to be done. This was absolutely the last straw. And if Anthea was going to move out of that ridiculous house she might as well move to Little Woodford.

So, thought Max, Abi was about to move into the area, as was Judith and now, very possibly, Anthea. She wasn't sure whether she was happy or terrified of the prospect of almost all her entire family living on the doorstep. She might end up as unpaid carer for both her mother-in-law *and* any grandchildren that might appear. Talk about being piggy in the middle. So much for a peaceful retirement. And then she felt a twinge of guilt for being selfish.

Gordon sat by his mother's bedside and stared at her battered face. Apparently, from what Dot could gather from the scene when she'd arrived – the rucked up rug, the broken china, the tray – his mother must have been carrying her supper tray into the sitting room when she'd tripped, gone headlong, probably catching her head on a footstool on the way down. She was now conscious but confused and concussed. Gordon wasn't sure if that was a good thing or not that she'd been out cold for so long. At least it would have stopped her from feeling frightened and alone. On the other hand, a blow to the head for someone of her age was no trivial matter. Actually, it would be no trivial matter for someone young and fit. The bruising was monstrous with her left eye swollen shut, the eyelid and her forehead were a livid red. The nurses had told him that it would soon go black, purple and shades of mauve and she'd have a 'bobby-dazzler of a black eye'. Her right arm, which rested on the bedcovers, was encased in a blue-bandaged plaster cast and under the covers her ankle was strapped up too because of a sprain. Beside the bed a monitor beeped with each heartbeat. She'd had an MRI scan and the results had been encouraging – or rather, nothing sinister had been detected. She'd emerged into consciousness just before he'd arrived at the hospital but they'd given her a fair bit of sedation and pain relief while they'd set her wrist and now she was sleeping. Gordon had been told that when she woke up, they were going to subject her to a battery of tests to ascertain that no lasting damage had been done. Providing that was the case, the prognosis was, despite appearances, quite good and, he'd been told by the medics, if no untoward complications surfaced as she recovered his mother was expected to make a good return to full health.

'But,' the female doctor had said, 'whether or not your mother can return to independent living is another matter. You've said that'll be what she'll want, but whether or not she'll be capable…'

'Good luck trying to persuade her otherwise,' said Gordon.

'I agree. There are strategies we can put in place to aid this but it'll only be a temporary solution. And we'll need to get an occupational therapist to assess her ability to perform simple tasks.'

Gordon nodded. That made sense. 'And if she can't?'

'Then we're going to have to persuade her that she'll need long-term assistance.'

'She won't like it.'

'If she can't make a cup of tea, or climb the stairs, there will be no alternative. Naturally, she could get a stair lift installed and employ a carer but there will come a time when even those measures won't be enough.'

And then what? wondered Gordon.

His stomach rumbled and brought him back to the present. His breakfast had been interrupted and now it was after two o'clock. No wonder he felt hungry. Of course, he was sure that the instant he left his mother's bedside she'd wake up but the canteen wasn't that far away and he only needed to grab a sandwich. He'd be there and back in a matter of minutes.

He pushed his chair back and got to his feet. What with the drive and now sitting still for a couple of hours, he felt stiff. He eased his back and stretched before he made his way to the nurses' station.

'Just going to get a bite to eat,' he told them. 'Back in a tick.' And while he was away from the ward, he'd phone Max. He'd promised to phone her on arrival but until now there hadn't really been a suitable moment.

Gordon headed down a long corridor which led towards reception and the canteen. Off it was a door into a sunny and sheltered courtyard garden. Gordon went into the fresh air, glad to be away from the smell of antiseptic and disinfectant, the incessant bleeps of the machinery and monitors and the incoherent rant of a dementia patient in a side ward.

He swiped his screen and pressed the phone icon.

'How is she?' said Max as soon as she answered.

'She's got a broken wrist and a very badly sprained ankle and concussion plus what are going to be some shocking bruises but assuming she doesn't pick up any infections they are expecting her to make a full recovery.'

'How long will that take?'

'They wouldn't commit themselves. Old bones take a long time to knit. Two months at least, probably considerably more.'

'Oh, Lordy, she won't like that.'

'No, and the worst of it is, with an arm and a leg out of action she can't possibly look after herself at all. She needs help for every aspect of her personal care.'

There was a silence as Maxine took in the implications. 'So, she's going to be in hospital for some time.'

'Or a nursing home.'

'Having nurses do everything for her.'

'That's the long and the short of it.'

'Your poor mum. It's her idea of hell.'

'Not that she knows this yet. She was unconscious when she arrived and what with the pain relief and one thing and another she's not really with it yet. In fact, right now she's asleep which is why I've had a chance to pop out and phone you. Anyway, there's nothing much I can do except sit with her till she surfaces and then try and comfort her while she comes to terms with everything and what her immediate future is going to be like.'

'Poor Anthea. She's going to hate it. No matter how sensitive the nurses are she'll be so unhappy.'

'But she'll have no choice. With one hand completely out of action feeding herself will be tricky and as for doing anything else…'

'Just ghastly. But I'm sure you'll be wonderful with her. If anyone will be able to get her to come to terms with the situation it'll be you. One thing Gordon, your mum is going to *have* to think about moving out of that house.'

'And I don't think this is the moment to mention it. Maybe when she's better.' He'd come to the same conclusion himself but it was a conversation he was dreading and certainly one he couldn't face on top of telling his mother that *every* aspect of her personal care, every single and intimate aspect, was going to be administered by nurses for the foreseeable future. 'How's the move going?'

'They're due here shortly. Getting the stuff in the van took longer than they thought and then the M25 played up… Abi didn't sound best pleased when I phoned her to tell her about Granny. But,' she added hastily so Gordon didn't get the wrong impression, 'it was the delays, not Granny she was irritated with. She was hugely sorry to hear what had happened and said she and Marcus will visit her just as soon as they can. Not this weekend, obviously but soon. She said to give Granny oodles of love.'

'I'll pass the message on. I'm off to get a bite of lunch now and I'll ring you again later today.'

Marcus drove the van onto the driveway of their soon-to-be temporary home, hauled on the hand brake and killed the engine. It ticked as it cooled.

'At last,' said Abi. 'We should have been here in time for lunch and now it's gone two.' She flicked the handle, pushed open the door and a waft of warm spring air, laden with birdsong, whooshed into the cab. She stretched, undid her seat belt and jumped down to the ground. 'And no Dad to help us carry the stuff.'

'It's not his fault,' said Marcus. 'Your poor grandmother.'

'I know, it's just she couldn't have picked a worse time.' Abi kicked at a stone on the driveway before she marched up to the front door and rang the bell. 'Well, we finally made it,' she said to her mum before she swooped in to give her a kiss on the cheek. 'Nightmare journey. I don't suppose there's a cup of tea available before we start unloading.'

'Of course. Come in the pair of you. Have you had lunch? Would you like a sandwich? I wasn't sure if you'd grabbed something on the way.'

Abi turned to Marcus who was following her into the hall. 'Mum's offering a sarnie.'

'That'd be lovely, Maxine. We've been on the go since the early hours.'

'What are you planning to put in it?' said Abi.

'Cheese?'

'Is that it?'

'I might be able to find something more exciting. I'll have a look.' Maxine went to the kitchen and began opening cupboard doors while Abi filled the kettle and plugged it in. 'So, what's with Granny?'

Maxine filled her in on the details, as much as she knew them.

'I pity the poor nurse who tries to wipe her bum,' said Abi.

'Yes, well... Anyway, let's not talk about that side of things,' said her mother.

'Stop being such a prude, Mum. It's a fact, isn't it?'

'Yes, but Granny Anthea would no more like us discussing her personal hygiene than she's going to like someone having to help her with it. She's a very proud old lady and from a generation where bodily functions simply weren't discussed.'

Abi sniffed. 'It's not going to make the situation go away, though, is it?'

Max found a tin of tuna at the back of a cupboard and fell upon it. 'Ta-dah,' she said as she brandished it.

'Err… we're vegetarian, remember.'

'Of course, silly me. Well then, it'll have to be cheese after all.'

Abi rolled her eyes. 'And supper?'

'Oh, yes. I've got some *Quorn.* I was going to make a shepherd's pie.'

'Thank you,' she said as the kettle came to a boil.

Maxine got out the bread and butter and began to put together the promised sandwiches, leaving Abi to make the tea.

'I shall have this,' said Marcus, 'and then make a start on the van. The sooner we get it unloaded the sooner we can go back to London and start making the flat presentable.'

'Actually, it's not that bad,' said Abi as she got the milk out of the fridge. 'Just a couple of walls that need a lick of paint but the carpets are in good nick and I don't think there's much else to be done other than give it a good clean.'

'That's good, darling,' said Maxine, 'because, as I don't have a car, it'll be difficult for me to get to yours and lend a hand.'

'You could come with us in the van.'

'I could but then I wouldn't be able to get back later

tonight and I am *not* going to sleep on your floor. Not at my age.'

Abi rolled her eyes again. 'I said, didn't I Marcus, that Granny couldn't have picked a worse time to go arse over tit? We'll just have to manage as best we can.'

11

Ryan opened the door of the pub for Amy and followed her to the bar.

'Evening,' said Ella, the new barmaid. 'What can I get you?'

'A pint of bitter and a large white wine, please,' said Ryan.

'Chardonnay, white Rioja or Cab Sauv?'

'Chardonnay, please,' said Amy. 'You're new, ain't you? I'm Amy and this is Ryan.'

'Ella,' said Ella as she pulled the beer pump for Ryan's bitter. 'Yes, started here a week or so ago. Still getting used to it all. I'm only doing a few shifts a week – just enough for Belinda to keep on top of the admin and the books. Who knew there was so much involved in running a pub?' She turned to get the wine bottle out of the fridge and poured a large measure into a glass. 'There you go, nine fifty, please.' She passed the two drinks through the pump handles and took the money in return.

'She seems nice,' said Amy as she and Ryan headed for an empty table in the corner. 'Pretty too.'

'Was she?' asked Ryan. 'Can't say I noticed.'

Amy punched his arm lightly. 'You fibber. Don't give me

that. And I don't know why your eyes were popping out of your head – she's far too old for you.'

'Is she?'

'Trust me, lots of crow's feet.'

'Didn't notice those either.'

'Was that 'cos you were staring at her tits?'

'I was not. Anyway, how could you think that when the most beautiful woman in Little Woodford is right here with me.'

'Give over.' But Amy looked smug, nevertheless and gave Ryan a kiss on the cheek to show she forgave him.

'Wotcha, Ryan. Can I join you or am I interrupting?'

Ryan looked up. 'Steven. Nice to see you, mate. Haven't seen you for an age.' He stood up to shake his old friend's hand. 'It must be months.'

'Probably. Last year, maybe?'

'Definitely.'

'Hey,' said Amy. 'Ain't you going to introduce me?'

'Sorry, yes of course. Amy this is Steven. Steven, Amy. Steven and I went to school together.'

'What? To the comp here.'

'No, the one in Cattebury.'

'I didn't know that's where you went to school.'

'You never asked,' said Ryan.

'Anyway,' said Amy, standing up and holding out her hand. 'Nice to meet you, Steven.'

Steven gave her a firm handshake and Amy winced.

'Blimey,' she said as she rubbed her knuckles. 'What do you do for a living? Break rocks with your bare hands?'

'Kind of,' said Steven. 'I'm a builder.'

'Cool,' said Amy. 'That's a well useful job. Not that I need one but if I ever get to move into anything that's bigger than my rabbit hutch I might. Not that that's likely.'

'I don't know,' said Ryan. 'Never say never. There's always a chance that we might need somewhere larger.'

Steven flicked a glance between the pair of them. 'Is there something you're not telling me, Ryan?'

'Not really. Ames and I are an item. I moved in with her a few weeks back.'

'Yeah,' said Amy, 'and if he keeps letching after that new barmaid he'll be moving out again, and all.'

'I wasn't.'

'Says you. Anyway, Steven, why don't you join us?'

'Cheers.' He put his pint on the table and hooked a chair out with his foot.

'What brings you to this pub,' asked Ryan. 'I've not seen you in here before.'

'Moved back, haven't I? I used to have a gaff on the far side of Cattebury, but I never liked it as much as I did here and when me and the missus split up it seemed a good moment to make a new start.'

'Sorry to hear that,' said Ryan.

'What? That me and Clare split or that I've moved here?'

'Daft bugger – that you've moved back obviously.'

'Git.' But it was said with a broad grin. 'Still fighting fires, Ry?'

Ryan nodded and sipped his drink. 'Yeah.'

'I dunno, how you do it. Don't you get fed up with working shifts and risking your neck?'

'That's rich coming from someone who works on

building sites. They're right up there in the list of the dodgiest workplaces on the planet.'

'And that's rich coming from someone who goes into burning buildings,' countered Steven.

'Look,' said Amy, fed up with being ignored, 'which of you has got the most macho job doesn't matter. It's not a contest.'

'It's all right, Amy. We fought when we were at school,' said Ryan.

'Friendly rivalry.' The pair grinned at each other.

'And who won the most?' asked Amy.

'I did,' said both men in unison.

Amy shook her head and rolled her eyes. 'What are you building right now, Steven?'

'I've got a job on that new estate near the station. I'm building a conservatory. Those houses are well titchy and as soon as people move in, they want an extension.'

'Them houses are all right. My mum lives in one.'

'Don't get me wrong,' said Steven, backtracking. 'They're nice houses but for people with kids at home, or expecting more kids, there's not a lot of space.'

'Yeah, you're right, I suppose. I clean for a woman whose daughter moved back unexpected, like. She's moved out again now but I know she found it tricky with everyone living on top of each other.'

'Exactly. Anyway, once this conservatory is done, I'm hoping to get a job renovating a cottage – well, it's called a cottage but it's pretty blooming big. The trouble is, it'll be good money but I'm not sure I want it.'

'Why's that?' asked Ryan.

'Because I'm not sure what I'll find when I start ripping back the old plaster and panelling and the couple want me to give them a fixed price. I've told them I can't work like that. Supposing there's dry rot, or rising damp or something structural? They seem to think it's just a question of fitting a new kitchen and a couple of bathrooms and giving the place a coat of paint but I've been in this trade long enough to know that things are rarely that straightforward.'

'And you've told them that?' said Ryan.

'Yeah, but they don't want to listen. I mean, what would I know? Only been a builder for twenty years but they're convinced they know better. I've told them they won't find a builder in the country who'd take on a job like that for a fixed price. Apparently, they're *thinking* about the price I quoted for the cosmetic stuff – the bathrooms and the kitchen and the paint and everything. I've told them we'd have to come to an agreement if I found anything else and they're *thinking* about that too. I mean, I can't foot the bill if I find they need a new roof. It's their responsibility, not mine, but they don't seem to see it like that.'

'Good luck with that,' said Amy.

'Cheers,' said Steven raising his glass. 'If I take the job on, I might need it.'

The next morning Maxine wandered down the garden to look at her studio and sighed. Chock-a-block. The boxes and furniture filled it so completely that some of the things were actually pressed against the windows. Ryan and Amy had assured Maxine it wouldn't be for long as they'd ferried the stuff from the van.

'We're going to be completing shortly and the building work shouldn't take long,' Abi had said in response to Maxine's query about how long her studio was likely to be out of action.

'Have you actually *got* a builder yet?' Maxine had asked. She'd spotted the glance exchanged between the pair.

'We've got some quotes,' said Abi.

'We just need to come to an agreement about contingencies,' Marcus added.

'Contingencies? I thought you said it was only cosmetic.'

'It is. But…'

'But?'

Abi explained about the builders' reluctance to offer a fixed quote. 'Anyway,' she added brightly, 'there's a builder called Steven we both think is good, his price was reasonable, he seems young – well, late-thirties – energetic and his references all checked out. And, the best thing is, he can start pretty much as soon as we exchange contracts which we hope will be next week.'

But, thought Maxine, why, if none of the builders would commit to a fixed quote, did she think that they probably knew more than Abi and Marcus about the problems an old house was likely to have and why did she think it didn't bode well?

The phone in her back pocket buzzed bringing her back to the here and now. She hauled it out – Judith.

'Hi, Jude, how's it going?'

'I think I might have found somewhere.'

'That's excellent news. Where?'

'Near the town centre. It's down a lane that runs between the bookshop and the florist.'

'I didn't know there were houses down there.'

'I thought you'd lived in the town for decades.'

'Yes, but living in a place doesn't give you licence to go exploring down back alleys and other people's private spaces.'

'Even so.'

Maxine couldn't be bothered to argue. 'So what is it? A flat, a house…?'

'A little mews house. Very sweet. And quiet. And…' Judith paused for dramatic effect, 'off-street parking.'

Maxine conceded that essential where town centre living was concerned. 'Well, done.'

'Thank you. I need to come and have a look at it for myself. Can I come and stay?'

Maxine's shoulders sagged. 'Jude… it's just…'

'I know, I know, you've got Marcus and Abi as well, but I only want to come for a night. Besides I haven't seen my niece for an age and it'll be lovely to catch up.'

'It's not just that, Anthea's had a fall, a bad one and Gordon's had to rush to be by her bedside.'

'It's not…?' The implication was left unsaid.

'No, she's going to be OK, eventually but it's going to take time and the poor old thing is terribly shaken up. She was on the floor all night.'

'Poor Anthea. But Gordon isn't expecting you to zip up to there to be the ministering angel.'

'No.'

'She really shouldn't have been living on her own, not at her age. What was Gordon thinking about, letting her carry on like that?'

'Come off it, Jude. You've met Anthea. Anthea does

what Anthea likes and a more stubborn old biddy I have yet to meet. However, I think even she will see reason now. When she finally gets out of hospital, we'll have to find her some sort of assisted-living flat near us. Quite apart from anything else, it isn't fair on Gordon to leave things as they are. He's either worried sick or charging up and down the motorway to allay his fears.'

'Anyway, back to me coming over… I've got a viewing on Tuesday so I'll come on over to yours after. If you want you can come and see the house with me. In fact, I'd rather like you to, you know more about old houses than I do, seeing the work you and Gordon did on yours.'

Maxine suppressed a sigh. Judith wasn't going to be dissuaded. She wondered if telling her they'd had to go veggie would dissuade her. Probably not; she might embrace it. Or if she didn't, she might insist her sister cooked two meals – meat-free and carnivorous.

'Honestly,' said Judith. 'If Gordon was there, you'd be cooking for four anyway and you wouldn't resent feeding him.'

'No, of course not.'

'Look, if you don't want me to come and stay, just say so.'

'Don't be like that, Judith, of course I want you to stay but, what with one thing and another, I feel more than a bit frazzled at the mo.'

'You need a distraction to take your mind off things.'

Like having yet another houseguest was going to achieve that. 'You said Tuesday.'

'Yes.'

'It's not great. That's my day in the charity shop and I

really couldn't make the time to see your house too, not as well as everything else.'

'You could bunk off just this once, surely? Let's face it, you're a volunteer, they can't bitch if you want a bit of time off. What are they going to do, dock your pay?'

'Except I'll be letting the team down.'

'Up to you.' Judith sounded put out. She didn't like being thwarted.

'Or you could arrange the viewing for when I get off. I finish at three.'

'I'll see.'

'Up to you,' shot back Maxine. It was hardly going to be difficult to do that, was it?

'I said, I'll see. I'll let you know how I get on. Just think, Maxie, soon you'll have almost all your family in Little Woodford. Won't that be lovely?'

'Yes,' said Maxine. 'I can't wait.' But her feelings didn't mirror her words.

12

It was Monday evening before Abi and Marcus came back to Little Woodford having finished sorting out their flat. Abi had a paint smear on her forehead and a stippling of emulsion up both forearms caused by the splash back from the paint roller. They both looked tired.

'Honestly, Mum, I don't think I've ever worked so hard in my life. We didn't get to bed till gone eleven last night and we were up at seven this morning to finish off.'

'I thought you said there wasn't that much to do.'

'There wouldn't have been with another pair of hands.' She paused. 'If you'd been there, we might have got it all done yesterday.'

Maxine wasn't going to take the flak for this. 'Or maybe we wouldn't. It's your flat and if we hadn't got it finished in one day where was I supposed to sleep?'

'But we would have done.'

Maxine wasn't going to argue. 'Go and get cleaned up. Supper'll be on the table in about half an hour. And please try and keep things tidy, especially in the bathroom, as Aunty Judith will be coming to stay tomorrow.'

'Aunty Judith?'

'Yes. I'm sure I told you that since Uncle Mike left her,

she's decided to move nearer to me. She's viewing a house just off the high street tomorrow and wants to stay over.'

'That'll be nice.'

'Yes, dear.' And while Maxine liked a family get-together as much as anyone she knew full well that the next evening, while she rushed around cooking supper, serving drinks and then clearing up again afterwards, Abi and Judith would be far too busy catching up with each other to contemplate that it might be quite nice if they lent a hand. But it would only be for one night and then Judith would be away, she could have a word with Abi about ground rules and order would be established for the remainder of her daughter's stay. Well, that was the theory at any rate.

Abi and Marcus went upstairs, dragging a couple of big suitcases with them, to wash and brush up before dinner. They had barely shut the door to their new bedroom when the phone rang.

'Oh, hello, darling,' she said when she heard Gordon's voice. 'How's it all going?'

'So-so. Mum's on the road to recovery but she's so miserable. And the nurses *will* call her sweetie or dearie or Anth and she hates it.'

Maxine could well believe it. 'Have you had a word with them, suggested something a bit more formal might be in order?'

'I do, but they don't pay any attention and then their shift goes off duty and another one comes on and then the nurses aren't the same from one shift to another because half of them are agency nurses. It's hopeless, Max.'

'I can see.'

'Max... what if Mum came to ours when she's well enough to leave?'

'Wha...' Maxine bit her tongue and took a breath. 'Do you think that's wise, love. Now I'm having to cook veggie stuff she won't like my food and, on top of that, what do I know about nursing? You've said she's completely incapacitated and do you think your mum would want me bed-bathing her and wiping her bum? Won't she be mortified that it's her daughter-in-law doing it? Wouldn't that be worse, in her eyes, than having a stranger doing it, someone she'll never have to see again?'

'The staff here reckon we can get a carer to come in twice a day to do the personal stuff, get her up and washed and dressed and give her meds and then again in the evening to get her ready for bed.'

'Would that be better?'

'Probably, yes. It'd probably be the same person. Here it's the constant stream of *different* nurses that makes it so awful. It's a succession of young girls, all of whom seem to think it's OK to be like she's her best friend and an equal, not a proud old lady with completely different standards. One called Mum, *Honeybun*. I thought she was actually going to have a fit. It's doing Mum's head in. Max, I don't think I've ever seen her so down. Not even after Dad died.'

'I'll think about it. I'm not ruling it out but it's a big ask. And, to be honest, I think it's a big ask for your Mum too. I mean, what happens if a carer doesn't turn up? It'll come down to me, won't it? And how would that go down? She might flatly refuse to let me anywhere near her. Frankly, if I were in that boat, I don't think I'd want Abi giving me the once-over with a soapy flannel – and she's a blood relative not an in-law.'

'Put like that...'

'Exactly.'

'If only I had a sister.'

'Well, you haven't.'

'We'll just have to hope the carers are completely reliable. If I could be the emergency back-up I'd volunteer in a heartbeat but me looking after Mum's personal care is a total non-starter.'

'No, I understand that. She's of the generation who would rather die than have a bloke, let alone *her son*, do that sort of stuff for her. And I'm not being tricky because I don't fancy the job but I've got Abi and Marcus here and I've got my other commitments, and my day at the charity shop each week, and my Art club is just getting going, and...'

'And how are Abi and Marcus?'

Maxine lowered her voice. 'They've literally got back here a few minutes ago. I'm in the dog-house because Abi thinks that if I'd helped, they'd have been finished yesterday. It's all my fault it took longer than they'd planned. But I think they may have found a builder and they're due to exchange contracts this week so, all being well, they'll be out of here before your mum moves in. *If* she moves in,' she added quickly.

'I think it'll be a week, probably two, before the hospital will even think about letting her out. You don't have to make your mind up yet. In the meantime, I'll have a look at private nursing and carers in our area. You never know, it might not come down to Mum having to move in with us, she may *have* to stay in hospital till she's better and they may say she's fit enough to go back home—'

'—and pigs might fly.'

'But, if she can't go back to her place, Mum coming to ours may be the only option till we can find a proper, permanent solution.'

'I'll think about it,' said Maxine, 'but I think it'd be better all round if it didn't come to that.'

She rang off and tried to turn her attention to cooking supper, but the thought that most occupied her mind was that while Judith had suggested it would be lovely to have almost all her family living in Little Woodford, it seemed to her that almost all her family were going to be living, not just in the town but in *her house*.

Maxine had to admit that Judith had been right to describe the house as really quite sweet – it even had roses growing round the front door which was made of oak planks with a diamond, bull's-eye glass pane above a shiny, brass dolphin knocker. Above each of the five windows at the front of the house was a brick arch which gave the house a slightly surprised look. The house overlooked a mews Maxine had never known existed despite all her years living in Little Woodford. It was reached via a low archway that joined two shops on the high street, just big enough for a saloon car to pass under. Easy to miss, which Maxine apparently had, as she must have walked past it on a regular basis for the best part of forty years. Once under the arch, the mews was wide enough for a parking space outside each of the three houses that were located there and it had enough room for the cars to turn round so reversing back through the entrance was unnecessary.

The estate agent, a young, fresh-faced man called Sam, who sported over-sized horn-rimmed glasses which made him look rather geeky, was waiting for them and let them in. The front door opened into a tiny hall with a cloakroom beside it and then into a spacious sitting room, empty but for a wood-burning stove and a flight of open-plan stairs with a glass and chrome banister. It was surprisingly light as attached to the back of the house was a large conservatory which, in turn, led into a completely enclosed garden.

'And it's south facing,' said Judith as she clacked across the floorboards in her leopard-print kitten-heels. 'Big, isn't it?'

'It's like a Tardis,' conceded Max.

'I think this might make a great dining room,' she said from the far end of the conservatory.

'The previous owner did,' interjected Sam. 'It's K glass, so energy efficient.'

'Really?' said Judith. 'That's good, I suppose.'

Max suppressed a smile. Judith had never given the least thought to anything being energy efficient in her life. If she was cold, she whacked up the heating, if she was hot, she dialled up the air-con. Leaving Sam to explain the ins and outs of the special glass to a bemused Judith, she returned to the sitting room and went through into an ultra-modern kitchen – all white Formica and more chrome. She wasn't sure she'd want all these shiny fittings which would need constant polishing but as Judith was certain to get a cleaner, such a detail wasn't going to bother her sister. She pottered up the stairs to the upper floor. It seemed there were two bedrooms, one double aspect with an en-suite, and a further bathroom. Once again there was a lot of white paint, glass and chrome but there was nothing about the house that Maxine felt Judith could find fault with. In fact, if she hadn't been so wedded to her own home, she could almost fancy down-sizing to a place like this herself – only somewhere that wasn't going to need so much elbow grease to keep it looking tip-top. The good thing about her own house was that it embraced the shabby-chic look – it was all about homeliness and comfort so a few fingerprints and some dust were part of its charm.

'I love it,' announced Judith when Sam had locked up and they were in Judith's little Mini. Maxine had baulked at driving there but Judith had complained that she wasn't getting her new shoes ruined tramping across the reserve.

'So, you're going to put in an offer?'

'Too right I am.'

Three days later Abi and Marcus stepped through the front door of Wisteria Cottage and looked at each other.

'I can't believe it's actually ours,' said Abi.

'I don't want to be a wet blanket but I think about three square metres are ours,' said Marcus. 'The rest belongs to the building society.'

Abi grinned at him. 'You know what I mean.'

Marcus put his arm around her shoulders and gave her a squeeze. 'I do. And it's going to be so glorious when it's all done up.'

'Let's have another good look round and a think about

things before Steven turns up. We'll have so many decisions to make once work gets going.'

'Like?'

'Like where we'll want electric sockets, like how we'll want the fixtures and fittings in the new bathroom – will we want a bath or just a shower or both? And then there's the kitchen; Judith was brilliant with ideas like having a proper wine-cooler in the kitchen and an ironing board that slides under the counter and that really thin pull-out unit she talked about for storing jars and spices.'

'But Judith is loaded. We're really going to have to think about the budget.'

'If this is going to be our forever house, we want to get it right first time.'

The pair climbed the stairs which creaked ominously.

'Do you think they're safe?' said Abi, giving the banisters a tentative shake. They seemed firm enough.

'The surveyor said so.'

They reached the landing.

'It seems even bigger than I remember it,' said Abi as she gazed left and right.

At the head of the stairs there were two doors, side by side, which led to two double bedrooms. Then the landing doubled back to the two bedrooms at the other end of the house, one a single and the other they planned to turn into the master bedroom with an en-suite.

Abi walked down the landing and flung open the door to the biggest bedroom, the one that would be theirs and looked at the wall to her right. 'You know, we could knock through into the box room and make ourselves a dressing room. Or a walk-in wardrobe,' she said wistfully.

'But if we have children it'll be a squeeze if we have visitors.'

'I suppose.' She stared at the wall again. 'But we could build in some lovely fitted units. You know, like the ones you see on the ads with special racks for shoes and those pull-down shelves so you can store stuff up high and still get to it easily.'

'I think they're quite pricy, too.'

Abi turned to face him, her eyes hard. 'If this is our forever house, as we keep saying it is, we are *so* not cutting corners.'

'But it's the kind of thing we could do later. We don't want to overstretch ourselves, do we?'

'We could always extend the mortgage.'

'We've already got a bridging loan,' said Marcus.

A shout from downstairs stopped them from arguing further.

'Hello,' the voice repeated.

Abi went onto the landing and called back down the stairs. 'Steven?'

'The front door was open.'

'Come on up.'

Heavy steps thumped up the creaky stairs. 'Hi, nice to meet you, finally,' said Steven. He clasped Abi's hand and gave it a firm shake.

'Good to meet you, too,' said Marcus holding out his hand. 'What do you think of the place?'

'As I said in my emails, superficially it's got a lot of potential but it's also going to be a bit of work. Obviously, I've got guys in the trade who can come in and do the specialist stuff; the wiring, the plumbing and that sort of thing but until we get it back to the bare bones, I can't see the whole story. I'd say it's a good idea you want to be rid of the panelling because it might be hiding all sorts of stuff.'

'But it's sound?'

'I would say it is *mostly*.'

Abi sighed. 'I think we were hoping for *entirely*.'

'Let's keep our fingers crossed.' He rubbed his hands together. 'OK, so the quote I gave you was to cover the broad outline of the things you want doing. Let me get my notebook, ruler and some other bits from the van and you talk me through the more specific stuff.'

After he clattered down the stairs Abi turned to Marcus. 'Have we made the right decision?'

'He seems a decent sort to me. And he's local. If he does a shit job his reputation round here will be ruined—'

'I'd make sure of that.'

'So he wouldn't dare. He'll be fine. We just need to make sure he doesn't go over time or budget.'

The pair went downstairs to start making the initial decisions for the first steps in the renovation.

They met Steven again in the kitchen.

'This is such a huge space,' said Abi. 'And I'd really love an Aga.'

'They are very pricy,' said Steven.

'I know, but…'

'Thousands. It'll completely blow your budget,' said Steven firmly. 'You can get some really fab range cookers for a massive amount less. And, to be honest, if you're going to be out all day at work, keeping an Aga running probably isn't that practical.'

'I think,' said Marcus, 'that's a decision we won't have to make right at the start.'

'So,' said Steven as he moved across the room and tapped the wall on the far side, 'this isn't load-bearing so if you want to knock through into the boot room and the pantry you could. You could also move the sink and put bi-fold doors or French windows on that wall which would let you see into the garden. It's quite dark in here,' he added. 'Not that this lino helps. Lighter flooring would make a huge difference.'

'Oh yes, the lino is the first thing that needs to go.'

Steven began to pull his steel tape out of its case and measure up the dimensions of the kitchen. He jotted down the measurements in his notebook. 'It'll be a lot of units if you have them along both walls. You might be better off with an island and a breakfast bar. Have you thought about what sort of style of units you want?'

'I had hoped for something very simple and modern. Clean lines, stainless steel handles, a stainless steel splashback behind the cooker, a stainless steel hood, that sort of thing.'

'Got any catalogues?'

'No. We've been round some show rooms, haven't we, Marcus? And an aunt of mine gave me some brilliant ideas for maximising space in the kitchen.'

'Hang on.' Steven tramped out to his van and returned a minute later with a couple of fat books. 'There's a trade supplier who does good stuff at sensible prices. Have a butcher's. While you do that, I'll have a good look round so I can make some suggestions about how we can make this place really work. Unless,' he said, 'you've already got a clear plan.'

'No,' said Marcus. 'Well, we've got some ideas but we

know nothing about building or buildings so what we'd like and what would work might be two totally different things.'

'More than likely,' said Steven with a wry smile. 'But if you're happy to take advice, this partnership might work very well.'

And while Abi and Marcus flicked through the pages, turning down the corners of the ones they wanted to mark, Steven went around the house, tapping walls, checking out the state of the windows, measuring up, looking at the electrics and making notes all the time.

After about half an hour he returned. 'Given that you don't want too much structural work done *and* the house is going to be empty my original quote for the basic building work stands. Obviously the cost of your new bathroom and the kitchen will depend on the fixtures and fittings that you choose. I've done a couple of sketches.' He flicked open his notebook and showed them his ideas for both. 'This is rough and ready but it gives you an idea. I can do something different or more elaborate if you want me to.'

Abi looked at his sketches. 'The bathroom won't have a window.'

'Good lighting and a decent extractor fan is all you need. Unless you really want a window. But cutting through the wall will be a big job – and an expense. It'll cost you enough putting in bi-folds in the kitchen.' Steven looked from one to the other. 'You told me you didn't want me spending more than thirty grand. And that's without any contingency.'

'Correct. And we're hoping that won't be necessary,' said Abi, firmly. 'And roughly how long till it'll all be finished?'

'Maybe six weeks, maybe longer. Even with contractors doing the specialist stuff it's still a lot of work.'

Abi looked at Marcus. 'But…' she started.

'It's still not *that* long,' said Marcus. 'And just think what we'll end up with.'

'I suppose. Best we don't tell Mum. She was arsey enough about us moving in, in the first place.' She turned to Steven. 'Are you sure it's going to be that long? Can't you do it quicker?'

Steven blew his cheeks out and pursed his lips. 'I'll do my best but I really can't make any promises. Until we get under the surface…'

An hour later, when they'd discussed the ins and outs of the configuration of the bathrooms and the kitchen and Steven had left to produce some proper drawings and some accurate figures, Marcus and Abi locked the front door behind them and prepared to go back to her mum's.

'I suppose,' said Marcus, 'it's a bit like a surgeon opening someone up and finding that the routine surgery isn't going to be quite as routine as he thought.'

'I would hope that doesn't happen very often. You'd think with x-rays and the like they'd know exactly what they're going to find before they start rummaging around.'

'But there's no x-rays for a house.'

'Really, Marcus. Stop being such a doom merchant. What can possibly go wrong?'

Marcus looked back at the house. 'No, I think you're right. It's all going to be fine.'

'But we must be absolutely on top of the project at every phase. I'm sure Steven is very good but you know what tradespeople are like – give them an inch and they'll take a mile. I've watched enough episodes of *Grand Designs* to realise that sloppy project management equals spiralling costs, so I will be holding Steven's feet to the fire every step of the way.'

13

The following Wednesday afternoon, Amy arrived at Olivia's to do the cleaning and saw Olivia's bike, propped up against the house.

'Bugger,' she muttered. If the bike was there, sure as eggs were eggs, it meant that its owner was too. Which meant, in turn, that she couldn't cut any corners nor could she make herself as many cups of tea as she fancied... or have a nip of gin. She rang the bell and waited to be let in.

'Not at work, Mrs L,' she said as the door was opened.

'Afternoon, Amy. No, not today. I've got to work over the weekend so I've got today off in lieu.'

'That's fair.' Amy slipped off her jacket and hung it on the coat hooks in the hall. 'The normal, today?'

'Yes, please. I thought I'd have a bit of a go at the garden today while you do the house. Not that it takes much to keep it tidy.'

'Not like your old place, eh?'

Olivia's smile tightened. 'No.'

Amy got out the polish and a duster. 'Ooh, I know what I meant to tell you. You know your mate, Mrs Larkham, the one what runs the art club...'

'I know Maxine Larkham, yes.'

'Would she have a daughter? Only, my Ryan's got a mate who's a builder – Steven, he's called – and he's taken on a job for an Abigail Larkham, doing up an old cottage out of town a bit.'

Olivia nodded. 'As Maxine's daughter is called Abi and I know she and her partner are moving back here it's probably one and the same.'

'Well, it seems your mate's daughter is a right piece of work. Never gives poor old Steven a moment's peace, he says. On his back morning, noon and night; how much is he spending on this? What's that going to cost? Poor bloke's ears are starting to bleed, he says.'

Olivia's lips pursed. 'Are you sure? Maxine is delightful and very easy-going so I find it hard to believe that her daughter is quite as bad as you make out.'

'Don't always follow that kids are like their parents. I mean look at Zac and...' Amy tailed off when she saw Olivia's eyes narrow. Well, Mrs L mightn't like it but there was no getting round the fact that her son Zac had been a right handful when he'd been doing drugs. Mrs L might like to think that *she* was a pillar of society but her son had let the side down and no mistake. He was *supposed* to be clean now but once a druggie always a druggie, in Amy's eyes.

'Despite what your friend Steven might think, there is nothing wrong with the client being on top of the costs when it comes to a building project. It's *very* easy for things to get out of hand and, at the end of the day, it'll be Abi Larkham footing the bill, not your mate.'

That's me told, thought Amy. 'Right, I'd better get on, Mrs L. Can't stand around all day chatting, much as I'd like to.' And I *would* like to chat all day, but not with you, you po-faced old bat.

While Amy was busy giving Olivia's house a good going over, Maxine rang Gordon's phone.

'How's it going?' she asked.

'Beyond slowly. I've had to go to the local superstore to buy more pants, socks and shirts. It seemed daft putting tiny loads through the washing machine so I could turn up at the hospital each day looking semi-decent. And Mum is getting more difficult and fed-up. I don't blame her. It's been almost two weeks now.'

'I can imagine. And I'm missing you too. Any chance of coming home for a couple of days?' The silence down the phone answered her question. 'It was only a thought.'

'Changing the subject how are Abi and Marcus? How are the ground rules?'

Maxine snorted. 'Oh, Abi was all sweetness and light and understanding when I mooted that we shared the cooking and the shopping and the bills and all that sort of stuff.'

'But?'

Maxine sighed. 'Put it this way, I apparently don't understand how insanely difficult it is to keep an eye on Steven, or how hard they are working re-landscaping the garden, nor how broke they're going to be when they've done the house because they're not,' Maxine's voice flew up about an octave as her indignation got the better of her, 'going to ruin their forever home with anything less than the best. I mean, what's wrong with buying a few second-hand pieces and then getting nicer things later when they can afford it? Like we did. God knows how long we ate off a pasting table and slept on a mattress on the floor. Like it matters. And don't,' she added, 'tell me to calm down because I'm finding it very difficult to maintain any sense of proportion at the moment.'

'I think I can tell that,' said Gordon. 'But we know how bad their garden is. They have masses to do there and it's all hard labour. And surely you'd be cooking for me if I were home so...'

Maxine knew he was right. 'Yes, but I wouldn't have to cook vegetarian. With you here I could insist they cook their own bloody food if they want to be different.'

'You could anyway.'

'But it's a faff just cooking for one... I'm finding it all rather irking.'

'I think I can tell.'

'If you were here, I wouldn't feel so ganged up on.'

'Maxine, I really don't want to row with Abi. It probably won't be for long.'

No, thought Maxine, of course you don't want to have it out with Abi – anything for a quiet life. Except he wasn't the one being treated like a skivvy. 'Fine,' she said in the way that meant things were anything but.

'Anything else going on? How's Judith's house hunt?'

Change the subject, why don't you? 'She's made an offer on the little cottage she saw which is a plus as at least she won't need to come and stay any more. And Steven, according to Abi, has made a good start on the house and nothing major has cropped up so far. Fingers crossed that there aren't any hitches and it all comes in on time and on budget and then we can get back to normal. And it won't come a day too soon.'

'Amen to that,' said Gordon.

Abi and Marcus had been working all day in the overrun garden of Wisteria Cottage when Steven had called them both in.

'You need to see this,' he'd shouted from the back door to where they were hacking back the undergrowth. They'd skirted past the skip, now filled with discarded kitchen units and a huge pile of lino that had been ripped up and went into the house.

There, in the middle of the floor was a raised trapdoor and a gaping hole. Abi went over to stare at the void.

'What the fuck is this, Steven?'

'What do you think? You've got a cellar.'

'A cellar? That's quite cool. And all that extra space.'

'I don't think this is a good thing,' said Steven carefully.

'Really? A bonus room that we didn't know about? What's wrong with that?'

Steven sighed. 'Because if no one has been down there for years there could be all manner of issues going on.'

Abi frowned. 'Is that why there was nothing in the particulars? The previous owners didn't want anyone to know about it till they'd got the money safely in the bank?'

'I think the previous owners didn't know about this cellar either. I don't know how long the lino has been down but there were two layers of the stuff and, to judge by the state of the bottom layer, I wouldn't imagine the original floorboards have seen the light of day since the war.'

'And you're not talking the Iraq one, are you?' said Abi. She took Steven's torch out of his hand, crouched at the edge of the hole and peered into the gloom that was illuminated in patches as she swept the beam round. 'What are we going to do, then? Put the trap door back, cover it up and pretend we know nothing about it?'

'God, no. That's the last thing you should do. I need to get down there and make a full structural survey. I need to know how big it is, the state of the timbers, if there's any damp, dry rot...' Steven shrugged. 'Quite apart from anything else I've got a feeling this could explain why your stairs creak so badly. If there's a lack of support under the stairs it could mean the whole house is sagging into the cellar.'

Abi and Marcus stared at him horror struck. 'The surveyor should have spotted this,' Abi managed to say after a couple of seconds. 'We'd never have bought if we'd known. The bastard,' she added through clenched teeth. 'I'll sue him.'

Steven shook his head. 'You won't get anywhere. He couldn't possibly have found this without starting to take the house to bits – like I'm doing. No way will a court find him to be at fault.'

'But this could cost us thousands.' Abi's face was ashen.

'Let's not jump to conclusions. I'll get a ladder and get down there. To be honest, I'm a bit surprised there aren't steps here or maybe there's another entrance somewhere else in the house—'

'Somewhere else? You mean, the house might be completely hollow underneath?' Marcus sounded as shocked as Abi looked.

Steven wrinkled his nose and pursed his lips. 'Let's not get ahead of ourselves. I'll get the ladder – back in a jiffy.'

Abi gazed desolately into the hole. 'What do we do if it is a complete disaster?'

Marcus put his arm around her. 'We have insurance; we had a full survey...' He paused. 'We've done nothing wrong. I think one way or another we'll be OK financially if it transpires that it's *really* serious. I expect we'll have to pay the excess, though.'

'How much will that be?'

'Off the top of my head? About a grand.'

'A grand?' yelped Abi.

'Right, let's have a proper look at this,' said Steven returning with an aluminium ladder over his shoulder. He lowered it into the hole, checked it was safe then swung his feet on to the rungs and began to descend. 'Let's have the torch,' he said to Abi as his shoulders reached floor level.

Abi passed it to him, waited till Steven got to the bottom of the ladder before following him down.

'Watch your step,' said Steven as she jumped off the bottom rung. He moved the light around the big space which smelt of must and mould and damp earth. The floor was lumpy and uneven and seemed to stretch away across the depth and width of the house. Behind him, lying on the floor was an antique looking set of steps – the original ladder down from the kitchen. He shone the torch up to the trap door and saw some broken fixings. That explained the lack of access.

'Good job the stairs had already fallen down. I wouldn't have wanted them to collapse with us using them,' said Abi. 'If this didn't have the potential of being such a total disaster,

I'd be delighted to discover I've got this extra space. But...'
she sighed heavily.

Steven swung the torch across the rest of the ceiling which
seemed to consist of heavy beams laid crosswise with the
boards of the kitchen floor above laid over the top. Mats
of thick cobwebs, covered in the dust of centuries, wafted
gently in the newly stirred air.

'I think,' said Steven, 'I'd like to see a couple of dozen
Acrow Props down here before I do anything else.'

'And what are those when they are at home?'

Before Steven could answer Marcus came gingerly down
the ladder. 'Thought I'd better see for myself how the land
lies,' he said as he joined them.

'I was just saying to Abi how we need to put some support
under these beams. There doesn't seem to be much holding
up the ground floor. Once those are in place I can retro-
fit some proper support but I don't want to do anything
with the rest of the house till this is sound. I need to know
what's going on with the beams and all.' He shone the torch
at the nearest beam and had a good look at it then touched
the edge of it with his finger and thumb. A chunk of wood
crumbled like ash. He didn't have to say anything. He went
further into the cellar to see what else he could find.

Abi turned and stared at Marcus in horror. 'Shit,' she
whispered.

'Shit, indeed,' he echoed.

'I don't think we should tell Mum and Dad about this
either. Not till we know exactly what's going on.'

'We can't keep it from them.'

'We can and we will. We said we'd only be with them for
a couple of weeks, remember and then Steve said it might

be more like six weeks and now this! If they think it's going to be *a lot* longer, they may get stroppy and insist we rent something.'

'You think?'

'Do you want to risk it?'

Marcus sighed. 'Maybe you're right.'

'There's no maybe about it.'

14

'I'm sorry,' said Anthea, her voice trembling and weak, 'but I don't want to stay here another minute.' The left-hand side of her face was still one massive multicoloured bruise but the swelling had largely subsided so at least her eye was fully open now. But the livid shades of her injuries were still a shocking contrast to her snow-white hair even though they were no longer black and purple but mauve and an unpleasant shade of ochre.

'Mum, you've got to. The nurses know what's best for you—' He was about to expand on the comment but his mother interrupted.

'Don't be ridiculous, Gordon. I doubt if the nurses know what would be best for a pet hamster let alone a ward full of old people with complex needs. There isn't one who looks as if she's old enough to have left school and why can't they understand that I'm not *sweetie* or *dearie* but Mrs Larkham. They've got absolutely no respect for their elders and betters and they talk to me as if I'm ga-ga and the food is a disgrace and there's never a moment of peace on this wretched ward...' She stopped and a tear ran down her face. 'I'm sorry, Gordon, but I just want to go home.'

'I think we both know that going home isn't going to be

possible for a while and I think you're being a bit hard on the nurses,' said Gordon, but he couldn't bring himself to disagree with all his mother's other points. 'But until your arm and your ankle have healed there is no way you can manage on your own. And, anyway, the nurses are still worried that until you're stronger you might be susceptible to some sort of infection.'

'I'm not stupid and I know my limitations,' snapped Anthea. She shut her eyes as if by doing that she could shut out the ghastly implications of her situation. After a couple of seconds, she opened them again and lasered her son. 'And this is the worst place for staying infection-free if you ask me. God knows what bugs and diseases are rife here. You hear such awful stories about Escherichia coli and necrotising fasciitis—' She saw her son's slightly startled look. 'You're surprised I know these things? That I understand what they are? Gordon, just because I am old doesn't mean I've lost my ability to read a newspaper.'

'No, Mother, of course not.'

She sighed. 'So what are you going to do about it?'

What indeed? The occupational therapist had said that independent living was completely out of the question for at least two months and then would it really be possible for her to move back into her old home? A nursing home might provide a solution but the chances of finding a suitable one with a vacancy in the immediate future seemed a very long shot. If she wasn't going to accept staying in hospital and moving to a nursing home wasn't on the cards, there was only one other option – his house. Anthea, living with him and Maxine? Jeez – on top of having Abi and Marcus? The trouble was, apart from wanting to be horribly selfish, there was no reason why he and Maxine should refuse. They had the space, they were both retired, they were both fit and healthy and they could afford visits from professional carers to help out. But it would be inconvenient, a tie, and they would have to be responsible for the rest of Anthea's care on a daily basis. But what alternative was there?

Gordon sighed. 'Mother, what do you suggest? The options are few. It's here or,' he paused, 'my place. Is that what you want? If it is, we'd need to sort out some professional care but Max and I will have to fill in the rest of the day – you know, in case you need it...' He let the implications of all that that entailed sink in.

Anthea lay back on her pillows and shut her eyes. 'And what does Maxine say? I've no doubt you've been talking about me to her.'

'Mum, she's as worried about you as everyone else is.'

'That didn't answer my question.' She opened her eyes and stared at her son. 'Let's face it, you won't be coping with... my needs. Not that I'd want you to. Apart from anything else, it isn't a man's work.'

Gordon nearly laughed. It was OK for his wife to demean herself and help another adult get on and off the loo but it wasn't OK for her son to do it.

'To be honest, Mum, Maxine was concerned about how *you* would feel about it more than anything else.'

His mother snorted. 'As, during the last two weeks, I haven't encountered a single soul who has had the *least* regard for my feelings, I find it a shock to find that anyone still cares one jot.'

Gordon rolled his eyes. 'Does that include me?'

'You're my son, you don't count.'

Wasn't that the truth. Although he knew she hadn't meant it quite like that – at least he hoped she hadn't. One could never be quite sure.

'But if Maxine does agree to look after you... I mean...?'

'Would I cope with her helping me to the loo?' Anthea shut her eyes again. 'I survived the Blitz, I can cope with most things. It won't be worse than what's on offer now.'

Gordon wasn't expecting his mother to show undiluted gratitude but reckoned it might be for the best if he gave Maxine an expurgated version of her mother-in-law's comments.

'I'll talk to Maxine again and I'll have a word with the nurses; see what they say about when they think you'll be fit enough to leave, providing there is a proper support mechanism. But, as Max isn't trained at all, they mightn't be in favour. All I'm saying is, I wouldn't hold my breath.'

'I don't want to hold my breath, I want you to just get on and do it. Am I making myself clear?'

Abundantly.

Maxine was setting out the community centre for another meeting of her art club. She had lowered the screen and was adjusting the lens on her projector till the photograph of a lake was pin sharp. It was a great picture; the sparkling water was surrounded by mountains, above which was a sky half-covered by towering thunderclouds while the other half was clear blue. In the foreground was a meadow filled with wild flowers and some spectacular contrasts of light and shadow. Maxine had taken the photo herself some years previously when she and Gordon had been on a holiday in the Swiss Alps and she'd used it a couple of times since as a basis for some water colours she'd done. She thought her class might enjoy interpreting the scene in paints too.

However, her mind wasn't fully on preparing the room. Gordon had told her that Anthea felt she could cope with Maxine looking after her in conjunction with professional carers. She'd tried to find a silver lining to that particular cloud – like the ones in the photograph – but she'd failed horribly. She didn't mind the idea of cutting up Anthea's food and helping her to eat, or looking after her on a general level but there was no guarantee that *all* of Anthea's personal needs would be covered when a carer was in the house. She'd coped with babies and nappies and then potties because it was all part of motherhood and joys had far exceeded the (literally) shitty bits. But this was going to be a completely different challenge which wouldn't be made easier by Anthea's formidable and somewhat tetchy outlook on life. Plus, there was the fact that, by no stretch of the imagination could their relationship be called *close*. Gordon was her only son and from the start Maxine had been aware that Anthea was unlikely to find any woman good enough for him but Maxine – dear God! An art student – was not what Anthea had had in mind *at all* as a suitable life-partner for him. She'd even, at the wedding, confided in one of Gordon's aunts, a confidence overheard and passed on by Max's best friend, that she gave the marriage 'five years at best'. Naturally, it hadn't helped matters. Not that she'd ever told Gordon about his mother's doubts. And even though they had celebrated their ruby wedding anniversary some years previously, Maxine thought that Anthea continued to harbour a faint hope that there was still time for Gordon to find a more suitable partner.

'Evening, Maxine,' said Olivia as she entered the hall.

Max jumped.

'Sorry, I didn't mean to startle you. I thought I'd come early so we could have a bit of a catch-up. I so enjoyed our chat a few weeks ago.'

'Yes, it was lovely. I did too. And you didn't really startle me – I was miles away.'

'A penny for them, then.'

Maxine shook her head. 'I need *a lot* more than that.'

Olivia put her sketch pad down on a nearby table. 'That sounds ominous. Anthea or Abi?'

'Both.'

'Has Anthea had complications after her fall? I mean, when I heard she'd spent an entire night on the floor of her house with a broken arm... at her age... Goodness she must be incredibly tough to have survived that.'

'No, no complications but I've just heard she wants to finish her recovery and her convalescence at mine.'

'But you've got Abi and her partner. Or are they moving out soon? How's their house coming on?'

Maxine shut her eyes and shook her head. 'I have no idea. All I know is they have got a builder in and work has started. They promised they'd only be living with us for a fortnight but that's almost up and there's no mention of significant progress at the house, so I can't see that time scale being stuck to at all. Of course I may be doing them and their builder a disservice but...' She sighed heavily. 'I love my family, I do, but I don't want them all under my roof. Despite your brilliant advice on wrangling boomerang children I've failed epically with Abi and now I'll probably have Anthea to deal with too.' She gazed at Olivia. 'I'm dreading it.'

'When's she arriving?'

'Gordon thinks he'll be able to spring her early next week. That's if the consultant OKs it. She's been there for almost two weeks so I imagine they'll be glad of the bed. And she's not developed pneumonia, or any other possible set-backs that someone of eighty-three who has had such a traumatic accident might expect, so I imagine the NHS will be only too glad to hand her over to the care of some willing relations.'

'I think you're a saint.'

Maxine sighed. 'Not really. I think *dutiful daughter-in-law* is about all I deserve as an accolade.'

'Anytime you want a shoulder to cry on – I'm here. I mean it.'

The door crashed open and a gang of other art club members thundered through, all chatting excitedly about their on-going art projects and then ooh-ing over the picture projected onto the screen.

Maxine gave Olivia's arm an appreciative squeeze before she nailed on a professional smile and greeted the newcomers.

15

Abi wandered down from the spare bedroom and into the kitchen dressed in a rather fetching silk dressing gown. The kitchen was filled with evening sunshine, a radio burbled on the windowsill and her mother was busy preparing the evening meal.

'I feel better for that shower,' she told her mother, who was chopping onions.

'Do you, dear? That's nice. How's the work going?'

'It would be going quicker if Steven hadn't taken the weekend off.'

'Darling, I think you're being a little unreasonable – he's allowed that much, surely.'

'Marcus and I kept going.'

'You're very dedicated, but you're still on gardening leave and it's your garden you're sorting out.'

'Was that meant to be funny?'

'Not really. Anyway, Steven's back on the job now so...?'

'So things are progressing.'

'Does that mean that you'll be able to move in soon?'

'Steven's not able to give us a date yet.'

Maxine looked at her daughter because she had a

deep-seated feeling that she wasn't being told the whole truth. 'What sort of kitchen are you going for?'

'Something plain and classic.'

'Have you ordered it yet?'

'Not exactly.'

'So, the *two weeks*...? Which was up today...'

'Oh, Mum, it was only an estimate. So, we're going to be a bit over. It'll be lovely when it's finished.'

Maxine didn't dare ask how much *a bit over* would amount to, and she could hardly throw them onto the street now the fortnight was up. 'Any news on the flat?'

'The estate agent says there have been a number of viewings and someone wants a second look. At least if we flog that we can dump the bridging loan.' She went over to the window and looked out. 'One day our garden will look as nice as yours.'

'It probably will. You and Marcus are working very hard on it.'

Abi flicked off the radio.

'I was listening to that,' protested Maxine.

'No, you're not, you are talking to me.' She turned and leant against the sink and saw her mother take a swig from a glass by her elbow. 'Not gin already, Mum. It's only half six.'

'Your dad and I often have a drink about now.' Maxine, defiantly, took another swig. 'Sometimes we have a second.'

'And then wine with your supper. *And* you went to the pub on Saturday. Without dad.'

'I met friends there. It's not illegal – or it wasn't the last time I checked.'

Abi took a couple of paces and leaned on the table. 'You *do* know about the government guidelines, don't you?'

Maxine laid her knife on the chopping board. 'Yes, I do. I am also an adult.'

'I know but just think about what all this booze could be doing to your health.'

'You make me sound as if I am a borderline alcoholic.'

'If the cap fits.'

'Oh, for God's sake, Abi. I will not be spoken to like this by my own child.'

'I think, you're the one being childish by being so irresponsible.'

Maxine took a deep breath. 'I'm not going to be lectured about my drinking habits.'

'It wasn't a lecture; I'm trying to be helpful. I was simply pointing out that maybe the pair of you ought to cut back a bit on the booze.'

'Really?' Maxine drained her glass and glared at her daughter. 'Well, while you are in the mood for being helpful, why don't *you* lay the table?'

'Now you want to punish me, is that it? Mum, I'm knackered. Have you any idea just how hard Marcus and I worked today?'

'Like I sat around and did nothing.'

'This is getting silly and I don't want to row with you. I'm going to watch the news.'

Abi went through to the sitting room and switched on the TV. Back in the kitchen, Maxine reached for the gin bottle.

★

The next morning, Anthea sat on the edge of her hospital bed while Gordon crouched beside her and eased her slippers onto her feet. He felt her wince when he put the slipper over her sprained ankle.

'Comfy?'

'Yes, thank you.'

'And everything is packed?'

'I didn't bring much. It was hardly a luxury break.'

'Right, let's get you into this wheelchair and start making tracks for home.'

Anthea tottered slightly when she got on to her good foot but Gordon had tight hold of her and lowered her safely into the chair.

'I hate this.' She tapped the arm rest with her plastered arm. 'It makes me look like a complete invalid.'

'Mum, you've got a broken wrist, a badly sprained ankle, a severe concussion and you've now got a face that looks as if you went head to head with Henry Cooper.'

Her bruises were faded but still apparent, particularly around her left eye. The glancing blow from the corner of the footstool had left its mark.

'I hope no one thinks I've been mugged.'

'Would that be worse than them knowing you tripped over a rug?'

'I don't want to be classed as a victim.'

Gordon was at a loss to follow the logic so busied himself with collecting her small suitcase of personal effects and checking that the bedside locker was completely empty. 'All set?' he said cheerily.

'Yes, thank you.'

Gordon wheeled his mother past the nurses' station.

'Bye, Anth,' said one of the nurses.

'It's Mrs Larkham,' she snapped back.

'Of course it is, dearie.'

Gordon increased his pace.

'I have never been so pleased to get away from anywhere in my entire life,' said Anthea as they headed for the main entrance and the car park. 'Now, you're sure you've locked my house up properly and emptied the fridge.'

'Yes, Mother. And Dot's going to go in and collect the post to forward on to you and water the plants and her husband will cut the grass and keep an eye on things. Everything is sorted and you're not to worry.'

Anthea sniffed.

Gordon knew that despite the fact he was over sixty, she still didn't trust him to be able to carry out her instructions any more than she had when he'd been about twelve.

They got back to Little Woodford in time for a late lunch. Once Gordon had handed over his mother to Max he went back out to the car to get in her case and some bits and pieces he'd gathered up from her house.

'I've made some tomato soup,' said Maxine, once Anthea was settled on a chair in the kitchen. 'And I got some nice bread from the bakery to go with it.'

'Made – or opened a tin?' asked Anthea.

'Made,' said Maxine.

'Actually, I rather like Heinz's.'

'I'm afraid you'll have to make do with mine. I haven't any of the other.' She switched the gas on under the pan.

'I'm sure yours will be quite nice, dear.'

Damned with faint praise. Maxine was tempted to get out the fridge magnet that her kids had once given her as a joke. She'd put it away as she didn't think Anthea, in the current circumstances would appreciate – *Be nice to your kids. They choose your nursing home.*

'Before we eat, is there anything you want to do? See your room, freshen up… anything?'

'Don't be so coy, Maxine, it sounds really quite common. And no, I don't need the lavatory. I went before I left hospital and I am not like a dog who needs to go several times a day. I am perfectly well aware that we're both going to find things distasteful and embarrassing but we've got to get on with it. It's only for the short term and, when it's over, we can go back to living our separate lives and we needn't refer back to this again, ever.'

Maxine leant on the table and took a deep breath. 'Just so we completely understand each other… I am doing this because I love Gordon and you're his mother. You and I know we both hate this situation and we're not, and never will be, bosom buddies, so let's not pretend we are, nor that we're being all brave and braced up and jolly hockey-sticks and working as a team. We're making the best of a bad job and that's that. But as long as you're in *my* house and *I* am looking after you, you can do me the courtesy of being nice to me. I'm finding the prospect of nursing you quite hard enough without *you* making it worse.' There, she'd said it.

'Oh,' said Anthea. For a moment she seemed to shrink and there was a pause while she regained her composure and her stature. Then she raised her eyebrows as she looked straight at her daughter-in-law. 'I'll give you your due; you've got more backbone than I thought you had.'

Maxine almost laughed. 'Is that a compliment?'

'Not really.'

Anthea drank her soup with the aid of a straw not being able to manage her soup spoon adequately with her left hand, and Maxine cut her bread and butter up into chunks so she could pop bite-sized morsels of bread into her mouth between sips.

'It's like being a baby,' she grumbled.

'It's this or starve,' retorted Maxine.

'Steady on, Max,' muttered Gordon.

'It's all right, Gordon, Maxine and I understand each other perfectly.'

Gordon cast a worried glance at both women before he returned his attention to his soup.

Later, when Anthea had been helped upstairs to her room for an afternoon nap, Gordon helped Maxine stack the dishwasher.

'What was that all about?'

'Your ma and I have had words.'

'Already?'

Max stopped slotting cutlery into the basket and straightened up. 'It's inevitable given that she's always loathed me—'

'That's not—'

'Take it from me, she does. We tolerate each other and we manage to be civil to each other in company but, trust me, there's no love lost. While you were putting things in her room before lunch, I read her the riot act.'

'Was that entirely necessary, Max? She's old and frail and recovering from a horrid accident.'

'She might be all of those things but she's still got a vicious tongue and I am *not* going to be belittled or slighted or put down in my own home. Sorry, Gordon, I know she's your ma but she can be truly horrid sometimes.'

'I know. I know she can, but I didn't think she took it out on you.'

'Because I haven't told you. Forty years... *more* than forty years I've taken it and tried to ignore it, told myself that even if you'd married nobility Anthea wouldn't have thought her good enough. And as for me, an *art* teacher...' Max rolled her eyes. 'Sorry, if I've burst your bubble of belief that your mum and I are mates but the truth is, we're not.'

'Oh, Max. I wish I'd known.'

'And done what? Had it out with her and risked falling out? She's not the forgiving sort.'

'No, I know.'

'Anyway, I might have failed with laying down ground rules with Abi but I've had another go at doing it, this time with your mother. Of course, she's probably going to ignore everything I've said, like Abi has. It's probably in Abi's genes – inherited through the paternal line, like some diseases – to be so tricky.'

'So it's my fault.'

'Of course it is. You're a bloke.'

16

The expanded household quickly settled into a routine with Marcus and Abi showering early and vacating the family bathroom by eight, leaving it free for Anthea to use later in the morning. Max would bring Anthea a cup of tea around the same time and the carer they'd managed to employ, a lovely jolly local woman called Pearl, arrived between half eight and nine to get Anthea washed, dressed and ready for the day.

'Bye, both Mrs Larkhams,' she'd call as she vacated the house. Always followed by something along the lines of, 'You two behave till I get back here this evening. I don't want to hear no rumours of you getting up to no good while my back is turned.'

At first Anthea would tut and frown at this bonhomie, but as she got used to Pearl and her good humour a rapport began to grow between them.

Anthea would then hobble painfully downstairs, helped by Maxine, and have her breakfast at which point Gordon took over some of the care, freeing up Max to deal with any housework or washing or shopping. She'd had to give up volunteering at the charity shop and she hadn't managed to read the book club book but she was hanging on to her art club because, 'I need something to keep me sane.'

A week after Granny Anthea had arrived, the family was sitting round the dining room table eating supper. Abi pushed a chunk of Quorn lasagne around her plate.

'What did you do to this, Mum?' she asked. 'It doesn't taste right.' She scraped some of the veggie mince off the pasta sheet before she ate it. 'Don't you agree, Granny?'

'It's not great,' said Anthea, 'but then I don't understand why we can't eat proper meat than get served this. I've no idea what it is and I'm not a rabbit and I'd like to know why can't we have beef?' She glared at Maxine.

'You know why,' said Maxine, 'and I've got quite enough to do without cooking two separate meals every evening. So, Abi, unless you want to cook your own vegetarian meals, you'll have to make do with my attempts. And if you don't like it you can lump it.' She returned Anthea's glare and then shifted it to her daughter. She leaned across to her mother-in-law, shovelled up half a forkful of mince so Anthea could use her left hand to eat it. She could manage to raise the fork to her mouth but she wasn't dexterous enough with that hand to cope with the fine motor skills needed for other aspects of feeding herself and she certainly couldn't cut up her own food.

'Get real, Mum. I can't be expected to do *all* the housework as well as working like a navvie.'

'I don't think anyone suggested that you should. All I said was, if *you* want vegetarian food that comes up to *your* standards of perfection then *you* might like to cook it.'

Gordon and Marcus exchanged a look.

'And if *you* cared,' retorted Abi, 'about climate change and the sort of planet, *you* are leaving to your grandchildren and the next generation *you* might see the need to stop eating meat too. But, oh no...'

'Frankly, right now, I haven't got time to care about that,' she snapped with more vitriol than was necessary, before she ate a forkful of her own lasagne and then prepared another one for Anthea.

Despite Abi's prediction about global warming the temperature around the dinner table dropped a couple of degrees.

'I was just saying...' countered Abi.

'Well, don't.' Maxine leaned forward, picked up the wine bottle and refilled her glass. She took a large swig, ignoring Abi's disapproving stare.

The rest of the meal was largely eaten in silence.

Afterwards Abi and Marcus stomped off to their room citing emails to write about their flat in London which, at last, had an offer on it, Anthea went to watch TV in the sitting room and Maxine and Gordon were left to do the clearing up.

'Again,' pointed out Maxine.

'Don't be too hard on Abi; she and Marcus are up to their eyes with the house and the garden.'

'Darling, I *know* that but she could still lend us a hand. I'm fed up with doing almost everything.'

'I help,' Gordon protested.

He did... a bit. Like now, but there was a lot of time when jobs needed doing and he wasn't around.

'And they've got to go back to work in a week or so,' he added.

'They were jolly lucky to get a month off in the first place.'

'Just as well, because they've needed it. Mind you, they have managed to get the worst of the work done in the garden.'

'So much for, *we'll be in in a fortnight.*'

They put the last of the plates and glasses in the dishwasher and Maxine slammed the door shut.

'I really fancy a pint,' said Gordon. 'Let's go to the pub.'

'I'm bushed,' said Max. 'I'd really rather have another glass here.'

'But we finished the bottle.'

Maxine opened a kitchen cupboard and pulled out a new one. 'And stuff what Abi says about our drinking habits,' she said as she unscrewed the cap.

'Which was?'

'She seems to think you and I are borderline alcoholics. Actually, not even borderline.'

'So, leave the wine and come to the pub with me; the walk'll do you good and there won't be any evidence to annoy Abi with. Besides, it'll blow the cobwebs away,' tempted Gordon.

'No, I'm too tired. I'll sit with your ma till Pearl comes back to get her to bed.'

'If you're sure.'

Maxine nodded and took her glass through to the sitting room.

Gordon shrugged on his fleece and headed for the pub, walking through the nature reserve in the dusky evening. There were a few dog walkers out and about, a couple of lovers walking slowly, hand-in-hand. From the copse, in the middle of the meadow he could hear the sound of kids being raucous – more than likely it was the local youths indulging in something slightly illegal – under-age drinking and maybe a spliff or two – but what else was there for them to do in a little town like this? He was still mulling about the lack of facilities for the young, when he pushed open the door to the pub. A few of the regulars were in but it was pretty quiet. He'd obviously hit on the lull between the people who came in for a drink after work and the people who came in for a drink before bed. He made his way to the bar where the new barmaid was serving.

'Evening,' said Gordon. 'It's Ellie, isn't it?'

'Ella, but close enough. And you're…?'

'Gordon.'

'Of course. I met you on my first day. You were with your wife. What can I get you?'

'A pint of bitter, please. Belinda not about?'

'She's gone to the flicks in Cattebury.' Ella poured his pint. 'She'll be back in time to help me close up. And that's three ninety, please.'

Gordon swapped some cash for his drink and leaned on the bar as he took his first sip. A couple of old boys from the allotment society were chuntering about white fly and there was another couple playing crib, but he didn't fancy joining either group nor did he want to sit at a table on his own. He leaned against the bar.

'What did you do, before you worked here?' he asked Ella.

'Shop work mostly, in Cattebury, but then my ex buggered off, I couldn't afford the rent on my own and… let's just say I've had to move back with my old Mum and Dad here in Little Woodford.'

'That's tough.'

'Tragic, isn't it?' Ella mopped some drips of beer off the bar. 'My age and back home with the folks.'

'If it's any consolation, my daughter and her partner have just moved back.' Gordon had another drink of his pint. 'They're doing up a house near here.'

'At least your daughter's got a partner and a house.'

'At the risk of being politically incorrect, and God knows, with the MeToo movement I don't know *what* I'm allowed to say, but I'd have thought you'd be beating men off with a stick.'

Ella blushed. 'You're very kind, but having been through a divorce I'm picky about getting involved again. I want someone who'll treat me right and look after me properly not just a random bloke who might take me out on a date or two and then move on.'

'I don't blame you.'

'How about you?'

'I got lucky. Been married now for over forty years.'

One of the old boys from the allotments came up to the bar.

'Evening, Gordon,' he said. 'No Maxine? Two pints please, Ella.'

'Evening, Bert,' said Gordon. 'Not tonight. We've got my mum staying with us and she's keeping her company.'

'I thought you said it was your daughter and her partner?' said Ella as she passed one of the pints between the pump handles.

'It's all of them. A total houseful.'

'How long for?' said Bert.

'A while, I think,' said Gordon with a heartfelt sigh.

'No wonder you've come out for a drink. I expect we'll be seeing more of you down here, then,' said Bert.

Gordon thought it sounded like a great idea. After all, a pretty woman to chat to, nice company and a beer – what wasn't to like?

Gordon could hear the shouting from halfway down the drive. He was tempted to turn around and go straight back to the pub, only Ella and Belinda had called *time*. He hiccupped softly as he put his key in the lock – or tried to. It took a couple of attempts. What the hell were Max and Abi arguing about, now? he wondered, as he managed finally to get the door open. He made his way to the kitchen where the two women were squaring up like a couple of cats. Any minute now they'd get their claws out and start raking chunks off each other.

'Good God,' he yelled above the noise.

'And you can keep *right* out of it,' said Maxine.

Undaunted, or maybe it was the drink that made him brave, he yelled straight back, 'Shut up, the pair of you!'

Maxine turned and glared but she stayed silent.

'What on earth is going on?' he asked.

'I clear up the kitchen, you and I stack the dishwasher, everything is tidy and I come to make a milky drink for *your* mother and I find madam, here, has been making sandwiches because she didn't eat her supper properly and was hungry and has left the kitchen in a total tip.'

'You are *so* exaggerating,' sniped Abi. 'It was just a few crumbs.'

'I am not.'

'Are. *And* you've been drinking.'

Gordon held up his hand. 'SHUT UP!' he roared. Silence fell again. He looked at the worktop with a crumb-scattered breadboard, a buttery knife and a dirty plate. 'Is this the cause of the argument?'

'Yes.'

'Don't you think you're over-reacting, Max?'

Max opened and shut her mouth.

Gordon picked up the board and swished the crumbs into the sink and then chucked the used plate and knife into the dishwasher. 'There. Solved.'

'That's *not* the point,' shrieked Max. 'And *don't* undermine my authority. This is *my* house.'

'Actually, I think it's *ours*,' said Gordon.

Maxine narrowed her eyes. 'For over a week now I have been a skivvy for everyone. Your mother, I don't resent because she's ill, but the rest of you…' She stopped and took a breath because her voice was getting shrill. 'As for the rest of you… I'm busy *too*, and I am *tired* and I have a *life* which I have had to put on hold – not that any of you give that the *least* bit of thought – and I am not here just to make life easier for *you* because *you* can't be bothered to shift for yourselves.'

'I think you're being a bit unfair on Abi—'

'Don't… don't you *dare* take her side.' Max's voice was now dangerously low. 'Again.'

'I'm not. I just want a quiet life not all this aggro.'

'It's what I want too but I'm not fucking getting it,' she snarled back.

'Mum!' said Abi.

Maxine rounded on her. 'And don't *you* dare tell me what I can and can't do, can and can't cook, or can and can't say!'

Abi looked close to tears. 'You're being unfair.'

'I am not. You criticise my cooking, my drinking and now my language.'

'It was a bit strong,' said Gordon.

'Right, that's it,' stormed Maxine. 'The pair of you can go to hell.' And she slammed out of the kitchen.

In the silence that followed Abi and Gordon stared at each other in disbelief.

'I've never seen Mum that angry before.'

'Me neither. I think you'd better apologise in the morning.'

'Hang on, she was cross with you too.'

'I'll make it up to her when I go to bed.'

Abi grimaced.

Gordon ignored her. 'Right now, I'm going to watch TV for a bit while your mum calms down and I suggest you make sure the kitchen is spotless.'

Abi sighed, snatched the dishcloth off the taps and began to wipe down the counter.

'And make sure you sweep up any crumbs off the floor,' advised Gordon.

'God, Dad, you're as bad as Mum.'

'Don't start a fight with me,' he warned. 'You don't want to piss off both your parents.'

Abi muttered something unintelligible as Gordon left the room. As he passed the dining room he caught sight of the whisky decanter on the sideboard. He was going to need a stiffener before he faced the rest of Max's wrath. He poured himself two fingers – well, maybe three – before he headed to the sitting room. He found an old repeat of *Family Guy* which would do nicely while he had his nightcap.

It was nearly midnight before he made his way up to bed. He didn't dare switch the light on – he didn't want to provide yet another reason for his wife to be cross with him so he slipped into the bathroom and got undressed there. It was as he was leaving the en-suite and a shaft of light from the half-open door fell across the bed he realised that she wasn't sleeping there. The row was obviously worse than he'd realised.

Oh well, it would all blow over in the morning. Feeling slightly sozzled he was asleep in an instant.

17

The next morning, after Abi and Marcus had left for Wisteria Cottage, Maxine got quietly out of the single bed in the box room and padded downstairs to make herself and Anthea an early morning cuppa. She'd lain awake most of the night, tense, miserable, angry and fed up and feeling, in turns, guilty about her reaction and livid at being taken for granted. As she waited for the kettle to boil, she tried not to get wound up again about the previous night's row but she was still finding it hard to believe that Gordon had sided, once again, with Abi not her. She had always known how he indulged his daughter and she'd found it quite endearing – well, mostly. But surely even *he* could see that Abi'd crossed a line. And when he'd told her that she was being unfair on Abi…! The very thought of what he'd said made her start to hyperventilate, again. Unfair! How dare he? She took long slow breaths to try and calm down. Just *how* was she being unfair? Abi was just swanning along as usual while she… she had lost half her house, her studio, her free time, her job… She took another calming breath.

Gordon mightn't want rows, he might want a quiet life but how about her? Didn't she deserve that too? And that was before she even contemplated the extra housework and shopping and cooking. And then there was the small matter that Abi could stuff washing into the machine, but the more lengthy and time-consuming process of taking it all out and hanging it up seemed to be entirely beyond her skill set.

The kettle clicked off and Maxine distracted herself from her black thoughts by making two cups and taking one of them up to Anthea who was awake, sitting up in bed and listening to the *Today* programme.

'Morning, Anthea.'

Anthea stared at her over her glasses. 'Morning. So what was all that about?'

'What?' Maxine plonked the mug on the bedside table.

'Maxine, I am neither deaf nor stupid. There were raised voices last night – an argument.'

'Oh, that.'

'Yes, that. You weren't arguing about me, I trust.'

'No, nothing like that.'

'Because I don't want to stay here if I'm not welcome.'

'Of course, you're welcome.'

'Good.' Anthea picked up her mug with her good hand and took a sip. It struck Maxine that now she knew she wasn't the cause of the altercation she'd lost interest in what was. Not that Maxine cared terribly. It wasn't as if it was any of Anthea's business.

'I need to tell you that I'm going out shortly, so when Pearl has got you sorted for the day, it'll be Gordon who'll get your breakfast ready. He was late back last night so I'm leaving him to sleep – you might have to tell Pearl to give him a bang on the bedroom door to make sure he's awake.'

'Oh.' Anthea sounded disapproving.

'I'm sorry, Anthea, but I think I deserve a day off.'

'If you say so.'

Anthea couldn't have made her opinion clearer if she'd actually said that Maxine was a slacker. She left Anthea's room, closing the door behind her slightly harder than was necessary.

Stuff them. Stuff them all, she thought as she showered in the family bathroom and dressed in her previous day's clothes to avoid having to go into her bedroom. The way she was feeling right now, the last person she wanted to encounter was her husband. She didn't think she would be held responsible for her actions. She went downstairs, gathered up her painting gear plus a portable easel and stool and headed out. As she picked up her handbag, she noticed her mobile phone and removed it. She wanted to be alone and that meant she didn't want to be badgered by Gordon or anyone else. She jumped into the car and reversed out of the drive. And if Gordon wanted the car, tough, she thought rebelliously as she drove down to the cricket pitch.

She chose a corner of the outfield which gave her a terrific view of the oaks that bordered it and the yews which edged the churchyard and yet was out of the way of passing walkers or any of the groundsmen. The dark, British racing green of the yew foliage contrasted brilliantly with the fresher, brighter green of the oaks and the expanse of verdant grass of the pitch and as she stared at the view, she felt her blood pressure lowering. She set up her easel, settled herself on her stool and began a preliminary sketch of the scene. Apart from a blackbird singing and a robin's staccato warning to incomers against encroaching on its territory, the silence was almost total. If she listened really carefully, she could hear a faint hum of cars on the ring road several hundred yards away, and now and again a soft breeze rustled the leaves. Maxine immersed herself in her picture to the extent she was even unaware of the chimes of the church clock as it recorded the hours and half hours as they passed.

A shadow fell across her watercolour and she looked up, startled and saw the vicar's wife.

'Heather!'

'I hope I'm not disturbing you.'

'You're not.' Maxine glanced at her watch. 'Blimey, is that the time?'

'I saw you from the bedroom window first thing and you're still here. I was about to make Brian and myself a couple of sandwiches for lunch and I wondered if you'd like to join us? Please don't feel you have to.'

'No, no, that'd be lovely.'

'Really?'

'I didn't think to bring a picnic and now I think about it, I'm famished.' She smiled broadly at Heather. 'That's really kind of you.'

'We hardly ever see each other outside the book group.'

'No, and I missed the last meeting and not being a church goer…'

'What's that got to do with it?'

Maxine thought probably quite a lot. 'But it'll be lovely to have a proper chat – and lunch too. What a treat.'

'I'm only offering a sandwich.'

'Even so.' After all the emotion of the previous evening, this unexpected kindness made Maxine feel quite moved. She turned away so she could dash away a tear without

Heather seeing it and busied herself putting her paints away and folding up her stool.

'I'll just dump this lot in the boot of the car. I don't expect anyone will be so desperate as to nick a second-rate watercolour but you never know.'

'That's *not* a second-rate watercolour. It's gorgeous. I love it. You completely capture the scene – which, by-the-by, is one of my favourites.'

'Then it's yours.'

'Don't be ridiculous. I can't possibly accept it.'

'Yes, you can.'

'I'll pay you.'

'OK, done.'

'How much?'

'One cheese and tomato sandwich.'

Heather grinned at her. 'It might have to be pickle not tomato.'

'Then the deal's off.' Max paused for about a second before she added, 'Joking.'

'Phew. And can I be cheeky?'

'Of course.'

'Would you sign it for me? Because, you know, when you're all rich and famous I can flog it to fund my old age!'

Maxine laughed. 'I think we'll both need to dream on.'

Heather helped Maxine gather up her bits and pieces before they both headed off to the vicarage.

'I'm back,' Heather called to Brian as she shut the front door behind them. 'Brian, I'm back,' she yelled again.

'I heard you,' said Brian coming out of the study.

Maxine had never met Brian, what with her not going to

church and him not attending the book club, but she was instantly struck by how kind he looked. Kind, but messy. His fringe stood up at all angles, his sweater which had a hole in the ribbing, had biscuit crumbs down its front and his baggy, saggy trousers had a mark near his right knee.

Heather stood next to him and brushed off the worst of the crumbs. 'Maxine, meet Brian, Brian – Maxine.'

The pair shook hands.

'Maxine and I go to the book club together and she's a super-talented artist.'

Maxine felt her face flaring. 'What Heather means is that I dabble in watercolours.'

Heather tutted. 'Don't listen to her, Brian. Now then, you come into the kitchen with me, Maxine. I think I might have a bottle of sherry somewhere if I can persuade you to join me in a little treat. Brian?'

'No, not for me, dearest,' said her husband. 'I'm writing a bit of a tricky letter and I need a clear head.'

Brian disappeared back into his study as Heather led Maxine through to the back of the house and the kitchen.

Maxine had never been in the vicarage before and was struck by the out-of-date decor. Not even shabby-chic but far worse and as for those ghastly green tiles!

Heather saw her looking. 'Grim isn't it? But it's weatherproof and the church commissioners have promised us we're in the queue for an update. Take a seat,' she said as she headed for a cupboard and rummaged till she found the amontillado. 'You will, won't you?' she asked as she looked for some glasses.

'Just a small one. I've got to get the car home later.'

Heather carefully poured two tots and handed one to Maxine.

'So... how's it all going? Olivia told me at Church last week that you've suddenly had your family descend on you. It's not easy when that happens, is it? Olivia had a desperate time with her Jade.'

The thought of what awaited her when she got back home made her tempted to neck her sherry in one go, so she removed the urge by putting the glass carefully on the table. She then took a deep breath. 'I think I could cope if it were *just* Anthea or *just* Abi and Marcus, but the fact that it's all of them...' This time she did allow herself a small sip. 'And last night I lost it – *really* lost it. I went batshit with Abi and then, when Gordon came back from the pub, I shouted at him too. Which is why I decided to spend the day painting so we can all calm down.'

'Very wise.' Heather gathered up the makings of the promised sandwiches and began to butter the bread. 'Dare I ask what was the cause of the row?'

'Bread crumbs.'

Heather snorted. 'I'm sorry,' she said straightening her face.

'No, you're right. Talk about a storm in a tea cup. But, the thing was, I'd left the kitchen spotless after I'd cleared up after supper and when I went back a couple of hours later it was a mess again. OK, just a few crumbs and a dirty plate but it was the *principle* of it all. The thoughtlessness.' She felt ridiculously close to tears – again. Maybe it was because she'd had such a rough night.

Heather put the bread knife down and gave her a hug. Maxine lost it and howled.

★

'I still can't get over Mum's attitude last night,' grumbled Abi for the umpteenth time that morning. She pulled off one of her gardening gloves and wiped her brow with the back of her hand.

'Change the record, Abs,' said Marcus as he loaded the wheelbarrow up with a pile of hedge clippings.

'It's all right for you. You weren't the one who got shouted at. *And* she swore at me.'

'She was very angry.'

'She was very unreasonable.'

'Your mum's got a lot on her plate right now.'

'And we haven't?' Abi tugged her glove back on and began cutting back the branches of an overgrown shrub with a pruning saw. The garden around them was starting to take real shape as they reversed the years of neglect. The beds were still full of mare's tail, bindweed, brambles and nettles, and the lawn was more dandelion than grass but at least now they could see that there *were* beds and a lawn whereas before the garden had mostly consisted of dense scrub. Abi had commented, when they'd first started on it, that she wouldn't be surprised if they came across a castle with Sleeping Beauty imprisoned in it.

'Your mum's got a point that we don't do very much to help,' reasoned Marcus.

'Don't you start.' She pulled off her gardening glove again. 'I need a break, I'm knackered.' She piled her gloves and the pruning saw on top of the wheelbarrow and headed for the house. Marcus trotted after her.

'Steven!' she called as she peered through the back door.

In front of her was a large hole in the floorboards with arc lights shining out of it and a couple of planks laid over it.

A muffled 'hang on' answered her from the depths.

'I'm going to put the kettle on. Want a cuppa?'

'Please.'

Abi went over to the tray balanced on a Workmate and picked up the kettle. A single tap protruded from the wall in the shell of the room that had once been a kitchen. Everything had been stripped out with the exception of a couple of sockets, the tap and some patches of dingy, cracked tiles which had been behind the sink and the range. It could have been hit by a bomb, thought Abi as she filled the kettle and plugged it in.

As the kettle spluttered, Steven emerged from the hole.

'How's it going?' asked Abi.

'Slowly, but I've got two of the replacement joists in position and with any luck I should get the third one in by next week. Once that's done the house will be stable and we can start getting anything else removed that might be infected. Dry rot is a bugger for spreading. Once we've worked out what needs replacing we can do that, *then* we can start treating everything against a recurrence, *then* we can start replacing the floorboards and *then*, when that's done, I can start on the kitchen proper.'

'And how long will that take?'

Steven sighed. 'We're talking lengths of string here. The last thing you want is to find a pocket of dry rot left and have to start again in a dozen years or so. It'll be a couple of weeks at least if I'm going to make sure we've got all the infected timbers out. Then we'll have to get a specialist team in to treat anything that remains *and* all the new stuff.' He shrugged. 'Maybe another ten days or so on top of that.'

'That adds up to almost a month.' The kettle clicked off but Abi ignored it. 'And it's already been three weeks.'

'You can't hurry this sort of thing – not if you want a proper job doing.'

'And in the meantime the bills keep going up and up.'

'Can't be helped,' said Steven. 'I'm doing my best.'

'I know, I know.' But she didn't sound happy.

'It'll be lovely when it's finished,' Marcus chipped in.

'But it's not the two week job you said it would be,' grumbled Abi.

'Two weeks?!' said Steven, incredulously. 'You're kidding me?'

Marcus looked embarrassed.

'What did you think I'd use for tools – a magic wand?' asked Steven before he muttered 'two weeks' again. 'Look, what with one thing and another, you'll be lucky to be moving in in under three months, maybe four or five is nearer the mark.'

'Five?' squeaked Abi. 'Mum's going to go ape.'

'Not if we don't tell her, like you suggested,' said Marcus. 'We don't want another row.'

Steven looked from one to the other. 'Things a bit tense, are they, with the folks?'

'You could say that,' said Abi while Marcus nodded, morosely.

18

After a good cry on Heather's shoulder, Maxine felt much calmer.

'Letting it all out can be very cathartic,' Heather had assured her as she passed her tissue after tissue.

'But I feel such a fool,' Maxine had said as she dabbed her eyes and finally pulled herself together. 'What on earth have I got to feel sorry for myself about?'

Heather returned to making the sandwiches. As she sliced the cheese and laid it on the buttered bread she said, 'You're tired, you've got a lot on your plate, your world has been turned upside down and you feel unappreciated and undervalued. It's enough to make anyone feel a bit low.'

Maxine sniffed and blew her nose. 'I'm sorry, you invited me in for a nice lunch and you end up giving me counselling.'

'Hardly. Besides, I'm a vicar's wife – it's in the job description.'

Maxine gave her a damp smile as Heather dolloped on pickle.

'I expect,' continued Heather, 'your outburst will have made your family have a good look at themselves and realise how much you do for them. They'll probably start helping out a lot more.'

'You think?'

Heather nodded as she sliced the pile of sandwiches into triangles. 'Now then, I don't think another sherry will put you over the limit and even if you don't want one, I do.'

After lunch, Maxine went back to the cricket pitch and carried on with her painting aware that she felt much calmer. Good old Heather, she thought. Had she instinctively known that there was a sheep in need of attention even if the 'sheep' wasn't one of her husband's flock? She finished her painting and then worked on some sketches to delay returning home.

It was almost five when she stretched and stood up. Time to go home and see how Anthea had fared under Gordon's ministrations. She packed away her stuff and returned.

'Where the hell have you been?' was the greeting she got from Gordon as she let herself in through the front door.

'Out.'

'Duh,' he said. 'Obviously. I was worried sick.'

Maxine dumped all her painting kit by the front door – she'd deal with it later – and hooked her handbag over the newel post. 'What? In case you had to cook supper?'

'Don't be silly.'

'I needed time to calm down, to take stock… a bit of *me* time.'

'You could have left a note,' he grumbled.

'I told Anthea I was taking a day off.'

'I know but…'

'But?'

'But I wondered if it was more than that.'

Maxine headed into the kitchen to make herself a cup of

tea. 'More than that? You didn't think I might have done something dramatic – like left home?'

'I dunno.' He sounded a bit sheepish.

'Come off it – and gone where?' She switched the kettle on.

Gordon shrugged. 'Your sister's?'

'No.'

'So you've forgiven me?'

Maxine turned around, leant against the counter and sighed. 'I wouldn't go that far.'

'But—'

'I was *very* angry last night. More so because you sided with Abi.' Gordon looked as if he was about to speak again. 'Shh.' She held up her hand. 'You want a quiet life? So do I and you not backing me up won't help. Why do I *always* have to be the bad cop where Abi is concerned? Abi needs to pull her weight around this house. If I wasn't coping with your mother as well, I might just be more loving and giving but Abi and Marcus can both cook, they are capable of going to the supermarket, of pegging out their own washing or even cleaning the bloody bathroom, but do they? No, it's muggins here. And I'm tired of it.'

'I see that.'

'And you could help out.'

Gordon's eyebrows shot up. 'I do. I help with the dishwasher and I do the garden.'

The kettle clicked off. 'You do. And you also play golf twice a week.' She made a cup of tea for herself ignoring Gordon's pained look. If he wanted tea, he knew how to make it.

'But I like playing golf.'

'I *liked* my day at the charity shop. I *liked* painting in my studio.'

'Come off it, Max, you went painting today.'

Max shook her head. 'You really don't get it, do you?' As she said it the front door crashed open and Marcus and Abi piled in. They toed off their muddy boots in the hall leaving clods of earth scattered over the tiles and clattered into the kitchen.

'What's for sups, Mum? I'm famished.'

'I've no idea. Whatever you fancy cooking. I'm tired too and I'm going to read a book on my bed. Let me know when it's ready.' She picked up her mug and headed upstairs leaving her husband and daughter looking bewildered.

A couple of hours later Abi called everyone to the dinner table.

Anthea took her seat and looked disdainfully at her plate of over-cooked, rubbery-looking omelette, bread and butter and some salad. 'Honestly, Maxine, is it fair that just because you're in a mood we all have to suffer?' Then she turned to Abi. 'Is this really the best you could do?'

'I didn't get much notice,' snapped back Abi.

'Someone of your age should have the gumption to be able to rustle up a decent meal from store cupboard ingredients. You didn't teach her very well, did you, Maxine?'

'Apparently not. Still, I did a better job on Abi than you did on Gordon. He can't even spell *cooking* let alone do it.'

'Enough,' said Gordon, slapping his hand on the table. 'Abi's done her best and we should all be grateful.' He glared at his wife who glared back.

Like the previous night's supper this one was also largely

eaten in silence and at the end, Maxine pointedly left her plate on the table when she finished and stamped upstairs to the box room. She had considered moving back into her own bedroom that night but that plan was off the agenda now. Half an hour later she heard the front door slam so she peered out of the window and saw Gordon stamping down the drive. She made a private bet that he was off to the pub – again.

While he was out, she moved her clothes across to the spare room. Until Gordon began to support her in her battle with their daughter and his mother, she wasn't going to move back.

On the Tuesday of the following week Judith left the solicitor's office in West Myring and resisted the urge to give a little skip. She also resisted the urge to go for a celebratory drink as it was a bit early in the day – even for her. She was chuffed because, having sold her old house, she'd now managed to complete on her new one and soon she would be moving to Little Woodford. For a while she'd been slightly unsure of her decision – Little Woodford was slightly further from London's West End and had rather fewer facilities than her current place of residence but, on the positive side, she'd have company in the form of her sister who would also give her an introduction to the local social scene via the medium of Maxine's large group of friends. And having explored it properly, whilst house-hunting, she had discovered its charm. OK, she wasn't moving there for the shopping but the pub was great, there was a high-class butcher, a bookshop, a decent cookware shop and some nice little independent stores that sold all sorts of quirky bits and pieces.

Rather than skipping down the high street or heading for the pub she restrained herself to pulling her mobile out of her handbag and ringing her sister.

'Hiya, Sis,' she said when Maxine picked up. 'How's things?'

'You don't want to know,' was the response.

'That sounds ominous. The family getting you down?'

'In a nutshell.'

'What? All of them? Even the sainted Gordon?'

'Especially the sainted Gordon.'

Judith had to repress a giggle. What on earth could a dull old stick like Gordon have possibly done to piss off her big sister? 'Want to talk?' Oh, please do. Judith longed to know what was going on.

'Not really.'

Bugger. 'Well, as you obviously need cheering up, I've rung to tell you I've exchanged,' said Judith. 'Isn't it wonderful?'

'Great.'

'You could sound more enthusiastic.'

'Sorry. No, it is great. Really. I've just got a lot on at the mo; Anthea is shit-stirring, Abi is being a complete pain and Gordon... Oh, never mind.'

'Is being a bastard?' Judith offered.

A loud sigh whistled over the airwaves.

'Come on, spill,' prompted Judith. 'A problem shared is a problem halved.'

'Gordon seems to find the easiest way to deal with things is to go to the pub or the golf course. And he certainly won't take my side against Abi and tell her to pull her finger out around the house because – and I quote – he wants a quiet life.'

'And Abi is daddy's little girl and the apple of his eye.'

'Exactly.'

'Which leaves you to deal with everything—'

'—And Anthea who is as tricky as ever.'

'That's not fair.'

'No, it's not. Even if he was around it wouldn't make much difference. Anthea has set views on the sort of jobs a man should do and looking after her doesn't feature. Pearl is wonderful, a treasure, but she can only do so much.'

'But Anthea must be getting better.'

'The bruises have gone, her ankle is mending although she still can't put much weight on it but at least she is semi-mobile and she's stopped needing me to get her on and off the loo.'

'Even so...'

'Even so, it's a lot of extra work – talk about fetching and carrying – and Abi and Marcus won't help citing the renovations to their cottage mean they are too busy. And even when I *do* persuade them to lift a finger, the atmosphere and bad feeling it causes makes it not worth the effort.'

'Oh, dear. You do sound a bit put upon.'

'I am. Very.'

'Come to mine. If you're not around Abi and Gordon will *have* to pull their fingers out. It'll be a bit chaotic while I sort and pack and do shit like that but you're more than welcome.'

'I could give you a hand with the packing.'

'Nice offer, but what you need is a rest not more work.'

'Seriously, it's the perfect excuse to leave them to stew for a day or two. I can't come before Thursday because of my art club so, maybe Friday, for a long weekend?'

'Really? Another pair of hands would be fab but what you need is a spa day not playing at being Pickfords.'

'What I need is to get away from my family before I lash out with the carving knife.'

'As long as you don't include me in family members you'd like to murder, then be my guest.'

Maxine waited until Gordon came in from the garden where he'd been tidying up the veg patch. He had mooted the idea of going to the golf course to play nine holes because the weather was glorious but when he saw the look on Maxine's face, he rapidly changed his mind. She offered both Anthea and her husband some late elevenses and when she'd carried the tray of mugs and the plate of biscuits into the sitting room, she broke the news.

'My sister is about to move house and I'm going to hers to help her pack. I'll be gone a couple of days – maybe more.'

Anthea opened and shut her mouth and then frowned. 'But... but...'

'But?' asked Maxine. 'But you'll have Pearl, or her stand-in, as always and you don't need me that much during the day. I'm sure Gordon can run up and down stairs for you and Abi can take over on the domestic front.'

Anthea snorted. 'That'll be interesting given her lack of any culinary skills.'

'Then Gordon will have to help.'

It was Gordon's turn to snort.

'Really,' said Maxine. 'If it had been me involved in an accident you'd *have* to cope. None of you are completely helpless – not even you, Anthea, not anymore. And I'm going to take the car.'

Gordon looked horrified.

'Sorry, love, but the train journey to Judith's is the pits. Besides, as you'll be looking after Anthea you won't need it to get to the golf course and I'm sure Abi and Marcus can do any shopping that's needed on their way home from the cottage.'

'But they're going back to work next week.'

Maxine rolled her eyes. 'Then they can do the shopping on their way home from the office. It's what we used to do. Or they can order it on-line. Jeez, Gordon, anyone would think I'm the only person on the entire planet who can do these basic things.'

'No... but...'

'And if all else fails, get take-aways.'

'Must we?' asked Anthea faintly, appalled by the idea.

'If Gordon and Abi can't be bothered to cook then you'd better get used to the idea,' said Maxine, knowing she sounded callous. But really, they were all grown-ups, they weren't completely incapable so why were they behaving like they were?

She then dropped her final bombshell. 'I'm off out. My friend Olivia has got a day off and she and I are meeting for lunch at the pub.'

'The pub?!' said Anthea.

'Yes.'

'But...?' she spluttered.

'What? I'm a woman so I shouldn't be seen in such a

place without my husband? Is that what you mean? It's OK for him to go on his own but not me?'

'I suppose it's the modern way,' conceded Anthea.

Maxine stood up and picked up her handbag. 'There's cold chicken and salad in the fridge and plenty of bread in the bin. I'm sure, between you, you can come up with something for lunch. I'll see you later.' And she swept off leaving Gordon looking somewhat shocked.

19

'No Gordon?' asked Belinda as Maxine ordered a glass of red wine.

'I'm meeting Olivia for lunch.'

'That'll be nice.'

'It will, won't it? Of course I see her at the art club and I *used* to see her at the book club, when I had the time to read the wretched books, but they're not things where we get to have a proper chat.'

'You and Gordon always used to come together but I haven't seen you here for weeks.' She put Maxine's order on the counter. 'Is everything OK – I mean, I know your place is a bit... crowded.'

Maxine sighed and leaned in closer. The bar wasn't full and the noise level was low and she wasn't sure she wanted any of the punters to be able to indulge in a bit of casual eavesdropping. 'To be honest, it's been getting a bit heavy.' She thought about telling Belinda she and Gordon had separate bedrooms but that would be over-share.

'Because of the family?'

Max nodded. 'You know that ditty – *Lizzie Borden took an axe and gave her mother forty whacks—*'

'*And when she saw what she had done, she gave her*

father forty-one,' finished Belinda, gleefully. 'It's not that bad, surely?'

'I've been tempted. Anyway, I've got a chance to escape for a few days so I'm going to stay with my sister.'

'That'll be nice. Six pounds, please.'

'I think it may be a case of frying pans and fires but I'm prepared to risk it.'

'I hope the risk pays off,' said Belinda as Olivia pushed open the door to the pub.

'Hello,' said Olivia kissing her friend on the cheek. 'What risk? I'm agog.'

'I'll tell you over lunch,' said Maxine. 'Now, what can I get you to drink?'

The pair had ordered their food and Maxine had updated a sympathetic Olivia as to the ups and downs of her family life when the door to the pub opened again and Amy sailed in.

'Hi, Belinda,' she called before she caught sight of her employer. 'Oh, hiya, Mrs Laithwaite. Skiving again?'

'No, Amy, I don't skive. I've taken a few days leave to enjoy this lovely weather we've been having, and to catch up with some personal admin.'

'That's nice.' She turned her attention back to Belinda. 'I'll have a large white, please. My Ryan's off shift so he's meeting me for lunch. Got just enough time to fit in a quick bite between the Post Office and cleaning for Miranda. Anyway, Miranda probably won't mind if I'm a minute or two late.'

'Really?'

'She's *a lot* better than she was when I started for her.'

'I suppose. Want to start a tab?'

'Yeah, that way Ryan might pay the whole bill.'

Belinda grinned, passed the wine over and entered the amount in the till.

Amy wandered over towards Olivia's table and chose a seat at the one next door. 'Lucky old you being able to pick and choose your days off.'

'It doesn't quite work like that.'

'Now I do for you, I have to get all my stuff done at the weekends. No days off for me. I'm not grumbling, mind, I like the extra cash.' She stared at Olivia's companion and Olivia took the hint.

'Amy, I don't think you know Mrs Larkham. Maxine, this is Amy.'

'You work in the Post Office, don't you?' asked Maxine.

Amy nodded. 'Maxine Larkham? You must be Abi's mum.'

It was Maxine's turn to nod. 'I didn't know you and my daughter know each other.'

'Oh, no we don't. I know *of* her. My bloke Ryan's got a friend who's a builder.'

'Steven?'

'That's the guy. He was telling us it's a big old job he's taken on for your daughter's house.'

'Oh? *Big old job?* I thought it was mostly cosmetic – doing it up, putting in a new kitchen, that sort of thing.'

'Cosmetic? Where did you get that idea from? No, he's going to be there for months. Mightn't be finished till the autumn, he says. There's a cellar full of problems. He mentioned something about dry rot. Sounds like rubbish to me – rot's caused by damp, everyone knows that. Anyway, from what he's told Ryan, he's almost having to rebuild the place from the foundations up. Didn't you know?'

Maxine took a very large gulp of wine before she answered. 'Let's just say, I do now.'

As Maxine walked home, she used the time to contemplate the implications of exactly what Amy had told her. Having quizzed Amy further, she understood that the problems with the house had come as much of a shock to her daughter as it had to her but it didn't explain the deception to her parents. Why hadn't she told her and Gordon? Although Max had a bloody good idea. Abi was worried about her parents' reaction – as well she might be. They were at daggers drawn now so what would they be like by the end of it? And this was assuming that Steven didn't find anything else wrong with the place.

She opened the front door and went to find Gordon. Anthea was fast asleep on the sofa in front of some mindless TV game show. Maxine took the remote off the arm of the sofa and turned it off. Anthea didn't stir. In the silence that followed she listened for clues as to Gordon's whereabouts. Nothing. She headed for the garden and found Gordon contemplating his compost heap, leaning on a fork.

'Did you know about the cottage?' she asked.

'Hello, dear. Nice lunch?' He smiled at her, possibly hoping for some sort of rapprochement.

'No, not really and you haven't answered my question – did you know about the cottage?'

'What about the cottage?' asked Gordon, patiently.

'About the cellar, about the rot, about the fact it's going to be months and *months* before Abi and Marcus can move.'

Gordon's smile faded. 'Months? Are you sure?'

'Not entirely – I heard the news via a friend of a friend. Well, a friend of the builder. I think we should get over there and see for ourselves.'

'What, now?'

'Yes, now.'

'What about Mother?'

'She's asleep on the sofa. I am sure she can cope with being on her own for an hour or two.'

Gordon nodded and Maxine went to wake Anthea and tell her they had to go out urgently.

'Here's my mobile number,' she said, putting a Post-It on the coffee table.

'But what if I have a fall and can't get to the phone.'

'Try not to.' Maxine was a bit sharper than was necessary but Anthea coming over all frail and helpless was the last thing she needed right now. 'We'll be back as soon as we can.'

Anthea merely sighed, picked up the remote and switched on the TV. Maxine had been dismissed.

There were several white vans and a couple of skips outside the cottage when they pulled up on the drive. The transformation of the garden was noticeable and it looked much bigger than it had on their previous visit. The cottage had also been transformed – into a major building project. Maxine's heart sank.

'It'll be lovely when it's finished,' said Gordon as Maxine opened the car door. She looked at the logos on the vehicles. One said 'Professor Timber – dry rot treatment a speciality' and another proclaimed it belonged to 'Kestrel Structural Repairs.'

Maxine pointed to the vans. 'That doesn't bode well.'

They headed past the vans and the skips to the front door which stood open. The sound of hammering and drilling spilled out. The pair entered and headed through the huge gloomy hall towards the kitchen which was flooded with bright light. They stopped at the door. Maxine was reminded of a picture of the Blitz she'd seen once; a house had been damaged by a bomb and a group of rescuers stood around a massive hole looking into the crater. In this case the men were builders and the hole was illuminated by three large arc lights on tripods.

'Shit a brick,' she whispered.

'Bloody hell,' echoed Gordon.

A bloke in a hard hat noticed them. 'Can I help?'

Maxine pulled her eyes away from the pit. 'Oh... yes... we're Abi's parents. We came to see how you're getting on.' She hoped she sounded bright and cheerful and not horrified. 'Maxine,' she added, sticking out a hand. 'And this is Gordon.'

'Steven,' said the bloke. 'Nice to meet you.' He shook their hands in turn before he turned and gesticulated at the massive hole in the floor. 'As you can see this is proving to be a bigger job than we imagined. Your daughter is very lucky that her insurance agreed to cover the cost but there was no way anyone – not even the previous owners could have known about this cellar – and your daughter is certainly the innocent victim in all of this. The main problem is the dry rot.'

'So Amy was right,' muttered Maxine.

'You know Amy, do you? Nice lady,' said Steven. 'The rot's infected a lot of the timber beams which support this floor and so the rest of the house. Good job we got to it when we did. Another few years and I reckon the entire building would have collapsed.'

'Isn't that lucky,' said Maxine through clenched teeth.

At this point the back door, situated across the other side of the void opened and in came Abi clutching a couple of empty mugs. Her eyes widened as she saw her parents. 'Mum, Dad, what are you doing here?' Her eyes flicked guiltily from one to the other.'

'We thought we'd come to see how things are progressing.'

Amy put the mugs down on a tray by a tap protruding from the wall and picked her way around the side of the hole to join her parents.

'Steven's got everything in hand,' she said.

'Oh, yes. We can see that. Tell you what,' said Maxine, 'why don't we leave Steven to get on – he doesn't need us under his feet – and you can show us how you're getting on with the garden.'

Abi didn't respond as she led them back out through the front door.

When they got back outside Maxine rounded on her daughter. 'Right, young lady – when were you going to tell us?'

'It's not our fault there's a problem with the house,' responded Abi.

'That is *not* what I asked,' said Maxine. 'To judge by what I've seen you must have known for days – weeks – that doing up this house is going to take much more time than you thought would be involved. A couple of weeks? Huh!

A couple of years more like.' Maxine's voice was starting to get screechy. She lowered it. 'You've been lying to me.'

'No, no I haven't.' Abi sounded genuinely shaken for a moment, then she regained control. 'Have you been drinking, Mum.'

'I met a friend for lunch and had one glass of wine and don't change the subject. When, exactly, *were* you going to tell us? Eh?'

'We were, honest. We were waiting for the right moment.'

'When?' snapped Max. 'Or did you hope that your father and I wouldn't notice that weeks were turning into months? Do you think we're stupid?'

'No, no of course not.'

'Steady on, Maxie, don't be too hard on her, she's having a tough time of it. This house is turning out to be more of a nightmare than a dream. You shouldn't blame Abi. This isn't her fault.'

Maxine stared at Gordon in disbelief and took a deep breath. He just didn't see it, did he? She wasn't cross about the state of the house, she was cross about being lied to, about being duped. By her own daughter. And that nothing was being offered to ameliorate the situation – no suggestion of moving all their kit out of her home, no suggestion of finding a place to rent... 'Fine. Fine,' she repeated. 'I can see I'm *completely* over-reacting.' She walked away from them back towards the car. Gordon and Abi exchanged a glance. 'This is obviously all my fault that I'm not being more reasonable,' she added as she opened the door. 'Come along, Gordon, we don't want to leave your mother alone for too long, do we?'

As soon as Maxine got home, she ran upstairs and pulled

a suitcase off the top of the wardrobe. A few minutes later Gordon came into the spare bedroom and saw her packing.

'What's going on, Max?'

'What does it look like?'

'But you can't just light out.'

Maxine stopped folding up a skirt and clutched it to her chest. 'Why not? I told you I was going to go to my sister's; I've just brought the moment forward.'

'But what about your club?'

'I'll cancel it for this week. Or they can carry on without me. Up to them. Frankly I don't care.'

'But Max—'

Maxine threw the skirt in the suitcase. 'But *nothing*, Gordon. I hate the person I am turning into because no one else seems to be prepared to confront Abi about what is going on. So it's me that has the rows, it's me that tries to lay down the law, it's me that has to be the bad cop. I never used to be like that, I used to be easy-going, relaxed about most things. Now I can see that you all thought I was a pushover, a bloody doormat which is why I've ended up being a sodding drudge.' She put on a silly voice. '*Oh never mind, Maxine'll do it, she won't mind.* Well, I *do* mind. I *mind* that you think Abi is in the right and I am in the wrong; I mind I do all the cooking, the cleaning, the washing, the pegging stuff out on the line and everything else because everyone else seems to think I don't have anything better to do. I've had enough of being taken for granted—'

'I don't.'

'What?' yelped Maxine. She gave a mirthless snort of fake laughter. 'You're the worst of the lot. I thought I could rely on you for help but all you do is tell me I'm over-reacting, being mean to Abi, that she's having a hard time of it. What about me, Gordon? What about me?' Yet again she felt tears close by. She stopped and took a deep breath. 'Well, maybe I am over-reacting, but I am tired and fed up and I don't seem to have any personal space anymore and...' And she stopped because the threatened tears couldn't be dammed any longer.

'Don't be like that, Maxie.'

She sniffed, gulped and used the heels of her palms to wipe the tears away. 'Why shouldn't I? You are either at the pub or the golf course, your hobbies are still OK, still sacrosanct. I've lost my studio, I've had to give up working at the shop, I've lost half my house, I've had my free time curtailed and no one seems to care – least of all you.' She went to the chest of drawers and grabbed several pairs of knickers which she chucked in on top of the skirt. 'So you can cope without me for a while, see how you like it when your mother sneers at your efforts—'

'She doesn't *sneer*.'

'Huh.' Maxine dragged some blouses off hangers and then put them and her pyjamas and a pair of shoes in the case. She flipped the lid over and zipped it up.

'You're really leaving us?'

'What does it look like, Gordon? And I'm taking the car.'

She bumped her suitcase down the stairs and trundled it over the hall tiles to the front door. She saw her painting stuff lying where she'd left it and after she'd loaded her case into the boot, she returned for that too. Just because she was going to help her sister with packing up her house it didn't mean she couldn't have some time off too. Besides, she needed the Zen-calm that painting always brought her.

Gordon had followed her and saw her put her easel in the car.

'I thought you were going to help your sister. You didn't say anything about painting.'

'I'm not allowed to, is that it?'

'No, that's not what I meant.'

Maxine slammed the boot shut and rested her hand on it. 'Do you know something, I don't actually care what you meant. Not anymore.' She got into the car, turned on the engine and lowered the window. 'I'll be back when I've calmed down. It might be a while.'

20

Two days later Olivia unlocked the community centre and wedged open the door. It was a glorious evening with the sun still high in the sky. If today, thought Olivia, was an indication of how July was going to pan out for the remaining thirty days of the month then it might be the start of a blinding summer. The temperature was perfect – proper Goldilocks weather, she thought, not too hot and not too cold. Across the way, the solid stubby Norman church tower cast a shadow over the graveyard, and the red valerian, which clung to the crevices in the drystone wall that surrounded it, bobbed and nodded gently in the faintest of breezes. Above her the rooks circled about their nests, their raucous, croaky calls echoing across the cricket pitch which was bathed in golden light. In the nets, on the far side of the ground the local cricket team was practising and the faint, clichéd sound of leather on willow and the muted shouts of encouragement only added to the perception that this was a flawless English evening. Olivia sighed contentedly. How could one not be at peace with the world when one viewed a scene like this? It was an ideal subject for a bit of landscape painting.

'Evening, Olivia.' Bill, one of Maxine's art group arrived.

A pleasant man of around sixty, Olivia judged, who wasn't the best artist in the group but whose lack of technical skill was made up for by his enthusiasm and a rather attractive and childlike naivety in his work.

'Hello, Bill,' she said. 'Thanks for coming.'

'So what's the plan for today?'

'Do you mind if I wait till everyone gets here, or I'll be saying the same thing a dozen times.'

'Fine by me.' He put his rucksack containing his painting equipment down on the floor. 'Nice evening.'

'Indeed. And I don't think that Maxine will mind us using the opportunity of such glorious weather to meet outside.'

'No. Who could mind about that?'

Olivia didn't like to break the news to Bill that, given the reasons why Maxine had buggered off, she probably wouldn't give a toss where they met – or what they did. Not that she was going to share *that* with the group. What had been going on in Maxine's private life was none of their business. In fact, Olivia didn't think it was really *her* business either but as Max, after she'd sent a brief email to everyone on Tuesday afternoon about her intended absence from the group's meeting, had followed it up with a personal email to Olivia with a longer explanation, she couldn't now pretend she didn't know all the gory details. In the last paragraph of Max's missive, after a run-down of all her gripes with her family – most notably what had happened at the confrontation at Wisteria Cottage – she'd told Olivia she'd gone to her sister's, ostensibly to help her move house but really that was just an excuse, she was going to switch off her mobile and she needed to get *right* away before she 'lost the plot'. Apparently, the encounter at the house had been pretty grim, made worse by Gordon telling her she was over-reacting to Abi's predicament. Still, the group didn't need to know that Maxine was having a monster fall-out with her nearest and dearest and, hopefully, time away would allow things to calm down.

Olivia nodded at Bill to imply that Maxine would be very happy with everything before she said, 'How about helping me get some of the tables and chairs out here on the grass, ready for the others when they arrive?'

Ten minutes later the rest of the group had pitched up in dribs and drabs and everyone was busy setting up their portable easels and sketch pads and some were even making preliminary drawings of the church – prior to painting it in watercolours which, Olivia had decreed, was their project for that week's art club. Not original, thought Olivia, but the group seemed happy and working outside in the balmy evening sunshine was a bonus. Olivia, concentrating on her work, didn't spot Heather strolling across the outfield of the cricket pitch.

'Evening, Olivia. Can I interrupt?'

'Heather, lovely to see you. Want to join us?'

'Goodness no. I can't even draw a straight line with a ruler. Do I gather Maxine isn't here?' Heather scanned the assembled artists.

'No, she had to cry off this week.'

'Good... well, not that she's cried off but I want to pick your brains and I don't necessarily want her to know.'

Olivia, intrigued, laid down her sketchbook and pencil and gave Heather her full attention. 'Pick away.'

'What do you think of this?' She produced a framed picture that Olivia hadn't noticed she was carrying. It was a watercolour of the scene Olivia herself was trying to capture, of the church and the trees set in a simple gold frame and a pale gold mount. Olivia thought it was exquisite.

'I think it's really lovely. It's also so good it makes me wonder why I am bothering. It's a fabulous picture. But if you want a proper opinion you really need Max, not me. Where did you get it?'

'Maxine gave it to me. She did it.'

Olivia took it from Heather's hand and examined it more closely. 'I saw another picture she'd done a while back – it was of her garden but we were busy chatting so I have to admit I didn't *really* look at it apart from thinking it was very pretty. But looking at this properly I can see this is good – or I think so... I'm no expert,' she added.

'I agree... that it's good, that is. Not that you're no expert.' She grinned at her friend as she took the picture back. 'It got me thinking... supposing we had an art exhibition?'

'An exhibition? I suppose we could. Why?'

'I had Max round at mine the other day and she sounded so down – really fed up. Unappreciated, undervalued... And she'd had a row with Gordon. Don't tell her I told you so, but I know you two are good friends, and I think you ought to know she had a good old cry on my shoulder.'

'Don't worry, she sent me an email saying something similar which is why she's not here. She hasn't just *cried off*, she's left home for a bit as she's had another, worse, fall out with her family. She found out via Amy that her daughter's house has serious structural problems and that Abi and her partner could be living with her and Gordon for the foreseeable future and Gordon didn't back her up when she got cross with Abi for not telling them... What with that and her mother-in-law...' Olivia sighed. 'She's gone to her sister's for a bit while things simmer down.'

'Amy? Why would Amy know about Abi's house? I mean, I know she's quite nosy but even so...'

Olivia explained about the lunchtime meeting.

'Trust Amy to let the cat out of the bag. I imagine Maxine was in the dark because Abi was waiting for a good moment to break the glad tidings.'

'Maybe. Or maybe Abi was hoping that Max and Gordon would get so used to her and Marcus living with them they wouldn't notice how long they'd been there.'

Heather nodded at the possibility of that being plausible.

'Anyway, back to your idea of an art exhibition...'

'Ah... yes... Given how put-upon Maxine is feeling, I thought that if we had an exhibition for local artists it might perk her up a bit. And given how good she is, her work would really shine. That would be bound to make her feel better about herself if all and sundry give her a pat on the back, say how talented she is and so on. And we could make it obvious that the art club was all her idea so that would be another feather in her cap. I can't see how it would garner anything but positive comments and give Max a real boost.'

'That's a great idea.'

'Thank you, I was rather pleased with it when I thought of it.'

'Always assuming Maxine's arm can be twisted.'

'I think if we emphasise it's about the art club rather than her, I think she'll be happy to join in.'

'So crafty,' said Olivia. Heather smiled at her assessment. 'Where do you think we should hold this exhibition?'

'The town hall.'

'Good shout, but won't they charge?'

'I think,' said Heather, 'that if the vicar's wife and an ex-councillor approach them in the right way there's a chance they might waive the fee. And especially if we offered to give some of the proceeds to a local charity.'

'Proceeds?'

'Oh yes, the pictures will be up for sale unless specified otherwise by the artist. I'd have paid good money for this.' Heather waved the little painting. 'Well, if I had any, that is. And, let's face it, there are lots of people in this town who do have money. Oodles of it.'

Olivia took this on board. 'Good point.'

'You and I need to go and see Miranda,' said Heather.

'Miranda? Why, because she's got oodles of money?'

'Partly. She's got some seriously high-end art works in her house which means I bet she's mates with a couple of proper arty types and what I really want is for a professional to value the paintings so we sell them at realistic prices. If Maxine's are worth what I think they might be, her family are going to *have* to take notice of her talent when the cheques roll in.'

'Wow – that's a brilliant plan. We could go tomorrow, if you're free. I've taken the week off to make the most of this lovely weather.'

'Perfect. Come to mine for a coffee and we can walk up together. Ten thirty? But Maxine mustn't know anything about this till we've got it all organised and got the rest of the art club on board. If we present her with a *fait accompli* I don't think she'll be able to refuse to join in.'

'This could really work, unless,' said Olivia, 'the art

group go all shy about showing other people what they've achieved.' She lowered her voice. 'To be honest, my kids brought home better pictures from nursery school than one or two of the group manage to produce.'

'Take it from me,' said Heather, 'they'll probably be the keenest to exhibit – that sort always are.'

'Ice and lemon?' asked Judith.

'Mmm, both please,' said Maxine. She watched as her sister finished making the gins and then took the drink offered to her. 'Cheers,' she said as they clinked glasses – very nice designer glasses. She took a sip. Wow! Judith didn't stint on the gin in a G and T. The pair went back out of the kitchen and into Judith's cream and pale green sitting room. Every time, in the past, when Maxine had visited with her child, she'd been terrified of the damage Abi might have wrought on the soft furnishings. Even now she worried about spilling something or having mud on her shoes. She put her drink down on a mother-of-pearl coaster.

'I ordered Thai, I hope that's OK?' said Judith.

'Frankly, Jude, as I've said before, if I haven't had to cook it, I don't care what it is and I care even less if it's got meat in it.'

'Do you cook every night?'

'Yes.' Maxine was slightly surprised by the question. 'Don't most people?'

'God, no. I mean, I can cook a bit, but it's such a faff, isn't it?'

Maxine had thought that the amount of take-away

food her sister had ordered in since she'd been staying was because they had both been working really hard during the day and packing, sorting, boxing-up, dumping... It had amazed her how much two people with no kids had managed to accumulate over the years.

'Have you never thought of getting rid of some of your old clothes,' she'd asked Judith when they'd been clearing out yet another wardrobe in yet another of Judith's spare rooms.

'But they're heirloom pieces,' Judith had protested. 'Some of these jackets cost a small fortune.'

Maxine didn't doubt it. 'You could have eBayed them. Recouped some of the outlay. Vintage stuff does really well on the internet.'

'But the effort, darling. The effort.'

And it now transpired that cooking was too much effort too. Thinking back, Maxine realised that whenever they'd gone to stay in the past, which hadn't been that often mainly because of her terror of what damage her child might inflict on her sister's house, Mike had always insisted on taking them out to dinner and lunch had rarely been anything more adventurous than sandwiches or soup. Now she realised it was because Judith hadn't been bothered to produce anything more taxing.

'Actually, I quite like cooking,' admitted Maxine.

'Really?'

'Yes, making something nice, listening to the radio... it's quite calming.'

'I bet Gordon isn't thinking so,' said Judith with a chuckle. 'I wonder how he's getting on?'

'I dread to think.'

Gordon had the sense to grab an oven cloth as he pulled the saucepan off the stove but he didn't think about the handle on the lid as he ripped it off. The heat from the metal handle seared his fingertips and he dropped it onto the tiled floor. His yell of pain was partly obscured by the clattering lid as smoke billowed out of the blackened pan and set off the smoke alarm.

'For fuck's sake,' he yelled as he switched on the cold tap and thrust the pot under it. The water sizzled and spat as it hit the scalding metal and steam joined the smoke. Gordon held his fingers under the cold water in the hope of reducing the effect of the burn. As the water cooled the damaged skin he gazed at the blackened contents in the pot. Ruined.

Abi raced into the kitchen. 'What the hell?' she shouted above the insistent piercing shriek of the alarm. She opened the back door, and the window and then flapped a tea towel at the white box by the ceiling. After a while it fell silent, leaving their ears ringing from the racket.

'What on earth have you done?' she asked.

'What does it look like? Burnt the spuds, burnt my hand, ruined a pan… God, I hate cooking.'

'Gordon? Gordon, are you all right?' Anthea's imperious voice cut through from the sitting room.

'Yes, Mother, I'm fine.'

'What's going on?'

'Nothing, I managed to set off the smoke alarm, that's all.'

'Is that all? That's all right then.'

Abi and Gordon looked at the charred remains of the potatoes. 'Supper's going to be late,' he said.

'Jeez, Dad, you're hopeless,' said Abi.

'Then, you do it,' snapped Gordon. His fingertips were throbbing despite the cold water.

'Keep your hair on. Why don't we get a take-away? Bin this lot.'

'Because your grandmother doesn't approve.'

'Stuff... 'Abi stopped because Anthea had appeared at the kitchen door.

Anthea sniffed the air. 'Have you burnt something?' She limped further into the room and peered into the sink. 'Can't you even boil a potato? Really, Gordon, you are hopeless. And why weren't you helping your father?' she accused Abi. 'And what don't I approve of?'

'Take-aways,' said Abi.

'Ghastly food, for ghastly, idle people.' She glared at Abi, daring her grandchild to argue with her elders and betters. She then turned and hobbled back towards the sitting room. 'And hurry up, I'm hungry.'

Gordon switched off the tap and looked at his hand. A livid red line, with puffy white lumps of incipient blisters on either side of it, ran straight across three fingers and his thumb. 'Ouch,' he said.

'And it's your right hand,' observed Abi. 'Want some plasters?'

'I don't think that'll do much good.' He switched his attention to the pan. 'And what are we going to do with this?'

'Bin it. Get a new one.'

Gordon picked it out of the sink, emptied out the water,

scraped what he could of the blackened spuds into the compost caddy and then chucked the pan into the bin. 'Done.' He went to the veg rack and picked up a load of potatoes and then grabbed the peeler. He made an attempt to peel them but the burns on his fingers made him wince. 'It's no good, Abi, you'll have to do these.'

'If I must.' She started scraping away. 'What are we having to go with these?'

'I made some mince, earlier. I thought I'd make a shepherd's pie.'

'I hope it's Quorn.'

'Yes, of course it is.'

'I hope you've cooked it better than the stuff Mum put in the lasagne.'

21

The next day, after Olivia had had a quick coffee at Heather's place and discussed some more details about the exhibition, the pair walked up the road, past the cricket pitch and onto the high street before plodding up the hill towards Olivia's old house.

'You must miss living in The Grange,' said Heather.

'More than you could possibly imagine. It's mostly down to the lack of space at the new house but I miss the garden—'

'Even though the old one must have been so much work.'

'Yes, despite that. And I miss not being overlooked, I miss the views.' Olivia paused. 'But the new place is easier to look after, cheaper to run so I've got to look on the bright side.'

'So… have you been to the house, since you moved out?'

'No. But I know they had a mass of work done because Amy has told me all about it.'

'Of course.'

'She suggested to me that I might like to try a bit of minimalism – less to dust, she says.'

Heather grinned. 'That sounds like Amy – always one eye on how to make life easier for herself.'

'You can't blame her, though. How many jobs does she hold down?'

'I know, and I don't. I *do* blame her for snarfing my best biscuits—'

'You're lucky it was only biscuits. She used to nick my gin!'

'Indeed. But I don't suppose she can afford many luxuries.'

'Her new bloke seems sound.'

'He's a fireman, isn't he?'

'Yes, called Ryan. Zac's met him and says he and Ashley get on really well.'

'I'm pleased. It would be good for Ashley to have a father-figure and a fireman would be a good role model. Not that Amy hasn't done a really good job of bringing up Ashley on her own.'

'She did a better job than I did with my Zac.'

'You did a fine job with Zac – he's come good in the end. It was only a glitch.'

'Hmmm,' said Olivia as the pair turned onto the drive to The Grange and scrunched over the gravel. Behind the house, Miranda's eco-friendly windmill turned slowly and gracefully in the light breeze and in the front, her rose bushes were covered in scented white blooms.

'Goodness, the roses are doing well,' said Olivia, enviously. 'I don't remember them *ever* being that good when I lived here.'

'But your roses probably never had quite as much manure fed to them as these ones have.'

Olivia snorted with laughter. 'Of course, that "delivery" she had last Christmas.' Some months previously, Miranda's constant protests against the ways of the town – the church bells, the farmer's market and other issues – had so alienated her to the locals that someone had taken it on themselves to dump a couple of tons of farmyard muck on her drive on Christmas Eve. 'Did they ever find out who did it?' she asked.

'There were rumours it was Harry.'

'Harry from the pub?'

'But nothing could be proved.' Heather rang the doorbell. 'Anyway, it made Miranda realise she couldn't fight a whole town.'

The door opened and Miranda appeared in an immaculate pair of white jeans and a black silk camisole. Her fabulous emerald earrings glittered on either side of her face. Both Heather and Olivia instantly felt like frumps in their ordinary cotton summer skirts and blouses.

'What a lovely surprise,' exclaimed Miranda. 'Come in, come in.'

Such a difference, thought Heather, from her first visit to welcome Miranda shortly after she'd moved in. When she'd mentioned the town's campaign to raise money to restore the bells Miranda had threatened her with legal action if they should ring again. But, as Heather had just remarked to Olivia, once Miranda realised she couldn't fight a whole town, the nicer side of her had emerged and lots of the locals now regarded her as an asset, if not an actual friend.

'Now then,' she said, as she led them towards the state-of-the-art kitchen, 'Can I get you tea or coffee? I'm afraid I've only got almond milk. I hope you can cope with that.'

Olivia was busy staring in amazement at the transformed house. When she'd lived there it had been filled with squashy sofas and thick rugs and bookcases. Now it was all shiny white surfaces, bare floorboards, chrome and glass. It was... impressive. But Olivia didn't think it'd be the least bit cosy in the dead of winter. On balance she'd stick to her own style and taste.

'Olivia?' asked Miranda.

'Oh... coffee, please. And don't worry about the milk. I'm happy with it black.'

Miranda set the coffee machine on the counter going – it wouldn't have looked out of place in Costa or Starbucks – then she turned and leaned against the work surface. 'To what do I owe this honour? It's lovely to see you, as I said, but I am sure there's a reason for your visit.'

'Busted,' said Heather. She put the carrier bag she had with her on the counter and drew out a small tissue wrapped package. Carefully she peeled off the paper to reveal the little watercolour. She handed it to Miranda.

Miranda considered it. 'Very sweet,' she said, after a few seconds. 'And very competently executed.'

'Oh.' Heather felt a whoosh of disappointment. *Very sweet* was a rather more dismissive opinion than what she'd hoped to hear, although the *competently executed* qualifier made up for it a bit.

'Sorry, but it's not really my kind of thing,' said Miranda. She pointed at the huge bold picture of stylised scarlet poppies which dominated a wall in the sitting area. 'I mean, from what I know about art, which isn't a great deal, I'd say this has been beautifully painted by someone good and I am sure there is a market for it, but it's not for me.' Miranda handed it back.

'We weren't expecting you to buy it or anything.' Heather put the picture back on the counter. 'We were rather hoping you might be able to help us find an expert who *can* evaluate it. We're planning an art exhibition – ostensibly for the art club; a bit of a competition… best watercolour, best landscape, best abstract, that sort of thing. It would be great if we could tempt some sort of art expert to come along and judge some of the paintings and maybe advise on the sort of price they might fetch. But what we actually want to do is provide a showcase for Maxine's work, like this picture here,' Heather tapped it, 'so it reaches a bigger audience.'

'This is Maxine's! I mean I knew she'd set up an art club but I had no idea she was any good.' Miranda put her hand to her mouth. 'Sorry – that came out so badly.'

'The thing is,' said Olivia, 'is that *no* one seems to appreciate just how good Maxine is – least of all her family. If the locals did, *and* she managed to sell some of her work then maybe it might change things a bit and perk her up and, most of all, it might stop her husband and her daughter treating her hobby as a bit of a joke.'

'Oh, poor Maxine. I had no idea. Well, that's a totally different kettle of fish. I can't make any promises but I do know a couple of gallery owners who might be persuaded to do a spot of pro bono judging in return for a weekend in the country. Do you mind if I hang on to this and I promise I'll have a word with them the next time I go up to London.'

'Yes, sure.'

'In fact,' mused Miranda, 'there's a chap who used to work for a place I occasionally frequent. He's set up on his own. Hang on…' Miranda pushed on a flat white panel beneath the counter and a hidden drawer slid out. Unsurprisingly, the drawer was divided into compartments and was tidily organised with a place for everything and everything in its place. Heather thought about her kitchen drawers which were shambolic – utensils, bits of string, half-used books of stamps, pens, a block of Post-Its…

'Ah… here we are.' She produced a business card. '*Dominic Harcourt*,' she read. '*Fine art dealer*. He might be the person.'

'It would be ace,' said Heather, 'to have a proper expert give a bit of a professional critique and suggest asking prices for the exhibits but if we don't find one, we can have the exhibition anyway.'

'I'm not going to make any promises,' said Miranda. 'The art world is a fickle place, it's also incredibly snobby, but I'll have a word with this guy,' she waved the card, 'and report back. Now… coffee.'

Maxine was blissfully unaware that she and her art were the subject of so much of her friends' interest as she helped Judith pack up a very beautiful and precious Royal Worcester dinner service in masses of newspaper. As they finished wrapping each piece, they placed them carefully in a box lined with bubblewrap.

'Dinner service? But you don't cook.'

'No, Maxie, but caterers do.'

God, how the other half live, thought Maxine. Not that she and Gordon had needed a dinner service for years although they occasionally had friends around for kitchen suppers; lasagne and salad and lashings of garlic bread – that sort of thing. Less fuss and hassle than the pretentious, showing-off dining that had been all the rage in the seventies and eighties when they had first married. Maxine almost shuddered at the thought. She still had some 'best china' but she couldn't remember the last time she'd got it out. Mismatched kitchen china was all they used these days.

Judith's mobile buzzed on the table beside them. Maxine still had hers switched off.

'Ooh, it's Gordon,' she announced as she picked it up. 'Shall I answer it, and are you "in"?'

'I suppose you'd better and, yes, I am.'

'Gordon!' trilled Judith. 'How lovely to hear from you... Yes, she's right next to me.' Judith passed over the phone.

'Hi,' said Maxine hoping her lack of enthusiasm was obvious.

'Max, darling, when are you coming home? It's been three days now.'

'I am quite aware how long it is and the answer is, I don't know.'

'But Maxine, we miss you.'

'You miss what I do.'

'OK, I'll be honest, that too, but I miss *you* more.'

'Really.' Maxine's 'scepticism monitor' red-lined.

'I do,' Gordon insisted. 'The bed's too big for a start.'

'Then move into the box room. The one in there is only two foot six. It'll be nice and cosy.'

'Max, come back.'

'No, I'm still angry.' She winked at her sister.

'Abi is really sorry. She and Marcus are going to rent a self-storage unit and clear out your studio.'

'Good.'

'Aren't you pleased?'

'They could have done that as soon as they found out the extent of the cottage's problems.'

'They're doing it now.'

'And so they should.'

'You're being harsh.'

'Yes. You lot have made me so.'

'We didn't mean to.'

'No, I'm sure you didn't but the drip-drip-drip accumulation of being taken for granted by all and sundry is going to take a bit of eroding away.'

'I can't make it up to you till you come back, Maxine. You *will* come back, won't you?'

Maxine let a couple of seconds pass before she answered. She wanted to make sure he was properly anxious.

'Max?' He sounded quite fraught. Good.

'Yes.'

His sigh of relief was audible.

'Probably after the weekend.' Which would be interesting with all of them under each other's feet and rubbing each other up the wrong way. Maxine was almost sorry she was going to miss witnessing it.

'Don't leave it too long. I do love you and I really *do* miss you.'

Hmm. 'Bye Gordon.' She hit the red phone symbol and disconnected.

Judith cackled with laughter. 'That told him.'

'But I shouldn't have to, should I?'

22

The next morning, Saturday, Miranda picked up her mobile and carefully keyed in the number on the little bit of pasteboard that she'd left on her counter by the coffee machine.

'Dominic? How lovely to catch you. It's Miranda Osborne. I think we met at your previous gallery.'

'Miranda, of course. You bought that stunning Bouraine ballerina.'

'You remembered.'

'Difficult to forget,' Dominic countered.

Indeed, thought Miranda as she gazed fondly at the figurine that had set her back the best part of four grand.

'Now, much as I'd love to chat, I have a possible business proposition. I have in front of me a watercolour by an unknown artist but I think it has real quality. I'd like your opinion.'

'Of course. Can you bring it into my gallery?'

'Absolutely.'

'And is it a one-off or are there other works I can look at?'

'There are but it may take me a day or two to get hold of them.'

'No hurry,' said Dominic. 'Give me a ring before you come up to town – just to make sure I'm around. And you know where my new gallery is, don't you?'

'I've got your card.'

'Great. Looking forward to seeing you.'

'And I look forward to seeing you too.'

Miranda finished the call with the usual niceties and put her mobile back on the counter. She knew from Olivia and Heather that there were a whole stack of canvasses and watercolours in Maxine's studio but she also knew that they were probably buried under her daughter's possessions. She wondered if it was possible to extricate them. Only one way to find out. She rang Olivia and asked her if she was free to accompany her to Maxine's place so the pair could liberate a few pictures.

'Of course. I'll cycle up to yours right now. I'll be with you in ten minutes.'

'I'll make some coffee.'

Half an hour later the two women crossed the Cattebury road and headed down the side turning that led to Maxine's house.

Miranda had never had cause to venture down this road and she was quite surprised by the size of the Edwardian villas set in big gardens with mature beeches lining the avenue. They weren't the kind of house she would favour for herself but she could appreciate their appeal. Very Sunningdale, she thought. Olivia turned into number five and Miranda followed her. The drive had a big white van parked in it and she could see, through its open doors that it was partially filled with a large sofa, a couple of dining chairs, half a dozen packing cases and a nest of tables – how twee, she thought, she didn't know people still had nests of tables. Maybe the prodigal daughter was moving out again and Heather and Olivia had got the wrong end of the stick.

She said as much to Olivia.

'I don't think so – I know Amy isn't the most reliable of sources—'

Miranda snorted.

'—but she had this from the builder himself.'

'Even so...'

Despite the fact the front door was open, Olivia rang the bell. A harassed looking man in his sixties appeared.

'Oh, Olivia.'

'Hello, Gordon. I hope this isn't a bad time...'

'No – well, no worse than any other time.' He looked at Miranda enquiringly.

'This is my friend, Miranda. I was telling her about Maxine's talent for painting and she's interested in seeing her work.'

'Really?!'

'Yes,' said Miranda, firmly. To judge by his stunned reaction, what Heather and Olivia had said about Maxine's husband paying no attention to his wife's talent was true. No wonder Max was so pissed off. She stuck her hand out. 'Nice to meet you, er, Gordon. If I may?'

Gordon took her hand and shook it.

'Dad! Can you move? This is heavy.'

Over his shoulder Miranda and Olivia could see two young people struggling through the hallway lugging a washing machine between them.

Miranda pulled Gordon out of the porch, onto the drive. They were followed by Olivia. Behind them there was a thump as the couple dumped the washing machine on the doorstep and leaned on it to take a breather.

'God, this is heavy,' complained the girl.

'My daughter and her partner,' explained Gordon. 'Abi and Marcus. They're moving their kit into a storage unit.'

'Oh.' Miranda brightened. So access to Maxine's studio was going to be possible – if not today, it would be shortly.

'We'll get it done sooner if we get some help,' said Abi looking at her father.

'Not right now, Abi. Maybe when our visitors have gone.'

Abi glared at Miranda and Olivia – Miranda raised her eyebrows at the girl and stared coolly back until Abi dropped her gaze. Maybe the strain of moving all her possessions – again – was making her so graceless. Even so, she felt another flash of sympathy for Maxine.

'Come and have a cup of coffee,' said Gordon, 'and then we can see if we can get to where Max kept her stuff.' He squeezed past the washing machine which was partially blocking the front door, followed by Miranda and Olivia. Miranda rather deliberately ignored Abi as she went into the house. The three of them went along the tiled hall – nice period features, thought Miranda – into the big kitchen with its stunning view into the garden and the nature reserve beyond.

'No coffee for us,' said Miranda. 'We've just this minute had one.'

'Oh – right... well, you'd better come and see if we can get into the studio. Although I'm not sure where Maxine kept everything.'

'I do,' said Olivia.

'Do you?' He seemed amazed by the information. 'I never paid much attention to what she got up to there.'

Miranda despaired for Maxine. Worse and worse. No wonder she'd taken herself off. Talk about being undervalued! 'Just one thing, Gordon,' she said, 'could you not tell Max we called. We've had an idea but it may not come off and we don't want to raise any hopes only to dash them.'

'OK.' Gordon sounded bemused. 'If that's what you want.'

'We do,' said Olivia. 'Mum's the word. And it's nothing sinister, honestly.'

'I believe you. I know you and Max are good friends.'

The three tramped out to the garden and across the lawn to the wooden summer house-cum-studio. They stood on the deck in front of it as Olivia looked in through the door at the muddle of Abi and Marcus's possessions.

'Can you get to where you need to?' asked Gordon.

'I think so.' Olivia squeezed in through the door and pushed a big cardboard box to one side. She then lifted a kitchen stool out of the way and handed it back to Gordon who dumped it on the grass. There was some huffing and puffing and after a minute or so she called, 'Can someone take this?' A canvas was waved from inside in the direction of the door.

Gordon took it and passed it to Miranda who gave it a glance before she stacked it carefully in a corner of the veranda. The paintings began to come out one after the other quite quickly and they had about twenty before Abi and Marcus returned to collect some more stuff.

'Do you mind?' sniped Abi as she pushed past her father.

'Sorry, sweetheart,' he answered as he scuttled out of her way.

'And what on earth are you doing with Mum's paintings.'

'Having a look,' said Miranda.

Abi rolled her eyes. 'Yes, but why?'

Miranda crossed her arms. 'Because, although *you* may not be able to recognise talent there are people here who can.'

Abi narrowed her eyes. 'Really? Well, I haven't time to discuss the art world, so if you'll excuse me?' She went into the summer house and emerged a minute later hefting a large cardboard box which she passed to Marcus before she grabbed another one for herself and the pair headed back to their van. Gordon seemed to have wandered off to pull up some weeds in one of the flower beds. Poor Maxine, her family couldn't be more uninterested in her painting if they tried. Miranda sighed.

'I don't suppose you can find some of Maxine's watercolours,' she said to Olivia.

'I'll have a go. I think her sketchbooks might be further in.' There was more huffing and puffing then, 'Eureka!'

A minute later, looking red-faced and tousled, Olivia emerged back into the fresh air.

'Got two,' she said, brandishing them.

'Great,' said Miranda. 'Let's have a look at them.'

Ignoring the fact she was wearing pristine white jeans she sat down on the step of the veranda and patted the wood to indicate Olivia should join her. Then, together, they began to flip slowly through the heavy watercolour paper in the first of the spiral bound books. There were a number of studies of the little town and the nature reserve but there were some stunning portraits too; one of Belinda leaning on the bar of the pub, another of Abi, and another of an old man with leathery skin, startlingly blue eyes and bad teeth.

'God, that's Bert Makepiece to a T,' said Olivia.

'Even I recognise him and I've only met him a couple of times. I almost expect the picture to talk, it's so lifelike. I think, on balance,' said Miranda, 'I shall take the water-colours up to London and leave the oils and acrylics. Partly because the sketchbooks will be easier to carry and partly because I think, she's a better watercolourist than oil painter.'

Olivia nodded. 'Sounds like a plan.'

'How many sketchbooks were there?'

'Quite a few – maybe a dozen.'

'So if Maxine comes back before I can return these,' she tapped the books with a perfectly manicured fingernail, 'she's unlikely to notice they're missing.'

'It's possible,' Olivia conceded.

'Then I'll risk it. I'll try and get up to town in the week.' Miranda closed up the sketchbook. 'Fingers crossed we're right about her talent.'

It was about three o'clock when Abi and Marcus drove away to their storage unit with a van full of possessions. Abi's heavy hints to her father that he might like to lend a hand with the unloading had failed to get picked up. And why should he? thought Gordon, as he watched the van turn out of the drive from the sitting room window. He had enough to do, what with his mother and the housework. He needed to get the vacuum cleaner out and give the ground floor a once-over in case Maxine pitched up – the kids had tramped through all sorts of muck as they'd shifted all their worldly goods through from Maxine's studio; he didn't want to give her more grounds for complaint. And then he'd have to think about supper. God, this housework malarkey was never bloody ending. Not that he was going to admit it to Maxine – she'd use it as yet another stick to beat him with.

He turned back and looked at his mother enjoying a postprandial snooze on the sofa. A whole month since her fall and still no word from occupational health about doing an assessment to see if it would be possible for her to move back to her home. He'd better get onto it on Monday morning and chivvy them up. Gah, another thing to do. *And* he'd have to go shopping. When was he going to get a chance to get back on the golf course? he wondered.

He left his mother snoring softly and went into the kitchen to think about the next meal. He opened the fridge door and looked at the contents as he tried to remember what he'd planned for supper that night. Oh yes, he was going to do macaroni cheese and a salad. And it was going to be quick to make, wouldn't need peeling, easy-peasy-lemon-squeezy – result. In fact, he could make it in advance, leave his mum in front of the TV for an hour and slip off down to the pub for a sharp half before coming home to heat it up and make the salad. Not that he'd tell his mum where he was off to because she wouldn't approve – no, he'd tell her he was off for a walk. And, with luck, Abi wouldn't be around either because she'd smell a rat and probably guess the truth. The last thing he wanted was her banging on about his drinking habits. She'd already remarked on the decreasing level in the whisky decanter and the number of wine bottles in the recycling. He was beginning to think that he ought to take a leaf out of Maxine's book and bugger off to get away from the nagging. Not that he could do anything like that till she got back, not with his mother to consider. And, even then, such a course of action wasn't really possible because Maxine would go bat shit. And he didn't want to risk that – not again.

Two hours later the mac-cheese was in the fridge together with a bowl of mixed salad. Gordon left his mother with the remote control and set off across the nature reserve. He assuaged his conscience with the knowledge that he hadn't *really* lied about going for a walk because that was what he was doing right now, wasn't it? The fact that he was only going to be walking for about a quarter of a mile was neither here nor there.

He pushed open the door to the Talbot and made his way to the bar. The place was almost empty but seeing as how the pub had only been open for about fifteen minutes it was hardly surprising.

'Hiya, Ella, and how are you?'

'Good thanks. The usual?'

'Please.'

Ella began to pour a pint of bitter. 'You've managed to escape from the burden of being a house-husband.'

'Only temporarily. Got to go back to cook supper in an hour.'

'Very domesticated. Three ninety, please,' she said as she put the pint on the bar.

Gordon winced as his burned fingers made contact with

the change in his pocket. He gingerly grabbed a handful and held the coins in the palm of his hand as he counted out the right money with his good hand and passed it over.

'Ooh, that looks nasty,' said Ella seeing the red weals on his fingertips. She took it in hers as she looked more closely at his burns. 'I bet that hurts. Ooh, you poor man. How did you do it?'

'In the kitchen.' He gazed at Ella. It was a long time since he'd been shown such sympathy. Maxine was great on the practicalities of basic nursing, but not given to much in the way of compassion. 'Get over it,' was more her mantra than 'ooh, you poor man.'

'Ella, could you collect some tonics from the cellar for me, please.' Belinda's voice cut across the moment from the far end of the bar. Gordon snatched his hand back and Ella rang up the sale.

'Of course, Belinda,' she said.

After she'd disappeared down the steps Belinda took her place behind the beer pumps.

'And how's Maxine?' she asked, rather pointedly in Gordon's opinion.

'Fine, thank you.'

'I hear she's gone to stay with her sister.'

Gordon nodded as he sipped his beer. 'Yes,' he answered. 'Back soon?'

'Probably.'

'Good.'

'My sentiment entirely.'

Belinda leaned on the bar. 'I wouldn't want the punters to get the wrong end of the stick and you know what this town is like for gossip...'

'I do indeed.'

'But they tend to notice things like married men making doe-eyes at the barmaid. And, by *barmaid*, I don't mean me.'

Gordon could feel his face flushing which was partly due to a slightly guilty conscience and partly due to being angry at the insinuation. It was true he liked talking to Ella but that was all it was. 'I wasn't.'

'Glad to hear it.'

The cellar door opened and Ella appeared at the top of the steps with a tray of shrink-wrapped bottles.

'Thank you, my dear,' said Belinda.

'Where do you want them?' Ella stared at the shelf of mixers which was, very obviously, full. There was certainly no room for another two dozen bottles of Schweppes.

'Put them on the side for the time being. They'll be needed later on.'

Gordon moved away from the bar and took a window seat. How could Belinda accuse him of making doe-eyes? OK, maybe he did spend a lot of his time at the pub talking to Ella if she was on shift but that was all it was – just chat.

23

Maxine dragged her case down the stairs of Judith's house which was surprisingly echo-y now so much stuff had been packed away. It was time to go home, the vast majority of the packing had been done and what was left the removal men could easily deal with. Besides, regardless of the difficulties that she'd run away from, Maxine was missing her home, her family and her friends. Also, it would be her art club evening in a few days and she couldn't really abandon them again. Despite the hard work, she'd had fun with her sister but she felt the gin and the take-aways were taking their toll on her waistline and, even though she'd had her painting things with her, she hadn't had a single chance to pick up a brush. If she was at home, even with Anthea's demands, she'd be able to escape if only for an hour or two.

'Thanks for all your help,' her sister said as the case thumped off the last step and onto the ground floor.

'Thank *you* for the gin, the shoulder to cry on and the chance to get away. I dread to think what I might have done if I'd stayed put.'

'The trouble with you and I is that we're too patient for too long.'

Maxine recognised that what her sister said was accurate about herself, but Judith… patient?!

'The things I put up with from Mike,' she continued. 'Honestly, looking back, Trina's welcome to him.'

'The other woman is called Trina?' Maxine asked, hoping she sounded innocent. She'd been very careful not to let slip that she knew anything about Mike's new woman or that she was pregnant because to do so would reveal that she'd spoken to Mike about the situation. She didn't think Judith would be best pleased to know her sister had gone behind her back.

'Yes, short for *Catrina*, I suppose. Not that I care.' She lifted her chin, defying her older sister to contradict her.

'Look, I've spent the last few days moaning about my lot and you've been a brick and listened. The last time I asked you about Mike and his new woman you told me it was none of my business. Which is fine. Truly. But talking does help… honest.'

'A bit late for that with you about to head out the door.'

Maxine propped her case against the hall wall. 'Not necessarily. I've not told Gordon I was thinking of returning today.'

'Want to catch him out?'

'Not really. I feel that if I arrive back unexpectedly, I'll get a truer idea of how he coped.'

'Not very well, if I'm any judge.'

'Come on, let's have a cuppa and you tell me about Trina. I'm agog with curiosity. All I know is she's a lot younger than Mike.'

'And pregnant,' said Judith as she led the way back to the kitchen.

'Pregnant?' Maxine was quite proud of how shocked she sounded even though she'd known for weeks. 'Crikey.'

'It seems he suddenly had an epiphany and discovered that all he'd ever wanted to be was a father.' Judith filled the kettle. 'Whether it was before or after the scheming little madam got herself up the duff I don't know. Anyway, that's the long and the short of it. And that's why he was happy about getting everything settled in double-quick time so the baby won't be a bastard. Of course, the baby's father is – and always will be – but it wouldn't be fair on the kid to be saddled with Mike's main characteristic on its birth certificate.'

Maxine hugged her sister. 'No, and that's very magnanimous of you. I'm sorry it turned out this way.'

Judith heaved a sigh. 'It's not all bad – the settlement is generous, things could be *a lot* worse.'

'Even so.'

'Yes. Even so...' She sighed again. 'The trouble is, I'm not good with my own company.'

'I know. My idea of bliss is being cast away on a desert island – no one to look after but myself, no one demanding a meal or some attention when I want to paint—'

'Bugger that,' said Judith. 'I'd want to top myself after day one.'

Maxine laughed. 'I know. But you're not going to be alone for long if I'm any judge. You're still beautiful, you're still pretty young, you're certainly very well off – I should think you'll have men queuing round the block.'

'Maybe.' She paused while she got a couple of mugs out and made the tea. 'Anyway, in retrospect, Mike wasn't that great. He could be a dull old stick. When we went on cruises, he spent half the time reading in the cabin or looking at the sea when there was *so* much to do on board. I had to drag him to everything because I wasn't going to turn up to things looking like Billy-No-Mates. And then he'd complain of being tired and go to bed at half-past ten. Half-past ten – I ask you! Things would just be getting going at that time of night but oh, no – Mike needed his sleep.'

'If he likes his sleep so much, I don't think he's going to like having a baby. They're not great in that department.'

Judith giggled. 'No, nasty messy little buggers too. And you know how Mike was a one for wanting things *just so*?'

'So tell me about Trina.' Maxine cradled her mug.

'Well... not that I got any of this from Mike but I asked a couple of mates to see what they could find out—'

'And?'

'And it seems she's some sort of mad, hippy-dippy, Green-voting, vegetarian, eco-activist.'

'And Mike's fallen for her?' Maxine's incredulity was no more faked than when Mike had told her similar things about Trina a couple of months previously.

'I know. Talk about mid-life crisis. I mean, if he'd shacked up with some young bimbo who was all teeth and tits I'd have been livid, but I would've kind of understood it. It's what men do, isn't it? Trade up to the latest model. But this Trina... I just can't get it. From what my friends tell me she's a total frump – Birkenstocks in the summer, wellies in the winter and tatty old jeans all year round. I mean, since when has Mike ever shown any desire to eat lentils or wear hand-knits?'

'Nowt so queer as folk. Gordon might have his faults but I'm pretty sure he's not got a wandering eye.'

'I thought that about Mike – just saying. Now then, are you staying for lunch or should you get going?'

Maxine looked at her watch. 'I think I should head off; have lunch at home. But remember you can talk to me any time. Honest. A problem shared...'

'I'm more of the *a-friend-in-need-is-a-pain-in-the-arse* school myself but you're probably right. And it's been nice having you here, having some company...' She gave her sister a hug. 'I never thought I'd say this but I'm actually looking forward to moving to Little Woodford.'

Just as Maxine was jumping in her car to drive back to Little Woodford, Miranda was on a train and heading to London, with Maxine's watercolours safe inside a large art portfolio – also Maxine's. She was quite excited on behalf of her friend although she told herself that, realistically, it was unlikely that Maxine was likely to be hailed as the new Damien Hirst or Tracey Emin but there was definitely something about her paintings, an energy, a *vibrancy* which made Miranda think they might sell. But first she needed to persuade Dominic to come along to Olivia and Heather's planned exhibition. When she'd phoned him to arrange this meeting, he'd sounded tolerably enthusiastic so she was guardedly hopeful.

While she sat on the train, she Googled the address on Dominic's business card and saw it was not far from Kensington Church Street. Perversely, her hopes plummeted somewhat. If he could afford the rent and rates for a gallery in that sort of area, he must be doing OK for himself. Maybe he might not be hungry enough to think a weekend in the country judging a local art exhibition was going to be anywhere *near* worth his time. Still, nothing ventured et cetera, et cetera. While Miranda was trying to weigh up her chances with him, her phone rang. Dominic.

'Dominic, I was just thinking about you and looking forward to our meeting this morning.'

'That's just it, Miranda...'

Her heart sank; she knew it, he was having second thoughts.

'I've got a problem at the gallery,' he continued. 'We've got a power cut. Terribly inconvenient. No lighting, no alarm system... Would you mind frightfully if we met somewhere else?'

'No, of course not. But what a bore for you.'

'And you.' There was a heavy sigh. 'The power company *say* they're doing everything to resolve the issue but they can't give me even a vague idea when we'll be reconnected. I've told them it'd better be before closing time otherwise they can pay for security – there's no way I'm leaving this place empty overnight without a functioning alarm system.'

'Goodness, no. How awful. So where do you suggest we meet?'

'The Royal Garden Hotel on Ken High Street. I'll meet you in the lobby.'

'At the same time we've got planned? Eleven thirty?'

'Perfect.'

Miranda disconnected. She decided that when they'd finished with the business part of the meeting, if Dominic had the time, *and* if he'd offered to help her, then she'd stand him lunch. It was the least she could do.

★

Maxine stopped the car in the drive and stared at the house. She was dreading her return. For a start, she was fully expecting the house to be a complete tip and she didn't think Anthea was going to welcome her with open arms. But, she also realised, she was slightly worried that the house *wouldn't* be a tip, that it was immaculate and that her absence wouldn't have been particularly noticed. She wanted them to find out that she was invaluable – not redundant. Not that she was going to find out if her status had changed by sitting in the driver's seat. Besides, it was lunchtime and she was hungry.

Maxine got out of the car, collected her bag from the boot and let herself into the house. She could hear the TV blaring in the sitting room which meant Anthea was downstairs – as she usually was at this time of day. Maxine thought about greeting her mother-in-law first but decided against it heading, instead, into the kitchen.

'I'm back,' she called. No way was Anthea going to hear her over the TV going at full blast but there was a chance Gordon might. Nothing. Maybe he was in the garden. She went out of the back door and tried there. Still no sign of him. Maxine felt a little stab of disappointment. There was nothing for it but to go and talk to Anthea and see if she knew where he was.

'The pub,' was the curt answer after Max had muted the TV with the remote in order to make herself heard. No additional *welcome back,* no, *did you have a nice time with your sister?* But, realistically, what did she expect?

'And how are you?' she asked her mother-in-law.

There was a sniff before, 'Getting there.'

'Good.' Maxine went back into the hall and collected her bag before she dragged it upstairs. She looked at the door to her old bedroom before she hauled it to the spare room. Gordon obviously hadn't taken her advice and moved into the smaller, cosier bed; the bed hadn't been made properly – or, at least, not to her standard – it needed a dust and a hoover and, when she went into the en-suite, it was much as she expected it to be, barely acceptable. Part of her longed to sort it out but part of her thought, *sod it*. If Gordon couldn't be arsed to keep up any sort of standard, why should she?

After she'd dumped her case and sent a quick text to Judith to say she'd got back safely, she went downstairs to the kitchen. The gin bottle in the corner of the work surface, between the kettle and the bread bin, glinted enticingly in a shaft of sunlight that fell through the window. And why not?

Just a quick snifter, she thought, in the words of her sister. She'd got used to a lunchtime aperitif during her stay at Judith's and, quite apart from that, she was rather dreading seeing Gordon. She was still cross at his lack of support, she was still angry about how he took her for granted but she'd been the one who'd walked out, left him to cope and she had a nasty niggle that she hadn't been quite fair. Would he resent it? Would he sulk? And would she deserve it if he did. She poured herself two fingers of gin, sloshed in some tonic and took a swig. Dutch courage.

'Hitting the bottle?'

Oh, Gawd, Anthea. She turned, fixed a smile on her face and lied. 'Just thirsty. Fancied a tonic.'

'Really?' The disbelief was almost tangible. There was a pause. 'I am assuming you're back to pick up the reins. Things have been dire since you left.'

'I'm sorry to hear that.'

Anthea raised an eyebrow. 'Really? I thought that was the whole reason for going – to make a point.'

'No, not really. My sister needed help before her move – the van comes in a couple of days.'

'Really?'

'Yes. *Really.*' God, the old bag was irritating.

'So, what's for supper?'

Lie or no lie about the alcohol content Maxine chugged at her drink to keep her blood pressure down. 'I don't know. You tell me.'

'There's precious little in the fridge.'

Spurred by this comment, Maxine strode across the kitchen and pulled open the door – a manky piece of mousetrap cheese, a couple of tomatoes, a selection of condiments, some milk and a half-used bag of mangetout. Even Gordon Ramsay would be pushed to make anything out of that lot. And she'd drunk a large gin which might have put her over the limit so she was not going to risk her licence by heading for the supermarket right now. And Gordon couldn't if he was at the pub. Well, if God had intended women to be tied to the kitchen sink, he wouldn't have invented take-aways.

'Assuming the children don't bring anything home with them when they come back from work, I shall pick up the phone and order in a take-away.'

'A take-away?!' Substitute the word 'handbag' and Anthea could have passed muster for Lady Bracknell.

'And why not?'

'Can't you shop for something?' she peeved.

'No. It was a long journey, I've had an exhausting time with my sister and, if I'm honest, I can't be bothered.' There was an audible 'tut' which Maxine ignored.

'But you always cook.'

'I might have done, but not tonight. So, any preference?' she asked brightly.

'For what?'

'Chinese, Indian, pizza…?'

'Is that the choice?' Anthea sniffed.

'No, you could have a burger or chicken wings or a kebab.'

Anthea rolled her eyes. 'A kebab?!' Another Lady Bracknell moment.

'The ones from the local guy are very good.'

'I'll take your word for it,' Anthea sneered. 'Frankly, my dear—'

I don't give a damn, thought Maxine.

'—I think I'd rather starve.'

'Suit yourself. Anyway, there's no need to make your mind up just yet, it's hours till supper. You might have a change of heart by then.' Maxine drained her glass and put it in the dishwasher – which needed to be run, she noted. She got a tablet out of the cupboard, shoved it in the slot, closed the cover, pressed the buttons and slammed the door. It whooshed into action as she made her way out of the kitchen. 'I'm going upstairs to unpack and possibly have a lie down. When Gordon gets home, tell him I'm back, would you?' Although, as she said it, she knew he'd spot the car on the drive and work it out for himself. Maxine tramped up the stairs feeling strangely liberated by the way she'd stood up to Anthea again. She must do it more often.

24

Miranda rang Olivia's doorbell and hoped Olivia was in. She glanced at her watch and saw that it was gone five thirty so there was a chance she might be. As she waited for the door to be opened, she stood back to look at the house and its neighbours in the street. Maybe the estate wasn't quite as tacky as she'd once thought although, as she gazed around, she was aware of a curtain twitching across the road. That was one thing she'd always been spared – nosy neighbours. Her apartment in Kensington had been three floors up and the nearest house to her new home was about a hundred metres away. She couldn't imagine what it might be like to live in such hugger-mugger conditions. Some of these houses were practically back-to-backs. She heard the door click.

'Miranda! How did you get on?' Olivia sounded genuinely happy to see her which Miranda found touching. She still hadn't got used to the genuine friendship of the local population – so different from the faked corporate closeness of her old acquaintances where everyone had been assessing everyone else for their usefulness in the back-stabbing business of getting ahead. She threw the door wide. 'Come in, come in. Sorry I was so long answering the door; I've only just this minute got back from work. I want to hear all about the gallery. What was Dominic like?'

Miranda laughed. 'I'll tell you everything, promise.'

'Sorry, it's just I've been on tenterhooks all day. Wine, tea, coffee...?'

'I'd love a glass of white.' For all Miranda's veganism, she was prepared to let her ethos slip when it came to socialising over a glass of something with a friend which might not necessarily be completely free of animal products.

Olivia led the way into the surprisingly large kitchen-diner with a small conservatory tacked onto it which made it superficially light and airy although, as Miranda could see at a glance, the amount of work surface and cupboard space wasn't that great. 'Take a seat,' said Olivia as she headed to the fridge and got out a bottle of Pinot Grigio. She grabbed a couple of glasses from a wall cupboard and sat down opposite her guest.

'Cheers,' she said after she'd poured the wine. 'Right, what happened?'

Miranda took a sip. 'The good news is that Dominic has agreed to come along and put a value on the paintings and judge a couple of categories; we thought best novice, best watercolour, best mixed medium and best abstract... I don't know what you think, but we reckoned it levelled the playing field a bit for the other painters. And naturally it's all dependent on dates and availability but, in principle, he's up for it.'

'Hurrah. Brilliant news.'

'And he likes Maxine's work. He's sure there's a market for it. He reckoned on the open market he might get five hundred plus for that little watercolour she gave to Heather.

Dominic hoped we wouldn't mind but he took a picture of Heather's watercolour to show some of his clients – to gauge the interest.'

'Five hundred or more? Wow! Not that Heather would sell, of course, but even so... Anyway, what was his gallery like? You said it's in South Ken.'

'I didn't see it. Poor Dominic was having a bit of a nightmare when I met him; they'd had a power failure and so all the lighting was kaput, the alarm system was out... We met in a restaurant and I bought him lunch to try and cheer him up.'

Olivia pulled her laptop across the table towards her. 'What's the address?' she asked as she lifted the cover and pressed the 'on' button.

'Why?'

'Google Earth. The nosy person's manna from heaven.'

Miranda laughed as she got out Dominic's card and pushed it across the table. Olivia tapped in the address and then hit street view. The camera footage showed two galleries – one each side of the road.

'It's probably one of these. Classy,' she said.

'Exactly. There's *a lot* of money in South Ken. Anyway, he's kept one of Maxine's sketchbooks because he wants to show her work to some other people. He's going to courier it back to us in a week or so. He really seemed quite keen on exhibiting her.'

Olivia beamed. 'But that's wonderful. So, all we have to do now is fix up a suitable date for this exhibition, persuade the rest of the art group that not only is it a good idea but also it's *their* idea, and then get Maxine on board.'

'The first thing is easy, I should think, and I suspect the second is too...'

'And the third should be because we'll tell Maxine that the art group won't play ball if she doesn't join in.'

'Really? Are you sure the others will go along with that – they mightn't mind that much?'

'Oh, yes,' said Olivia. 'Because I'll tell them that's what they're going to say if they know what's good for them.'

Miranda grinned. 'Brilliant.'

Maxine lay on her bed in the spare room, reading a book and trying hard to ignore the sounds of her family moving about downstairs. She knew, if she surfaced, she'd be expected to take up the slack, make decisions, make meals, retake control and she wasn't ready to yet. Let them carry on, she told herself as she adjusted her pillow and returned to the story. But it was difficult to concentrate when raised voices drifted up the stairs and a door slammed. She was wondering what was going on when she heard heavy feet on the stairs – Gordon, she suspected – and then a knock at her door. She thought about feigning sleep and not answering but the chances of being left in peace were vanishingly thin.

'Yes?'

Gordon pushed open the door. 'You're back,' he said. No, *hello, darling*, noted Maxine.

'Obviously.'

'Mum said you're not planning on cooking tonight.'

'As there isn't anything in the fridge to cook *with*, I said we might have to have a take-away.'

'Mum's not a fan.'

'Oh dear,' said Max, without a shred of sympathy in her voice. 'And, as I'm not the only able-bodied adult in this family, I don't know why you think it should be exclusively my job to supply meals.'

There was a pause before Gordon said, 'We've missed you, Max.'

Tempting though it was to say *good*, Max restricted her reply to, 'Well, I'm back now. But,' she added as Gordon's face brightened, 'I'm tired after my drive from Judith's and I've been working very hard helping her pack up. I'll get back into harness tomorrow but right now I haven't got the energy.'

'That's the thing, Max, we all feel a bit like that.'

'What did you do today? When I got back your mum told me you were at the pub.'

Gordon's face flushed. 'Might have been,' he muttered.

'You didn't think to re-stock the fridge before you went there.'

'I thought Abi and Marcus might do a shop.'

Maxine stared at him. 'Oooh look, flying pigs.'

'It's their turn,' he countered.

'And their excuse this time is?'

'They had to go and see the house before they came home – and then they felt too tired.'

Maxine shook her head. 'Diddums,' she said harshly. 'Doing things when you're tired or fed up or unappreciated are all part of being an adult.' She stared at Gordon. 'I've been coping with that for the past thirty years or so, ever since I had Abi, but I don't think anyone has noticed. That was one of the reasons I buggered off; since Abi and Marcus moved in, they've reverted to being kids again – expecting me to do everything, just like the old days. Olivia warned me this would happen – she was so right. Well, tonight *I* am too tired to be bothered so that is why I suggest we order a take-away.' She held up her hand. 'I don't care if your mother doesn't like them, she can eat what she's given and be grateful for it. I'm sure that was her mantra to you when you were growing up.' The look on Gordon's face told Maxine she was right. 'And as Abi and Marcus can't be bothered to shop, they can pay for it.'

'That's not going to be popular,' said Gordon.

'I don't care. I'm her mother, not her best friend, and for once she can do as she's told.'

'When did you start being so harsh?' muttered Gordon as he left the room. Maxine almost regretted coming home.

A couple of days later Olivia rang Maxine's bell on her way home from work.

'How are you?' she asked when Maxine answered it.

'It's like I've never been away.' She ushered her friend inside and led her through to the kitchen. 'Tea? Coffee?'

'I'd love a cup of tea.'

Maxine called through to the sitting room to see if Anthea wanted a drink before she put the kettle on and pushed the door closed.

'Your ma-in-law is still with you, I see.'

Maxine rolled her eyes. 'Indeed. Although, finally, there is light at the end of the tunnel; Gordon's gone to her old house today to meet an occupational therapist to see what can be done to make it suitable for Anthea to move back. Frankly I'm not holding out much hope but, I suppose if the health people say it's *completely* unsuitable, it gives us the green light to flog it and find something that *is* suitable nearer here.'

'And what will Anthea say about that?'

Maxine leant against the counter. 'I don't really care. I know it sounds harsh but it'll make our life endlessly easier and it'll give her a big pot of money to employ carers or cleaners or whatever she needs to make life comfortable. And, frankly, I think she will be as glad to see the back of me as I will be of her.'

The door banged open. 'Are you talking about me,' demanded Anthea.

'Yes,' said Maxine. 'I was telling Olivia that Gordon's gone to your house to meet the occupational therapist.'

'And about time,' said Anthea. 'The sooner I can move back the happier we all shall be.'

'Hear, hear,' echoed Maxine.

Olivia shifted uncomfortably as Anthea hobbled back to her lair in the sitting room.

The kettle boiled and Maxine made the tea, taking Anthea's to her, before she suggested that Olivia might like to join her out in the garden where they could sit on the studio veranda in the sun.

'Sorry you had to witness the altercation,' said Max. 'Never nice to be the outsider on a domestic.'

'Hardly a domestic.'

'Even so.'

The pair settled themselves in the chairs on the summer house deck and sipped their tea.

'Now, Maxine,' started Olivia, 'I hope you don't think I'm interfering...'

'Sounds ominous. Why?'

'Well, at the last art club meeting, the one you missed, the rest of us had a bit of a chat,' Olivia lied fluently, 'and we thought we'd like to hold an exhibition of our work.' The truth was that she'd emailed the group, swearing them to secrecy about the plan she and Miranda had cooked up and basically ordered everyone to join in. Luckily, apart from one or two, everyone had been pretty enthusiastic and even the doubters had come round after a bit of gentle arm-twisting.

'That's a lovely idea.'

'But the thing is, and we're adamant about this, we won't do it unless you exhibit too.'

'Oh.'

'Oh?'

Maxine paused and looked deeply embarrassed. 'Look, it's not that I don't want to but I've been painting all my life—'

'—and you think it'll be unfair on the others if your work is there as a comparator.'

Maxine blushed. 'Well... yes. But that sounds so big-headed.'

'Supposing I was to tell you that we plan to sell the work and that, so far, we're all agreed on giving a percentage of the proceeds to local charities. If people are prepared to pay more for some work than others it'll mean more money for the good causes.'

'Money to charity?' Maxine still sounded unsure. 'Not that I've ever sold any of my stuff but, yes... I suppose.'

'And Miranda has offered to pay to get all the entries framed uniformly to make the whole thing look more professional. You know as well as I do what a difference a decent frame makes to any picture.'

'Goodness, that's generous. I mean, I know she can probably afford it but that *really* isn't the point. It's incredibly kind of her.'

'I happened to mention it and she asked about how we planned to exhibit the stuff and... Well, I think she's knows about art and art galleries and stuff...' Olivia tailed off. She didn't want to reveal just how much Miranda knew or how she was helping in other ways.

'Even so, it'll make all the difference. You *have* been busy.'

'It hasn't taken much organising to be honest.'

Maxine raised her eyebrows. 'Hmm.'

The pair sipped their tea in silence for a few seconds, enjoying the late-afternoon July sunshine before Maxine spoke again. 'Have you got a venue?'

'The town hall. And because of the local charity aspect the town clerk says we can have it for free.'

'Better and better.'

'He's going to let us know which weekend in August we can have it.'

'Best I look out a few pictures then. And at least I can get to my old sketchbooks now all the kids' clutter has gone.'

'Has it?' said Olivia feigning ignorance. She looked behind her as if to check the veracity of her host's statement. 'Oh, so it has.'

'The bonus of throwing a total strop was that they finally hired a self-storage unit. They're still under our roof for the foreseeable future but now I've got my studio back I feel as if I can cope. Not that I'm telling the family that. I want them to carry on thinking I might bolt again at the least provocation – it'll keep them on their toes.'

'Talking of bolting… you said you'd gone to your sister's to help her move house. How's that going?'

'She should be arriving tomorrow if it all goes to plan.'

'So, Gordon's away, your sister is moving house tomorrow, Abi and Marcus are still here…'

'Don't,' said Maxine. 'And to think, only a few months ago I was revelling in how quiet and ordered our life had become. God, if I could turn the clock back.'

'Still, it'll be nice to have your sister around.'

Maxine didn't answer.

'Won't it?'

'She's not terribly self-sufficient.'

'Oh.'

As soon as Olivia left Maxine's she pedalled to Miranda's hoping, as she went, that her friend and co-conspirator was in.

'Olivia, what can I do for you?'

'Good news and bad news.'

'Come in and have a seat, do. Can I get you anything?'

Olivia shook her head. 'Just had tea at Maxine's. The good news is she's on board with the exhibition, the bad news is she's going to go through her pictures.'

'And she might spot there are some missing,' finished Miranda.

Olivia nodded. 'Do we know when we can expect the book back that Dominic kept?'

'I'll chivvy him up.'

'Good. In the meantime we must return the other one. One missing sketchbook might be attributable to the chaos of Abi moving her furniture in and out but two might be tricky.'

'That's easy,' said Miranda. 'I'll drop the one I've still got back while she's at her art club tomorrow. I'll use the opportunity to reiterate to Gordon that this exhibition is an art club idea and *nothing* to do with you and me.'

'Although I told her about your offer to get the framing done.'

Miranda tilted her head slightly making her emerald earrings dance. 'I think we can explain that away as the actions of a local philanthropist. Not that I saw myself in that role when I got here,' she added wryly.

'Erm... no,' agreed Olivia.

'Things change.'

'When are we going to tell her about Dominic and his role valuing stuff?'

'Not until quite close to the day. We'll pass it off as a serendipitous coincidence. A happy alignment of the stars that my art-dealer friend happened to be in the area that weekend.'

'You think she'll fall for that?'

'Why not? It isn't as if I've any involvement at all with the art group. And I think she'll be so busy as the exhibition gets nearer, she won't examine any of the details too closely. It'll be fine. Trust me.'

25

Gordon shut the door of his mother's house behind the occupational therapist and thought about what she'd said about it. She'd said that externally it was a truly lovely place, which it was given that it was a beautifully proportioned late Georgian or early Victorian building, with a wisteria covering the mellow stone facade. A dream home, she'd added slightly wistfully, before she'd announced that internally it was *far* from a dream home for a frail octogenarian. Actually, what Jolene, the health professional, had said was the house was *completely* unsuitable for a frail octogenarian and a total nightmare from an occupational health point of view, unless some major alterations were made. However, as the property was Grade II listed and, given the scope and scale of the alterations, it was going to be months and months before the relevant planning permissions were likely to be in place and even more months before the building work would be finished, it made the whole prospect of sorting it out to make it suitable almost a non-starter.

Gordon sighed as he walked back into the glorious dining room with its open fire, wood floor and beautiful cornicing and wondered what it would look like converted to a downstairs bedroom with hoist over the bed and an en-suite wet room which was what Jolene had said would be needed for the coming years.

'If your mother wants to carry on living here then the house will have to be future-proofed,' Jolene had insisted. 'A stair lift, some ramps and a few grab-handles simply aren't going to cut it.' She pointed out that the first floor had random floor levels with steps in unexpected places between rooms and along corridors, the lighting was atrocious and the floors were all uneven. 'And suppose there was a fire? How on earth would your mother get out in an emergency?'

Gordon had seen the sense of what she'd said but such alterations would cost thousands. Given that the house was set in a big garden surrounded by a neat beech hedge, around the corner from the local shop, the pub and about half a mile away from the primary school, when the inevitable happened and it had to be sold, it would be perfect for a family with young children who were more likely to want a functioning dining room than a downstairs DIY care facility. Surely, any such self-respecting purchaser would want thousands knocked off the price to convert it back? Gordon sighed.

'There's a certain amount the local NHS Trust will be prepared to fund – it's far more advantageous for all concerned to keep people in their own homes – but, I'm afraid, certain alterations are beyond our scope.'

'Just what help can we expect?' asked Gordon.

Jolene had looked at her watch and said that it was getting late and she needed to get going and it would be better if he phoned her department in the morning when the options could be discussed at length.

'We might need to do another site visit,' she added.

As he watched Jolene drive away, Gordon knew in his heart what the obvious solution was; scrub the alterations, sell the place now and move Anthea into somewhere purpose-built near Little Woodford. But somehow, he didn't think persuading Anthea was going to be an easy task.

He looked at his watch; five thirty and the village shop shut at six. He made his mind up – he'd buy a ready meal, raid his mother's wine cellar for a bottle of something and stay the night. If the local health people needed to do another visit there wasn't much point in driving all the way only to have to return almost immediately. Besides if he slept on the problem, he might come up with something different – or better – as a solution.

As he walked to the shop, he rang Maxine and told her the gist – that a lot of work would need to be done and he wasn't sure it would be worth it. 'And I'm going to stay the night here. The occupational health woman thought they might need another look so there's no point in coming home.'

'Oh. Only Judith is moving in tomorrow...'

'And?' Did Max hope he'd rush back to be at his sister-in-law's beck and call? 'She's got a firm of professional movers to do the job. Anyway, you didn't tell me you expected me to help.'

'No, I didn't, but, you know what she's like. After they've gone, she might change her mind and want things put in different places. She can't possibly move big pieces of furniture by herself. It would be nice if we could help her out a bit.'

'God, Maxine, nothing will have to be moved instantly,

will it? Surely Judith can wait a day or two if she needs a hand. It's not exactly life or death, is it?' It had been a long day and he was tired and he didn't want flak.

'No, you're right. It's better if you stay the night.'

That was big of her.

'Just one thing Gordon, what should I tell your mum?'

'That it's complicated, it's going to be expensive and it probably isn't going to be worth it.'

'She's not going to be pleased.'

'No.'

'I may leave it for you to tell her.'

'If you think that's for the best, that's fine,' he lied. Bugger, he'd hoped Maxine would break the news – it was a conversation he *really* didn't want to have.

The following day, as the shadows began to lengthen, Judith generously tipped the Pickfords' men who had finished unloading, picked up a large swathe of polythene that had been ripped off her sofa as they'd squeezed it through her tiny hall, and shut the front door with a sigh. It was done. She'd moved. She was in her little mews cottage. She looked around at the mess. Sure, the big pieces of furniture were mostly all in the right place; the three-piece suite, the dining room table and chairs, the side board, the coffee table... but everywhere there were half-unpacked boxes, crumpled newspaper and bubblewrap, piles of china, stacks of pictures, clusters of ornaments... She didn't want to even think about the upstairs. She'd made up her bed but the spare room was almost inaccessible due to the mounds of bed linen, duvets, towels and boxes full of her clothes.

She sighed as she pushed up the sleeves of her shirt. Staring at the chaos wasn't going to get anything done but she felt utterly daunted. Where on earth did she start? Randomly she picked up a vegetable dish and lid off the dining table and put it in the sideboard, then a pile of plates followed by the gravy boat and the soup bowls. Half an hour later her best china and glassware had been sorted and the dining table was almost clear. She made herself a gin and tonic as a reward and then started on her kitchen equipment – not that there was much but she still needed to think about where best to store her pots and pans, her everyday china, where her coffee machine should live, where to stash the cleaning cloths, the bin bags… the minutiae of ordinary, everyday living. That done she had a go at her books. She didn't have that many so they were quickly squared away leaving an empty packing case which she set about filling with all the packing detritus that was strewn over the surfaces and floors. She'd just about filled it to capacity when she noticed her gin, virtually untouched, on the mantelpiece. The ice had melted and the fizz had gone from the tonic but she took a slurp regardless as she slumped onto the sofa, still partly covered in yet more polythene, and let out a deep sigh. She hadn't felt this tired for as long as she could remember. Maybe it wouldn't have been such a push if Maxine had been bothered to help her, but she'd cited Anthea, Gordon's absence and a need to prepare for her wretched art club as reasons why she couldn't. Wouldn't, more like.

'Come off it, Jude. I've just spent days packing up your old house. I don't remember you helping Gordon and me when we first moved here.'

'Maybe because, back then, I was still a schoolgirl.'

'Hardly.'

'Almost.'

'Anyway, I can't help today so that's that. Gordon and I'll come over at the weekend and give you a hand then. He's back home from Anthea's place this afternoon, all things being equal, but he'll have had a long drive and he won't want to start lugging furniture around.'

Judith had had to accept that was the best offer she was going to get, but the knowledge of future assistance didn't help with how tired she felt right now.

She looked at her little ladies Rolex. Good grief, nearly eight. It had been a long day but she hadn't realised quite how long. If she'd been back in her old house, she'd have picked up her phone and speed-dialled her favourite take-away but she hadn't acquainted herself with any of the ones on offer around Little Woodford. It would have to be the pub. For a second, she thought about ringing Maxine and Gordon and asking if they wanted to join her – the last thing she wanted was to eat alone but then she remembered Maxine's sodding club. Bugger. No chance of having some company. Instead she downed the rest of her gin, armed herself with her Kindle, grabbed her handbag and got herself ready to leave her new house. Out of habit she checked her appearance in the mirror in the downstairs loo before she left. Jeez – she looked like Lady Macbeth after a long night on the battlements. She dragged a comb through her hair, pinned it up into a make-shift bun and momentarily considered trudging upstairs to put on some make-up but then decided she really was too dog-tired to bother even with that. She made sure she had the new bunch of keys, shut the front door and walked the hundred yards along the high street to the Talbot.

When she pushed open the door, she was pleased to see it was comfortably busy but not rammed and that there was a small table squashed into a corner that was free. Perfect for a singleton. She ordered a large glass of red wine and the slow roasted pork and mash before she took a seat. As she did, she looked back to the bar where the very attractive barmaid, was chatting to the locals. Or was that 'chatting up'? She was certainly flirting, although, why shouldn't she? thought Judith. She contemplated the woman and quickly came to the conclusion that they were of a similar age. It's the neck, thought Judith – always the giveaway. She rubbed hers. Despite the lotions and potions she smoothed on, she knew she had a touch of the old turkey neck herself, but not quite as noticeable as the barmaid's, she thought smugly, before admitting that the barmaid probably couldn't afford the sort of products she could.

She settled herself more comfortably at the table, switched on her Kindle and began to engross herself in the latest exploits of Jack Ryan – now *that* was a real man – as she took the occasional sip of her wine.

'Excuse me.'

Judith looked up to see the barmaid proffering a plate of food in her direction. Quickly she moved her bits and pieces off the table and pushed her now-empty glass to one side to leave space for her supper. 'Thank you,' she said. 'And another glass of Merlot, please. Sorry, and your name is...?'

'Ella.'

'Lovely to meet you, Ella. I'm Judith – I've just moved

here and I think there's every possibility this might become my local.'

'That's nice. I'll bring your wine right over, Judith.'

'Cheers, sweetie.' Judith tucked in with gusto before the woman came back with her drink. The food was delicious but she made herself eat it slowly, alternating mouthfuls of pork with pages of text and sips of wine. She was in no hurry to go home where there wouldn't be much else to do but go to bed – unless she fancied doing more unpacking. It was as she reached for her glass some fifteen minutes later, as she swallowed the last mouthful of pork, that she heard a voice she recognised drift into her psyche. Gordon! How nice to have a bit of real company to interact with. A book was all very well but not the same as a proper conversation. She looked over to where he was standing at the bar and froze. She mightn't have a slew of A levels or a university degree but she was top of the class when it came to body language and what was going on between him and the pretty barmaid couldn't have been more blatant if there had been a neon sign pinned to him flashing 'Phwoar'. And what was worse, the barmaid was the same. Her *light flirting* with the other pub goers had shifted up several gears into *take me I'm yours* territory.

Fucking hell, she thought, swiftly followed by, now what?

26

Maxine arrived home from her art club, unloaded the car and dumped everything in the hall before she went to the kitchen to pour herself a glass of wine. Generally, she came home from her art club feeling energised but not this evening; she still felt completely weighed down and browbeaten by the events that had happened earlier, before she'd left home. Even the club's excitement about the prospective art exhibition hadn't bucked her up. She leaned against the counter and necked most of the glass – sod what Abi said about her drinking – before she refilled it and carried it through to the sitting room.

'You're back,' observed Anthea, switching off the television as Maxine joined her.

'I am.' Max hoped the TV going off wasn't a precursor to Anthea wanting to rehash what had happened shortly before supper. 'Where's Gordon?'

'Where do you think?' Her tone was terse. 'Running away from reality.'

Maxine could hardly blame him. She'd run away from reality too if she had the chance but she had nowhere to run. And there was no escaping that what he'd told his mother, when he'd arrived back from her old home late that afternoon, *was* reality. It might have been an unpalatable reality but it was pretty much the only option; Anthea would have to sell up and move into something more appropriate. It was that, or live with them for months and months, while planning permission was sought, her home got converted, while her health might well deteriorate further and while she'd be shelling out tens of thousands of pounds for a house that, in all likelihood, she would only continue to live in for a few years at the very most. Financially it made no sense whatsoever. Her reaction had been one of a blank refusal to believe him, followed by an accusation that he was exaggerating the situation to make her sell for his own benefit.

'You want your inheritance early!' she'd accused. 'You've been after it for years, ever since you wanted me to sign that dreadful power of attorney document.'

'Don't be so bloody ridiculous, Mother. Why? Why would I want your money? This house is paid for, I've got a pension, we're comfortably off...' He'd spluttered to an indignant halt before he'd regained his momentum and shouted, 'We simply don't need it.'

'You're taking advantage of me because I'm old and alone,' she'd shouted back.

The pair eyeballed each other angrily. If they'd been cats, their tails would have been fluffed up like bottle brushes. Gordon dropped his gaze first.

'For fuck's sake,' he'd muttered quietly, but not quietly enough.

'Don't you dare use that language to me.'

For a second Maxine thought he was going to swear at his mother again but he turned and headed for the back door.

'I'm going into the garden,' he'd said as he slammed it behind him.

When Maxine had served up a mushroom risotto fifteen minutes later, he'd insisted he was too busy to come in and that he'd rather eat in her studio.

'That's petty,' she'd told him.

'I'm not going to sit there and be accused of trying to fiddle her out of her money.'

'Suit yourself.' Maxine had felt too weary to try to dissuade him.

Supper had been eaten by the rest of them in an uncomfortable silence and Maxine had been glad of the excuse to flee to her art club leaving Abi and Marcus to clear up. Thankfully, with everyone tiptoeing around in embarrassment after the earlier row, Abi hadn't made the least fuss.

Now, sitting on the sofa, Maxine became aware of Anthea staring at her. God, she didn't want another set-to. She took a large gulp of her wine and then considered following Gordon to the pub. Had she not been quite so tired it would have been an extremely tempting idea. She decided to try and move away from the subject of her husband onto safer ground. 'Were you watching anything nice?'

'Moving wallpaper,' was the response. It seemed Anthea was in no mood to discuss her evening's viewing. 'And some woman called while you were out.'

'Who?'

'No idea. She didn't stay. It was all very clandestine if you ask me.'

'Really?'

Maxine would have asked for more details but Anthea spoke again. 'Look, Maxine, next week the cast comes off my arm and, all being well, my ankle will be given a clean bill of health too, so there is no reason on this earth for me not to move back home.' She saw Maxine open her mouth but she overrode her, imperiously. 'No, I don't care what you have to say; I am an adult, I have all my marbles and I have lived in that house for decades without mishap. What happened was an unfortunate accident and it won't happen again.'

'You don't know that,' said Maxine.

'You seem to be implying that I make a habit of falling over. As I rarely drink – unlike *some* people,' she stared hard at Maxine's wine glass, 'I think the chances of that happening are vanishingly small.'

Maxine leant forward, picked up her glass and drained what was left. 'Do you know,' she said, 'I hardly drank at all until recently but given the circumstances of my life right now I think it's surprising I don't drink even more than I do. And,' she added, 'I really don't think that how much I drink is anyone's business but my own. Not yours, not my daughter's, no one's.'

'If you say so, Maxine. Although, call me old-fashioned, but do you really want your nearest and dearest to think of you as a drunk?'

'I don't see you having a go at your son about how much he drinks.'

'He's a man, it's different.'

Maxine was lost for words so she stamped into the kitchen and defiantly refilled her glass.

'Typical,' said Anthea when she returned.

'Do you know, maybe you're right. Maybe you should move out before either of us does or says something we both might regret.'

'I think,' said Anthea coldly, 'that particular ship has sailed. It's obvious you've had enough of me.' She held up her hand and added, 'And don't argue. I may be old but I'm not stupid.' She sounded breathless. Maybe the effort of being so vitriolic was tiring her.

Maxine almost laughed. Arguing about having had enough of her mother-in-law was the last thing she'd been about to do.

Anthea pulled at the neck of her blouse. 'If this house wasn't so hot, I could catch my breath.'

'Are you too warm?' asked Maxine.

'Aren't you? Although I'm so tired I probably won't have trouble sleeping. Where is Pearl? I'm exhausted and I want my bed.'

'She'll be here in a minute.'

'Good.' She plucked at her blouse again. 'The heat,' she muttered weakly. 'I can't breathe.'

'Would you like a cold drink?'

'And risk needing the lav in the night? Absolutely not. And don't change the subject.'

Maxine took another slug of her wine. She didn't think it was she who had changed the subject but Anthea, talking about being hot and tired and breathless. She sighed – as always, everything was her fault. As calmly as possible she said, 'I'm afraid the issue of whether you go home or not is between you and Gordon. I'm not getting involved.' Although, what she was actually thinking was, *I don't care how you do it but I wish you'd just go. Get out of our lives. Leave us. I've had enough.*

Did Anthea mutter *coward*?

She looked at the clock on the mantelpiece. Nine thirty. Thank God, almost time for Pearl to come round and help put Anthea to bed and high time Gordon was back from the pub. Given the awfulness of Anthea's earlier accusations and the ghastliness of the row, she'd thought about softening her attitude towards Gordon and moving back into the double bed. She felt they could both do with a sympathetic cuddle. On the other hand, she felt exhausted by the day's events and, as he'd been down the pub most of the evening, she wasn't sure she wanted her sleep to be disturbed by his snoring. Maybe tomorrow.

The pair lapsed into a sullen silence.

Five minutes later Pearl rang the bell then let herself in almost immediately exuding good humour and energy.

'Evening, ladies. I trust you all had a good day. Come on now, Anthea, my dear, let's get you up the stairs.' She must have sensed the atmosphere because her smile and her bonhomie shrivelled.

'Thank you, Pearl for asking but no, it was a simply awful day. And tell my daughter-in-law that I am almost capable of fending for myself again *in my own home.*'

Pearl glanced nervously between her charge and Maxine. 'I think it's a bit late in the evening for that sort of discussion,' she said firmly.

'Dear God, another coward,' said Anthea, loudly enough to be really heard this time.

'A decision like that is way above my pay grade,' said Pearl, supporting Anthea as she got her out of the armchair. Despite her support, Anthea stumbled. 'Steady now,' said Pearl.

'It's all right. Don't fuss, I can manage.'

Pearl shot a look over her head to Maxine who responded with a sympathetic smile. Anthea was being even more difficult than usual.

'But you must have an opinion,' insisted Anthea. She seemed to be breathing heavily again.

'You wouldn't want to hear it.'

Anthea looked deflated. 'Then I shall have to fight my battles on my own.' She leaned on Pearl. 'It's been a long day and I feel quite tired. Never,' she panted, 'have I felt quite so glad to be going to bed.' She did look tired – exhausted.

Pearl led Anthea towards the door and the stairs. 'Let's not worry about things like that now. Let's get you washed and sorted and tucked up.'

The pair left the room. No wonder Anthea felt knackered, Maxine thought, she did too. Maybe it *was* the weather. On the other hand, it wasn't *that* hot. She slumped back in her chair and listened to Anthea and her carer make their ponderous way up the stairs.

Maxine sipped her wine and tried to work out how they could move Anthea out of their house if returning her to her own home was out of the question – which it was – when there was an almighty crash from upstairs followed by a cry of help from Pearl.

'Maxine, Maxine, come quickly, Anthea's collapsed.'

Maxine thumped her glass down and shot up the stairs to find Anthea, grey-faced, clutching her head and struggling for breath, lying across the bed. Beside the bed the lamp was lying on the floor, the china base shattered. She was moaning softly.

'It hurts,' she whimpered. 'My head hurts.' And her face was oddly misshapen as though one side had got too close to a candle and had melted.

'I'll call an ambulance,' said Maxine, diving across the corridor to the main bedroom to grab the phone by the bed.

'Yes, ambulance,' she gabbled as the call-handler picked up and asked *which service?* 'I think my mother-in-law's just had a stroke.'

Judith waited for Ella to be busy serving another customer at the other end of the bar before she made her way to the counter and feigned, she hoped, convincing astonishment at seeing her brother-in-law leaning against it, nursing a half-empty Guinness.

'Gordon! How long have you been here?' He jumped. Who's got a guilty conscience? she thought.

'Judith? What on earth...?'

'I know! Surprise! I didn't see you come in.' Which was true, although she didn't tell him she'd been keeping an eye on him from the moment she *had* clocked him.

'But...? I mean...? Of course,' he remembered. 'You moved today, didn't you?'

'Top of the class, Gordon. And I couldn't face cooking so I came here.' She yawned. 'It's been a long old day.'

'Yes, it would have been.' He still looked slightly shifty and uncomfortable.

'And you thought you'd nip out for a sneaky pint while Maxine's busy with her art club. Yes?'

'Kind of.'

'Don't blame you.' She smiled at him. 'I don't know how you and Maxie are coping now you've got half your family living with you. It would drive me demented.'

'It's not easy,' he admitted.

Ella came over to their end of the bar and Judith asked for her bill.

'Everything all right?' Ella asked as she tapped a code into the till.

'Just delish, darling.' She handed over her credit card and completed the transaction. Ella handed her the receipt and then went to serve more customers.

Once she was out of earshot, Judith turned back to her brother-in-law. 'Frankly,' she said, giving him a hint of a conspiratorial wink, 'I'm amazed you don't spend more time here, rather than saving your forays to the pub for when Max is away painting.' She nodded at Ella and lowered her voice further. 'Quite apart from the beer, the view's not bad.' She snorted a dirty laugh that was a dead ringer for one of Patsy Stone's phnaar-phnaar guffaws.

A flush shot up from Gordon's neck to his hairline.

'Not that *you've* probably noticed,' she added. 'Not an old married type like you.' His discomfort was almost tangible. She was about to twist the knife further when Gordon's mobile rang.

'Excuse me,' he said as he fished his phone out of his back pocket. 'Hi, Abi. What's up?'

Judith saw the colour drain from his face.

'Shit. Yes, I'll come right back.' He ended the call and looked up at Judith, a stricken expression masking his face. 'It's Ma,' he said. 'She's had a stroke.'

27

Judith was pushed to keep up with Gordon as he strode across the well-worn paths of the nature reserve towards his house and every few steps she had to half-break into a run. The sense of urgency increased as they reached the hill that led to the gate into their road and saw blue lights flashing eerily off the trees.

Gordon crashed into the house and was met by an ashen and crying Abi. In the background lurked Marcus looking uncertain. Judith felt sympathy towards him – she felt uncertain too. What *was* she doing here? What on *earth* could she do to help? This was a family tragedy and she was virtually an outsider.

'How is she?' Gordon demanded as he hauled his key out of the lock.

Abi shrugged. 'I don't know. Mum's upstairs with the paramedics.'

Gordon took the stairs two at a time as Judith gave her niece a big hug. 'Anthea's in good hands now. Paramedics are miracle workers,' she said as she stroked Abi's hair.

Abi snuffled into her shoulder. 'I suppose,' she said indistinctly.

'Marcus,' said Judith. 'Be a love and put the kettle on.'

If nothing else it'd give him something to do for a minute or two; stop him looking quite such of a spare part. She pulled Abi into the kitchen and pushed her down onto a chair before handing her a roll of kitchen paper.

'Tea or coffee?' asked Marcus.

Frankly, after that race across the reserve, Judith wanted a brandy. 'Coffee, please.'

'Tea,' said Abi. 'Do you think Granny is going to...?'

'Live?' said Judith as robustly as she could. 'Knowing your granny as I do, I should think there's every likelihood.' Although, as they all knew, she was old and frail and there was no guarantee, but Abi needed reassurance right now. Positivity. They lapsed into silence. Marcus dispensed mugs of tea and coffee and they sat around the table, clutching their hot drinks and listening to the noises upstairs. Finally, there was some much louder clattering and the paramedics began to transport their kit out of the house.

'Excuse me,' said Judith waylaying one of them as she came down the stairs for the second time.

'Yes?' said the woman who was clad in a green coverall which sported lurid dayglow bands round the arms and legs.

'How is Anthea?'

'Very poorly.'

'Will she be all right?'

The young woman smiled. 'It's a bit early to tell,' she said. She hefted a large carry bag of kit higher onto her shoulder and took it out to the ambulance before she came back and ran back up the stairs. The two ambulance crew then manoeuvred Anthea from the first floor, strapped to a special sort of wheelchair. Her skin was candle-wax pale and, if she was conscious, she gave no sign. Gordon and Maxine followed and behind them was a stranger –Anthea's carer, presumed Judith.

'Gordon, you go in the ambulance with your mother,' said Maxine, 'I'll get Abi to drive me to the hospital in a minute. And Pearl,' she continued, 'thank you for being such a rock till the ambulance got here. I don't know what I'd have done without you.'

Through the open front door Judith saw Anthea being transferred onto a proper stretcher as Gordon jumped into the back of the vehicle. She turned her attention back to the conversation in the hall.

'No worries, Max. It was a pleasure to help,' Pearl was saying.

'You must be so late for your other charges.'

'The agency sorted out cover for them. The old ducks don't like their routine being too messed about with.'

'That's good. I don't suppose we'll be seeing you again for a while.'

'No.'

There was a momentary awkward pause before Judith saw her sister give the carer a big hug. 'Thanks for everything. I know she wasn't the easiest of patients but you were a star.'

'It's all part of the job. Don't you worry. Now, I'll get off and you get yourself to the hospital.' Pearl left, skirting the ambulance that was still parked outside the front door, before she jumped into her little car and headed off.

Maxine shut the front door and slumped against it, her eyes shut.

'Max? Are you OK?'

Maxine opened her eyes. 'Judith? What on earth...?'

'I was having supper at the pub. I was there when Gordon got the call. I came over in case there was anything I could do.' She walked along the hall and held her arms out to her sister. Maxine fell into them, the tears starting to flow.

'Oh, Jude. I feel so guilty because this is all my fault.'

'There, there,' soothed her sister. As she comforted Maxine, they saw the flashing blue lights that were visible through the leaded window in the front door, move away. Then, as the ambulance joined the main road, the ululation of the siren started.

'I came back from Art club and she was being difficult and all I could think was that I wished she would just leave us. Go away. But I didn't mean it to be like this, not ill, not in an ambulance. You believe me, Judith.'

'Oh, Sis. Don't be silly. Of course you didn't want it to be like this. We all know that.'

'But if I hadn't thought it, if I hadn't wished her gone...'

'She'd still have had a stroke,' said Judith with conviction. 'She's old, she's frail, she's not in the best of health—'

'And she and Gordon had an awful row.'

'There you go. Nothing to do with you.'

'I suppose.' Maxine blew her nose and dried her eyes. 'This isn't getting me to the hospital. Abi?'

Abi stood up, her car keys already in her hand. 'Come on, Mum. Let's get going.'

'And both of you,' said Maxine. 'Don't say anything about me saying I wanted his mother gone. It won't help matters.'

'Of course not. Anyway, why would I?'

After they'd gone the house seemed empty and quiet. So many people, so much drama and then ... nothing.

'I'd better make tracks too,' said Judith.

'I'd run you home,' said Marcus, 'only Abi's got the car.'

'I'll be fine. And the walk'll do me good after all that excitement.' Actually, Judith was putting a brave face on things. In the light of the lack of a lift, her second preferred option would have been to be beamed back to her cottage by a crew member of the starship *Enterprise*. Thank God, she was wearing trainers. No point in smart shoes on a day when you're moving house, had been her rationale earlier in the day. She hadn't expected it to have paid off quite so well.

Miranda was entertaining Olivia in her kitchen when they heard the ambulance siren wail. Their conversation paused momentarily at the sound – an uncommon one in Little Woodford.

'You know, when I lived in London no one paid the least attention to blues and twos,' mused Miranda. 'I suppose it's a good thing that they're so unusual here that when an emergency vehicle goes past, half the population stops and gawps.'

'One of the many advantages of not living in a heaving metropolis,' agreed Olivia. She flicked through the pages of her notebook before she snapped it shut. 'I think we've pretty much covered everything. You've got the town hall, and our chief judge organised, the art club are all on board and they'll get their pictures—'

'Maximum of three.'

'Maximum of three to you a fortnight before the show, ready for you to get them framed.'

'And everyone's happy with the style – a single white mount and a plain black frame.'

Olivia nodded. 'It's up to them to choose something that won't get lost with a pale background. Heather is going to get the WI to provide tea and cakes, and that, I think, is that. Oh, and well done for getting that sketchbook back into Miranda's studio.' She picked up her notebook and slid it into her handbag.

'Excellent. That's that then.' She smiled at Olivia. 'And before you go, I rang Dominic earlier and asked about the other sketchbook. He's promised to courier it back to us shortly then all we have to do is get it back into the studio like the other one. After that we just have to persuade her to allow Dominic to see the rest of her work so he can make overtures about exhibiting her properly.' She made it sound so simple.

Gordon was pacing the corridor outside the Resus unit when Maxine arrived.

'How is she?' she asked as soon as she reached him.

'Being assessed. Apparently, because the paramedics arrived so quickly things are a lot better than they might have been, but she is still very ill. She's in a bad way; it's touch and go.' He gave his wife a bleak smile. 'She's in good hands and they're doing their best.'

'That's what I told Abi. I told her to go home, by the way. There's no point in her having a sleepless night as well.'

'No. Although I don't suppose she'll sleep much anyway.'

The pair lapsed into silence as they both gazed at the door to Resus, both wondering quite what was going on behind it.

'Let's take a seat,' said Max, taking Gordon by the hand and leading him over to some rows of blue padded chairs. 'There's no point in pacing up and down. It won't make things happen differently. I'm sure they'll tell us as soon as there's any news.'

He nodded. 'I shouldn't have rowed with her.' He slumped onto one of the seats.

'It probably didn't help matters that she and I had an argument too.'

Gordon looked at his wife and sighed. 'What about?'

'She said I drink too much and I pretty much told her she'd driven me to it.'

'You did *what*?'

'And your point is? And what's more, when I suggested she might like to take issue with your drinking habits, she said it was different for a man. For God's sake, which century is she from?'

'The last one,' said Gordon. 'She's got different standards.'

'I'll say so.'

'I know you two don't see eye to eye but you should make more of an effort to cut her some slack.'

Maxine could feel her blood pressure rising. 'Why me? Why am I the villain of the piece?'

'Because she's old and frail.'

Maxine bit her tongue.

'And you do drink quite a bit.'

'Jeez, Gordon that's pots and kettles. You're down the pub almost every night.'

'Only for a pint or two.'

Maxine narrowed her eyes. 'Says you.'

'Anyway, this doesn't change the fact that you had a go at my mother.'

'It was self-defence. I'm sorry Gordon and I've said this before, but I am not going to be belittled and ticked off in my own house by a bloody visitor.'

'That's my mother you're talking about.'

'And I'm your *wife*.' She glared at Gordon. She didn't trust herself to stay calm and reasonable and besides, as Gordon seemed to be blaming her for his mother's condition, it was probably better if she didn't stay where her presence might make things worse. She picked up her handbag from the floor and walked away. Gordon, she noticed didn't ask her where she was going or offer any sort of apology. Sod him, she thought as she headed for reception. When she got to the automatic doors, she pulled out her phone and rang the number of a local taxi company. Both he and his poisonous mother could shove it.

28

By the end of the following week Anthea was still clinging on to life in a high dependency unit and Gordon seemed to be spending most of his waking hours at the hospital by her bedside. Which suited Maxine fine because she was still angry with him. She tried telling herself that he had been stressed and frightened about his mother's condition but now things seemed to have stabilised he'd had lots of opportunities to apologise and yet, to judge by the way he looked at her, he was waiting for her to say sorry. Well, he could bloody wait.

Judith's house was getting straighter by the day but there was a finite limit to how much sorting and unpacking she could do in a day. She would have spent some of her spare time with her sister, but Max seemed to be in such a constantly filthy mood it was easier to keep out of her way. Judith put it down to worry about her mother-in-law although she found it a bit surprising that Maxine didn't visit along with Gordon. Maybe there were restrictions about the number of visitors patients in intensive care could have at any one time. With time on her hands and her curiosity about Gordon and the luscious Ella unsatisfied, she decided to do a spot of detective work to find out if her suspicions were right about what the woman was up to. Besides it wasn't much of a hardship to while away the odd lunch hour in a welcoming pub with a decent selection of gins. It took three visits to the pub before she managed to find Ella working behind the bar on her own. She was sure that Belinda might tell her about her new barmaid but there was every possibility that Belinda might also want to know why Judith was taking such an interest. Before she shared her suspicions with anyone else, she wanted to be sure of her facts.

Judith was no fool and didn't think Ella was attracted by Gordon's youth, looks or charisma. On the other hand, his house and his bank account might be quite a draw. A woman of her age without an engagement ring or wedding band and who worked in a pub might well consider her life to be in a bit of a rut. What better way to solve the problem than with a meal ticket out of it? And one of the pub's regulars – with the right sort of encouragement – might be the person to supply it. A part of Judith didn't blame her. After all, she'd been a kept woman almost all of her life; she'd never done a day's work, had hardly ever lifted a finger for herself and yet had had a husband who had been more than happy to fund her lifestyle for the best part of twenty-five years. Even when he'd lit out, she'd hardly been left a pauper. No, finding a well-heeled man wasn't to be sniffed at – except when that well-heeled man belonged to someone else.

Judith hitched herself onto a bar stool, ordered a large G and T, and smiled at Ella as she was handed the drink.

'And one for yourself?' she offered.

'Thanks, I'll have a tomato juice.'

Ella rang up the drinks and Judith passed over her card to be tapped on the machine. 'Cheers,' she said as she raised her glass. Then, 'It's quiet today.'

'It always is on a Thursday.'

'Do you do a lot of shifts here?'

'It's the day job. Well, and the evening job too, quite often.'

'It must be quite nice being able to lean on a bar, chatting to the locals.'

'Belinda says if I've got time to lean, I've got time to clean.'

Judith laughed. 'As it's her pub then I suppose it's her rules. Is she a good boss?'

'I've had worse.'

'And the locals?'

'Some of them are OK.'

'Then I hope I fall into that category.'

'You've been all right so far. But didn't you say you're new to the area?'

'Only moved in recently.'

'Lucky you to be able to afford somewhere.'

'I downsized, but yes I am. The house prices are pretty massive, aren't they?'

'Tell me about it. And as for renting... How are the likes of me supposed to afford anything?'

'It must be difficult.'

'It's impossible.'

'So where do you live?'

'With my folks. I ask, I mean, at my age.' Ella sighed theatrically. 'I mean, I haven't always but... well... circumstances changed; he lit out, I couldn't afford the rent, you get the picture.'

'I do indeed and I sympathise. I had to move for similar reasons. Men, eh?'

Ella rolled her eyes and took a sip of her drink. 'Men,' she agreed.

'Still, there must be a few good sorts out there.'

'If you can find 'em.'

'But, if you don't mind me saying so, I'd have thought you'd have a whole slew of blokes to choose from.'

'Thanks.' Ella preened slightly and then tossed a brunette curl over her shoulder. 'The thing is, picking the right one. Once bitten twice shy and all that. I want the right sort of man who's going to treat me in the right sort of way so I can live in a nice house in a nice area with nice things around me.'

'Nothing wrong with setting your sights high,' said Judith while she actually thought Ella needed a massive reality check. 'And how do you plan to get that?'

'I need to find Mr Right, that's how,' said Ella. 'In the meantime I'm picky about who I date. I mean, I don't want to be tied to some loser when the right bloke does rock up. It's all about being ready to grab the opportunity when it comes along.'

'Nothing like being focused,' said Judith. Nothing like being a piece of scheming work either, but she made herself smile at Ella. 'Anyone on the horizon?'

Ella smirked. 'There might be. Got to play my cards right, that's all.'

'Good luck.' But if it's my sister's husband I hope you burn in hell. 'Cheers.'

*

The one good thing about Anthea being in hospital, Maxine decided, was that with Gordon being so preoccupied with visiting her in the car, Abi and Marcus were forced to shoulder more of the shopping burden. Maxine could pop out and bring home the occasional pint of milk or a loaf of bread but a big shop for four adults was out of the question with only Shank's pony for transport. Naturally the downside was a certain amount of grumbling but, for once, Abi had the sense to tone down her chuntering when her parents were around.

When they weren't, Abi let rip.

'It isn't as if we're not working full time,' she complained to Marcus over Friday lunch in the staff canteen at work, a week after Anthea had been admitted into the stroke unit.

'*And* we're dealing with our own house. I mean, we really don't have enough hours in the day to earn a living *and* project manage *and* do all the bloody shopping. And we've got to do another massive shop again tomorrow.' She shovelled in a forkful of baked potato and cheesy beans. 'What about us having a weekend off, that's what I want to know? Seriously, Marcus,' she said indistinctly before she chewed and swallowed, 'I've got better things to do with my Saturdays than tramp around the effing Tesco in Cattebury.' She sighed before she ate another forkful. 'I think it'd be an idea if we move into the cottage just as soon as there's heating, lighting and running water. Stuff the mess and everything else – if we're there, Mum can't expect us to run around after her and Dad.' She ate some more.

'I don't know, Abi,' said Marcus. 'Won't it be easier for Steven to work without having us and our possessions underfoot?'

'We only need to take a few bits and pieces.'

'But cooking and washing and all that sort of stuff…?'

'We should go over and have a good look at the house. We've not looked at it in that sort of light – we've only concentrated on having it properly completed and when that's likely to happen.'

'I don't know—' Marcus started. He took a deep breath. 'And you said, and I quote, *I couldn't live in a place that was over-run with builders.*'

'That was then, this is now. Besides, don't you want to be independent again, because, frankly, I can't wait?' She stabbed the air with her fork to emphasise her point. 'A bit of mess and muddle is nothing compared to what we have to put up with at the moment; being treated like skivvies – worse, *unpaid* skivvies.'

'It's not that bad and your mum and dad are in a pretty stressful situation.'

Abi rolled her eyes. 'Dad's sitting by her bed, listening to the machines beeping, reading the paper to her in case she can hear what's going on and Mum's swanning around at home doing bugger all from what I can see. Neither of them is hardly rushed off their feet, are they?'

Marcus kept quiet.

'So that's a plan then, we'll go over to the house after work and see if it's possible to move in. Mum and Dad will have to fend for themselves tonight. I'll text them and tell them that we'll be too busy to cook supper. And you and I can grab a bite somewhere so we can make plans without them interfering.'

'Come off it, Abi, you're making it seem like your mum and dad are out to thwart us. And, let's face it, when we moved in, you were upset because you felt they didn't want us there. Now you're cross because they *do*.'

Abi scraped up the last few beans off her plate. 'Don't be ridiculous, Marcus. I don't know where on earth you got that idea from.' She stood up, picked up her empty plate and glass and put them on the tray. 'Finished?'

Marcus had to grab the last of his sandwich off the plate as Abi whipped it away.

'Apparently, I have,' he mumbled as he stuffed the last morsel into his mouth and followed her out of the canteen.

'I'll meet you in the car park at five and we'll go straight to the house,' she ordered as she peeled off the main corridor towards her office.

'Yes, dear.'

'We're going to have to have another go at the garden,' said Abi as they got out of the car at Wisteria Cottage. 'That's if we'll be able to find the time, given all the jobs Mum wants us to do for *her*.' She surveyed the length of the grass and the weeds which seemed to have over-run all the flower beds again. 'That was the one good thing about living in the flat – we only had to worry about inside stuff, not the outside stuff as well.'

'But it'll be lovely to have somewhere to sit out on nice summer evenings, to have barbecues and maybe to have a kick-about with the kids when they come along.'

'Yeah, well, that won't be for a while. We can't possibly afford kids with all this to pay for.' She ignored Marcus's look of disappointment.

'We could always increase the mortgage when it's finished. The house'll be worth a heap more than we paid for it.'

Abi's snort of derision told Marcus what she thought of that idea.

'Let's go in and see what's left to be done,' she said marching to the front door and getting her key out ready to unlock it but the door was already open. The place smelt of glue, dust and something pungent like white spirit.

'Coo-ee,' called Abi as she strode in. There was no reply. 'Good job we came round if Steven has left this place unsecured. We could get squatters. What was he thinking of?' she said as she made her way into the kitchen where she stopped and stared about her. The transformation from the bomb site to what almost looked like a proper house was striking. Most noticeable was the floor in the kitchen – the boards were back down, the gaping hole had gone although a proper trapdoor had been installed which, when Abi pulled it open, revealed a real set of steps leading down to the cellar.

'Coo,' said Abi, dropping the door back into place as she heard the sound of heavy boots clattering around in one of the outhouses joined to the kitchen. 'Steven? I didn't see your van.'

'It's round the back. Easier to load and unload my kit rather than drag it through the rest of the house.'

'But you should have finished half an hour ago. We can't afford overtime, you know.'

'Just finishing up for tonight. And don't worry, it won't go on the bill.'

'Good.'

'So, what do you think?'

'The kitchen's looking good.'

'It's coming together.'

'When will you be able to start fitting the units?'

Steven laughed. 'There's a way to go yet. We've got to get all the rest of the timbers treated, including all the new stuff *and* what's in the roof, then we've got to get the wiring done, and as you know I've only just made a start on the upstairs plumbing to get in your new en-suite... As I said, you'll be lucky to get away with moving in before the autumn.'

'That's the point. We want to move in before then.'

Steven stared at her in astonishment. 'But you've just said you can't afford the overtime.'

'That's right, but we want to live here while you do the work.'

Steven's look of astonishment morphed into one of horror. 'No. No way.'

'This is our house, Steven so I don't think it's up to you.'

'Fine, if you want it that way, but you'll have to find another builder.'

'But...'

'I'm serious, Abi. You can live in a caravan in the garden but I can't have you here in the house with everything else going on. Quite apart from any health and safety issues, working round your living space will be a nightmare for me and my sub-contractors.'

Abi's lips were clamped together so hard they went white. 'I see,' she said eventually.

'Steven has a point,' ventured Marcus.

Abi glared at him. 'We need to talk,' she snapped. 'We're going,' she said, stating the obvious as she swept out. 'There are plenty of other builders around. I'll phone you tomorrow,' she shot at Steven as she left with Marcus trailing after her.

'A pint of bitter,' said Steven as he leant wearily on the bar of the Talbot. Thank God it was Friday – two days off.

'You sound like you need it,' said Ella as she poured the drink. 'And we don't see you in here that often, either. It's Steven, isn't it?'

'Yeah, it is.' He smiled at her. 'Good memory. And you are?'

'Ella. And that's three ninety, please.' She handed the pint through the beer pumps as Steven fished in his pocket for the cash. 'Cheers,' he said as he made his way over to an empty seat in the window and slumped onto it.

God, he thought, that bloody Abi was a piece of work and no mistake. Spoilt little cow. Every time she came over to the house, he ended up feeling like he'd done nine rounds with a prize fighter. He took a long draught of his beer and wondered if it would be all that bad if he did get sacked from the job? The money was good, it was a long-term project and the security was great but was it really worth it? He leaned back in his chair and stared at the ceiling as he weighed up the pros and cons. The phrase *que sera, sera* popped into his head. True, he acknowledged and, if Abi sacked him, so be it. He lowered his eyes and looked towards the bar as he gave up contemplating his future employment prospects and turned his attention to Ella. If she were a bit younger, he could fancy asking her out. On the other hand, if roles were reversed, he wouldn't think twice about asking out a woman who was his junior by a few years. Would it be so bad to be a toy boy? He watched her covertly as he sipped his drink and was rather disappointed when her face lit up as a new customer, a bloke of about sixty or so, went to the bar. She hadn't smiled at him like *that* when he'd asked for a drink. Her father, maybe, mused Steven. The new guy turned around and scanned the customers in the relatively empty bar before he met Ella at the open hatch through the counter and dipped in to give her a kiss – on the lips, and although it wasn't a proper snog it wasn't a peck either. So, no way he was her father – totally over-affectionate for a greeting between relatives. As he stared, he realised, with a physical jolt, that he recognised the man – Abi's dad – so *definitely* not a relation. What the fuck…? And him a married man and all. The randy old goat!

'Wotcha, Stevie-boy.'

Steven turned in the other direction. 'Ryan! Nice surprise, buddy. And Amy. Let me get you both a drink.'

'No, you're all right. My round and let me get you a refill.'

'No, can't. I've got the van in the market square.'

'Leave it parked there overnight and walk back to your place. The traffic warden's never out before nine and even then, you get two hours grace.'

'That sounds like a plan. I could seriously fancy drowning my sorrows,' Steven said gloomily. 'I may not have a job come Monday?'

'Not have a job? Bloody hell. Seriously?'

'Seriously.'

'Now look, I want to hear all about it but let me get the drinks in first.'

And when Ryan returned with two pints and a large Chardonnay he and Amy were regaled with the trials and tribulations of working for his current employers.

'I mean,' said Steven, 'he's not so bad but her...' He took a slug of his second pint.

'So,' asked Amy, 'are you still working on that big old job at that cottage? The one with the dodgy cellar?'

'That's the one.'

'I met the mother the other day. Maxine Larkham?'

'That's her and, funnily enough, her old man is at the bar. I recognise him because him and his missus came over to see the place shortly after I started work on it. I thought they'd been happily married for *ever* but I've just seen him snog Ella, so what's going on there?'

Amy stared at the oldish bloke Steven had indicated. 'If he's snogging the barmaid his wife's not going to be a happy bunny. Poor cow, because no way can she compete with *that*.' Amy shot a vitriolic glance at Ella who was still flirting shamelessly.

29

The next morning Amy was pottering through town, on her way to the Co-op to get some essentials like milk and bread. She was scanning her shopping list, trying to make sure she hadn't forgotten anything, when she nearly bumped into another pedestrian.

'Sorry,' she said automatically as she side-stepped out of the way. She glanced up and saw Olivia Laithwaite. 'Mrs L. Sorry,' she repeated. 'Nearly bashed into you, there.'

'It's all right, Amy. I could see you weren't looking where you were going.'

'How are you, Mrs L? I hardly never see you now you work proper hours like the rest of us. I bet you don't miss the shift work. My Ryan was on nights this week.'

'Poor man.'

'Oh, it's not so bad,' said Amy airily. 'He gets a proper night's kip if there isn't a shout. It's not like being a copper when they have to be out and about patrolling.'

'I suppose.'

'When I left to come out he was home making himself and my Ashley brunch – a proper fry up.'

'How very domesticated.'

'He is.' Amy beamed. 'Hey, while I think about it... your mate, Mrs Larkham...'

'Maxine? What about her?'

'I saw her old man at the pub last night.'

'So?'

'So – and you mustn't breathe a word of it...' She paused as she considered whether she should go on. Maybe not. 'No, there's probably an explanation,' she said out loud.

'For what?' Olivia sounded mildly irritated.

Oh, what the heck. 'Well, old man Larkham was snogging the new barmaid and—'

'Don't be silly, Amy, Gordon wouldn't do something like that.'

Amy raised her eyebrows. 'You didn't see it, I did,' which she knew wasn't strictly true but Steven had and why would he lie? 'Anyway, as I said, it's probably something and nothing. Forget I said anything.' The town hall clock chimed and Amy looked up at it. 'Blimey, is that the time? I must fly. See ya.' Amy belted off into the Co-op leaving Olivia staring after her.

While Olivia was feeling utterly dumbfounded in the centre of town, so was Abi – only she was in the car with Marcus as they drove to the big supermarket in Cattebury. They'd been discussing Abi's ultimatum to Steven the previous evening.

'And you're *not*,' said Marcus, 'going to ring him and tell him we're moving in because we're *not* looking for another builder. That's *not* going to happen and that's that.'

'I don't get it. I don't understand why you won't back me up.'

'Because I don't agree with you.'

'You can't like living with Mum and Dad any more than I do. I mean, look at us now – being made to do a shop for them when we've got far better things to do with our weekend.'

'I think you're being unreasonable; we're going to eat this food too.'

'I am *not* being unreasonable. Besides, it'll be much easier for everyone if we move into the cottage – and we can keep a proper eye on Steven.'

'If we move into the cottage Steven will down tools. And we'll still need to buy food.'

'Not as much.'

'For God's sake, Abi, buying four pints of milk instead of two is hardly difficult.'

'That's not what I mean.'

'And your mum cooks most of the meals which means we don't have to.'

'That's not the point. I don't know why you're arguing with me when you know I'm right.'

'You're not.'

Abi swivelled in her seat to stare at her partner. 'Of course I am.'

'If you move in and Steven goes, I'll go too.'

Abi went white. 'You wouldn't,' she whispered.

Marcus risked a quick glance at her before he looked at the road ahead again. 'I love you to bits, Abi, but right now you're making it very difficult to like you. Steven is a brilliant builder and, if we lose him it could be weeks

– months – before we find someone as good to take his place, which will put the whole project back so it might not be finished before the winter. Is that what you want, to be camped out in a place with precious few facilities and probably no heating, for months and months?'

'That won't happen.'

'Huh.'

Abi looked at Marcus and saw a look of determination on his face which she didn't recognise. She opened her mouth and closed it again. 'It was only an idea,' she said.

'But not one we're going to use. Now phone Steven and tell him.'

Abi simmered but did as she was told then threw her phone back into her handbag. 'Satisfied?' she snapped and glared through the windscreen, missing the look of utter relief on Marcus's face.

As Abi and Marcus drove into the supermarket carpark in an angry silence, Olivia was ringing the bell on the Talbot. Inside she could see Belinda hoovering the carpet. She waved at her friend through the bullseye glass panes in the door.

'Desperate for a drink?' asked Belinda with a grin as she opened the door.

'Certainly not,' said Olivia.

'Joke.'

'I know, but this is serious.'

Belinda shut the door and shot the bolt. 'What is?'

'I've just heard something really, *really* disturbing.'

'And?'

'About Gordon Larkham and your new barmaid.'

'Oh.' Belinda's smile vaporised. She didn't look surprised either which spoke volumes.

'Oh? You *know*?' Olivia was aghast.

'No, no I don't, not really, except...' Belinda paused.

'Except what?'

'I caught him making sheep's eyes at her a while back.'

Olivia sat down on a nearby chair. 'He was *what*?'

'It was hardly jumping into bed with her.'

'No, but...'

'And I warned him off.'

'Well that obviously worked because Amy was full of if this morning. Apparently, he and Ella were, in the words of Amy, snogging last night, in the pub.'

'Snogging? Are you sure because, as far as I know, Amy's never met Gordon so, in which case, how on earth did she recognise him?'

'*She* didn't but she was having a drink with the bloke who is doing Abi's building work and *he* did.'

'Oh shit.'

'My sentiments, exactly.'

The two women exchanged a horrified look.

'So what do we do now?' said Olivia.

Belinda shrugged. 'What are our choices? I suppose we can do nothing and hope it goes away. We can warn off Gordon – but I did that before and he doesn't seem to have paid any attention. Or I can warn off Ella.'

Olivia nodded. 'But do we tell Maxine?'

'Maxine?! Why?'

'Because if Amy knows it's the equivalent of a splash headline on the front of a tabloid. The whole town will know in a couple of days. Word is bound to get back to her. You know what this place is like.'

Belinda rolled her eyes. 'You're right. But I'm sure Gordon hasn't actually *done* anything. A bit of light flirting in a public place is hardly a full-on affair.'

'It's gone beyond flirting if they were kissing. No smoke without fire,' added Olivia gloomily.

'You think?' Belinda shook her head then added, 'Of course Gordon and Maxine have been under a lot of strain recently what with her mother-in-law, and Abi moving back in, and now having to spend hours at the hospital on top of everything else.'

'It's no excuse though, is it? Look at me and Nigel – and I didn't bugger off and find some toy-boy gigolo because I was feeling the strain of him almost bankrupting us.'

She didn't notice Belinda struggle to hide a smile. 'No, absolutely not. If the tables were turned and it happened to be Nigel,' said Belinda, 'would you want to know? Especially if it didn't turn out to be anything physical.'

Olivia thought about it. 'Not that he would – not that he'd *dare* – but, on balance, yes. Because, if I found out that the whole town knew, and I was the only one in the dark – to think people might be laughing at me behind my back...' She shook her head. Olivia was very aware of what it was like to lose one's standing in the town. 'The only good thing about that business with Nigel was that I found out before the town did. By the time it was common knowledge, we'd lost almost every penny we had and I'd come to terms with the situation; I'd made a plan to sort it out. As far as I was concerned the worst was behind me.'

'Given what you've just said, I think you need to tell Maxine – or confront Gordon and tell him to 'fess up.'

Olivia sagged. 'Neither option is a conversation I want to have.'

'You're sure of your facts?'

'You witnessed something that made you uneasy and why would Amy make such a story up? On balance, I think the story's got legs.'

'Then, good luck,' said Belinda.

With Gordon at the hospital and Abi and Marcus, having done the shopping, now dealing with the garden at their new property, Maxine was alone in the house. She had a list of jobs she needed to do and afterwards, if she had time, she was going to examine her paintings to sort out what she planned to exhibit at the upcoming show in the town hall. She was revelling in the deep peace the solitude was giving her; even after a week of Anthea's absence she still loved having an empty house. She'd forgotten how much she liked her own company.

Then the doorbell rang.

'Bugger,' she muttered as she went to open the door. She hoped it was a delivery or something else that could be dispensed with quickly. Her heart sank a little when she saw Olivia on the doorstep.

'Olivia! How lovely,' she lied. 'Come in. Tea? Coffee?'

'A coffee would be lovely. I see the cars have gone – I assume Gordon is up at the hospital and the children...?'

'And the children are out too – gardening at their new

house. I was just revelling in having the place to myself. Not something I've enjoyed for weeks.'

'And now I've ruined everything.'

'Don't be silly.' Maxine put on the kettle and got out the mugs.

'And how is Anthea?'

'Much the same. Very poorly but stable is the official terminology.'

'Oh dear. Dare I ask what the prognosis is?'

Maxine shrugged. 'Who knows? She's old, she had a bad fall recently, she's so heavily sedated she's out of it most of the time, hospitals are inherently unhealthy places to be... I'm not holding my breath, but I think Gordon is.'

'You poor things.'

'Yes, well...'

'Maxine, I need to own up. This isn't really a social call.'

'Oh?'

'No. This isn't easy...'

'I'm being sacked as the leader of the art group?' Maxine offered.

Olivia shook her head. 'It's Gordon. There's a rumour... at least, it's not really a rumour as Belinda seems to have some evidence.'

'A rumour of what?' Maxine's voice was cold and hard.

Olivia told her what she knew, about Amy and Belinda being witnesses and about Amy's unofficial role as town crier and the concomitant implications. Maxine sagged onto a kitchen chair as she finished.

'Shit,' she whispered.

'I thought you'd rather know than not.' Olivia sat down

on a chair opposite. 'I didn't think you ought to be the one person in the dark if this rumour gains momentum – and, given that Amy is involved, it surely will.'

'I'll take your word about Amy. She's obviously got previous from what you've told me.' Maxine leaned back in her chair and contemplated the ceiling for a second or two. 'And Ella's a beautiful woman. You can't blame an old codger like Gordon having his head turned by the attentions of the likes of her. Who wouldn't?' Maxine stared at Olivia as a tear trickled down her cheek. Eventually she said, 'Things are tricky between us but I didn't think they were *that* tricky.' She shook her head. 'What should I do?'

'This is outside my skill set,' said Olivia. 'But I think you need to talk to him.'

Maxine shrugged. 'Are you *sure* this is true?'

'I think so. Belinda has seen them conversing a little more deeply than she felt comfortable with and Amy… well, she's the most gossipy person on the planet – worse even than Susan Carter in *The Archers*—'

'Who?'

'Never mind. And Amy sometimes gets the wrong end of the stick—'

'Well, then. She's talking about the wrong person.'

'But this isn't the sort of story she'd make up. And the bloke she was with – Abi's builder – was sure it was Gordon.' Olivia leaned forward and took Maxine's hand. 'I know you want to think this is all a pack of lies, and I really *do* think it's just a bit of flirting, window shopping maybe, but if you have a word with Gordon maybe it'll stop it becoming anything else.'

'Maybe.' Maxine looked bereft. 'But what if it's already gone beyond that?'

'No. I mean when... how?'

'I was away at Judith's for days, remember. And he spends *a lot* of time at the pub. And then, the other evening, the night Anthea had her stroke, when I got back from Art club she told me Gordon had had a female visitor while I was out. She said it all looked a bit clandestine.'

'Really?' Maxine didn't notice Olivia's expression of guilty horror. 'I'm sure it was nothing. It could have been anyone, a canvasser perhaps. And she didn't stay, did she?'

'Anthea said she didn't, but...'

'No. And regardless of anything else,' insisted Olivia, 'it can't have been Ella – wouldn't she have been working?'

'Maybe. I have no idea what her shifts are at the pub.'

'And that's another thing. If she and Gordon *are* carrying on then they're doing it at the pub so there can't be any hanky-panky there, can there? Think about it.'

'Maybe. But you know what they say – where there's a will there's a way.'

Olivia shook her head. 'Not Gordon. I'm sure of it.'

'That's what my sister thought about *her* husband. Right up to the moment *he* left her for a younger model.'

'I don't know your brother-in-law but Gordon's not like that, I'm sure.'

'Funnily enough, that's exactly what Judith said about hers.'

'Talk to Gordon. It can't make things worse.'

'You think? What if everyone's wrong and he's innocent? Me accusing him of straying is hardly likely to make things better between us. They're bad enough as they stand.'

'Surely not.'

Maxine sighed heavily. 'I remember a day, back in the spring, when I thought life couldn't be rosier; happily married, lovely house, a daughter settled with a nice partner... Well, the gods must have been having a right old laugh because from then on, it's just been one blasted thing after another. Did the Greeks call it hubris – getting one's comeuppance for being smug?' She looked bleakly at Olivia. 'We're sleeping in separate bedrooms, we're barely talking... Frankly, I don't see how things might get any worse – unless Gordon does actually bugger off with that little madam.'

'Where is he right now?'

'At the hospital, with Anthea. Or, at least, that's where he told me he was going.'

'He wouldn't have lied.'

'Why not? – the perfect opportunity. I said that I had stuff to do; a bit of housework and then sort out some paintings for the exhibition. He said fine, so I said, take as long as you want. I couldn't have given him more of an open goal if I'd tried.'

Olivia shook her head. 'I'm sure he's at the hospital.'

'Maybe.'

Silence fell till Olivia said, 'So, have you gone through your pictures yet?'

'No. And now, frankly, I'm not in the mood.'

'But you need to get them to Miranda by Monday at the latest or she won't have time to get them framed.'

Maxine shrugged. 'I don't know I can be bothered.'

'But Max! The art club will be devastated if you don't

join in. Supposing we do it together, now. Supposing I help you choose?'

'I'm not sure.'

'What else will you do? Sit here and imagine the worst?'

'Probably.'

'It won't help matters.'

'Maybe not. But haven't you got things you need to do?'

'Not anymore.'

Maxine realised she was being offered a true hand of friendship. 'Then that'd be nice.' She glanced at the kitchen clock. 'No... no, it's hopeless. It's lunchtime and I've got nothing to offer you except toast and a tin of soup.'

'That'd be fine. That's settled then. While you heat the soup, I'll go and find your sketchbooks from the studio, shall I?' At least, thought Olivia, with Maxine being so distracted, she might not notice that there was one missing; the one that still hadn't arrived back from London. And Maxine's statement about the mystery visitor confirmed that Miranda had safely returned the other sketchbook. Although its return might have caused other doubts and problems. Poor old Maxine.

30

By two o'clock, Maxine and Olivia had shortlisted three of her paintings for the exhibition, and Gordon wasn't back from the hospital – or perhaps, thought Maxine, the hotel room, or Ella's bedroom or wherever he might otherwise be. Being with Olivia had kept her mind off what her husband might be up to, but now she had no such distractions. Maxine thought about worrying and pacing the carpet for the remainder of the afternoon and decided against it. She picked up her phone and dialled her sister.

'You in?' she asked.

'Hello, sweetie, and yes, I'm fine, thank you for asking and yes the unpacking is going well, and yes, I'm at home.'

'Sorry, Judith but this is an emergency. Can I come round?'

'It's not Anthea, is it?'

'No. I'll be ten minutes.'

'Oh... but...'

But Maxine had killed the call, grabbed her door key and was heading out of the house. The nature reserve was full of post-lunch dog walkers and their pooches, summer sunshine, butterflies and wild flowers but Maxine was oblivious to it all as she strode purposefully along the paths to the other side, then down the road that led to the town centre. By the time she reached her sister's little cottage she was perspiring lightly and close to tears as, during her walk, she'd had nothing to think about other than her husband's infidelity.

'So what's all this about?' asked Judith as she opened the door. She saw her sister's stricken face and, while she was ushering her sister into her house, she reached into the downstairs cloakroom, picked up a box of tissues from the shelf over the basin and handed them to her.

'It's Gordon,' said Maxine after she'd blown her nose vigorously.

Judith took Maxine by the arm and pulled her into the sitting room and pushed her onto the sofa. 'Gordon? What's the matter?'

Maxine threw the box of tissues on the coffee table and dabbed her eyes. 'I've heard... there's a rumour... Olivia says that he and that new barmaid...'

'Are a tad over-friendly?'

Maxine stared at her sister, aghast. 'So you've heard about it too?'

'Sorry to be the bearer of bad tidings, but I've *seen* it.'

'You *what*?!' Judith's ears rang from the pitch and the volume. 'And you didn't tell me?'

'Sweetie, it was the night of Anthea's stroke. It was hardly the moment.'

'But since? It's been ages.'

'What I saw was just a bit of flirting and he can't have been to the pub since so...'

'He hasn't had any opportunity?' Maxine finished for her. 'It doesn't excuse what *did* happen.'

'She's a pretty woman, his home life is difficult—'

'And me? What about my home life? I'm the one who did the heavy lift with his bloody mother, I'm the one who was racing around after my effing daughter and her waste-of-space partner...' Maxine glared at her sister. 'Well, thank you very much.'

'I know, I know.'

'And you, for one, should have understood what with Mike buggering off with Trina.'

'But Gordon *isn't* buggering off with Ella.'

'Not yet.'

'He won't.'

'Oh yeah? And what makes you the great expert.'

'Because he loves you too much.'

Maxine's tears spilled over again. 'I don't think he does any more. We sleep in separate bedrooms, we barely talk, he thinks I'm some sort of harridan because if I'm not tough with Abi then no one is and she just takes us for granted. I rowed with his mother just before she had her stroke so he's blaming me for it even though he and she nearly came to blows only a few hours earlier... It's all ghastly.'

Judith pushed the box of tissues back towards her. 'He's a bloke and his daughter has had him wrapped around her little finger since the day she was born. He wants a quiet life. He wants his crossword on a Saturday, his feet up in front of the fire, a lovely wife who cooks him nice meals and nurtures him like she always has, who potters around in her studio while he potters about in the garden.'

Maxine gave her sister a watery smile.

'And now what's he got?' continued Judith. 'His routine's been disrupted, his house has been taken over by outsiders, namely his daughter and his mother, and his lovely wife is run off her feet by their demands and is the only one fighting to maintain things as they used to be. At odds with this is Gordon, the man who loves the quiet life, who thinks it'd be easier to let everyone have their own way rather than have the confrontation because he doesn't realise how ghastly life would become if they actually got it – which you do. And because of *all* of that you're not you're old smiley, placid, kind self.'

'You're not wrong there,' snuffled Maxine into her hanky.

'Instead, you're ratty and tired and short-tempered—'

'Gee, thanks.'

'—and, well… Ella isn't. What he *hasn't* done is look at *why* you're ratty and tired et cetera, et cetera. Nor has he stopped to consider why Ella is flirting with him.'

'I'm not with you.'

'To coin a famous line from the late, lamented Caroline Aherne who, when she interviewed Debbie McGee asked, *what first attracted you to the millionaire, Paul Daniels?*'

Maxine slowly lowered her hanky and stared at her sister. 'You mean…'

'Darling, you know I'm very fond of Gordon, but he's no spring chicken, is he? Nor is he George Clooney.'

'He's no millionaire either.'

'But he's highly desirable if you're a very attractive, recently single, middle-aged woman, back living with her elderly parents doing a pretty crap job—'

'How do you know this?'

'Because of my suspicions I've been chatting to her at the pub. *Know your enemy* was one of Mike's favourite sayings. Anyway, as I was about to say, she's very determined and ambitious and completely ruthless, if I'm any judge and she wants a bloke who can give her the lifestyle she wants – and Gordon is a contender if I'm any judge. To be honest, she makes Melania Trump look like a complete novice in the gold-digging stakes.'

Maxine stayed silent for a couple of seconds, then she murmured, 'The cow. But Gordon wouldn't…? He wouldn't, would he?'

'Leave you for her? No chance.'

'But then,' said Maxine, 'if you'd known about Trina you wouldn't have thought Mike would've left you for her.'

'No, no I was wrong there.'

Maxine's tears started again. 'So, you could be wrong again,' she wailed.

'This isn't remotely the same,' Judith said firmly, although she didn't explain why. 'And Ella is deluding herself if she thinks that Gordon might leave you and I am going to make it crystal clear that if she carries on carrying on, it will be my sole purpose to make her life here utterly miserable. Belinda will sack her, no one will talk to her, she'll be a social pariah and marked out as a scarlet woman. And that's just for starters.'

'You could do that?' Maxine forgot her troubles for a second in admiration for her sister.

'Probably not, but she doesn't know that. Would you risk it?'

Maxine shook her head. 'Shit, no.'

While Judith was comforting Maxine, Miranda sat on the patio of her home, shaded from the wonderful summer sunshine by a massive umbrella and trawled her way through art appreciation sites on her laptop. It was all very well having Dominic coming to the town to judge the imminent exhibition, but Miranda needed some help and advice on how to stage the event plus the best way to display the exhibits given their limited resources. She was sure Maxine would have some ideas – as an art teacher for years she must have made sure her pupils' works had been shown off to its best advantage for parents' evenings and the like. Not that Miranda wanted this to be in the same league as a parent's evening – no way. She wanted Little Woodford's inaugural art exhibition to be up there in the Championship, or preferably the Premiership and not wallowing down in the Isthmian League. Certainly having everything in uniform frames was an excellent starting point and the town hall's display boards were quite smart but, from her research so far, lighting also looked key. And that was the problem – the town hall lighting was dire; just three rather grim Victorian light clusters hanging from the ceiling. Maybe they could hire in some uplighters or some portable spotlights. The trouble was it was more expense and, while she didn't resent spending money on the show, she didn't want to make the exhibitors uncomfortable by playing Lady Bountiful too overtly.

Maybe she needed to look at other exhibition spaces – places not primarily designed as art galleries – and see what had been done with them to make them suitable. She reached for her laptop and Googled *pop-up art galleries*. A list of possible websites filled her screen. She clicked on one which was labelled *The Lamb and Flag* – presumably a pub somewhere. Miranda gazed at the images – dark, dingy, crowded... absolutely nothing to be learned from this place. She moved on to the next. This one seemed to be in a disused warehouse so plenty of space that had been used to good effect but some of the pictures seemed quite lost on the huge, stark, white walls. No. She shut the site and tried a third. Better by far. It was an exhibition in a village hall – so not so dissimilar from what was at her disposal. The space was neither too big nor too small and the display boards were a soft shade of grey which seemed to compliment all the pictures and, it seemed to Miranda that there was no extra lighting provided other than the very ordinary ceiling lights. Miranda considered it at length and decided that with a slightly darker shade of grey the contrast between the pictures and their background might be sufficient to allow them to get away with the existing lighting in the town hall. The only trouble with that was the display boards at their disposal were covered in royal blue felt – far from ideal. Maybe she could get a bolt of cheap grey cloth and re-cover them on a temporary basis with the aid of a staple gun. It was a possibility that deserved consideration.

And while she was considering this option she clicked on another website for a temporary gallery – and a picture of Bert Makepiece filled her screen.

Maxine's picture of Bert Makepiece.

Miranda did a double-take before she regained her composure and scrolled down. And there was Belinda, and Abi, and the church, and the cricket pitch... All the pictures in Maxine's sketchbook – the one they'd lent to Dominic – were up for sale as signed and numbered limited editions. For sale at between two hundred and six hundred pounds.

Bloody hell! Frantically Miranda whooshed the cursor back to the top of the page – *Miles Smith Fine Art* said the banner.

How had this Miles Smith got hold of Maxine's paintings? And who the hell was he? Had Dominic done some deal with him, cut Maxine out? Or had Maxine already sold her work and kept quiet about it? But that wasn't a possibility as that sketchbook hadn't seen the light of day since the spring, buried as it had been until she and Olivia had rescued it. No, this was all Dominic's doing. The bastard. Miranda almost threw her laptop onto the patio table as she got up and raced into the kitchen to find her mobile. Five seconds later she was dialling his number.

The number you are dialling is unavailable an electronic recording told her.

'I bet it bloody is,' muttered Miranda. She returned to her laptop and typed in *Dominic Harcourt*. A slew of similar names came up but nothing that seemed to be relevant to the art world and certainly nothing that related to the gallery in South Kensington. She tried *Dominic Harcourt fine art dealer*. Still nothing. She dropped the word *fine*. Zilch. She typed in the name of the street where his gallery was supposed to be and Google produced two contenders which, when she dug a little deeper, weren't owned by Dominic Harcourt nor seemed to have ever had anything to do with Dominic Bloody Harcourt. And that, thought Miranda, explained why they hadn't met there. The story about the power cut had all been a ruse to keep her away.

Miranda sat back in her chair and tried to think logically. If his card was a work of fiction and his phone number no longer worked how could she get hold of him? Who might be able to help? Eureka – the gallery she'd bought the Bouraine ballerina from, Dominic's old employer… they might know something. She returned to her tidy kitchen drawer and found their business card and rang the number. Thank God art galleries were invariably open on a Saturday.

'The Holland Art Gallery, how can I help you?' asked a young female voice with an improbably plumy accent.

'May I speak with Emanuel?' asked Miranda. Emanuel Holland was the owner and director. Nothing like going to the top, she thought.

'He's with a client right now. May I ask what it concerns?'

'Could you tell him that it's Miranda Osborne calling – and it's a private matter.'

'Miranda Osborne,' repeated the girl. 'And your number?'

'He knows it.'

'Oh, right. I'll let him know.' Her attitude had changed in a heartbeat from one of giving Miranda the brush-off to deference.

'Could you tell him it's rather important?'

'Certainly.'

Ten minutes later, Emanuel was on the line.

'Miranda! Sweetie, so long since I've spoken to you. And how is rural living? Aren't you pining for the bright lights of London?'

'Sorry to disappoint you, Emanuel, but no.'

'Tut. I'll just have to put on something spectacular to lure you back.'

'I'm sure you will. Now, I'm going to disappoint you again but this isn't a social call. I want to talk to you about one of your previous employees – Dominic Harcourt.'

'Oh dear, you're going to be joining *me* in the

disappointment stakes; I've never employed someone of that name.'

'But I met him at your gallery; he sold me the Bouraine ballerina.'

'Dominic *Smith* did.'

'Oh. But his card says Harcourt.'

'I can't help that. But it's not illegal to change one's name.'

No, thought Miranda, who knew for a fact that Emanuel had been given the name Eric by his parents.

'Anyway,' continued Emanuel, 'why do you ask? Or should I say *what's he done now*?'

A feeling of unease seeped through Miranda. 'Why do you say that?'

'Because we had to let him go.'

'Dare I ask why?'

'Dodgy deals, selling stuff using our name but pocketing the commission, failing to pass on the whole commission on other sales, creative accounting... need I go on.'

Dominic Harcourt, Dominic Smith, Miles Smith... It had to be him. And every one of his personae was dodgier than the last it seemed. 'And you didn't tell the police?'

'Bad PR. And he said he didn't understand the system, he'd received no training from us in financial matters, he wasn't being fraudulent, just naive, that he thought, as he'd made the sales himself, *he* was entitled to the commission *not* the gallery... You're the lawyer, you tell me if he'd have been convicted?'

'Tricky – and you're probably right. I know ignorance is no defence in a court of law but try convincing a jury.'

'Exactly. So, what's he done now?'

'If I'm right, I think he's reproduced some pictures by an

unknown but, in my opinion, very good artist and he, under yet another name – *Miles* Smith – is selling off signed and numbered limited edition prints.'

'Sounds like him. And you're sure the artist doesn't know?'

'Pretty sure. She's got a whole studio full of sketchbooks and paintings that, as far as I know, have never seen the light of day until very recently.'

'And *if* the pictures are signed, and *if* you're right and the artist doesn't know, the signatures must be forged.'

'And that's a charge he can't wriggle out of by pleading ignorance.'

'No way.'

'Small comfort,' said Miranda, 'especially for the artist whose work he's nicked.' She wondered how she was going to break the news to Maxine. Jeez, and on top of Anthea's stroke. *When sorrows come, they come not single spies. But in battalions*, she thought. Poor Maxine; yet more bad news to cope with.

31

Olivia had not long been back from Maxine's when her doorbell rang. She got up from the kitchen table where she'd been doing some personal admin and went to answer it. One look at Miranda told her something was amiss.

'It's Dominic,' said Miranda with no preamble.

Olivia was at a loss to understand what was going on. 'What?'

'I'll show you,' said Miranda grimly, leading the way past Olivia and into the kitchen where she plonked her laptop on the table and switched it on.

'What's the matter?'

'Quite a lot.'

The laptop fired into life and Miranda tapped some buttons. 'There,' she said, swivelling the machine round for Olivia to see.

'But that's... that's Bert. That's Maxine's picture.'

'Exactly.'

'But...?'

'Dominic's nicked it. And a bunch of her other stuff.' Miranda tapped the touch pad and the screen showed a montage of the work on offer.

'But they're signed. Surely, that means Maxine must know about this.'

Miranda raised an eyebrow. 'I thought that for a second, but remember he took a photo of Heather's little watercolour. Maxine's signature was on that. I'll bet my bottom dollar he used that to forge the others.'

Olivia peered at the screen and whistled. 'Just look at the prices.'

'I know. He's got ten or so of her pictures, and if he's got a hundred prints of each, and if we reckon the average price is about three hundred quid a pop...'

'That's thousands.'

'Around three hundred thousand if he sells them all.'

'Bloody hell,' whispered Olivia. 'And it's all our fault.'

Miranda shook her head. 'My fault.'

'The idea for the exhibition was mine.'

'I suggested Dominic should judge it.'

'It doesn't matter whose fault it is – Maxine is a victim here.' Olivia stared at the screen again and at the examples of her work. 'So this Miles Smith...?'

'An alter ego of Dominic. He's also gone by the name of Dominic Smith too. And it seems our Mr Harcourt – or Mr Smith – has previous.' She told Olivia about her earlier phone call to the Holland Art Gallery.

'What can we do?'

'The Met Police have an art fraud and crime department.'

'Really?'

Miranda nodded. 'But whether they'll be interested in taking on something that involves an unknown amateur—'

'—who had no idea her pictures might be worth anything.'

'Exactly. And it was sheer chance I found Maxine's stuff on the internet.'

'But you *did* find it, she's being ripped off and, whichever way you look at it, it's fraud.'

Miranda nodded. 'Now what?'

'You mean, do we tell Max or report it to the police or both?'

'Yes, all of it. And telling Maxine isn't going to be pleasant; we nicked her sketchbooks, we conspired to get her work in front of a bigger audience—'

'—a much bigger audience if things had panned out properly.'

'Well, we've achieved that,' said Miranda. 'But in doing so she's dipped out massively. The only good thing I can see – a *tiny* bit of silver lining – is that Maxine is really good if this guy thinks he can get all this money from her stuff. She's better, much better than we ever imagined.'

Olivia sighed. 'It doesn't alter the fact we need to talk to her. But let's leave it till tomorrow, eh? I think she's had enough bad news from me for one day.'

'I'm sorry,' said Miranda.

'Ah... of course, you don't know about Gordon, do you?'

Miranda's brow creased. 'Gordon?'

'I'll make us tea and fill you in.'

Maxine heard the click of a key in the lock.

'Hi, Max. I'm back,' called her husband.

Maxine sat by the kitchen table, nursing a cup of tea that had long since gone cold and wondered, for the umpteenth time, whether she should have it out with her husband or pretend she was still in the dark.

'Hi, Maxine,' he called again not having had a response to his initial greeting.

'In the kitchen.'

He ambled in, not a care in the world. 'Oh, tea. That's an idea. Has the kettle just boiled?'

Maxine shrugged. 'About an hour ago.'

Gordon stared at her full cup. 'But…?'

Maxine got up and chucked her cold cuppa in the sink.

'Is something the matter?' he asked.

Yes, massively. And the instant she thought that, she knew she couldn't pretend. She was going to have to have the conversation she was dreading and this was the moment to do it. 'You tell me.'

Gordon failed to spot her tone of voice. 'No, no, I don't think anything's the matter. The hospital says Ma's still critical and may be in for weeks and, if and when she gets discharged, we're going to have to sort out proper care – but you know that.'

'Oh, so you *were* at the hospital.'

He stared at his wife. 'Of course I was at the hospital. Where else would I have been?' There was silence. 'Maxine?'

She took a deep sigh and stared out the window. She didn't want to look at him while she made the accusation. 'I thought you might have spent the day with Ella instead.'

'Ella?' He was trying to sound innocent.

Maxine turned back and saw his face flare. Gordon had always been a shit liar, she thought. 'Yes, Ella. Ella from the pub.'

'I know Ella.'

'And just *how well* do you know Ella? Biblically?'

'Bib...' Gordon's face colour-changed from beetroot to ashen like a chameleon on fast-forward. 'No! No, of course not.'

Maxine believed him – being such a shit liar, no way could he have been so convincing if *that* wasn't the truth. Not that she was going to cut him any slack just yet. 'Really? Because that's not what's being said around the town.'

'Don't be ridiculous. What's being said around town and who by?'

'Belinda, Olivia, a woman called Amy.' She paused for effect. 'My sister.'

'Your sister?'

Maxine nodded. 'Uh-huh, she affirmed. 'She saw you with her the night Anthea had her stroke.'

'She couldn't have. I mean, she was at the pub but not...'

'But not when you were canoodling with the bar staff?'

'I wasn't.'

'That's not Judith's version. And what's more, since then she's had a bit of a chat with your Ella.'

Gordon lowered himself into a chair. 'I... she... it's nothing,' he finally managed to get out.

'I don't think Ella thinks so. According to Judith, Ella wants you plus your house and your money – or rather, she wants my husband plus *our* house and *our* money. To be honest, I'm not sure she knows how she's going to achieve it. I'd like to say *over my dead body* but I wouldn't put it past the scheming tart not to think that's a good idea. From what Judith has learned you are a means to an end and I will be collateral damage.'

'Now you're being ridiculous.'

Maxine snorted. 'I don't think it's me being ridiculous.' She stared at her husband. 'Think about it. Gordon, much as I love you – and I do, although it's been a bit of a stretch just recently – as much as I love you, you are not the catch you once were. You're pushing sixty-five, a bit overweight, going bald and getting a tad craggy—'

'Steady on.'

'But I don't care because that's *you*. That's how you are. My husband.' Maxine could feel her eyes pricking. 'The love of my life, or I thought you were till recently. And I compare myself to Ella and I can see why you're attracted. Why wouldn't you be? She's a beauty. She's got the face, the figure... everything.' She gestured to herself. 'And I... I'm older, greyer, more lined. Maybe I haven't looked after myself like I ought to have done – like Ella or Judith. If I'm honest, I'm a frump compared to them. So it's no wonder you're flattered by her attentions. But she's not after you for your body or mind; to Ella, you're a meal ticket. And when she's got what she's wanted, she'll spit you out.'

'That's really harsh, Max. I really don't think she's like that.'

'Really? She's middle-aged, she's living with her parents, she's desperate.'

'I don't think she's as nasty and as scheming as you're making out.'

'She is.' Maxine saw the anguish on her husband's face as he came to terms with reality. 'Look, I can understand. She's beautiful, she's charming and she made you feel like you are fifteen years younger. She flirted with you which is something I don't suppose has happened to you for years. I have days when I feel like I'm about twenty-six – and then

I catch sight of myself in a mirror and I'm back in the real world.'

Gordon gave Maxine a weak smile. 'You're still twenty-six to me. You're still the beautiful young art teacher I fell in love with back then. You always will be.'

'Except when Ella's around.'

Gordon was silent for a moment as he assimilated the truth of his wife's accusation. 'Possibly.' He sighed. 'I can't believe I've been so stupid.'

'Neither can I.'

Gordon gave her a weak smile. 'I just...'

'No, don't try and explain. It happened, no one died, you were led on, you were encouraged, you fell for it. You didn't actually *do* anything very much although what you *did do* was pretty hurtful.'

'I didn't mean... I didn't think.'

'I know. And it's my fault too.'

Gordon looked baffled.

'It is. I've been horrid to live with – even Judith said I've been a cow lately.'

'Not really.'

Maxine smiled wanly at her husband. 'Not really? A nicer response might have been, *no, you've been a sweetheart, kindness itself despite everything.*'

Gordon smiled back. 'It's been a bit tricky. But the worst must be over. It can't be that long before Abi moves out and it's unlikely Mum will be coming back.'

'I'm sad about your mum, obviously, but I won't deny it's a relief.'

'She didn't make life easy.'

'No. It was hell.'

'It was.'

Maxine reckoned that might have to do as an apology. 'Maybe we've weathered the worst of the storm.'

'I hope so.'

Maxine got up from her chair and went to the door.

'Where are you going?' asked Gordon.

'I thought I'd move my stuff back into our room. Let's start afresh – after all I honestly don't think anything else can go wrong, can it.'

As she was ferrying her belongings from the spare room back to the master bedroom her mobile in her jeans' pocket pinged. Miranda. What on earth did she want?

Can Olivia and I see you tomorrow? Need to talk about your paintings x

Something to do with the exhibition, she thought. Well, given that it was only a fortnight away there were probably a number of things that needed sorting out.

Of course, she texted back. Coffee here? Ten?

Xx was the reply.

When Maxine woke up the next morning, she realised how much she had missed sleeping next to her husband. She rolled over and spooned against him.

'Morning,' he yawned.

Maxine kissed his shoulder. 'Morning,' she replied. 'Tea?'

'No, not just yet. Don't spoil the moment.'

She stayed snuggled next to him for a while more and heard his breathing deepen before a gentle snore whiffled over the duvet. Very gently she eased herself away and out from under the covers before she grabbed her dressing gown and padded down to the kitchen to put the kettle on. No more making tea in the altogether, she thought, or not for the foreseeable future, not with Abi and Marcus in the house. But that was going to pass and not a moment too soon. Oh, for the quiet life again when they could please themselves and their house had been their own. As she waited for the water to boil, she thought back to the day, back around Easter, when she'd been caught by Abi, drinking milk from the container and wearing diddly-squat. Four months in actual time but a lifetime in events.

She made the tea and returned to the bedroom where Gordon was still sleeping. And why not? It was still early, but with her friends visiting for coffee and aware that she hadn't managed to finish the housework the day before, Maxine felt she needed to get up and get on. Besides, with Abi and Marcus in the next bedroom there was no chance of any connubial relations to celebrate their reconciliation. She put Gordon's mug on his bedside table and slipped into the en-suite to take a quick shower. On her return to the bedroom, wrapped in a towel he was sitting up in bed sipping his tea.

'Why the urgency?'

'Because I've got friends coming for coffee, I haven't hoovered the carpets, I don't think we've got any decent biscuits in the house so I need to pop out and get some and all this has to be done by ten.'

'You still don't want to visit Mum, then?'

'Given how things were between your mother and I at our last encounter I don't think my presence would be helpful.'

'She—' Gordon started to protest but Maxine cut across him.

'It won't be.'

'Maybe. And there's no point in both of us wasting a whole day. I'm really not convinced she's got a clue that anyone's there. I sit there because I feel I ought to – that the staff will think I don't care about her if I don't but I don't think I'm achieving anything.' Poor Gordon sounded sad and helpless. He sighed. 'I suppose, if Mum is still out of it, having been seen to do my duty, I might come back at lunchtime. It'd be nice to go to the pub together.'

Maxine raised an eyebrow. 'A show of solidarity in front of Ella?' she queried.

Gordon went brick-red. 'No... I just thought it'd be good to get back into the old routine. Anyway, it's usually Belinda behind the bar on a Sunday.'

'Which is true. Yes, I'd like that. I'll meet you there – twelve thirty.'

'It's a date.'

Going to the pub was a tiny glimpse of their old routine and it made Maxine feel quietly happy – like she did when she saw snowdrops or daffs in the spring. The first signs of things getting better after a long winter of gloom.

32

Two hours later, Maxine's moment of quiet happiness was completely forgotten as she sat at the kitchen table and stared, open-mouthed at the images of her pictures on Miranda's laptop.

'So let me get this straight, you arranged for a professional art dealer to judge our exhibition with a sweetener that I might want him to represent me in selling my work.'

Miranda nodded. 'That's about the size of it.'

'And you didn't think to ask me first?'

'Because we thought you'd say no,' said Olivia.

'With good reason, as it turns out,' snapped Maxine pointing at her stolen pictures.

'But you're so good,' insisted Miranda.

'And completely under-rated,' added Olivia.

'Maybe I like it like that. It's a hobby. I like doing it, quietly, on my own but now…'

'We're sorry,' said Olivia.

Maxine stared at her two friends. 'I suppose you want me to forgive you. To say everything is fine, it doesn't matter you pinched a couple of my sketchbooks, that this was all done behind my back, is that it?'

'We were hoping that Dominic would value the stuff

in the exhibition and put a realistic price on your work. That way it might make your family appreciate just how good you are but also raise even more money for the local charities.'

Maxine shook her head. 'And now this guy is flogging my pictures – pictures of my friends and family – to all and sundry and cleaning up at my expense.' She expanded one of the pictures on the screen and peered at it. 'And that's my signature. How the hell...?'

'He forged it. He must've done,' said Miranda. 'We think he copied it off the watercolour you gave Heather. We showed him it and he took a photograph *to get an expert opinion* from another art dealer.'

'This gets worse and worse.' She slumped back in her chair. 'The only thing I'm grateful for right now is that my entire family is out and they needn't know exactly what's going on till I've got some sort of handle on it all.'

'You've got nothing to be ashamed of,' said Olivia. 'This is *our* fault.'

Maxine frowned deeply. 'It may not be *my* fault, I may be the innocent party here but I've still got this horrid feeling that I've been...' she paused, searching for the right word, '*violated* somehow.'

'Oh, Max.' Olivia was aghast. 'We *never* meant...'

'I know. And it's foolish. You're right I should be chuffed to bits there are people out there prepared to pay silly money for my pictures but I feel guilty about that too. They're being duped as well.'

'Now you're being silly,' said Miranda. 'If people are willing to pay that sort of money it's because they really like your work. Trust me there's a lot of choice out there, they don't have to.'

'Yeah, well...' Maxine didn't sound convinced. 'On the other hand we can't tell from this website if anyone has actually parted with any cash yet.'

'There's a police unit which deals with art crime,' said Miranda.

'They won't be interested in small fry like me.' Maxine's phone rang. She glanced at the caller ID. 'It's Gordon,' she said as she accepted the call. She listened for a few seconds before she said, 'Oh, dear God. I'm on my way.' She put the phone down. 'Anthea's just died.'

Later Maxine didn't have much memory of being frog-marched from her house to Miranda's and shoved in her friend's car. Considering she'd never liked her mother-in-law, Maxine was taken aback by the emotion that now swept through her. Maybe it was because she knew how dreadful Anthea's death would make Gordon feel. Maybe it was guilt that her last words to her mother-in-law had been angry ones.

'You ought to ring your daughter,' said Miranda as she pulled out of her drive and onto the Cattebury road.

'Yes, yes, I should.' She fumbled around in the bag to find her mobile and then hit the buttons to get Abi. Tearfully she broke the news and listened to Abi's sobbing response.

'Marcus and I will meet you at the h-h-hospital. We'll b-b-be as quick as we can.'

'Poor Gordon,' said Maxine after she'd blown her nose.

'He's going to be distraught. This wasn't unexpected but it's still a shock.'

'Deaths always are,' said Miranda. 'It doesn't matter how much time you've had to prepare – it's the finality.'

They drove in silence for a few miles.

'I'm sorry I was so angry about my pictures,' said Maxine. Miranda reached over the central consul and patted Maxine's knee. 'In retrospect you had every right to be. We got carried away with trying to make everyone else see what we could see – that you're really good.'

'I don't think so.'

'You see… there you go again, doing yourself down. You are. Honestly.'

'But you know what they say – *those who can, do; those who can't, teach.* And I'm a teacher. QED.'

'Bollocks,' said Miranda. 'Rembrandt had dozens of students and nobody can accuse him of not being any good.'

'I suppose.' Maxine didn't sound convinced.

'I mean,' said Miranda, 'when Olivia and I dug out your work not even Gordon or Abi seemed to take the slightest interest in your portfolio. I'm sure you love them to bits and they you, but it was *so* telling they thought it was *your little hobby* and not worthy of any sort of attention.'

Maxine shrugged. 'But it is… *my little hobby*.'

'Not if you can sell your stuff for real money.'

Signs for the hospital began to appear at the roadside.

'Nearly there,' said Maxine with relief. 'And we don't need the money – real or otherwise.'

'That's not the point. I don't suppose Hockney needs the cash but he still paints because his fans want to see new work and it's what he does.' Miranda turned into the hospital grounds.

'Now you're being fanciful. I don't have fans.'

'You might now.' She slowed the car right down to a crawl as she was confronted by signs with so much information on them it was almost impossible to pick out what was relevant to her. 'Where to?'

'Take the next right. Drop me at reception – it'll be perfect.'

The indicator ticked and a few seconds later they were outside the front door.

'Think about what I said,' Miranda instructed as Maxine unbuckled her belt and jumped out. 'And I hope Gordon's not too devastated. His mum had a good and long life and a dignified death. I think that's what we'd all like.'

Maxine felt her eyes pricking as the reality of Anthea's death reasserted itself. 'Thanks for the lift and the pep-talk.' She slammed the door and raised her hand in farewell as Miranda drove away.

Over the following ten days Maxine had no chance to have any thoughts about painting, Dominic Harcourt or the town's inaugural art exhibition because, when she wasn't comforting a bereft Gordon, the pair of them were racing around trying to organise a funeral and sort out Anthea's affairs.

In order to do the latter, they drove north some days after her death to evaluate what might need doing. It transpired the answer to that question was 'a lot'. Maxine and Gordon had had no idea of the extent of the problem as, superficially, the house was neat and tidy; no hint of the chaos that lay beneath the polished mahogany and behind the doors of the closed up spare rooms. Once they had let themselves into the house and had started going through the various rooms, the scale of the job became apparent within the hour. Her filing system consisted of papers, bills or correspondence randomly stuffed into drawers, and the cupboards in the spare rooms and the attic seemed to be full of clothes that hadn't probably seen the light of day for decades and on which moths must have been feasting for a similar length of time. In amongst everything were some good bits of furniture and some nice silver but, other than that, Gordon and Maxine reckoned most of Anthea's possessions were fit only for the skip. There were moments of light relief as they found bizarre items that Anthea had squirrelled away: petrol coupons from the 1973 oil crisis; tins of soup with a forty-year-old 'best before' date; a suitcase containing old Tupperware boxes; a drawer full of liberty bodices. As each weird gem was unearthed, they found themselves laughing uproariously – their exaggerated mirth probably the release from the deep underlying sadness at having to do this job in the first place. They'd planned only to stay in the house overnight but as each hour passed the task seemed to get bigger rather than diminish.

Dot, Anthea's cleaner, and her gardener husband were stalwarts and helped out as much as they could with their local knowledge and contacts, organising the delivery of skips, getting in a local firm of house-clearance specialists, and sorting out a painter and decorator to freshen up the tired and dated decor. They also promised to be around to oversee the contractors when, Maxine and Gordon had to go back to Little Woodford to sort out final arrangements for the funeral on the Thursday and then get on with their own lives.

They were driving back home when Maxine's mobile pinged. She pulled it out of her handbag by her feet and stared at the screen. 'Bugger,' she muttered.

'Something the matter?' asked Gordon from the driving seat.

'Not really. That was a text from Olivia asking me if I'm going to be around for the art exhibition. Of course… it's this weekend. What with one thing and another I'd forgotten all about it.'

'Art exhibition?'

'Didn't I tell you about it?'

'Apparently not. What's it all about?'

'It's for the art club members.'

'Oh, them.' There were a couple of beats of silence. 'Is this why Olivia wanted to look in your studio some time back?'

'Yes.'

'I wondered if she'd told you. She and a mate of hers – someone called Miranda – wanted to look at your paintings. Only, they said I wasn't to say anything about it.'

'Yes, I know all about it – or, more accurately, I got to know about it finally.'

Gordon stared at the motorway ahead. 'They seemed quite excited about your stuff.'

'Don't sound so surprised.'

'Sorry.'

'I suppose I might as well tell you why I know about their

visit, why you were sworn to secrecy and why they took some of my sketchbooks. They took them to a London art dealer.'

That perked up Gordon. 'No kidding.' He sounded impressed.

'No, I'm not. And the reason for the subterfuge was they didn't want me to be disappointed if my work didn't turn out to be quite as saleable as they thought it might be.'

'And...?'

'And it turns out my pictures really are rather good and very saleable.'

'But that's great!'

'But sadly, the dealer they took them to turns out to be a complete and utter shyster who has nicked a whole book of landscapes and portraits and he's selling prints of my pictures fraudulently on the internet.'

Gordon turned and stared at his wife unaware that the car was veering out of its lane. The blaring of a horn brought him back to his senses and he swerved back on course. 'You what?'

Maxine told him what she knew.

'And he's charging how much? For prints?'

Maxine repeated the sums involved.

'Fuck me,' whispered Gordon. 'For *your* paintings?'

'You're sounding surprised again.'

'Sorry. Sorry,' he repeated. 'I've just never thought of you as—'

'A proper painter? Someone with any talent?'

'No. No, of course not. But you're an art teacher.'

'Stop digging,' said Maxine, more amused than disappointed.

Gordon lapsed into an embarrassed silence for a few miles. 'So,' he said, 'this art exhibition…?'

'It's at the town hall on Saturday and it's so the art club members can exhibit some of their work and we'll be selling the paintings with some of the proceeds going to local charities.'

'Are you flogging your work?'

'That's the plan.'

'How much for?'

'Given what that git Dominic thinks a mere print is worth I did think of asking rather more for an original.'

Gordon whistled.

'But then, this is Little Woodford so I thought I'd be more realistic.'

'How realistic.'

'Two hundred – each.'

'Still a tidy sum. Fancy your paintings being worth real money.'

'You've started digging again.'

33

The funeral was a low key affair at the local crem attended by the immediate family, Dot and her husband and Pearl. Anthea's remaining friends in her village were too old and frail themselves to travel and almost everyone else in her ancient address book had died or had gone ga-ga. It was sad that there were so few people to celebrate her life but they were comforted by the fact that, as Miranda had pointed out to Maxine, she'd had a 'good death'.

The mourners returned to the house for a buffet lunch and the seven of them sat around Maxine's big kitchen eating sandwiches, drinking wine or soft drinks depending on who had to drive, and reminiscing about Anthea until Pearl left to go back to work – 'They could only give me a couple of hours off' – and Dot and her husband hit the motorway hoping to get the worst of the journey over before the rush hour struck. Abi helped her mother put clingfilm over the remaining food and to stack the dishwasher.

'There,' said Abi, as she put in a tablet and slammed shut the door. 'Anything else?'

'No,' said Maxine looking around her and instantly spotting a plate that had been missed. She put it in the sink to wait for the next dishwasher program. 'How's your house?'

Instantly Abi was wary. 'Are you going to have a go at me about moving out?'

Maxine glanced at a half full bottle of red wine on the counter and was tempted to pour herself a glass. Did everything have to be so confrontational? 'I'm asking because I'm interested.'

'Really? Your interest usually stops short at how soon we can move out.'

'Yes, that's partly true but surely you want to move out too?'

'Too right we do.'

She glanced again at the bottle. No, don't. 'Has Steven given you any indication of when that will be?'

'September.'

'Next month.'

'I suppose.'

'That's great news.'

'If there aren't any more hitches.'

'I think,' said Maxine, 'Steven would have found anything else by now.'

'Maybe.'

'Are you going to go over this weekend?'

'No point really. We did a lot to the garden the last time and we can't do anything to the inside while the plaster is still wet.'

'Plaster – that sounds like a big step forward.'

Abi nodded.

'So, if you're at a loose end this weekend—'

'God, what do you want us to do now?'

'Nothing. But there's an art exhibition in town and some of my pictures are going to be in it.'

'Yours?'

Like father like daughter, thought Maxine. 'Yes, mine. I thought you might like to come along and have a look.' Abi looked sceptical. 'There's no entrance fee.'

'Oh, well... Maybe.' Then, 'Did Dad say something about you getting ripped off by some con artist?'

'I've not been ripped off like I've had my bank account hacked but...' and Maxine told her daughter about Dominic.

'And you've let him get away with it?'

'Not really, but Granny died just as I found out about it and Daddy and I had a lot to deal with.'

'Best you get back on it.'

'And how do you suggest I do that? It's not as if he's selling my pictures from a physical shop. I can hardly go and knock on the door of an internet site and demand reparation.'

'There must be a way.'

'If you're so clever, you do it.'

'God, Mum! As if I haven't got enough on my plate what with work and the house and everything. The thing that amazes me is that he thought your pictures were worth nicking.' And with that Abi went upstairs to her bedroom leaving Maxine reaching for a glass.

The summer weather broke the day of the art exhibition and the glorious sunshine they'd experienced for weeks gave way to drizzle. Gordon was glad because his garden had been suffering in the drought but Maxine reckoned that the chances of the townsfolk turning out in numbers in the rain to look at some pictures had been drastically reduced.

Never mind, she told herself as she walked across the soggy nature reserve. People hadn't bothered to look at her pictures in the past; it wouldn't make much difference to her if they didn't now. Except Miranda and Olivia had put a lot of effort into organising this exhibition and it would be a shame if their endeavours went unnoticed and unrecognised. She felt a twinge of guilt as she walked; she should have done more to help, and she would have done if she hadn't been wrapped up in Anthea's death. She hadn't even been over to the town hall to help them hang the pictures. She'd make it up now by giving *all* her proceeds to charity and by helping with the clearing up. It was the least she could do.

She got to the town hall an hour before the exhibition was due to start and was surprised to see a number of trucks parked in the market square. That won't be popular with people coming into the town to shop later on, she thought, as she pushed open the front door. As she went in she could hear movement in the main chamber and made her way up the stairs.

'Cooee,' she called, her voice echoing on the bare stone treads. 'Miranda? Olivia?'

She pushed open the door to the council chamber and found a young man with a massive reel of cabling busy plugging in some seriously large lights that were spaced in between the big display boards where the pictures were hung. The uniform frames made the exhibition look incredibly professional – Maxine was impressed.

'Gosh,' she said before she turned her attention to the young man. 'And you are?'

The lad put down his cable and stuck out a hand. 'Josh. Josh Barratt – I'm from *Upper Circle*.'

'Who?'

'The arts programme.'

Maxine was none the wiser. 'What?'

'*Upper Circle* – it's on TV. We cover the arts, everything; film, theatre, literature, exhibitions, the lot.'

'And?'

'And we're doing a programme about undiscovered talent.'

'But... why?'

'I dunno. I'm just the lighting man. Me? I obey orders, go where I'm told and fix the lights. You'll need to ask the producer. Now, if you'll excuse me.'

As he turned away Maxine could hear several more sets of footsteps on the stairs and then a group of half a dozen people entered the chamber, including Miranda. Apart from Miranda, who was dressed in her customary white jeans and black top, the others seemed to be trying to emulate butterflies with jewel colours, brilliant scarves, and oversized jewellery.

'Maxine, you're early,' exclaimed Miranda.

'I thought I ought to help as I've done nothing so far.'

'You've had other things to think about,' said Miranda.

'And what's going on? Who are all these people?'

'A TV crew.'

'But why?'

'They're going to do a programme about the art club.'

'But... why?' Maxine was completely dumbfounded.

'Because your art club is representative of art clubs up and down the country and is a perfect example of amateurs being a huge source of unrecognised talent. Think *MasterChef* with paints rather than food.'

'But why *our* art club.'

'Because I asked them to come.'

'But...'

'Because I let you down. Because it was my fault your paintings were stolen, because the police weren't interested—'

'I told you they wouldn't care about an amateur.'

'And because I have contacts in the trade.'

'Really?'

Miranda nodded. 'The first rule of anything has always been it's who you know, not what you know. And I know all sorts of useful people.'

'How?'

'Oh... one just does. But, in this particular instance, via a chap called Emanuel Holland who owns a real pukka gallery. Sadly, I knew he wouldn't want your watercolours as he doesn't take contemporary works or I'd have offered your portfolio to him. But, he has a huge circle of friends and acquaintances especially in the media so – Bob's your uncle.' Miranda grinned. 'The thing about the arts is that most success is predicated on talent and luck – with luck being the most important and most elusive aspect. You need that lucky break to get you from standing in the wings to being in the spotlight. And today,' and Miranda gestured to some of the huge free-standing lighting rigs in the town hall, 'I have every intention of putting your work in the spotlight. Well, and the rest of the art club's stuff too, of course, but as you are the stand-out star of the show I think the focus will be on your pictures.'

'But... but I'm ... I don't... No!'

'Why not?' Miranda was baffled.

'Because... because...'

'Because you feel you're not worthy? Because you're not good enough?' Miranda stared at Maxine. 'Balderdash!'

Miranda's vehemence silenced Maxine.

'Now then,' continued Miranda, 'I need to introduce you to some folk and in particular to Isadora, the producer and she's also their main interviewer.' She took Maxine's arm and led her to one of the bright butterflies who were gathered in the corner of the chamber, pouring over some paperwork.

'Isadora, this is Maxine.'

The woman, a thirty-something stick insect with purple and turquoise eye make-up which matched her purple and turquoise hair highlights and contrasted with her vermilion and yellow kaftan turned and beamed at Maxine.

'Wonderful,' she trilled. 'So delightful to meet you. Miranda has been telling me all about you and your club. Such talent.'

'They're a great bunch,' said Maxine with enthusiasm.

'I was talking about you.'

Maxine could feel herself blushing. 'No...'

'No false modesty, please.'

Maxine wanted to tell her there was nothing false about her modesty but decided that there was no point.

'Now then, we're going to need to interview you – just a few words about why you set up the art club, where you meet, how often you exhibit your work, general stuff about it and the members. And we need you to sign a release form allowing us to broadcast the material we film.'

'I suppose. I don't know about the members all being happy about their work being included.'

'Oh, don't worry about that; that's all been taken care of.'

'They all know about this?'

Isadora blinked slowly. 'Of course. You can't think this is all spur of the moment.'

Maxine had assumed it was. Surely an arts magazine programme had to be prepared to respond to events as and when they happened?

'Miranda proposed this to us almost a couple of weeks ago, didn't you, Miranda.'

While she'd been up at Anthea's house Miranda had been organising this. And hadn't shared a word of it to her although, clearly, the rest of the art club had been in on it. Why?

Maxine turned to Miranda. 'Why didn't you tell me?'

'Because you'd have said *no*. Honestly, Maxine, sometimes you're your own worst enemy. I reckoned that if I produced a *fait accompli* you'd have no choice.' She gestured to the hall, the lights, the crew that were setting everything up. '*Et voila.*'

She was right.

'Now then,' said Isadora, 'I think we need to give you a quick once-over with some powder and lippy.' She clicked her fingers and a young kid with a toolbag of make-up brushes hung around her waist appeared. 'Darling, work your magic on Maxine, here.'

'But...'

'But nothing,' said Isadora. 'TV lights are very unforgiving. Giselle will make sure you don't look too hagg— Giselle will make sure you look your best.'

Maxine allowed herself to be led away into a quiet corner where Giselle sat her down and began to work. It was going to be rather more than lippy and powder, Maxine realised, but it was rather nice to have someone gussie her up.

After the calm of being made up, which took a good quarter of an hour, it all got rather hectic. First Maxine was interviewed and each question seemed to involve several takes, then they did some cut-away shots so it looked as if they had more than one camera, then Maxine was asked to talk about some of the paintings in the exhibition and halfway through all of this the public was allowed in. First it was a trickle, mostly friends and relatives of the art club members but then, as word spread around the town that a TV company was filming, it was as if someone opened the sluice gates and a flood poured in.

Finally, Isadora finished with her and Maxine was free to grab a cuppa from the WI table in the corner.

'Isn't this a triumph?' enthused Heather as she handed over a large mug of tea to Maxine.

'It's all a bit bonkers if you ask me.'

'Miranda says loads of the paintings have been sold. The

local charities are going to really benefit from this. You must be thrilled.'

Maxine wasn't sure she was. It was all ridiculously surreal. She finished her tea and went to look at the pictures that the club members had chosen to exhibit. Framed, mounted and beautifully lit, some of them were really rather good. Maxine felt a bubble of pride that her little group had come so far in a few months. Just think what they might achieve in a few years. And, gratifyingly many of the pictures had little red dots on the frames indicating they'd been sold. She looked at the price tags pinned discreetly to the side of the exhibits. Mostly they seemed to have been valued at between twenty to fifty pounds – although the frames had to be worth at least a tenner of that, thought Maxine. She drifted along the display stands and saw her work at the end. All three pictures had dots. Coo. She felt even more chuffed and somewhat relieved. It would have been rather embarrassing if no one had wanted to buy her work. And then she realised almost simultaneously that she'd not discussed with Miranda or Olivia what price tag she'd decided on. She peered at the little paper label of the nearest one and her jaw dropped. Five hundred pounds! And someone had paid it?! Hell's teeth. She looked at the other two price tags and read the same.

'They were almost the first to go,' said Miranda behind her.

Maxine spun round. 'But that's a ridiculous amount of money.'

'It isn't for pictures of that quality,' said Miranda.

'Come off it.' But Maxine couldn't deny that someone

– or even several people – had been prepared to shell out for her work.

'Well done, darling,' said Gordon, joining them. He had Abi and Marcus in tow. 'We'd have congratulated you earlier but you were busy being interviewed.'

'Thank you.' Maxine still felt quite dazed.

'Darling!' Judith bowled up, arms outstretched. 'What a clever, *clever* big sister I've got. I can't tell you how proud I am of you. And look,' she tapped one of the price tags with her ruby-red fingernail. 'Look at the prices you've commanded.'

'I know. It's mad, isn't it?' But Maxine couldn't help grinning broadly. She looked around at her smiling family. They weren't such a bad lot and it was lovely to be appreciated. It made up for all those times of *not* being appreciated.

'And it must make up for that con artist nicking your other stuff?' said Gordon.

'Yea, it rather does. Although I'm still livid he did, and there seems to be no redress but worse things happen to people.'

'Well done, Mum,' said Abi. 'I've got to admit I'm a bit surprised at how good people think you are but hey, they do. No accounting for taste. And talking of taste and people who rate your work... have you got anywhere with that slimeball who nicked your stuff?'

Maxine sighed. 'I haven't a clue where to start. Why do you ask?'

'Because you should. He's making money out of you and it's not right.'

'No, it's not, but what's done is done.'

'Which means you've not done anything.'

'No.'

Abi sighed. 'Mum, you're hopeless. Thank God you can knock out some more pictures to recoup your losses.'

Maxine didn't know whether to laugh or cry.

34

Abi and Marcus left the exhibition and trudged back across the nature reserve to the house. The rain had stopped but the sky was overcast and a sharp breeze harried the lowering clouds swiftly across it while the tall, tawny grasses that fringed the paths dripped into the puddles. Abi thrust her hands into her jacket pockets.

'Mum is hopeless,' she told Marcus.

'That's being unfair. Her paintings were lovely. I thought you said she wasn't any good.'

'No, I wasn't talking about her art stuff. I mean about going after the bloke that nicked her other pictures.'

'But she's right – what can she do?'

'If he's selling them on-line there has to be a way of getting in touch with him. She hasn't even looked at that option.'

'Look, if your mother wants to let it go, I don't think it's for you to interfere.'

'No? Well, from what Olivia told me, this bloke could be making thousands out of Mum. Our family should have that money, not him.'

Marcus noticed that Abi hadn't said *my Mum should have that money.* 'If you're so keen, you do it.'

'Mum said that. Like I've got the time.'

'It's only an internet search.'

'I don't even know his name.'

'Then find out – those two mates of your ma's, Olivia and the other one, they'll know.'

'I suppose.'

'It'd be a way of thanking your ma for putting us up all this time.'

Abi snorted. 'Huh, she should be thanking us for everything *we* did when Granny was in hospital.'

Marcus sighed heavily. 'Yes, dear.'

The next morning, after breakfast, Abi announced she was going for a walk.

'Shouldn't be too long,' she said as she put on her jacket and let herself out of the front door.

Maxine continued to load the dishwasher as Marcus said he was off up to their house to check on the progress made the previous week and Gordon disappeared into the garden to see what effect the rain had had on his wilting herbaceous border.

Abi strode along the road and headed for The Grange. As she crossed the road, she heard the church clock strike eleven. Not too early to be visiting on a Sunday she decided. She walked up the drive trying to work out how long it had been since she'd last been here, when she and Tamsin had gone to school together. Ten years, fifteen? Ages, anyway. Not that she'd been *that* friendly with Tamsin – Tamsin Laithwaite was a deal too set on getting her own way if her ideas or plans differed from Abi's. A bossy-boots, like her mother, thought Abi. She rang the bell.

She was taken aback when the door was opened by someone other Tamsin's mum, Olivia. But she recognised her – the woman who'd got in the way then they'd been moving stuff out of her mother's studio.

'Oh, sorry...' she started. 'Only...'

'Yes?'

'Is Olivia in?'

'Olivia Laithwaite. Sorry, she hasn't lived here for ages.' The woman stared at her. 'You're Abi Larkham, aren't you?'

Abi nodded as a penny dropped. 'Of course, Mum said something about Olivia moving only I forgot. I was friends with one of her daughters and used to come here a lot when I was at school. But, actually, you might be able to help. You and Olivia came to see Mum's pictures in her studio, didn't you and you set up that exhibition together too?'

'We did.'

'So you must know about that awful man who nicked Ma's stuff.'

'I do. Look, would you like to come in.'

Abi nodded and followed Miranda inside. 'You've got the advantage on me – I'm sorry but I don't know your name.'

'Miranda – Miranda Osborne.'

'Nice to meet you... properly.'

Miranda led her to the kitchen area. Abi gazed at it with undisguised envy and instantly felt a pang of dissatisfaction with the one she'd chosen and which she'd been so excited about. *This* was a dream kitchen – hers was nowhere near, not in comparison.

Miranda pushed on a concealed drawer and it magically slid open. She picked out a business card and handed it to

Abi. 'This is the man – don't bother with the number, it doesn't work. And he also goes by the names of Miles Smith and Dominic Smith. But it's Miles Smith on the website selling the paintings.'

'What have you done about it?'

'I've informed the Met Police's Art and Antiques unit.'

'Oh?'

'I'm not holding out much hope – the unit is very small and, sadly, I'm afraid your mother's paintings don't command the sort of money that makes it likely for them to take an interest.'

'Oh.' Abi got out her phone and Googled Miles Smith. A montage of the pictures in the virtual art gallery filled her screen including several of her mother's. At the bottom of the page was an email address. She pointed to it. 'Have you tried this?'

Miranda shook her head. 'No.'

'Okay,' said Abi. 'I've got an idea. It may not work and I'll have to get my partner to use his email to write to him – can't risk him twigging I'm the oh-so-great Maxine Larkham's daughter. Although why there's such an interest in her stuff beats me.'

'Really?' Miranda's voice hardened. 'Well, if that's everything...'

Abi found herself being ushered back towards the front door.

'And may I offer you a word of advice,' said Miranda as she opened it and Abi stepped over the threshold.

'Of course.'

'You obviously know nothing about art and wouldn't recognise talent if it introduced itself and shook your hand, so please don't denigrate your mother's work. It makes you look stupid, which is, frankly, extremely unattractive.' And with that she clicked the door shut leaving Abi utterly lost for words.

By the time Marcus had returned from the cottage she'd regained them and, in the privacy of their bedroom, the pitch of her voice made Marcus wince more than once as she relayed, with increasing indignation, what Miranda had said to her.

'I mean, how *dare* she?'

'You have been quite harsh on your mum,' said Marcus, carefully.

Abi had been expecting unalloyed support and got defensive. 'No, I haven't.'

'When you suggested we could take over her studio you said her art was just some third-rate watercolours.'

'So?'

'So, they're not, are they?'

'Well, I don't know about art, do I?'

'Then Miranda has a point – you shouldn't sneer at something you don't understand.'

Abi was feeling raw and hard done by after the strip that Miranda had torn off her and now Marcus's unexpected support of Miranda had the effect of vinegar being dripped onto the wound.

'I didn't sneer,' she yowled.

'You did. You do… all the time. I haven't said anything before because I love you very much and I put it all down to the strain of the move and the renovations and everything else but it's got to stop, Abi. You've been horrid to your mother, you've taken her for granted, you've talked to her in a way I'd never dream talking to my mum.'

Abi started to sob. 'She's been horrid to me too.'

'She's had the patience of a saint and if she *has* snapped then it's because you pushed her to it.'

Her crying ramped up a notch. 'How can you say that? How can you take her side?' Her face was going red and blotchy with tears.

'Because it's the truth. Look at yourself, Abi, take a long hard look at yourself, because Miranda is right – you're becoming very unattractive. And if you don't change your ways I don't know if I can stick this relationship out.' And with that he stomped out of the room leaving Abi sobbing on the bed.

For the rest of the morning Abi stayed in her room with little to occupy herself except thoughts of what Miranda and Marcus had said. She was very subdued and quiet when she came down to Sunday lunch.

Maxine plonked a large puff-pastry-wrapped sausage shape on the table. 'Vegetarian beef Wellington,' she announced.

'Thank you, Mum. It looks delicious.'

Maxine's gaze flew to her daughter. 'Are you all right, Abi?'

'Of course.'

'Fine.' Maxine didn't sound convinced as she sliced the pie and handed the portions round. There was an uneasy silence as everyone tucked in. The conversation, such as it was, was sporadic and largely consisted of comments like 'pass the spuds, please,' or 'anyone for anymore?'

When the plates were empty, Abi got up and told her mother to stay put – she and Marcus would clear up.

'Go and sit in the sitting room. We'll bring you coffee,' she added.

Her parents, looking bemused and bewildered, did as they were told.

In the kitchen with the door shut, Marcus began stacking the dirty plates in the dishwasher. Abi put a hand on his arm to stop him.

'We need to talk.'

Marcus straightened up. 'Okay.'

'I'm sorry.'

'Really?'

'You're right – I have been a bit of a cow recently.'

'A bit?'

'All right, a total cow. It's just…'

'Yes?' he encouraged.

'Okay, I'll admit it, I'm a control freak and what with the house – our house – and living here… I've *lost* control. I suppose my coping mechanism was to get all angry with everything.'

'And everyone.'

She nodded. 'I want to make it up to you.'

'Not just me,' Marcus reminded her.'

'No, I know. I think I've got a plan for Mum and that git and how to rescue her work.' She gave Marcus a brief outline. 'What do you think?'

Marcus considered it for a moment or two. 'I think it might work. But, when you do finally go to meet him, you're going to have to take Miranda. She's the one who knows Dominic or Miles or whoever he is, she's the one who showed him the paintings and let him borrow them so she's the one who can say he definitely nicked them.'

'No, no way. I can't see that woman again. Not after what she said to me.'

Marcus raised his eyebrows. 'If you want to atone, you're going to have to or I don't think your plan's got a chance.'

35

Over the next week Abi considered what Marcus had said about needing Miranda's help but she couldn't face another encounter. She reasoned that there was no urgency as Miles or Dominic or whatever he was calling himself wasn't going to do away with the evidence – not if it was providing him with an income. Although there was no way of checking his sales – there wasn't a ranking to show which pictures he was offering were his best-sellers like on an Amazon page. But as the days slipped by it became harder to pluck up the courage and easier to let the whole matter slip onto a back burner. On top of that she had her day job and, because the major structural work had been done on the house, she and Marcus were now bombarded with daily emails from Steven about where they wanted electrical sockets, light switches, what sort of door handles, what colour grouting...

The first week passed with Abi making no move and then the next and August slipped quietly into September. The excitement of the art exhibition and the filming by the TV crew waned, along with Abi's indignation about her mother's work being ripped off.

'Do I gather,' said Marcus, as they drove home from work

one evening, the autumnal sun already low in the sky, 'that you're going to do nothing about that crooked art dealer?'

Abi coloured slightly. 'I... well... it's not that easy.'

'That's not what you said when you told me your plan.'

'Maybe I was over-confident.'

'Maybe you're running scared of Miranda.'

'No.' Abi saw Marcus glance across at her. 'Maybe a bit.'

'You're going to have to move soon. Once that TV programme gets aired you may find that chummy gets sufficient enquiries about your mum's work and scores enough on-line sales that he won't be interested in what you're offering. If he's making thousands of pounds through the internet, a paltry fifteen hundred quid mightn't be worth the risk of revealing his actual address.'

'I suppose.'

'I don't think there's any *suppose* about it. Your mum needs her portfolio back so *she* can make the killing on the back of the publicity the programme will bring, not him.'

Abi sighed. 'We don't know the exposure will do any good.'

'You want to risk it?'

'No,' she conceded.

'So, you'll contact him tonight, as you planned, and if he responds you're going to promise me you'll go and see Miranda,' he said sternly.

'OK, I promise.'

Once they'd got in, Marcus opened up his laptop and found Miles's website. He clicked on the *contact me* button before he swivelled the machine round to face Abi.

'Off you go,' he said.

Abi flexed her fingers and took a deep breath.

'What are you waiting for?' asked Marcus.

'I need to think how Granny Anthea would write to him,' she said. 'I need to channel my inner *old lady*. She stared at the screen for a second or two before she began to type, her fingers flying over the keyboard.

Dear Mr Smith, I am very interested in some of your limited edition prints but I regret I am unable to buy them as things stand. I am old and old-fashioned and I do not believe in credit cards or on-line transfers of funds which are the only options you allow me in order to purchase them. There are three prints I am particularly interested in with a total value of £1500. If I were to send you a cheque along with details of the three pictures would you send them to me in return? Obviously, I would allow you the time for the cheque to clear first. I appreciate payment by cheque is almost unheard of in this modern age but I would be most grateful if you would indulge an old lady this once. I look forward to hearing from you. Yours sincerely, Millicent Stockwell. P.S. I am using my son's laptop and email and he will pass your message back to me.

'There,' she said. 'What do you think?'

'I think that's just the ticket. I also think he's greedy enough to send you an address so you can send him the cheque.'

'Supposing it isn't his address – supposing it's *poste restante*, or a friend's house, or anything.'

'It's a risk, I agree. But as we're going to use the address to confront him rather than send him some dosh all we're risking is our time. If he's there, eureka, if he's not...' Marcus shrugged.

'Shall I press send?

'Go for it,' said Marcus planting an affectionate kiss on her forehead. 'Well done.'

The reply was waiting for them when they returned to their bedroom after supper. Abi's excitement that her quarry had taken the bait was tempered by the knowledge that she now had to face Miranda.

'Tonight,' ordered Marcus. 'Before you get cold feet.'

Too late for that, she thought as she trudged through the dark up the drive to her nemesis's front door and triggered a security light.

'Oh, it's you,' was the harsh greeting she got from Miranda.

'Hello, Miranda.'

'What can I do for you?'

'It's about Miles... Dominic – the art dealer bloke.'

'And?'

'I may have got somewhere.'

'Have you indeed?'

'I've got an address – Croydon.'

'Interesting, because I did a bit of digging too. I rang an ex-employer of his...' Miranda paused. 'Maybe you should come in.'

Abi stepped back over the threshold with a feeling she was a fly getting too close to a spider but, after her last encounter, she was too intimidated by Miranda to refuse.

'He used to work,' said Miranda, 'for an acquaintance of mine called Emanuel Holland – an art dealer. Emanuel still had his details on file including a photocopy of his passport and a couple of photocopies of utility bills to prove he wasn't some illegal immigrant when he was taken on.'

'And?'

'He was born in Merton, his real name is Dominic Smith and the address he supplied was for a place in Croydon. He obviously has an affinity with south London.' Miranda sounded bewildered.

'Whereabouts exactly?'

'I'll get the details,' said Miranda. She left Abi standing by the door as she disappeared across the huge living space to more concealed drawers. A minute later she was back with a file. 'To be honest, I thought you were going to give up on this. I was about to start making more enquiries myself. I had a message from Isadora yesterday – the producer and presenter; the programme is going to be screened in a couple of weeks, and I felt someone had to make a move sooner rather than later.' She showed Abi the address she had.

Abi's heart sank. 'It's not the same – he lied to me.'

'Or he's moved. He was let go from the Holland Gallery for financial impropriety a while back. Come,' ordered Miranda imperiously and she led Abi to the kitchen and pulled out a stool by the island and flipped open a Macbook. She clicked on an icon and Google Earth opened. 'Let's take a look,' she muttered to herself. She typed in the post code and the app zoomed down from the heavens to pinpoint a road in south London. 'And the other one...' she typed in a second code. 'Gone up in the world, hasn't he?' she observed to herself as the app swooshed across to another, smarter street. 'Who says crime doesn't pay?'

Abi peered over her shoulder. 'Nice.'

Miranda snorted. 'But not bought with legitimately earned money I'll be bound. I wonder how many people he's conned.' She swivelled round on the stool. 'How did you get his address?'

Abi told her about the email via his website.

'Good plan. Greed – it gets them every time. Can't resist another buck. Well done.'

'Will you come with me and Marcus to confront him – to get Mum's portfolio back? We don't know him, we've never met him. If he denies everything, we won't have a leg to stand on. But if you're there…'

'We ought to report it to the police – this is fraud.'

'But it'll take an age to get her pictures back if we do that – and the TV programme may go out before they make a move and he'll make even more money out of her.'

Miranda considered Abi's argument. 'You have a point. Legally, we only know *for sure* he's defrauding your mother – we can *surmise* that she's one in a long string of victims but we have no proof of that. I suppose, if we were to demand he returns her work and any unsold prints, we could be considered to be acting within the law, especially if he hands everything back voluntarily.'

'Really?'

'I'm not a criminal lawyer but I would say we have right on our side. And this is also a matter of copyright – your mother's. If he ceases and desists to use her work then we can say justice has been done.'

'Do you think we can get him to agree?'

'He's not a thug, he's an art dealer. And there'll be three of us and probably only one of him. When are you going to go?'

'Saturday.'

'Count me in.'

★

Abi and Marcus didn't have much time to think about the up-coming confrontation as the days preceding it were filled with their day jobs and trips to their house in the evenings to check out the finer details of the work that remained.

'It's looking good,' said Marcus, his voice echoing in the unfurnished rooms. Upstairs, the walls had been painted uniformly white and the carpet fitters had put down pale grey carpets throughout, while the new en-suite and the pre-existing bathroom had been kitted out with white suites, white tiles and subtly pattered floor coverings. The house looked terrific and smelt of fresh paint.

Abi was going through each room with a notepad and pen, logging any defects and faults, not that there were many, and ticking off completed jobs on the decreasing list.

'It'll be perfect when it's finished,' she said happily. 'Worth all the heartache—'

'And the money.'

'Thank God for house insurance.'

The pair padded down the stairs and into the now bright, light hall area, rid of its dark panelling and through to the huge living space that incorporated a kitchen in the corner.

'I can't wait to move in,' said Abi.

'Two more weeks,' said Marcus.

Abi grinned at him. 'That's what we thought back in April.'

'This time it really is. Your parents will be pleased.'

The mention of her parents made Abi's smile fade as it brought something else to the forefront of her mind. 'And tomorrow we're off to Croydon to get Ma's pictures.'

'I know. Got to hope it all goes according to plan because

if it does, and we can get those pictures, it'll be a good way of making everything up to her.'

Abi started to make a tart retort. 'Considering what Mum...' She stopped, remembering Marcus's previous comments about being sneery and unattractive. 'You're right. It can't have been easy for her and Dad either.'

Marcus gave her a squeeze.

'We're off out for the day,' said Abi to her parents after breakfast.

'Somewhere nice?' asked Maxine.

'London.'

'That'll be lovely for you. Have fun.'

Abi didn't tell her that *fun* was very unlikely as they headed out to the car. Two minutes later they'd picked up Miranda and were headed for Croydon.

'Not a place I know,' observed their passenger from the back seat. It was mid-morning when they arrived outside the address. The street consisted of a long row of identical Edwardian terraced houses, each with a tiny front garden, a porch over a front door, and three windows – two upstairs, one downstairs – facing the street. They had to park the car a couple of roads away as the kerbside was crowded with the residents' ones. Marcus and Miranda hung back a few yards leaving Abi to ring the bell – they didn't want Dominic recognising Miranda and they felt Marcus might be intimidating. A woman on her own... not scary. But Marcus and Miranda were ready to leap forward as soon as the door opened. If it did.

As she pushed the bell, Abi's heart was thumping even harder than when she'd visited Miranda the second time. She waited for a good few seconds before the door opened.

'Yes,' said the man who answered it.

'I'm Maxine Larkham's daughter,' snarled Abi stepping forward, ready to put her foot in the door as Marcus and Miranda rushed the ten yards along the pavement from where they'd been waiting.

Dominic,' said Miranda as she turned up the path.

Dominic's worried expression turned to one of shock. He made to shut the door but Abi had got her foot in the way and a second later she was joined by the other two and between them they were able to push it open wide. Dominic rushed backwards along the hall.

'I can explain,' he whimpered as he cowered against the newel post.

'What?' said Abi. 'About being a thief, a fraudster and a crook?'

'Yes... I mean no...'

'You've stolen Mum's pictures and you forged her signature.'

'I didn't mean any harm.'

Abi rolled her eyes. 'Bull shit. You can add *liar* to my previous list.'

Dominic seemed to shrink further.

Miranda stepped forward. 'You're lucky we haven't got the police with us. But that could change if you don't give us what we want.'

'Which is?'

'Maxine's paintings and all the prints you've had made. Every last one. Because if I ever find you've deceived me,

I'll have the fraud squad round here so fast they'll break the sound barrier. Do I make myself clear?' Maxine glared at him.

Dominic nodded, his face ashen.

'So where is everything?'

'Through here.' Cowed, Dominic led them through a scruffy galley kitchen with dirty crockery piled in the sink and a smell of stale cooking into a tatty conservatory at the back with several pasting tables scattered around the space. On each table was a pile of prints – some Miranda recognised, Maxine's. In a corner were a couple of dozen cardboard tubes ready to mail out the rolled-up pictures.

'And the originals?'

Dominic pulled the sketchbook out from under the prints.

'And is this everything? Because if you're lying…'

'I'm not, I swear.'

'There don't seem to be very many,' said Miranda as she leafed through them. 'How many did you have printed of each?'

'Just twenty – to see how they sold.'

Miranda sniffed. 'I'm not sure I believe you.'

'It's true. I can show you the bill from the printer.' Dominic began scrabbling around in a pile of paperwork near the cardboard tubes. 'Here.' He sounded really scared.

Miranda took it and looked at it. 'This could relate to any of these pictures.' She gestured the other piles of prints.

'But it doesn't. Look at the date. A week after we met.'

'Hmm. I'll believe you. But my threat still stands. One whiff of you ever selling anything of Maxine's ever again and I'll blow the whistle so loud you'll be deaf for life. Understand.'

Dominic nodded vehemently.

The three of them began to gather up the prints and the sketchbook, the big A3 sheets of paper being awkward and unwieldy. It took them a couple of minutes before they were sure they had everything.

They headed towards the front door.

'And I hope,' said Miranda to Dominic as they reached it, 'I never have to have anything to do with your ever again. Scum of the earth, like you, should never have been allowed out of the primordial swamp.' She swept out followed by the other two. Once they'd reached the car, popped the boot and dumped the piles of art work they indulged in a group hug.

'You were magnificent,' said Marcus. 'Even I was scared of you.'

'I'll take that as a compliment,' said Miranda. 'But it was a team effort and we got a result.' She slid into the front seat of the car, which Abi had rather thought of as her place – being the driver's partner – but she wasn't going to argue. Having witnessed another example Miranda's capabilities, she wasn't going to risk it.

36

The first weekend in October was going to be, thought Maxine, one for a lot of celebrating. And considering she'd already had quite a *big* celebration when Miranda, Marcus and Abi had returned, triumphant, with her pictures she was starting to feel thoroughly spoilt. Not something she'd felt for quite a while – it made a pleasant change from feeling like the put-upon underdog. But, with Marcus and Abi finally moving out on the day when the TV programme was going to be screened in the evening, she felt it was only right that she and Gordon had planned to pop a champagne cork – or two – on their own. Home alone with fizz! It seemed more – a lot more – than the best part of six months since Maxine had been feeling smug about her life given that, apart from Abi and Marcus moving in, they'd also had to deal with visits from Judith and the presence of Anthea. One way and another, since April, Maxine's spare rooms had been in almost constant use.

She couldn't wait to get back into their old weekend routine; lie-ins, pottering round the house and garden, a bit of painting, lazy lunches at the pub... Oh, the bliss of the quiet life.

She picked up her mid-morning tea off the counter and

wandered out into the garden, heading for her studio. The autumn colours in the nature reserve were starting to look spectacular – brown, russet, gold, bronze... Her fingers itched to have a go at capturing them. She opened the door and her phone pinged in the back pocket of her jeans. Belinda.

I've fixed up a tv in the function room. Fancy joining me and some regulars to watch your programme?

Oh. She and Gordon hadn't considered that. Fizz on their own, or celebratory drinks with a bunch of mates? She went to see what Gordon fancied.

'Sounds like a perfect excuse for a bit of a party,' he said, leaning on his spade in his vegetable patch. 'I know we planned a quiet night in but... well, this could be more fun.'

'I'll tell Belinda that we'll be there, shall I?'

'Sounds like a plan.'

The following evening, they made their way across the dark nature reserve with just the dim half-moon for illumination. Not that they needed much light – they knew the reserve so well they could almost have made the journey blindfold.

Maxine took Gordon's arm. 'I'm having second thoughts about this,' she admitted.

'Why?'

'Because they may have edited the programme to make us all look like complete numpties. Once you've signed that release form they can cut and paste and do anything with the footage; take things out of context, have a voice-over that is disparaging or plain rude – think *Come Dine With Me*. I kind of wish I'd never agreed to this and we'd stayed at home.'

'It'll be fine,' said Gordon, but inwardly he knew she might have a point.

They opened the door to the pub and were greeted by a huge press of people. Maxine recognised most them as they were either friends, pub regulars or members of her art club. Judith was there too, raising her glass in a toast, as were Heather, Olivia, Jacqui and Bex. She was relieved to see that there was one notable absence – no Ella.

'Drinks are on me,' said Belinda as she poured a large glass of red and a pint of Guinness.

'Don't be daft – you haven't seen the programme yet, it might be ghastly,' protested Maxine.

'You'll be a star, I know you will.'

But Maxine was still having doubts.

'Besides,' continued Belinda, 'you're famous already.'

'Don't be daft,' she said again.

'Honest. I Googled you straight after your exhibition and found you've got your own Wikipedia entry and then a whole bunch of your paintings came up. I even bought one. Look!' She produced a tube from under the bar and hauled out one of Dominic's prints – Maxine's portrait of Belinda. 'I couldn't resist. I know it's only a print but it's signed by you so almost as good as the real thing. I'm going to get it framed really nicely and hang it over the fireplace.'

Maxine was totally blown away by Belinda's support but, knowing the truth about this picture, she resolved to let her have the original.

Belinda leaned across the bar and winked. 'I bet you're selling loads. You're going to be vying with Miranda as our richest resident if you carry on like this.' She turned away to serve another customer.

Maxine wondered how much money she might have made if the cash from the prints had gone into her bank account not that conman's but then she'd never thought of selling her paintings – or making and selling prints of them. Maybe, in some respects the wretched Dominic had done her a favour because she was certainly considering flogging her work now.

She was joined by Judith.

'All set for your big moment?' her sister asked.

'Not really.' She repeated the doubts she'd voiced to Gordon.

'Look a fool? You? You won't. Anyway, even in the unlikely event you do, people have short memories.'

'Really?'

'Oh yes.' Judith checked Gordon was busy chatting to another regular before she lowered her voice. 'It seems Ella has already forgotten your Gordon. My spies tell me she's working in a pub in Cattebury and has her hooks into solicitor there.'

'Belinda sacked her?'

'She didn't have to.' Judith tapped the side of her nose. 'She got the hint and moved on. I don't think she felt that welcome here.'

'Thank you.'

'Mum!'

Maxine turned at the sound of her daughter's voice. 'Abi. I didn't expect to see you here. And Marcus.' She was genuinely touched to see them. 'I thought you'd have been too tired from moving furniture to come.'

'Couldn't miss your big moment, could we Marcus? Isn't this exciting!'

For the umpteenth time in a couple of weeks Maxine wondered why her daughter had become so much less difficult. She'd asked Gordon if he'd spotted the transformation.

'I think you're exaggerating, Max,' he'd said. 'She wasn't that bad. I know she had her moments but, on balance, things weren't so very dreadful.'

Maxine had wanted to remind him how often he went to the pub to escape the rigours of three generations under one roof, of the row than made her move out to her sister's for a few days but then she channelled her inner Elsa – let it go, she'd thought.

Belinda rang the bell behind the bar to get everyone's attention. In the silence she said, 'I'm not calling *time* but it is time to see the programme.'

Maxine led the way up the stairs to the function room where she and Gordon were ushered to the front. Almost everyone else in the bar trooped in behind them and the little room was filled to bursting.

Belinda switched on the TV and dimmed the lights and a couple of minutes later the opening titles to the show appeared on the screen.

This was a programme that was new to Maxine and Gordon so they had no idea what to expect and Maxine sat on the edge of her seat not sure if it was fear or excitement that was stopping her from relaxing.

As the theme music died away, Isadora appeared on the screen. 'This evening's programme is brought to you from the idyllic market town of Little Woodford.' A cheer went up in the pub, doused by a gale of shushing. She described the town's attributes, its architecture—

'Get on with it,' a heckler called. 'We all know about that.'

The audience laughed.

'And it also boasts an enviable number of clubs and societies. Most recent of which is the town's art club set up by the super-talented amateur artist and art teacher, Maxine Larkham.'

Another cheer erupted. Maxine's face burned with pleasure and embarrassment and Gordon gave her such a nudge of pride she almost spilt her wine.

There then followed a head shot of Maxine.

'Gosh, Mum,' said Abi who was sitting behind her mother, 'You do glam up well.' Maxine could have cried.

'So, Maxine,' said Isadora, 'what gave you the idea for this club?'

And Maxine explained about her own passion, the pleasure it gave her and how she wanted to share it with others. As she spoke there were cut-away shots to various pictures of the group's work and then, after Maxine's interview, other members of her club were also interviewed before it was back to Isadora.

'Britain has a long history of producing top-rate artists and this little group shows that there is a lot more raw talent to still be discovered, thanks to people like Maxine Larkham.' And as the segment finished a close up of one of Maxine's landscapes filled the screen.

Maxine sat, stunned as the viewers around her went ballistic. 'Oh, my,' she whispered as tears of total happiness fell unchecked.

When things had calmed down and everyone had trooped back down to the bar, Maxine found herself the centre of attention for some time. As the crowd around her thinned, Abi and Marcus came and said their congratulations and their goodbyes, citing exhaustion from the move and the need for an early night. It wasn't long after that Judith managed to squeeze her way through the press to talk to her sister.

'You're going to have to set up another art club, aren't you?' she said. 'Half of Little Woodford is going to be beating a path to your door wanting to be taught by the great Maxine Larkham.'

Maxine laughed. 'We've got vacancies for a few more in the current group but I shan't expand beyond that. Besides, what this group has achieved is down to them, not me. I can teach technique but no one can teach talent.'

'Very profound,' said Judith.

Gordon escaped from a corner where he'd been having his ear bent by Bill, one of Maxine's group who was slightly the worse for wear, about 'wunnderful Maxine and her dedicashun. She's sho lovely. Don't you think your wife is wunnerful, Gordon. I do...' While Gordon was delighted Bill thought so highly of his wife the conversation seemed to be on a loop that was going nowhere.

'Fancy another?' he said noticing Max's glass was almost empty.

'Tempting—'

'Yes, please,' said Judith. 'A large G and T – easy on the T.'

'Max?' he asked.

'I think I've had enough,' said Maxine.

'But this is a party. You're celebrating,' insisted Judith.

'Sure?' said Gordon. Maxine nodded. Two minutes later

he was back with Judith's drink but not one for himself, Maxine noticed. Judith, with a new drink in hand, dived back into the thick of the party leaving Maxine and Gordon alone.

'I'm tired,' she told him. 'All this emotion and attention has worn me out. I'm not used to this sort of thing.'

'Me neither, and I've only been on the periphery. It's nice, though, and I'm very proud of you. You were such a star in that programme, and that Isadora woman obviously thinks you're the next Turner.'

'Hardly,' said Maxine. 'But she did tell me I ought to submit to the Royal Academy summer exhibition.'

'Really? But that's wonderful.' He drained the last dregs of his drink. 'I'm so sorry I never realised that you were as good as you are.'

'But you don't know about art. You know about oil fields and geology and stuff like that.'

'But I've got eyes.'

'Honestly, it doesn't matter. And seriously, I knew I was competent, quite good even because people like my stuff, but I didn't know till that git Dominic took me for a ride that it was properly saleable. Not for real money.'

'So, what are you going to do?'

Maxine put her empty glass down on a nearby table. 'Well,' she said, taking Gordon's arm. 'After we've had an early night and a *very* long lie-in in our empty nest, I'm going to take a leaf out of Dominic's book and set up a website selling originals, limited edition prints and I might even take commissions.'

'Really?'

They moved to the door of the pub and slipped outside

into the dark, chilly night. Maxine nodded. 'Miranda's going to help with a website – she's got friends in the art business who she's already tapped up for advice. She assures me it's not difficult these days and there's lots of on-line help too. Once it's up and running it'll be a nice little earner.'

'You don't need to earn. I mean, the sale of Mum's house will see us right for ever.'

'I know that but, if and when Abi has a family, I thought she could take over running it, because she could do it from home. She could have a nice fat percentage of the sales and if she works from home, she mightn't need us for any child care. Win-win.'

'Not only a super talented artist but a genius.'

In the dark Maxine smiled smugly to herself and then quashed it. The last time she'd felt smug the gods had done their best to ruin it all and she wasn't going to risk it happening again. Instead she gave Gordon a peck on the cheek. 'Thank you for the compliment, darling. Come on, Mr Larkham, let's make best use of having our house back.'

'Let's,' said Gordon happily as they headed for home.

About the Author

CATHERINE JONES lives in Thame, where she is an independent councillor. She is the author of nineteen novels, including the Soldiers' Wives series, written under the pseudonym Fiona Field.

Acknowledgements

Writing is a solitary business but I am blessed to have a wonderful team behind me who I can totally rely on for encouragement, advice and support when needed: Rosie de Courcy, my editor at Head Of Zeus, who has the sharpest mind in the business and who makes such brilliant suggestions for the tweaks to make the story and the characters so much more 'right'; Laura Longrigg, my agent, who is always there if I need her and who listens to my ideas before steering me in more sensible directions; Rhea Kurien at Aria for her enthusiasm and knowledge of the digital market and her belief in me; for my friends in the RNA who get all the ups and downs of this writing business and throw some of the best parties in the industry; and my Chez Castillon buddies – Janie Millman, Katie Fforde, Benardine Kennedy, Jo Thomas, Jane Wenham-Jones and Judy Astley – who have made me laugh more than any group of people I know. A debt of gratitude and very possibly a large drink is owed by me to all of you.

I also need to thank Dr Pat Smith for the advice about the medical side of this book. Pat, if it's still not right, this isn't your fault – I am bad at taking notes so I may have misinterpreted what you said.

And last but not least I need to thank Mr Jones for being patient when I bang on about writing, about plots, about characters and anything to do with fiction. He is a non-fiction man through and through and he really doesn't get the fantasy worlds I like to create but he still listens – well, he says he does...

Hello from Aria

We hope you enjoyed this book! If you did let us know, we'd love to hear from you.

We are Aria, a dynamic digital-first fiction imprint from award-winning independent publishers Head of Zeus. At heart, we're committed to publishing fantastic commercial fiction – from romance and sagas to crime, thrillers and historical fiction. Visit us online and discover a community of like-minded fiction fans!

We're also on the look out for tomorrow's superstar authors. So, if you're a budding writer looking for a publisher, we'd love to hear from you. You can submit your book online at ariafiction.com/we-want-read-your-book

You can find us at:
Email: aria@headofzeus.com
Website: www.ariafiction.com
Submissions: www.ariafiction.com/we-want-read-your-book

 @ariafiction
 @Aria_Fiction
 @ariafiction

Printed in Great Britain
by Amazon